MW00477091

Heiresses of Russ 2011

Heiresses of Russ 2011

THE YEAR'S BEST LESBIAN SPECULATIVE FICTION

edited by
JoSelle Vanderhooft
and Steve Berman

Lethe Press
Maple Shade, New Jersey

Published in 2011 by Lethe Press, Inc.
118 Heritage Avenue • Maple Shade, NJ 08052-3018
www.lethepressbooks.com • lethepress@aol.com
ISBN: 1-59021-395-5 / 978-1-59021-395-7 (library binding)
ISBN: 1-59021-396-3 / 978-1-59021-396-4 (paperback)

Set in Minion and Gondola SD.
Cover and interior design: Alex Jeffers.
Cover image: Olena Vizerskaya.

Myth, Transformation, and Women Loving Women in 2010

INTRODUCTION BY
JoSELLE VANDERHOOFT

When Steve Berman, the publisher of Lethe Press, and I started putting together the inaugural volume of *Heiresses of Russ*—so-named in honor of recently departed Joanna Russ, arguably the most important feminist and lesbian essayist and fantasy and science-fiction author of the last century—I did not anticipate that we would ultimately assemble something like a lesbian version of Ovid's *Metamorphosis*...if Ovid's lesbian *Metamorphosis* had been shot in the arm with 30 ccs of third-wave feminism, spun around on a postmodern tilt-a-whirl, and given an overwhelming palette and an endless blank canvas.

But so we did.

The dozen stories you hold in your hands now, gentle reader, are all about transformations—of the grandiose kind, the subtle kind, the literal and the figurative kinds. Now, of course, transformation is to fantasy what salt is to good eating; Ovid knew this and so did folklore's anonymous originators and adaptors, long before modern fantasy was a spark in Granddaddy Tolkien's imagination. Whether it's Daphne turning into a laurel tree or the seven brothers in the Grimm tale "The Three Ravens," transformations and transmogrifications are nothing new, though I would argue that they are perennially interesting.

And for that matter, that they are important for queer individuals, and lesbian and bisexual women in particular.

Despite the gains that the LGBTQ movement has made across the planet, many lesbian, gay, bisexual, transgender, and otherwise queer youth growing up feeling like they are damaged, evil, dirty, and—perhaps most traumatically—alone. And while heterosexism makes anvils of us all, I think that cisgender lesbians and bisexual women experience a particularly nasty side of it. As women, we're expected not just to love men, but to hunger for the joys of motherhood and childbearing, domesticity, and everything labeled "feminine" or "girly." Oh, yes, even in 2011, even as I sit here writing this. It's difficult to quit those Victorian habits, you know. As Jewelle Gomez's most famous creation, the vampire Gilda, discovers in "Storyville 1910." And while many lesbians and bi women do want these things, we don't want them in the socially appropriate way. And freeing ourselves from those internal and external pressures takes courage, patience, and the willingness to leave the familiar and embrace the unfamiliar.

In short, our conflicts with heterosexism (emphasis on the sexism) reshape us, and transform us from the inside out—hopefully in positive ways. It's a horrible crystal with many hideous faces, and nearly all of the protagonists of these twelve stories spend time looking into its depths. The fact that some of them spend time as birds, cats, does, and imposter princesses is simply a larger metaphor for the transformations that queer women face in life.

The confusions and frustrations of being—and becoming—adolescent lesbians provide the framework for Georgina Bruce's "Ghost of a Horse Under a Chandelier" and Steve Berman's arresting retelling of *Swan Lake*, "Thimbleriggery and Fledglings." In the first, a creative young writer and artist named Zillah struggles to shape her own coming-out story—and her romance with her best friend, Joy—with the inspiration of her favorite comic book character, the "radical black, woman-loving superheroine" Ursula Bluethunder, and the help of a magic book that can make her attempts real. "Thimbleriggery" casts Odile, the "black swan" daughter of the sorcerer von Rothbart, with the "white swan" Odette (here called Elster) as lovers, in a story about father-daughter conflict, heterosexual privilege, and the power dynamics of sorcery, with results that are as tragic as they are triumphant.

Likewise, Ellen Kushner's "The Children of Cadmus" recasts the myth of Actaeon, the ill-fated son of Aristaeus and Autonoë of the equally ill-fated House of Cadmus whom virgin goddess Artemis turned into a stag for spying on her while she bathed. Here, Kushner focuses equally on Actaeon's lesbian sister Creusa, and in doing so touches upon the issues of gender presentation and gender identity with which lesbians frequently wrestle, particularly when they identify as butch or as another identity typically codified as male.

Sometimes, the transformation is a little less obvious. Rachel Swirsky's outstanding novella "The Lady Who Plucked Red Flowers beneath the Queen's Window" takes the theme of transformation in several different directions—all of them as unsettling as they are thought-provoking. The Lady in question is Naeva, a powerful sorceress from a matriarchal society that could well be a more sinister version of Sally Miller Gearhart's *Wanderground*. Here, men are "worms" kept only for their sperm, and most childbearing is left to a subclass of women called "broods." When a treacherous spell imprisons Naeva in the limbo of the spirit world, she must wrestle—in deeply imperfect, problematic, and ultimately human ways—with values dissonance in an ever-changing world and the flaws of her own deeply sexist civilization. To get any more specific would ruin the surprises, so let me just say this: this tale deserved its Nebula Award.

Finally, in the haunting, Colette-inspired "Black Eyed Susan," author Tanith Lee herself undergoes a transformation into the voice of Esther Garber, a Jewish lesbian writer who takes a job as a maid in what appears to be a French hotel during the 1930s. Here she encounters a spectral woman whose presence ties into both the hotel's mystery and the threads of unspoken desire that bind its staff.

And, of course, for stories where protagonists do not directly transform, the societies around them are often in flux. N.K. Jemisin's "The Effluent Engine" posits a world where the Haitian revolution ultimately succeeded and the fledgling nation is now struggling to maintain its independence against U.S., British, and French forces who would like to see it crushed. Meanwhile, the revolution and steam technology are changing the world for Haitians and black Americans alike, including the lesbian daughter of Toussaint L'Ouverture. Meanwhile, Nora Olsen's "World War III Doesn't Last Long" follows the transformation of a relationship between two lesbians against the backdrop of a nuclear war.

These are just some of the transformative journeys taken by the stories in this series that will be an ongoing tribute to the spirit of Joanna Russ's oeuvre. It is my hope that these stories help you to explore not only what it means to identify as a lesbian, but more broadly what transpires when exterior forces transform us while interior forces question everything we thought we knew about what is right and good with the world.

JoSelle Vanderhooft
Fort Lauderdale, FL
Autumn 2011

Ghost of a Horse Under a Chandelier

GEORGINA BRUCE

The way to get where Zillah goes is written in a book. Zillah keeps the Book hidden in a bookcase, slipped in amongst the others. Sometimes she loses the Book, and then she has to search through the bookcase, turn her room upside down, and squeeze her hand down the back of the bed looking for it. Other times the Book stands out, a bright red stripe glowing among the black and brown and cream-coloured spines.

It's easy to lose the Book because it's always changing. There isn't an author's name on the cover. And every time Zillah opens the Book it's different. Everything is different, even the title.

Today, it starts like this.

∽

The ballroom of the Grand Hotel by candlelight is amber and sepia, drifting into darkness at the edges like an old postcard. It smells of stale water, tallow, and dust. The ruby carpet is threadbare and shiny, and the plaster has been knocked off the walls, leaving bare brick in places, water-stained and sick. But in the candlelight the room still has a certain romance.

Hanging from the ceiling is a skeleton of a chandelier; the crystal gone, the bronze peeled away. But tonight, as if for a special occasion, there are candles in all the empty holders, and they glow pale yellow, smelling of scorched hair as they burn away the cobwebs on the steel bones.

Under the chandelier, a horse flicks her grey and silver tail, stamps her feet and snorts. Steam pours from her nostrils and rises up to the ceiling in billowing white clouds. The horse is made of fragile, wavering lines, which soon dissolve into the shadows.

Zillah has never told anyone about the Book, but she thinks that she might one day tell Joy. If there is anyone trustworthy in the whole wide world, it must be Joy.

After school they sit in the library together, their knees touching under the thick wooden desk, and scour history books and comic books for lesbian heroines. They find very few, but they know they are there, somewhere, hidden behind the flourished capes, buried beneath the piles of burnished trophies and medals won by men.

"We could be lesbian heroines," says Zillah. "We could be in a comic book."

"Artists are all sicko pervs," says Joy.

"You're an artist," says Zillah. She shows Joy what she's reading, pushing the book over the table.

It is *Ursula Bluethunder*, Zillah and Joy's favourite comic book. Ursula Bluethunder is a radical black, woman-loving superheroine, whose mission is to establish a lesbian separatist nation with money that she steals from banks using her superior intelligence, strength, and martial arts skills. She likes hanging out in libraries, too.

Joy sighs. "I want to live in New Free Lesbiana. I wish Ursula Blue-thunder was in here right now, browsing in the reference section."

"She might want one of these books." Zillah leans forward, over the desk. "She'll come over and say, hey you women, have you got…this, er," she flips over a book to read the cover, "*Women in England, 1760-1914*, and we'll be like, sure, take it…."

"No, she'll be like, hey are you two *lesbians*? I've got my horse outside, let's go!"

"Yeah, and then you'll be all like, stop, stop! I need to get my passport…."

"And she'll go, no need, young lesbian, for New Free Lesbiana is open to all women who love women!"

"Women who love women," says Zillah, smiling.

And the librarian raises her head and tuts at the two girls, who giggle, covering their faces with their books.

Joy's drawings are full of character and strong, confident lines. Even Zillah's mom, who doesn't believe in giving the girls any praise in case they become conceited, has to admit that Joy's got talent, although she doesn't understand why she wastes it drawing comic books instead of proper pictures.

Sometimes Joy draws Zillah. She draws quickly, soft pencil flickering over the creamy paper, and in a few strokes she manages to capture Zillah's likeness, her way of sitting, the frown line between her eyes when she's thinking. Zillah blushes red under Joy's appraising looks, gets hot cheeks and sweaty palms. When Ursula Bluethunder is attracted to someone, she never hesitates for a second. She makes her feelings plain. Zillah can't imagine what it would take to be like Ursula Bluethunder. She doesn't have the guts.

And Joy says, "What's up with you?" and Zillah says, "Nothing." But then the drawing shows her all lit up in a hot flushed energy field, and Zillah can't meet Joy's eye.

The two girls are in Zillah's bedroom, which is in the attic. It has its own door with a little staircase behind, and then at the top of the staircase, an archway where Zillah has hung up a silvery beaded curtain, so that when you walk through the silver falls all around you in a tinkling rush. Zillah has painted the room in indigo and silver and hung up blue-violet tie-dyed throws she bought from the North Laine, and put candles everywhere, and crystal teardrops and coloured glass. There's a big mattress with a patchwork throw and a limbless teddy called Tigsy that Zillah laughs at but secretly still loves.

Joy is sticking her pictures onto pieces of card. She's making a comic book called *The Hotel*. *The Hotel* is full of ghosts, broken connections and failed love affairs. The drawings are murky and sepia, water-stained and shadowy. In *The Hotel*, Zillah is a Seeker. That means she can find ghosts, and talk to them. Her job is to seek out the lost souls of women who love women, and help them to find peace with her everloving kiss.

"There's the horse," Zillah says, pointing to one of the pictures, and Joy nods, concentrating on what she's doing. All Joy's drawings have horses in them. She and her mom have stables and they ride horses on the Downs at the weekends. Their favourite horse is called Andrea Dworkin. Joy's mom named her after her heroine. Joy loves Andrea Dworkin best, but she rides all the horses. She has to, because people pay to keep their horses in the stables and have them ridden by Joy and her mom. It's no hardship, because Joy loves horses.

Zillah doesn't see the point of having a horse and paying someone else to ride it. On the other hand, she's hoping that Joy will invite her over one weekend and teach her how to horse ride.

"I don't get it," says Zillah, after a while of looking over Joy's shoulder. "Is it supposed to be like a fairytale or something?"

"I guess," says Joy, her head bent over the pages, braids falling across her face. "I guess it's kind of personal."

"Oh. I liked the one where we grow gills and dive under the sea and free mermaids from the evil Patriarch Fish."

"An artist has to grow," says Joy, mocking herself and meaning it at the same time. "I can't keep drawing Fish People. It's boring."

"I liked the Fish People." Zillah flips through the stiff cut-and-pasted pages. "You're not even in this one."

"I'm in there somewhere," says Joy. "Look harder. You're the Seeker."

But Joy puts down the drawings and Zillah lies back on the bed, putting her feet in Joy's lap. Joy strokes the tops of her feet. She squeezes her toes and rubs her soles, pressing into the sensitive spots, and Zillah tries not to squirm, or breathe too heavily, like some kind of perv. Is this a friendly foot rub, or a sexy one? Do people give friendly foot rubs? Is there a cure for being in love with your best friend? She wishes she was Ursula Bluethunder. She wishes she was brave and fearless and never confused. She has her eyes closed, concentrating on the sensations that run up from her feet to her thighs and the feeling of getting wet between her legs, and she can't help letting out a small sigh.

Then Zillah's mom comes in with a tray of sandwiches and orange juice and Joy pushes Zillah's feet from her lap and Zillah sits up straight. They both smile at Zillah's mom, who puts the tray on the edge of the desk and picks up Joy's drawings.

"Why don't you ever have any boys in your drawings?" asks Zillah's mom, who has probably never even heard the word "dyke" and would drop down dead on the spot if she knew her daughter was one.

Joy shrugs. "I don't really like boys." Zillah grins and Joy winks at her.

"Oh? Well, I suppose there's plenty of time for that," says Zillah's mom. She puts the drawings down long before she gets to the one of Zillah the Seeker kissing a ghost in the Hotel lobby. In the picture, Zillah the Seeker is sitting opposite the ghost. Their knees are touching, and so are their lips, but only faintly. You can just see her tongue snaking into the ghost's mouth. Later, when she's alone, Zillah looks at the picture and masturbates quickly, effectively. It feels like this is what Joy intended, a message, a secret sign. Could it be? Ursula Bluethunder would know, but she's not there to ask.

The ballroom of the Grand Hotel is dimly lit and cold. The chandelier makes a pale sun in the centre of the ceiling, radiating a little light around the middle of the floor, but Zillah the Seeker pads silently into the dark corners, carrying out her intricate search. All of her senses are alive, sending wavy tentacles of feeling into each corner, nook, and crevice. Right now, she doesn't know exactly what she's looking for, but she'll know when she finds it. She won't have any doubt. She knows everything that happens in the Hotel; and when someone checks in, it's her job to find them in the dark.

There, now; there is something in a trembling shadow behind the door. She picks it up and holds it in her palm: a small flat stone, on which a picture is painted in faded blues and greys. A cloud swirls above a derelict pier, over a flat grey sea. Zillah the Seeker knows the cloud is supposed to be a thousand starlings, circling around and around.

∾

"I'm getting soaked," says Joy. Rain streams down her face, runs in rivulets between her cornrows, hangs in fat drops at the end of her braids. They are leading horses along the beach at Littlehampton. The sea is the colour of wet slate. Zillah's horse, Edmund, has his head down, and Joy's horse, Andrea Dworkin, is licking water from Edmund's neck. Zillah is looking for treasure. It's not like Brighton, where you find nothing but stones and shells and tin cans and crisp packets. This is a real beach. She picks up a small flat stone and licks it, scraping it over her tongue.

"Tastes of the sea," she says.

"Freak," Joy says, and brushes the rain out of her eyes. "Pebble-lick-er."

Zillah shrugs and puts the stone in her pocket. "A souvenir," she says.

"A souvenir of this rainy, miserable day," says Joy. "That's sweet, Zills."

Zillah can't work out if she's being sarcastic or not, so she doesn't say anything, just keeps her head down. But Joy grabs her hand and squeezes, and says, "I know, let's play Ursula Bluethunder! I'll be Ursula, and you can be my new lesbian recruit."

They've played this game before, but never with real horses. It's stupidly exciting to watch Joy galloping along the water's edge towards her, splashing through the surf, shouting slogans at the top of her voice. Zillah tries to keep her face straight and not laugh, because she knows that would spoil the game for Joy, but later, as they canter across the beach towards New Free Lesbiana, Zillah shouts over to Joy, "I bet you play this all the time, don't you?" and Joy laughs, throwing her head back in the rain. Zillah thinks, if she really were Ursula Bluethunder, she would have kissed Joy by now.

In the late afternoon, when they get off the train at Brighton station, the weather is worse. It is raining hard and the sky is dark, and the streets smell of chip papers and salt, stale beer and drifting tobacco smoke. Zillah swears. She's left her jacket at Joy's house, and the cold rain is making her shiver.

"You idiot," says Joy. "Can't believe you forgot your coat in this weather." And then she grins and says, "Come on then! I'll race you." She starts running before she stops speaking, calling back to Zillah over her shoulder. Joy's a fast runner, but Zillah's faster, and by the time Joy gets to the house, Zillah's already waiting under the porch, shaking her head and sending showers of rainwater arcing out around her.

"You run like a superhero," says Joy.

"I am a superhero," says Zillah, striking a superhero pose. "Super-Zills!"

"GodZillah," says Joy, and laughs at her. "Let us in, then."

Zillah's mom isn't home from work yet, which is probably a good thing because she wouldn't be impressed with the girls tracking rainwater all through the house as they make their way upstairs to Zillah's bedroom. They empty their pockets of stones and shells, making a little messy puddle of beach in the middle of Zillah's homework, and get changed into T-shirts and dry their hair. Zillah's hair is very short, cut close to her scalp, and dries quickly, but Joy's cornrows are starting to frizz and unravel. She sits cross-legged in front of the mirror trying to fix them.

"You should get one of those plastic rain caps that old ladies wear," says Zillah.

"You should shut up." Joy turns back to the mirror and tugs at the ends of her braids, which are starting to curl up. "I should just get dyke hair like my girlfriend."

Zillah has never heard Joy use the word "girlfriend" before. She feels hot and hopes she isn't blushing. "It's not dyke hair," she says. "It's superhero hair. How am I supposed to save the world with an asymmetric bob?"

"A what now? Forget it," says Joy, pushing the mirror away. She means, forget trying to fix her hair. "It's ruined. Have to get my mom on the case."

Joy's mom is great at hair. She was the one who cut Zillah's hair short, even though it sent Zillah's mom totally batshit. Joy's mom doesn't ever listen to the other mothers. She does her own thing, which is probably why Joy is that way, too, not really seeming to care what people think. Zillah has a slight crush on Joy's mom, which she's never mentioned to Joy. It would make things weird. And she can't take the risk of Joy actually spilling the beans. Sounds crazy, but Joy and her mom don't believe in having secrets.

Zillah believes in secrets. Zillah has secrets that would make your head explode, if she ever told you.

The two girls stand at the attic window and look over the rooftops towards the sea. The old pier is silhouetted on a grey and gold sky, and thousands upon thousands of starlings are dancing over it. They look like iron filings, following the pull of a magnet in long sweeping spirals.

"It's beautiful. I'm going to paint it," says Joy.

"It's so beautiful I want to eat it," says Zillah. "It would taste of salt and...."

"Fish...."

"Starlings."

They look at each other, and laugh. Joy says, "Mmm, gamey." They're standing so close, pushed up together in the narrow window bay. Now would be a great time to go in for the kiss, thinks Zillah, if only this were some kind of television series or corny story. She can feel her lips tingling, and the proximity of Joy's mouth. What if Joy doesn't kiss her back? What if this ruins their friendship forever? Joy doesn't look away, not even for a second, and the moment stretches out into infinity: unknowable, unbearable, delicious.

∾

At midnight, Zillah the Seeker blows out the candle and climbs under the blanket with the telephone. She sits with her knees pulled up to her chin, the blanket over her head, and can't tell if her eyes are open or closed. The telephone's bell jingles slightly as Zillah the Seeker pulls it towards her. She picks up the receiver and holds it to her ear.

The receiver is heavy, made of black Bakelite, and there is dust in the curved mouthpiece that she disturbs with her breath when she speaks.

"Hello?"

The silence inside the phone washes up against her ear, wave on wave, until after a while, she can hear sounds. Voices, music, a distant soundscape that makes her think of a television left on in another room.

"Hello," she says again, as loudly as she dares, which is not very. This time there is a crack, like a bone breaking, and then clear as anything, Joy's voice.

"Hey Zillah, is that you?"

The sound of Joy's voice, with a smile in it, makes Zillah the Seeker's heart beat a little faster.

"Where the hell are you? I've been calling your house all morning. Your mom thinks she's got a stalker. And your jacket's still at my house. Aren't you cold?"

"It *is* cold here," says Zillah the Seeker. "But I don't really feel it so much." She tucks her feet in and curls up tighter under the thin wool blanket. Once upon a time, she lived in a house that was warm even in winter. But it's hard to remember.

"When are you coming over? I miss you. Stupid or what?"

"Not stupid." She pictures Joy sitting on her bed, big jumper over her pyjamas and fluffy bed socks on her feet.

"I wish you'd come over. Ride horses." Joy's voice becomes quieter, a little despondent. This conversation always ends the same way. Like all conversations on the dead telephone, fading into the past. "Hey Zills, remember that day we went riding in the rain."

"Sure," says Zillah the Seeker. But Joy can't hear her, anyway.

And then there is the click of the receiver going down, and for a few moments there is the wire humming, a nostalgic and beautiful sound. Zillah the Seeker listens closely, imagining a world where you could pick up any phone and hear that noise, and in the background would be your mom, cooking rice and chicken in the kitchen, and your homework would be on the floor in the living room and the TV on. But the humming grows quieter and fades into silence, and eventually Zillah the Seeker puts down the phone. That is the curse of a Seeker, to always be alone in the dark.

Zillah finds she can't stand being in love. She gets angry. The infuriating uncertainty. The not knowing. She mutters that it's not fair. If only she could know what Joy feels; if her thoughts were written in bubbles above her head, or spelled out in capital letters under every scene. Zillah has nothing, no proof of love. Only the nearly moments: hands brushing together when they walk, a certain lingering closeness when they hug hello. Zillah feels she is going mad with the nearness of things.

When Joy telephones to ask her to come out to the stables that weekend, Zillah only says she might, and then says 'bye and puts the phone down quickly before Joy has a chance to say anything else.

She doesn't know why it's suddenly all Joy's fault, but it is. She's so angry that she can't bear the thought of her anymore, but at the same time she wishes she could take everything back, ring her up and say sorry, and laugh. They could spend the weekend riding horses, drawing comics, and getting their hair cut by Joy's mom. All weekend Zillah is imagining what they would be doing right now, if she was over at Joy's place. The imaginings turn into passionate speeches, where Zillah tells Joy how she feels and demands to know where she stands with her. She cites every ambiguous moment, every paralysing look, everything Joy has ever done or said to make Zillah question herself. As if Joy is to blame for all of that. And then Zillah is sorry, and they both cry, and then, at last they kiss.

She knows she is being stupid and unfair. But she can't help herself, until on Sunday afternoon, her anger finally fades, leaving her sorry. She sends Joy a text message, taking half an hour to come up with the words in the right order. The text says, *sorry. Luv u. C u tmz? Xx.*

But Joy doesn't text back, and Zillah cries herself to sleep.

Someone is riding a horse through this story. Zillah the Seeker can hear the sounds of hooves under her sleep, and the colours of her sleep are all horse colours: tan, sable, palomino, Black Beauty and sorrel. The horses throw her and she wakes up with a headache like stallions charging back and forth inside her head.

She is shaking. The bed is so cold that there is hoarfrost on the blanket. The dead telephone is like a black iceberg in the middle of the bed, too painfully cold to touch.

She has never fallen asleep in the hotel before. That was a mistake. A very bad mistake.

The word stammering in her mouth is "No." She says it over and over to herself, out loud, her voice shaking and her teeth buzzing together, again and again until the room is full of no, and no is in her hair and when she takes a big gulping breath, she inhales particles of her sorrowful no into her lungs.

She has never before lost the one she sought. She cannot contemplate failure now.

Someone is riding a horse through this story. Probably Joy. She's one of those girls who always loved horses, and her mom encouraged her. She gallops over the downs on Andrea Dworkin, who was once magnificent, and still runs hard and fast but not so strong, because she's old. And Joy, trusting her horse to be bold and brave, keeps riding her harder, pushing her over the sucking mud and along the wet paths. Joy's head is full of Ursula Bluethunder stories.

Ursula Bluethunder is a talented horsewoman. It's said that a horse taught her to ride, and that she communicates her intentions through her strong muscled thighs and her shifting weight, so subtly that she and her horse are like one fluid being, one horsewoman hybrid. Joy aspires to this mastery, imagining herself so connected to Andrea Dworkin. But the old horse is too nervous, not trusting enough. When they canter along the road, her hooves hesitate on the smooth surface. And when a car drives by too fast, wheels spinning in the wet, horn blasting out loud and wild, Andrea Dworkin rears and slips, and throws Joy off her back onto the slick black tarmac.

It's Joy's mom who comes to the house to bring Zillah's jacket back. She doesn't have to do that. She walks right past Zillah's mom to get to Zillah, and folds her into a deep hug. They stand together like this for a long time, Zillah's arms pressed to her sides, Joy's mom pulling her in tighter and tighter until Zillah can hardly get her breath.

When she finally lets go, she looks Zillah right in the eyes and tells her, "They had to shoot Andrea Dworkin. Her leg was broken. I'm really sorry. I know you loved her."

"You loved her too," says Zillah.

"That's right," says Joy's mom.

When Joy's mom goes home, Zillah runs upstairs to her attic bedroom. She goes to the bookcase and runs her hand along the titles, bump bump under her fingers, touching every book. It's not there. She tries again, going backwards from the bottom shelf. But the Book is hiding. Zillah jumps up and grabs the top of the bookcase, spilling the books onto her bed. She picks up each book and throws it to the side, until she is crying so hard that she can't make out the titles, and she kneels down at the end of her bed with her face pressed into the covers.

"I don't want to be in this story anymore," says Joy.

Zillah looks up. Joy is sitting cross-legged at the end of the bed. Her hair is in cornrows again, neat and pretty. "I don't want to be yet another dead lesbian in some stupid story. You can do better than this. Think of Ursula Bluethunder. She would never let this happen."

"It's your story," says Zillah. "Your hotel. I thought this is what you wanted."

"You're the Seeker, Zillah. I thought you should work this out for yourself."

❧

The horse looks too insubstantial to ride, made of pencil and crayon and pastel, but Ursula Bluethunder sits astride her, as solid as anything, her powerful thighs clasping and controlling. She stretches out a hand to Zillah the Seeker, and lifts her onto the back of the horse in one smooth, flowing movement.

Zillah the Seeker wraps her arms around Ursula Bluethunder's waist, and the horse walks out of the ballroom at a sedate pace. But once she gets to the lobby doors, the horse rears up and leaps right off from the top of the steps. Zillah the Seeker wants to scream, but the air is whipped out of her lungs as they plunge towards the ground. There is a clatter of hooves and Zillah the Seeker flies up from the horse's back, but holds on tight to Ursula Bluethunder, who is laughing. They gallop through the narrow, twisted streets, charge through the Laine and along the cobbled alleyways towards the promenade, leap over the sea wall and canter along the path, and then they stop.

The pier flickers black against the indigo sky, haloed by a spiralling charcoal cloud. Zillah the Seeker reaches up and scoops a handful of birds out of the sky. They taste of salt and fish, wood and metal, sugar and cigarettes; they taste of Joy's mouth, her tongue, circling and circling around hers.

❧

It is not an infinite, unending moment of bliss. Their teeth clash and their tongues are too wet and Zillah keeps her eyes open the whole time, not quite believing this is happening. She's expecting fireworks, a transport of ecstasy, thundering hooves, or something. But it's nice. More than nice.

"About time," says Joy, and laughs at Zillah's expression. The rain falls harder against the window, making everything outside look impressionistic, like a painting. The dark pier with the intricate broken dome, and the smoke curl of birds drifting above, are blue and grey, blurred with rain.

"I thought you were never going to kiss me." She slides her hand around Zillah's neck and they kiss again, and this time it's better, sweeter, deeper, and Zillah feels the warmth snaking down her throat and into her veins. They kiss for a long time, standing in the attic window, whilst outside the starlings dance and turn and twist into shapes, even briefly forming the shape of a heart, before disappearing into the night.

At least, that is what it says in the Book.

When Zillah's mom finds out that Zillah and Joy are dating, she's inconsolable. It's the twenty-first century, everyone says. Chill out. But Zillah's mom is just nuts about that kind of thing. No one else cares. Even Zillah manages to get over herself. She finds out that the world doesn't end when she gets up the nerve to kiss a girl. If anything, the opposite.

Zillah hides the Book in the bookcase, and for a long time it stays hidden. She decides that life is more interesting than stories in a book. Eventually, she forgets the Book altogether, and it gets truly lost, bought and sold and shipped overseas and back again. Zillah wouldn't know the Book today if it landed in her lap.

Today, it ends like this.

Storyville 1910

JEWELLE GOMEZ

An unusual fog enveloped the city. It cushioned the cobblestones with its damp blanket; and the cast iron balconies that draped so many of the buildings became almost invisible. Gilda slipped into its folds as she watched the windows of the building that used to be her home—Woodard's. It was late enough in the evening that lamps should have been burning inside. She expected to see movement—women fluttering together after supper, getting dressed or dallying. The piano player usually arrived in time to eat before warming his fingers in front of the parlour fire; by now a few soft notes of music should have been drifting through the amber-lit windows. But all was dark and silent, just as it had been the previous two nights she'd watched, concealed behind the fog and the tall gate of the house across Rue Carondelet.

Before she'd left Yerba Buena, Sorel and Anthony had tried to dissuade her from coming back; too many things had changed in New Orleans, they said. But things changed everywhere. She might never bring herself to return to Mississippi where she'd been a slave, where her life had begun seventy years earlier; even now a sense of terror gripped her chest when she considered it. But Gilda's need to know it was possible to start fresh was too strong to keep her from New Orleans; it was a beginning of sorts.

Memory of Woodard's and the house full of women who'd become her family sent a spray of warmth through her that almost dispelled the gloom of the fog. She knew she'd see no sign of Minna, Bertha or the others, but she could hear them in her head. Singing around the piano, clinking wine glasses, teasing each other like the children they were. She heard the seductive laughter that attracted the gentlemen; she also remembered the rustle of their skirts as they scurried away whenever other madams, especially Miss Lulu, arrived to visit the owner of Woodard's. Miss Lulu and Woodard's Madam would sit together in sipping coffee in the parlour's late afternoon light; two more different women could be found nowhere. One was obsessed with hearth and home as if she was the old woman in the proverbial shoe; the other was a tough talking, showy entrepreneur. But both were making a world for themselves and the girls in their charge. However, Gilda knew that Woodard's was a bordello of a different type; the women here learned how to live outside the confines of the roles they played. Their Madam and her partner, Bird, tutored and trained with the precision of cavalry officers; and many left Woodard's to make their way in the world armed with the most significant valuables—self-worth and self-defense. One, Gilda, left with the gift of long life.

Woodard's had two benefits—if was just far enough away from the Storyville District and its pleasure houses to suffer less scrutiny by pious citizens. It incurred a higher rate of payoffs—officials always needed their share—but the men of New Orleans knew the establishment was worth the extra carriage ride. Alongside the standard fare, Woodard's vibrated with literate conversation and an aura of safety.

Miss Lulu's Mahogany Palace, as it was called, was another place altogether. Certainly more sumptuous, it too was legendary. Miss Lulu was known less for her erudition or generosity, and more for her astute business sense and fearless bargaining with anyone in the District. When Gilda was a girl Miss Lulu wore the tignon decreed for all women of color and turned it into a crown which sprouted feathers and jewels of every caliber. Despite the obvious differences between them and their establishments Miss Lulu's visits were regular. Woodard's Madam was a small, plain, pale woman whose only adornment was the way her face changed from grim determination to total engagement when she smiled. It was a change that could warm a room or send shivers of terror.

Sitting in Woodard's shadowed parlour, Miss Lulu's pale, octoroon features were almost lost beneath the flappery of her adornments; she looked like an exotic animal that'd wandered into a country parlour and couldn't find her way out. Yet when one listened to their voices together—the slightly accented Lulu and the carefully flat tones of Woodard's Madam, it was clear the two women had forged a bond of friendship across Canal Street that was both personal and political. They kept track of new fashions as well as the trickery of politicians over the hot brews served up by Bertha the cook.

Gilda peered up at the windows again as if a lamp might be lit now. She knew Woodard's Madam had gone to her true death and surely the girls and Miss Lulu had all gone to their natural rest by now too. It was Bird she was searching for. Bird, Woodard's other Madam, had helped give Gilda long life. Now she needed to see her to restart this life with its endless road. She'd never shaken her sense of abandonment as she'd watched Bird's narrow back atop the horse as she rode away from Woodard's so many years ago.

Now she could feel Bird's essence heavy in the fog surrounding her and emanating from the house itself. But faced with the dark windows and silence she was unsure of her next step. She'd been adamant in her need to come, if only to gaze at her former home. Sorel and Anthony were deliberately vague about the current occupants of the building, one of many they owned; they'd only say it still functioned as a benefit to young women.

Anxiety pierced Gilda's woolen jacket and cap, more chilling than the fog. She turned away from Woodard's and walked back toward the French Quarter wondering if they had been right—looking back was a waste of her time. But time was something she had more of than she could ever use. Gilda noted that her need for the blood was slowly gripping her chest and lungs. She'd been so focused on the past she'd ignored the other, more physical urging.

Gilda took several deep breaths, taking in the cool, damp air, letting it slow down her body's needs. Long strides carried her away from Rue Carondelet and toward the establishments of Basin Street. There she stood in the shadow of an overhanging balcony, so still she was almost invisible. Any who might catch her movement would see only a young, dark-skinned boy in cap and trousers dusted with the dirt of the road. She held a thin cheroot as if waiting for a light and listened to the thoughts of the men who passed or lingered near the entrance to the saloon several yards away.

One hesitated and turned to her.

"Are you all right, boy?"

"Yes sir," Gilda answered in her lower register. "I'm just hoping to get a light for this here."

"Ahh…you looking to celebrate Jack Johnson?" the man said with a slow smile.

Now Gilda hesitated. The man seemed kind; he'd stopped to ask about her and there was no predatory sense in him. But the world had gone crazy since Jack Johnson won the heavyweight championship. White men wrapped up their worst hatred and insecurities in the black boxer's win over his white opponent earlier in the year. Gilda didn't want to engage with another one who blamed the world's ills on a black man's success.

"Hey, he won fair and square, I say. Let's light up together."

Gilda repressed her huge smile that might break her façade. Instead she proffered the cheroot and gazed into the man's eyes as he searched his pockets for his own and a match. She quietly pulled his thoughts from him so she held his consciousness as well as his arm, guiding him away from the street into the alley behind them. Once in the deeper shadow she probed further and discovered the man was as thoughtful as she'd intuited. He did not have a heavy curtain between his whiteness and the many other colors of New Orleans' citizenry. She deepened the veil over his mind and quickly pressed him against the wall of the saloon where the music from inside pulsated through the damp wood frame of the building. His breath slowed to an almost imperceptible rate as she sliced the side of his neck and pressed her lips gently to the blood as it rose to the surface. This was the true color of life and it continued to amaze her.

She drew the blood in and searched his mind for what she might leave in exchange as she had been taught. Except for a small worry about a business deal that lurked far in the back of his mind he was amazingly content; there was little Gilda found she might share in exchange. But she must leave something especially for one who seemed to be so kind. It was no small thing to not be consumed by pettiness and race hatred, each person who was devoid of these diseases made it easier for others to live. In her short life—less than a hundred years—Gilda had seen so many succumb she was infinitely grateful that this man was not one of them. So, in the final moment she left him with her sense of gratitude. It flooded his body, replacing the blood she'd consumed and created a fluid well-being that would course through his veins the rest of his days.

She sealed the wound on his neck; walked him back to the street and leaned against the wall still some way from the entry to the saloon. Gilda listened to his breath return to normal; in his head he heard the echo of Gilda's voice: "Merci, mister," as she slipped away. The fresh blood filled her with new life, making her earlier indecisiveness feel distant. She rounded the next corner onto Bourbon Street and followed it toward Canal where the area became less lively; she took her time and observed the subtle changes. Some buildings leaned slightly as if they were settling into the marshy landscape. Fewer of the small houses were open; their shutters were drawn against the night air. But the pulse of the city was much the same, laced with the remnants of French culture and the pervasive sound of syncopated pianos and mournful horns. Her earlier anxiety was drained away by each note that floated out to greet her so she kept an easy pace until she reached Carondelet.

Gilda imagined that making the transition from bordello to school should have been somewhat easier given the location outside the District but Anthony and Sorel were reluctant to talk of the past with Gilda, always urging her to look to her future. She stepped back into the shadow to gaze again at the building that had been her home, hoping she'd learn more soon. As she watched she recognized some of the changes: the heavy red drapery that should have hung at the parlour windows was replaced by more muted tones now. The upper windows were framed by white lace and now window shades.

One fluttered slightly.

Gilda blinked at the darkness. Yes, there was a very slight movement; more than could be assigned to a random breeze making its way through the seams of the building. A chill crossed her shoulders, supplanting that layered on her by the enveloping fog. She listened more closely and understood what she'd only sensed earlier—it was too quiet. There was no sound at all; nothing came from the house not even the natural whine of wood settling, mice scurrying or window glass loose in its sash.

Bird?! Was that possible? Bird inside cloaking the house so no one of their kind would know she was there? So Gilda wouldn't know? She looked up and down the street again, now noting the emptiness. Clearly the street had been shielded, preventing random or unnecessary pedestrians from wandering onto the block. It had not held her back but she now understood why the fog was so unrelenting in this spot.

She lifted her gaze once more to scan all of the windows. Someone was there. If they refused to open the door, she'd go inside anyway. She'd come a long way from Yerba Buena to see the home that belonged to her family…Sorel, Anthony, Bird…no one could refuse her entry. Deep inside she understood that until she looked upon the place that had been her first refuge her heart would not be healed. And she wanted to feel whole again.

She moved out of the shadow, then stood on the step in front of the door, her hand raised to swing the door knocker on its brass plate. It too was new, less ornate than the one Gilda remembered. Before she could signal her presence the heavy door opened. Standing in the doorway was an imposing woman, of fair complexion, wearing a dark dress like she was mourning. Her head was wrapped—as if it were still 1850—in a black tignon adorned by one small expensive brooch.

"Finally you develop the courage to make yourself known!" The curl of her Creole voice was immediately familiar.

Gilda's breath left her lungs is if she'd been punched. Even though she saw immediately it was not Bird, there was no mistaking who it was—Miss Lulu!

"Cat got your tongue?" Lulu said with a soft bayou lilt and a stern grin that did not evoke mirth. She then stepped back from the door, saying no more and walked into the parlour. She did not look back. Gilda came up the step and crossed the threshold of the house that had been her world after she escaped from her life of bondage on the plantation in Mississippi. She closed the door behind her and felt the loosening of the fog and the cloaking which had been used to prevent her sensing life within the house.

"Miss Lulu?" Gilda said with the voice of a child.

"Lulu will do just fine, girl. Or I say Gilda now, eh?"

Gilda understood at once that Lulu was one of them. But the mystery of it was overwhelming. How could Anthony and Sorel have kept this news from her? Why did they keep it from her?

"They didn't want you dwelling so much in the past, child." Lulu's voice rang the same unmistakable haughtiness. "You'd chosen to abandon Woodard's.…"

"I did not abandon Woodard's!" Gilda almost shouted, stung by the accusation. "I left it in Bertha's charge, and her daughter's."

"Mortals! And what were they to do with it on their death beds? Someone had to step in."

"But what of Mahogany Hall?"

"Things are changing around us, which you would know if you had kept us in mind rather than chasing after that ridiculously inappropriate woman you were warned against by Anthony."

The wrenching inside her told Gilda this was true. She'd escaped from Woodard's almost as she'd escaped from the plantation. She'd left behind her friends because her heart was broken…the ones who'd given her long life were gone—one for the true death, the other to take to the road alone. And in Yerba Buena she again had her heart broken. She'd become obsessed with one of their family who was more insidiously destructive than any of their kind she'd known. Her desire for the woman had made Gilda's brain as foggy as the street outside was now.

Gilda was having a difficult time knowing how to put down roots in a life which required her to keep moving so the mortals didn't discover her secret. Who was real? What was permanent? It was a life that assumed she'd outlive everyone she grew to care about and was filled each day with the calculated risk of heartbreak. Was it easier to not care?

"Would you like a tisane?" Lulu said in a gentler voice.

"Yes, I think so," Gilda answered, sounding again like the child she'd been in this parlour decades earlier.

"Come."

They walked through the dining room to the kitchen, which like the parlour felt so much smaller now. The rough, round wood table still stood at its center marked by years of chopping and hot pans.

As Lulu pulled the kettle from the back of the stove to a full flame Gilda sat on one of the stools at the table and looked around at the room. It was almost the same. One of the pots was new, the cups and saucers that Lulu took from the cabinet were new as well.

"From my kitchen," Lulu answered Gilda's internal question. "They were the only thing I brought with me from Mahogany. I didn't need to be there any more. Too much noise…I was tired."

"Sorel asked you to come to Woodard's?"

"No. Anthony came to settle who would take over. I knew who... what he was. Those private conversations I had with your Madam revealed much over the years, especially toward the end as she understood her lifetime was over and she would take the true death."

"Anthony!" It was incomprehensible that her dear friend Anthony would have done these things in secret, all the while she was living with him and Sorel in Yerba Buena.

"He took many trips as you may recall. That is our way. And you were...preoccupied."

Gilda noted that Lulu said "our." She looked up at Lulu through the steam of the kettle as she poured hot water on the herbs in the pot. The steely strength of her shoulders was then apparent beneath the coal-black sateen of her dress. Her eyes, always a pale gray, had darkened somewhat and flecks of orange flickered behind her gaze.

"Anthony is smart and not sentimental. Unlike so many of our family."

The chilliness that had always been at Lulu's mortal core tinged her words with frost and made Gilda wonder if Anthony's choice was as wise at all. Was Lulu a good choice for their family, could she uphold their principles of long life?

Lulu sighed deeply and sat across from Gilda and returned her stare without expression.

"Only time will tell, yes?"

"I wish you'd stop doing that. I prefer to have my conversations out loud and to keep my thoughts to myself." The harshness of Gilda's tone matched her memory of Lulu.

"I'm sorry. I've been alone here a long time. I...." For the first time Lulu seemed unsure of herself.

"Where are the girls...the students? I understood that this was now a school."

"A home for destitute jeunes filles au coleur. It functions much as Woodard's did without the drinking and gentlemen. Only reading, sewing, cooking and woodworking.

"Woodworking?"

"Of course, your Madam would be furious if we didn't teach the girls all the arts…carpentry, shooting, fishing. They are as accomplished now as ever."

"And where are they?" Gilda asked again.

Lulu's voice dropped slightly, "I've sent them to the farmhouse. I knew you'd come; I thought it best we talk alone." The room rang with the anxiety of her words.

Gilda was flushed with the memory of the farmhouse. It was where she'd hidden after escaping from the plantation, leaving behind everyone who was in her family. There she'd been discovered and brought to Woodard's. The farmhouse was where Bird and her Madam, as Lulu referred to her, had retreated to be alone together, like parents on much needed vacation. The farmhouse was where Gilda had been reborn into this long life. It was there that the blood had been exchanged and she sickened enough to expel all that was mortal from her body, then awaken as part of the family to which she now belonged.

Despite her own proscriptions Gilda caught herself trying to listen to Lulu's thoughts, which were still masked.

"Why?"

Lulu again took a deep breath and poked a finger—no longer adorned with gleaming rings—under the edge of her tignon to scratch at an imagined itch.

"Bird was here, you were right about that; but she is long gone, on her journey again. She left something for you."

Gilda held her expression carefully neutral, not revealing her deep hurt that Bird had come and left—again without her.

Lulu moved smoothly to the drawer that held the cutlery, removed a paper-wrapped object and handed it to Gilda.

"She's a handsome woman," Lulu said in what sounded more like her old self. "Your Madam could have made a lot of money with her, cherie. Let me say that. Breathtaking! Oh, I understand their relationship, but still…."

Gilda was almost relieved to recognize the old mercenary Miss Lulu as she calmed her hands so they wouldn't shake when she unwrapped the tissue paper from the packet. She did it more slowly than necessary, wanting to extend the moment as if Bird herself would be inside. Bird—her other mother—the only one she felt could help her bridge the worlds.

Inside the paper was a knife whose blade was slightly curved and handle was a bright shade of green glass. Inside the paper was written: "Turkey is quite far away" and nothing more.

Gilda laughed fully for the first time in weeks. If she'd had tears they would have risen in her eyes. Instead she laughed until she could no more and fingered the edge and smooth handle with joy.

"I wouldn't have taken you for a gal who likes weapons, not from what I've heard."

"Not weapons. But a knife is an important thing for a journey, isn't it?"

"And important for cutting loose from the past."

"You must teach the girls this, I'm sure," Gilda said carefully side-stepping Lulu's comment.

"Oh they know how to handle all kinds of knives, I assure you."

Gilda re-wrapped the knife to savor later when she was alone.

"And why was Bird here?"

"The District...Storyville...as you know was created as a convenience for the religious and the politicians. It made them comfortable to believe they knew where all the sin was located." Lulu laughed at that. "Outside their own boudoirs, I mean." Lulu's laugh was harsh like the ripping of fabric.

"But with their regulations come graft, more corruption than ever before. And soon it will be over. I can feel that in the air. Les Americains...*ptuh!*"

Lulu made the spitting sound that many used to before Louisiana was part of the Union. "Les Americains" was an epithet still heard in the French Quarter late into the century.

"Storyville is seeing its last days, I assure you. I don't know when but I can feel them pushing our life into the Gulf just like they pushed the Africans into leg irons."

"But perhaps the District has become too much, the violence, drinking...."

"Those are just a part of it. It is the music we must worry about. Where will it go when all the pleasure palaces have closed? The sanctified don't want it in their homes; they curse our music like it comes from the Devil."

Excitement rose in Lulu's voice and her face flushed with her passion. "There is holiness in this music. I learned that as I listened every night to the magic of the pianos and the horns...."

Gilda understand Lulu's worry; this was not a country that recognized its treasures, especially those that came wrapped in dark skin. The compelling melodies and rhythms had a blood trail from the bordellos, across the Mississippi, through the cotton fields and back to Africa. It was not a music to be easily stripped of its meaning.

"Why did you think we needed to be alone to talk of these things?"

"I simply wanted the time to get to know you. Bird spoke of your sadness."

"What does she know of that?"

"You speak as if you two are not forever linked. You are looking for a renewal of your faith, I think."

"Faith?"

"In the family, our values. In yourself."

"And Bird thought she must leave me to this search on my own."

"I don't believe you are on your own, gal, if you noticed."

Gilda almost laughed at how easily Lulu's hard edge made her feel like a girl again.

"What is that?' Lulu was suddenly alert; her eyes blazed orange and she was still as stone listening. "Girls."

Lulu was away from the table, through the narrow back hall and at the rear door before Gilda could respond. She pulled open the door which led into the alley with a swift hard movement but did not let it slam against the wall. On the doorstep stood two young girls, chilled and frightened. Their faces were painted, and they wore dresses totally impractical for the foggy dampness surrounding them—no coats or shawls, just sheer fabric between them and the night air.

Lulu grabbed one by the arm and pulled her in, the other came too as if they were attached. She then slammed the door shut, shaking the door jamb. Gilda watched quietly not wanting to interfere, listening to the situation. One was older but tall for her age, which Gilda sensed was about twelve. She had dark, angry eyes that glared out from their kohl-stained rims. The younger was perhaps nine despite the way her wispy brown hair was pinned up in a complicated style much beyond her years.

"What's happened?"

The two girls trembled and their teeth chattered so hard they couldn't speak. Gilda took her cup from the table and passed it to the smaller of the two. She looked up at the taller girl before she took the cup and sipped the hot liquid as quickly as she could. Then she passed it to the taller one, who was wary, but then she sipped too until the trembling lessened.

Lulu pulled a shawl down from a hook in the hall, wrapped it around both of them, and pushed them deeper into the kitchen. She repeated her question in the exact same tone as if she understood they were already too frightened to be bullied.

The taller girl pulled the shawl more tightly around them both, giving herself something to do as she decided how to speak.

"What are your names?" Gilda finally asked hoping that simple question would open the door.

"I'm Colette...."

"Your real names," Gilda said softly.

They looked at each other maybe to see which would remember her name first.

"I...I...Clementina. I was Clementina and this here is my baby sister, Jinny."

"Well sit down and join us, Clementina and Jinny, we're about to have a little late supper, what about you?" Lulu spoke with the authority of one who took care of many frightened girls.

The two bundled together in the same chair, holding on to the shawl as if it was a life line and they were swimming in the Mississippi. Lulu stoked the fire on the stove and threw some meal in water when it boiled. She soon served them a bowl of porridge decorated with immense pieces of butter and sprinkled with brown sugar. They took turns with the same spoon, carefully not knocking the spoon against the bowl so their meal was silent.

The Miss Lulu that Gilda remembered had never been known for her patience or caregiving skills, but she waited with Gilda for the girls to calm themselves with the hot food before she spoke.

"You gals must be from May Tuck's place over on Bourbon."

That made their eyes open wide with fear.

"Don't worry I'm no squealer!" she said laughing; then looked at Gilda. "May likes her girls to have good manners…no banging the cutlery on the plates and all that. She got a mean old man, though. He'd be enough to run me out into this foul fog," Lulu continued as much for the girls as for Gilda.

Clementina and Jinny tried not to look like they wanted to disappear. They glanced at Gilda, not able to conceal their curiosity. Gilda's traveling clothes were covered in road dust and she still held the hat that camouflaged her femininity when she was on the road.

"I'm going out back to look around, make sure everything's…quiet while you all get settled." Gilda decided they might loosen up more quickly if they were dealing only with someone they knew. "Lock the door behind me," she said as put on her hat.

She felt Lulu lift the veil she'd drawn around herself and the house. Gilda would be able to hear the girls' story as Lulu extracted it from them.

Gilda walked to the end of the block and got her bearings; she felt relief being outside again after so many nights on the road. Music wafted from windows and doorways all though the District, where the pleasure and gambling houses were corralled by the law after Gilda left. Some were lavish, filled with marble fireplaces and chandeliers—living up to the name palace, as Lulu's had. Others were cheap waystations, little more than barns, in some cases, where girls worked in "cribs" for their quick sexual transactions.

Girls with no place to go or anyone to protect them always ended up in the District. That had been true at Woodard's too; however there the girls were given the choice of what work they could make theirs.

As Gilda moved in her wide-legged walk through the Storyville District she understood what Lulu said. Now she could feel the place closing in on itself. There was desperation around the houses thicker than the fog. The laughter was tinny and fearful. But the music was exactly as Lulu had described it—vital and regenerative. She made her way toward May's house on Bourbon and stood beneath the graceful curving iron balcony in front. So many slaves had bought their freedom with their work on these elegant architectural delights that Gilda could imagine their sweat was in the fog that swirled around her.

She listened to the laughter inside that reminded her of Woodard's. Then she heard the piano clear and sharp like the sound of a baby's first cry as it emerges from the womb. The playing had an urgency and purity she'd never heard before; and she sensed that the feeling in the piano player was somehow connected to things going on above him in the upper rooms. Gilda moved around to the side of the house and stood beneath an open window. She could feel the chaos inside and before she heard the words of the argument she was certain it was caused by Clementina's and Jinny's flight.

"I told you not to make them do that! We got other girls like to touch each other. Ain't no need."

The woman's voice, Gilda assumed it was May, was high and tight like she was tired of the argument but had to hold her ground.

"They girls like any others, they do what I say!"

His voice was petulant, needing to prove his mastery of the women and the situation.

"They sisters. You can't make them do that to each other."

"They girls, sisters don't matter. If the customer want to see it; they do like they told!"

"No, you can't do that."

The crack of the man's hand on May's face and her gasp were so loud in Gilda's ear she had to hold onto the brass hitching post at her side to steady herself.

"I'm telling you, Rusty, you can hit me if you want, but you gonna lose us some more girls if you don't listen."

Good for her, Gilda thought. But the next slap was harder. Gilda looked up at the window and gauged the distance—too high for most, but not for her. Instead she circled until she found an open side door. She let her mind reach that of the piano player as she asked, "Shall I come in and help May?" His response, "Yes!" was silent and puzzled but welcome. She slipped inside and climbed the back stairs, followed by the sound of the piano as if it was searching too. When she found them she listened to the energy of the couple on the other side before tapping softly.

"Come." The woman May said trying to keep the tears and anger out of her voice.

Gilda entered quietly as they glared at each other. He was red with anger and May was furiously thinking what she might use to hit him. They both looked surprised when they saw it was a stranger rather than someone from the household. She closed and locked the door behind her.

"Who in the hell are you?"

Gilda held the man in her gaze. She willed his silence within three seconds and May looked puzzled but not afraid.

"You one of them voodoo, ain't ya?"

"Yeah. Do you want this man?"

"What you mean?"

"Do you need him here or is there someone else who might be better?"

Gilda didn't want to totally catch May up in her hypnotic gaze because she wanted her to feel free will as this decision was made.

"I can't leave him here. He'll kill you or someone soon. You can see that, can't you?"

"Yeah. He's got a big temper and a little brain.

"So…."

"So…who are you and what you doin' in my house."

"You said I could come in."

"I ain't truckin' with no voodoo so you can carry your ass right out of here, boy."

Gilda admired the woman's hard edge, which she needed to survive in the world of Storyville.

"I think the piano player might work out better," Gilda said.

"What you know about it?"

Gilda could hear embarrassment in the woman's voice; clearly this was not a new consideration.

"This one is going to cause you trouble. That's what I know."

"He's got his uses."

"You don't need an enforcer if you treat the girls right, May. You know that.

"Now you teaching me my business? I said get out!"

Gilda was unsure what to do next. She looked at the man Rusty as he stared in her direction unseeing. She could take him with her and risk May raising the alarm. But she couldn't take his blood and implant a new idea of changing his ways while she stood here in front of May.

"I'm going but don't let him hit you again. He'll never stop."

Gilda started toward the door then turned back to May, "And let me get this one for you." Gilda drew back her left arm and hit Rusty with her fist, a move she'd had to practice more than once on the road. She could feel his consciousness return just as he was flooded with the pain of her blow. He crumpled to the carpet like a doll and May laughed.

Gilda turned on her heel and disappeared through the door before May could register that it was even open.

When she reached Woodard's Gilda was exhausted, but this time she felt excited because the lights were on in the parlour and she knew Lulu was waiting for her.

Together she and Gilda closed up the house—pulling the shutters, damping down the stove and locking all the doors—as if they'd been through these tasks together for years. It wasn't until they had Clementina and her sister Jinny swaddled in blankets, a rug and deep silence in the back of the buckboard and the four of them were headed out of town to the farm that Lulu spoke.

"Remind you of anything?"

Gilda saw herself as a runaway slave, swaddled as Clementina and Jinny were now. The safety she'd found was here for them too. For the first time she felt pride; pride to be part of a family with not just power but with a patient hand on the future.

There were seven girls at Woodard's now, aged three to fifteen. The three year old had been found as a premature infant in a basket tied to the back door one evening when Lulu returned from her search for the blood. Within months the baby's color had deepened and it was clear that in some white household in New Orleans what had been explained first as a cold, then as indigestion, had emerged as a mulatto baby unsuitable for their front parlour. But Woodard's was known as the house where girls went who had nowhere else to go.

"We're the Ursulines for les jeune filles des colouers. You know the convent that teaches the girls. We have become that for our colored girls who face uncertain parentage or poverty and do not want to grow old in the District."

"The aging process is quite fast there, I can see," Gilda sighed thinking about little Jinny's mature hair and Clementina's darkened eyes.

"We've been safe at Woodard's, in part because of the protection our family can provide, but also because I turn away no colored child. And there are many with colored children to dispose of. Where conscience will not allow them to drown them in the Mississippi they may bring the child to me."

"But there are so many mulattos and quadroons in the French Quarter, why would anyone want to…?"

"Like everything else, the time is different now. And no one wants the inheritance of their legitimate children or their political careers jeopardized by the dark child of a mistress. Or others who just can't feed the issue from a rape. I can't keep up with them all and have sent some, the boys, of course, out to Sorel and others."

"Yes, I've met those who worked in his salon."

"I know the hatred the whites and even the blacks feel for us...our fair skin, our hair. We are a reminder that each one of them—white and black—is a fool, believing their color is the best! Look what happened after that prize fight, people went crazy!"

Unconsciously Lulu snapped the reins of the horses with anger at the scorn smeared on Jack Johnson's win.

It was hard for Gilda to recognize the coolly calculating Lulu of the Mahogany Palace in this woman who assessed the political climate so perceptively. But Gilda could not argue with her. She'd seen the veiled looks of distaste for her in Sorel's salon—looks from whites because her skin was dark and from blacks because she did not dress her hair to make it look less African.

"They will destroy this country, I assure you. But we have to care for and educate our young or we'll disappear."

Lulu was right; all sides had wrapped themselves in self-righteous hatreds for each other and for their own. She didn't know if Lulu's mission to bring enlightenment to those who straddled both worlds would work but it was no less powerful or effective than others she'd heard expressed.

"I'm afraid that I wasn't able to convince May to rid herself of the man...."

"Rusty?"

"Yes, he's the one who caused the girls to run away. So we may expect some trouble."

"All the better that we're here at the farmhouse for several days. I can show you what skills the girls have gained...even planting!"

"If Rusty comes out here...."

"We'll plant a new idea in his head," Lulu said almost with humour.

"He's not so easily persuaded."

"Can't say as I've met a mortal yet who can resist our...our charms."

With that Gilda saw that Lulu had little experience in this type of confrontation. She finally understood that Bird had drawn her here not only to revisit her past but to also aid Lulu in preparing for her future.

They rode the remainder of the way in silence and arrived shortly at the farmhouse which stood on high ground far enough outside of town that it felt like another place altogether. It was as brightly lit as Woodard's had been dark. Lulu descended from the buckboard with an elegance that only she could pull off and waved Gilda back until she knocked on the door. Clearly a signal had been arranged to assure the girls' safety.

After the exchange at the door the light around the farmhouse softened. The protective circle had refracted the light from the lamps, causing them to glow more brightly. Gilda pulled back the rug and handed down the smaller child to Lulu and then took the bundle that was the older girl. As they moved to the farmhouse door so Lulu released them from the veil of sleep in which they'd been wrapped, tighter than the blankets. They woke with a start on a small settee, the same one Gilda remembered falling asleep on many times in years past.

The young women of Woodard's, varying in shade from deep cocoa to café au lait, stood alert and wary as Lulu and Gilda unwrapped their two packages. The young women tried not to hover and stare but they were as curious about the newcomers as any children would be. Each face was full of light and life, just as Gilda remembered the girls when she lived at Woodard's. The oldest girl, Hilda, had her dark red hair swept up in a tight bun like a schoolmarm, and ordered the others around with the same practiced tone.

Clementina's and Jinny's eyes widened as they observed silently. Hilda shooed all of the girls from the room as Lulu sat on a small stool in front of the settee. Gilda stood back by the window; rawness tightened her throat when she recognized Lulu's posture as the same she'd faced when here with her Madam and Bird decades earlier. She broke from the memories and listened to the sounds seeping in from the night until Lulu's voice drew her back into the room.

"Now you gals are welcome to stay with us, but there's one thing. You got to say you're colored. You understand?"

"I ain't no nigrah!" Clementina almost shouted, echoing the outrage she'd heard in the voices of her elders.

"I'm not asking you. I'm telling you. You got two choices: if anybody asks you you're both quadroon…you know what that is don't you?"

Jinny nodded quickly as she asked, "I like being a quadroon…. Rusty say they the best springs in the mattress." The old term and the metaphor sounded both incongruous and vile in the child's mouth.

"We don't talk about girls that way here, Jinny. But being a quadroon ain't a bad thing, I assure you.

"You say your grandmammy was black or you going back to May and Rusty and there ain't nothing I can do about it."

Clementina, whose mouth was open in protest, stopped her next words and looked down at her little sister before speaking.

"He made us do things we ain't supposed to, that's why we come to your house, Miss Lulu."

"I know, child," was all Lulu said as she watched Clementina making up her mind. Gilda was pleased that Lulu didn't try to corral the child's thoughts and bend them to agreement. Their decision had to come from inside.

Clementina examined Lulu's face, then her gaze moved down, measuring all she was being asked to be. Her calculating assessment was chilling to Gilda as if the colored woman stood on the auction block in Congo Square being assessed for her value by a child.

"I don't know how to be a nigrah," Clementina said finally with tears in her voice.

"Why, you'll just watch me and the other girls, Clementina. Haven't you ever played pretend?"

"No."

"I played pretend. I like it. I want to be colored, please. Please!"

"Yes, it'll be fine for you to play but Clementina has to play too or it won't work."

"Please, let's be colored and stay here!" The complexity of Jinny's request was totally lost in the childlike sound of her voice and her sincerity.

"We'd best make some decision soon, Lulu. We're about to have some visitors."

"Clementina?"

"Can I keep my name?"

"Which?"

"Clementina. I like that so much better than that other...."

"Yes, of course, Clementina. No one should be able to take your name from you. No one can take away who you really are inside. And it's inside that matters. Not outside. Remember that."

"All right, we'll be...we'll be colored."

With that Lulu yelled for Hilda, "Now, Hilda, now!"

The sharp crack of her voice brought the girls back into the room with blankets in hand. Hilda was outside and had the storm door to the root cellar open in seconds. A cellar was an unlikely thing in the waterlogged parishes but long ago Woodard's first Madam had constructed an underground room that appeared to be simple dirt but that resisted encroachment of the persistent underground waters. Gilda helped the girls descend into the dark which was lit only by one small lamp held in Hilda's steady hand; as she did so she breathed in the scent of the soil, a sprinkle of which lined all of her clothes. In the breath was the memory of her own hiding here, her own rescue. She hoped this one would turn out as successfully as hers.

"Candle out, Hilda," Lulu said in a placid voice that Gilda recognized as the gateway to the somnambulism that would keep them still and quiet until she awakened them.

"Sleep is all around...in your head and in the air. There is no walking or waking, only sleep. Until I bring the light."

Lulu blew out the candle, gently lowered and bolted the door, then turned back to the house. "I hear them now—five or seven, I cannot tell. The horses make it muddled."

"I am good with horses," Gilda said.

It was here that both understood how much older Gilda was than Lulu. Gilda had been on this path for several more decades than Lulu, and she'd traveled. Not yet as much as she planned to, but she'd seen the Pacific Ocean and the great forests and deserts in between New Orleans and Sorel's salon. Lulu's skills were confined to the intricacies of the New Orleans landscape. Not small but less than the world beyond and the future to come. Gilda's return was not that of a child, but a teacher. In that turning of circumstance Gilda felt the first balm, warm against her injured heart.

Lulu poured them each a shot of whisky and settled before the fire. In her life with Sorel and Anthony, Gilda had only learned to drink champagne, but she accepted the drink with curiosity. Sorel had confirmed that they had no need of nourishment, but desire of it was another matter. The finest champagne stayed chilled in his establishment at all times. Clearly Lulu's taste ran more to the grain rather than the grape.

Lulu threw her head back, swallowing the golden liquid in one gulp, then said, "I don't think we'll have time for sipping."

Gilda let the first burning of the drink slide down her throat and enjoyed the heat as it spread throughout her body. Intrigued, she took another sip as the quiet was broken by the pounding on the door.

Gilda remained by the window and pulled her hat from her jacket pocket. It was helpful to have something in her hands and it would confirm their impression that she was a boy. Lulu opened the door with a smile as if she always entertained late night visitors.

"Mr. Rusty. And who are the gentlemen with you?"

"Never mind about them. I think you got something or some things that belong to me."

"Far as I can tell, Mr. Rusty, folks don't buy and sell folks no more. So if you mean Clementina and Jinny, they can't actually 'belong' to you. Unless you they daddy."

"Them gals work for me. They owe me and May so don't play words, Miss Lulu. I know you know how the business works, even if you like to pretend you retired."

"Let me say this again. They don't belong to nobody. And they come to the school to get some learning, like all the other colored girls we got there."

"We went by the…. What you mean colored!?"

"We only take colored girls at Woodard's, you know that, Mr. Rusty."

"Them gals ain't colored, you crazy!"

"Look at me, Mr. Rusty, you saying I ain't colored?" Lulu looked past Rusty into the pack of white men. "Why, ain't that Mr. Daniel who bartends over at Gertie's? And I'm seeing Sam who work out front that Bourbon Street crib. You all know me; you even worked for me once, Sam, didn't ya? Now long as you known me ain't I been colored?"

"You simple heifer...." Rusty stepped across the threshold before the men in his gang could respond to Lulu. Gilda stepped forward away from the window so she was clearly visible. What he saw was a tall, dark, muscular young boy with a steely gaze, who seemed vaguely familiar. He tried to place the face but his memory had been blocked. He couldn't remember that it wasn't May who slugged him, but his hand went to his swollen jaw as if it had a memory of its own.

"You takin' in nigrah *boys* now. Or is this a personal project?" Rusty said salaciously.

"This is my cousin."

Gilda held tight to her cap and cast her gaze down at the carpet as they expected and listened, not to Rusty, but to the men behind him. They were restless. Having been whipped into excitement with free drinks and the tale of stolen whores they were now unsure what they were meant to do with the colored madam/school teacher in what felt like an empty farm house.

"Now Miss Lulu, where are them gals?" Sam called out almost solicitously.

"I sent them over to my cousin in Assumption Parish, that's why Gil...why Gil is here. He come back to work for me on the farm while they help out my aunt. And I think the new girls got some relatives over there."

"They ain't got no relatives over there!" Rusty yelled, impatient with the details.

One of the men lit a torch that flamed above their heads ominously.

"I ain't got time for this back and forth," a voice from the back said angrily. "Rusty, what we doin'?"

Gilda's face did not reveal the terrifying image that flooded her mind: the girls in the farmhouse cellar—locked in sleep behind a bolted door. They could not risk fire.

"Miss Lulu, you want me to catch the tea kettle?"

"Yeah, Gil, would you," Lulu answered, listening to Gilda's fears. She kept her eyes on the restless men as Gilda moved across the room and to the kitchen. Once out the back door, she circled the house and stood far enough behind the man with the torch so he didn't sense her there. She did not want the evening to end in blood but she could feel it rising in the five men. Liquor along with disdain for Lulu and the girls was swirling around in their guts. They needed some valve to release the heat and the prospect of torching the farmhouse was becoming more attractive with each moment.

"Mr. Rusty, you killin' their spirit, don't you care about that?" Lulu began

"Shut your mouth and give me my girls."

Lulu felt Gilda evening her breath and drawing each man into synchronization with her. She ignored Rusty and caught the thread of consciousness that Gilda flung out to her from behind the men. She held onto the thread, hoping Gilda knew what she was doing. Despite the seasoned nature of her mortal life Lulu was young in this new world; she'd never tried to control so many at once.

Gilda wove her line of control back and forth and around the men, linking each time with Lulu until they were all like one living organism corralled by her. She held them so tightly the air thinned; the torch went out and their breathing became shallow. She reached out to the horses the men had tied together behind her. Her silent request to them was answered as the horses moved quietly in concert back down the road, ambling slowly enough so that Gilda and Lulu could follow, nudging the pack of men between them.

It was an eerie procession; the horses moved as if they were in a military funeral, muffled and dignified. Gilda and Lulu walked in step with the men between them barely breathing and stiff legged like the zombies that many in New Orleans feared. A short time later they turned off the road, following the lead of the horses. At one point Gilda sensed someone else in the nearby dark but couldn't risk breaking her concentration to explore. That trouble would be met when this work was done.

The horses stopped abruptly in front of the still waters of a swamp, just as Gilda had requested of them.

"Go," Gilda said to Lulu.

Lulu pulled back, letting Gilda hold the men as she plucked Rusty from the group. Her eyes swirled gray and orange as she spoke to Rusty in a sweet Louisiana voice, "Don't you remember, Rusty, them gals…they colored?" She gave him one more chance to let go of his quest.

Even in her thrall he could not back away from the certain danger that lay ahead of him. It was just like the city officials who couldn't see the sin that lay outside the District, wouldn't acknowledge the damage they themselves created by letting women be used and abused and not protecting them. The energy and music that lived in the District needed their nourishment; instead they sucked it dry.

Lulu recognized the waste as clearly as Gilda.

"Nigrah bitch, I should have killed you and those so-called…."

Lulu sliced through the vein in his neck as it bulged with rage. The blood spurted onto her clothes and disappeared against the black of her dress. She encircled his shoulders gently in an embrace which would be the last he ever felt as she drank from him. Before the end she searched for a change of heart; finding none, she then went deeper looking for some good thing he might want or need she could exchange for and leave him with his life. But there was nothing, only his hatred and determination to bend the two children to his will, gutting them of their lives.

She drank deeply, taking in his anger, his refusal to see what lay in front of him, his anger at her, his anger at May. It all drained from him with his blood. At the end Lulu looked into his empty eyes one last time to find some innocence in his soul that she would keep within her always, just as they'd been taught to do.

When it was done she looked back at Gilda, who recognized she'd just witnessed Lulu's first kill. Lulu lifted him easily, tossed him into the swampy water and watched it float in the darkness of the watery garden. The swamp water filled his blood-spattered white shirt, ballooning it out around him. Then his head bucked upward eerily as his body was snatched from below with a speed and force that meant one thing—alligator. When all traces finally disappeared Lulu laughed deep in her chest.

"Devilish man!"

She turned back to Gilda and stopped smiling, understanding that Gilda was not one to laugh at the death of anyone. Gilda watched and listened to Lulu closely to be assured all was done as it should be. Lulu closed her eyes to secure his face in the furthest reach of her mind knowing she would have to visit those images sometime to re-ground herself in the knowledge that all life ends in death. As she placed the image inside, she understood for the first time the depth of her power and that her responsibility lay with the dead as well as with the living.

"That was a terrible thing," Gilda said out loud in a low even tone. Her words sparkled on the line of thought that wove its way around the men holding them tightly in an imagined incident they would report, embellishing the telling each year.

"Rusty was always too smart for his breeches. We told him not to go wandering into the swamp. Drunk he was. We tried to catch up with him. He just had to show off. Then he was gone. You could never tell Rusty nothin.' "

Gilda's words embedded themselves in each man's brain deeper than the real memories they'd carried for decades. One by one they climbed their mounts as they were directed by Gilda. They pointed their horses back toward town without noticing Gilda or Lulu. One of the men took a last look toward the black swamp, then said, "Damn, you could never tell Rusty nothin'!"

"Come on, it's too damned cold out here."

"Here, take a slug of this."

The words floated on the air as the men rode away, trailing Rusty's horse to return to May.

Gilda moved back onto the road and listened for the breath she knew was out there. The one who'd hung back and watched. He'd followed but remained hidden. Lulu took her cue from Gilda and remained quiet as Gilda scanned the dank brush on either side of the path that was barely a road.

"Ah!" Gilda said and walked briskly toward a cypress shrouded by moss. "You should step out now."

A tall, thin, youngish man stepped away from the tree onto the dark path, barely suppressing his fear. He wore a somewhat nice formal jacket and his cuffs were white, but he was covered in leaves and twigs he'd picked up on his journey from town.

"And who you be?" Lulu said roughly.

"The piano player," Gilda answered a little surprised. Then she laughed. "You're the one playing in May's salon, aren't you?"

"Yes, ma'am." He was puzzled to be known to this unknown black girl. Despite her cap and her manner he could see she was a girl and felt like he should know her.

"What are you doing out here!"

"I followed Rusty 'cause I knew he was following trouble. I don't like to see May worried so."

"Well, you won't see her worried much anymore." Lulu said with a chuckle.

"Are the girls all right?"

Neither Gilda nor Lulu answered. They listened inside of him to see how genuine his concern might or might not be.

Assured he was asking out of kindness they both simply nodded. Then Lulu said, "They come to live with me now, at the school."

"That's good. May couldn't figure out what to do about…."

"The music is our legacy, you know that don't you?" Gilda interrupted.

"I been thinking that, not in those words but I'm trying to get it wrote down and teach some young folks, when you can get them to sit still!" he said, laughing nervously, not sure what had happened at the swamp's edge shrouded by the trees.

"Maybe you can come teach my girls to play?"

"Girls?"

"I can pay."

"If they's able to learn, I'm the one can teach 'em."

"Then it's settled," Gilda said, once again using the soft tone that could find its way inside any mortal's mind.

"You better get back to work, you been out having a smoke too long. May will be worried and the salon will be too quiet without you at the piano. They love you playing."

"I got to get back, the salon...."

"Yeah," Lulu said pulling her skirts up around her ankles as she turned to head back to the farmhouse. "We'll see you at Woodard's. Afternoon is best. Ask for Hilda."

"You know that you should take good care of your hands," Gilda continued in the hypnotic tone that threaded through his thoughts. "You can't go around hitting things...or people...or your playing days are over."

"You sound just like my mama," the piano player said with a smile as he backed away and went in search of his horse, already barely able to remember the encounter.

Gilda and Lulu moved side by side in the moonlight which brightened as they got away from the cover of the trees and closer to the open road.

"What are you going to do about Clementina and Jinny?"

"It'll be interesting to see what kind of colored girls they make!" Lulu laughed, then hesitated as if finding her words. She closed her eyes and still saw Rusty's eyes open in surprise as she'd opened the vein in his neck.

"It is never easy, nor should it be," Gilda interrupted Lulu's effort to frame her thoughts.

Lulu didn't present the many questions she had about what had happened. Those she'd deal with later. Now she turned back to more mundane topics giving herself time to become used to what she'd just done and who she'd become.

"I think it's important for the girls to learn music, don't you?"

"No life is ever fully realized without music. There is no peace, no progress, no invention, no legacy without music. According to Sorel."

"You think Yerba Buena would be a good place to make a new start?" Lulu was having an uncharacteristically difficult time expressing herself. "Maybe I want to go out to live near Anthony and Sorel. Maybe in another two or three years. It'll be time for me to disappear from here and I'll bring Clementina and Jinny with me. Hilda will be ready by then."

"Hilda?"

"Yeah, that gal's a born schoolmarm! And if I can do it, anybody can! She already got a gift…seeing things."

"Miss Lulu, you are a world of marvel."

Lulu sighed deeply, relieved that Bird's and Anthony's promise of Gilda's help as a teacher had been fulfilled.

"I'm sorry you didn't get to see Bird."

"I will," Gilda said softly.

"I know she cares about you. I could tell she was thinking about you most of the time she was around. She wasn't sad or anything like that, just had you on her mind…like she was touching you."

Gilda stared up at the moon, knowing that somewhere Bird did too. She was the one who'd given her the final blood, bringing her into this family, making them eternally connected. Seeing Lulu's way with the girls made her better understand that connection. Lulu's easy way of talking about Bird's visit and feelings for Gilda made Bird's need to move out into the world alone feel like less of a rejection, less of a mystery.

Gilda would stay a while to help Lulu learn the things she needed to know just as Bird had helped her. Together they'd decide if Hilda really was the right one. Gilda was now comforted that she'd be able to learn New Orleans again from her new perspective, no longer a frightened child escaping her past. But then, as it did for them all, the moment would come for Gilda to find her own path; to create her own journey rather than chase some else's.

"I will," Gilda repeated to herself as Lulu unlocked the cellar door.

Her Heart Would Surely Break in Two

MICHELLE LABBÉ

Much later, when she is a queen, she will remember it this way, and regret:

It begins with a breeze lifting tendrils of her hair as Eleanor straightens in her saddle, but she does not brush them away from her eyes. She must be a statue, immobile and perfect, before Catriona, the new handmaid. Catriona, who is not really a handmaid at all but a trumped-up goose-girl, the only servant the castle can spare to go with the princess on her journey to the prince's kingdom. This chit of a girl is to be Eleanor's companion, and not Nurse, who has raised Eleanor, who still guards her fierce as a mother bear. The princess is given no choice in the matter. So Eleanor, from her height in the saddle, looks down

and hates the handmaid, hates the wild-haired, sun-browned creature slumping in her saddle, hates her with the force of a flood, a gale,
a wildfire.

So Eleanor throws her shoulders back in the way her mother has
taught her, but a tremble remains in her chin and she blinks suspiciously little. For courage she must snake one hand to her bodice,
where she has nestled the handkerchief that is her mother's part-
ing-gift, white silk marked with three perfect circles of her mother's
blood. The ritual is only folk-magic, and the princess is not sure she
trusts it. But when her soft fingertips brush the still-crimson stains,
she rises taller in her saddle, astride her white mare. She imagines
she hears the fabric rustling, whispering to her, as the horse's hooves
thud down the ill-paved path. *Oh, if your mother only knew.* Eleanor
closes her eyes and imagines her nurse at her side.

The roughness of Catriona's voice after the princess issues her first
command is enough to jar her from her reverie. She has never heard
it before. *Fetch the water yourself, if you've a thirst,* Catriona says, and
Eleanor, startled, does. She dismounts, bends forward, hair unbound,
locks trailing in the stream, laps creek-water in a motion both graceful and awkward.

As she straightens, water dripping down her chin, thinking of her
mother—*Oh, if your mother only knew*—she meets the handmaid's
eyes and for a moment, she knows. It is finished, then. In Catriona's
eyes Eleanor can see her own story reflected, her own anger. This
goose-girl asked to become a handmaid no more than Eleanor had
asked it, and Eleanor is contrite. But there is something else, too,
in the sharpness of Catriona's features. Eleanor wonders why she
thought the handmaid plain, when her eyes are that bold, brilliant
blue. Bluer than the eyes she has imagined the prince might have.

We're the same, you and I, Catriona says in that same rough voice,
and it is true, suddenly, Eleanor believes. With a swallow she re-
members to breathe.

Take off those clothes, you won't be needing them, Catriona begins,
but Eleanor's hands are already fumbling at her stiff beaded sleeves,
her eggshell-blue bodice. Catriona's disrobing is easier. Underneath,

Eleanor discovers, the handmaid is not freckled but marble-white, with glimpses of blue veins at her wrists, the tops of her thighs. Her hair falls around her like a bird's nest strewn to the wind. She stands, and her blue-moon eyes do not look away.

Eleanor's hands tremble so that she can barely undo her laces. She shivers, though it is the height of summer, and then Catriona's warm, callused hands are at her waist. Eleanor tenses at the unexpected contact, then wills herself to relax, release the taut muscles around her navel. The handmaid's fingers are deft and practiced on the laces of Eleanor's bodice, as if she has done this before. Eleanor does not notice when her mother's handkerchief slips out from between her breasts as the bodice parts, for then Catriona's hands are on Eleanor's quick-flushing cheeks, drawing her gaze up, and she sees Catriona's tongue dart over her chapped lips so they glisten. Eleanor can no longer tether herself, and she catches Catriona's sunburnt lips with her own soft ones, still wet from her drink at the stream.

Both girls now are gasping for air as if they have just escaped from drowning. Fabric rustles, hands tremble, as they shed their last garments, their trappings of rank. Both girls are the same now, as Catriona said, both smooth and milky with flashes of pink at their fingertips, their lips, their breasts, like ripening berries. Later on, when they have finished, they will don each other's clothing, and they will not be able to distinguish princess from handmaid, but for now, they draw to each other, thrill to each other. Eleanor feels the sweat beading at the small of her back.

A breeze passes by, but they do not notice, their limbs entwined. It catches up the forgotten handkerchief, the drops of blood still crimson-fresh. It rises in the air, begins a lazy descent into the stream where Eleanor knelt to drink. But Eleanor does not see it. Her eyes are closed. Her mouth is agape. She does not hear the handkerchief's refrain as it sinks under the surface of the water, as the current bears it away.

Oh, if your mother only knew....

☙

Black Eyed Susan

ESTHER GARBER

Black Eyed Susan first passed me in the corridor, just after the old woman had pushed me into it. Black Eyed Susan's eyes were black as ink from outer space, and she stared a moment, coldly with them, at me. But the old woman was still there, poking the twigs of her fingers into my side.

"What? What is it?" I mumbled to her. I had become confused, but already Black Eyed Susan had turned the corridor corner and was lost to view.

"In there," rasped the old woman.

"Where? Why?"

"There, *there.*"

Across the corridor was a door, one of many. "There?"

Like a mouse all in black, though not a black like Black

Eyed Susan's, the old woman continued to push me forward as if I were on wheels, towards the door.

It was marked *Private*.

"But—" I said.

Sharply, leaning past me, she rapped on the door with her horn-rimmed knuckles. For a mouse, the old woman was quite large, but for a woman quite small, shriveled down nearly to a husk, but a hard one.

From within the room a male voice said, "Enter. If you must."

The old woman turned the handle of the door, thrust me through, and slammed it at my back.

A big, warm room, fire in its grate, armchairs strewn about. Behind a polished desk piled with ledgers and papers, a man of average age and some indications of wealth, eyed me over his spectacles.

"Who are you?" he inquired, without interest.

"My name is Esther Garber."

"And?"

"I've come to work at the hotel."

"And so?"

"Monsieur, I was pushed into this room by an old woman."

"Ah!" A bark of laughter burst, beneath his narrow mustache. "Granny at her old tricks."

"Oh, was it your grandmother then, Monsieur?"

He drew himself up, removed his glasses, and scanned me intently. "I am the Patron. This hotel is mine. Normally you'd have no dealings with me. All that is seen to by Madame Ghoule, whom, I assume, you have already met when hired. However, the old lady you refer to, Madame Cora, will tend to drag to my notice any new girl on the staff I might, she supposes, fancy."

My face became blank. I met his eyes with all the hauteur of Black Eyed Susan's. Knowing, nevertheless, that if he must have me, then he must, since it was generally the safest way. Besides. I needed the job here, lowly as it was. My money had run out; and beyond the clean windows of the Patron's boudoir, light snow was already falling on the little French town.

He said, smiling with disdain, "Well, what do you think?"

"I'm surprised," I said, manifesting I hoped a halfway ordinary feminine reaction.

"Don't be," said the Patron. "My grandmother is mad, of course. Anyway, you're not my type—" what he actually said was, *not my bite of biscuit.*

I should now be modestly insulted, perhaps. I lowered my gaze, and thought of ink-black eyes, floating there between me and the patterned carpet.

He said. "What did you say your name was?"

"Esther."

"And your duties here?"

"Bar work, and some kitchen work, so I was told."

"And why then are you up here at the top of my hotel—aside, of course, from Madame Cora, who will have waylaid you somewhere between here and the ground floor?"

"I'm to sleep at the hotel, so Madame Ghoule informed me."

"Of course. Very well then. I wish you a pleasant stay," incongruously he added.

So I was dismissed, opened the door and came out, looking uneasily about for mad Madame Cora. But there was now no sign of her, no sign of anyone.

The entire hotel, which called itself *The Queen*, had a forlorn winter appearance, and few guests. Madame Ghoule, for it had been she who interviewed me, was a formidable barrel of a woman. The interview had consisted of her terse remarks on my proposed duties, and the evidence that I looked too skinny to be able to do any of it; was I therefore strong enough? I lied that I was, which she at once accepted. "You will keep no tips for yourself for the first fortnight, that is our policy here. I hope that is understood." I said it was. "After that you will receive your portion of tips from the communal dish." I knew, having done such work previously, the "portion" would amount to only slightly more than the initial fortnight's nil.

Walking back along the corridor, I found myself, instead of taking the back stair downwards to my allotted room, turning the corner.

But Black Eyed Susan had vanished entirely. She might be in any of the rooms, or none. I knocked quietly on each closed door I now passed. But stopped this after one was suddenly flung open, and an irate man in shirtsleeves cried, "Have you brought my beer? Where is my beer?" I apologized, and told him it would shortly arrive. "I have been waiting here half my life," he ranted, "for one tankard of bloody beer!"

Below, on the third floor, when I reached it, I located my room. The bed had been made up—then unmade and left open—and the sheets seemed to have been slept in only that morning. Some long-ish, dark brown hairs lay on the pillow, and bending over it, I inhaled a faint musk of violets.

Hadn't just such a scent wafted by me in the wake of Black Eyed Susan?

I thought, with abrupt alarmed excitement, that maybe she and I were to share this room. The bed was easily wide enough. But there were no personal items put about (aside from the dark hairs). It was an awful room, in fact. Bare floorboards, on which somebody had thrown a single rough shabby towel to act as a rug, an overhead elec-tric light without a shade. The windows had tawdry curtains, and outside the town was settling grimly into the icing of the snow.

I made the bed again, and went along to the bathroom, which lay another floor down. Only the cold tap would run, though the hot made urgent chugging noises. I did the best I could with myself, then went back all the way downstairs.

The bar, where I was to begin, was in the charge of a tall, thin woman. She sat in a sort of open kiosk to one side sewing things, which changed color over the days and nights, from white to red to grey, but which even so never revealed their intentions. To me they looked most like bags for octopuses. Nevertheless, despite the octopus bags, she kept her scalpel of an eye on the room, calling out with no warning, in a shrill voice, either to me or the male wait-er: "Window table wants serving. Make haste with the coffee." Such things. The customers, who came and went from the street outside, or ambled in from the hotel itself, tipped her in preference to us, and

I saw the loot always go directly into her pocket. Her name was Mademoiselle Coudeban.

At intervals I was retrieved from the bar to wash up dishes or floors, scrape potatoes and peel onions, or pour boiling water on beetles below the sinks. After a day or two, I was also sent to lay tables, and next carry plates into the restaurant, under the large, chilly eyes of the Chief Waiter.

At six, midday and seven in the evening, I ate in the kitchen, at one edge of a littered table. These meals were gratis, but consisted of soup, bread, and sometimes cheese. Three chambermaids also came down to feed in this way, but they were given pieces of pies or meats already prepared for the paying customers. I was obviously too new for this treat.

The chambermaids questioned me eagerly. I was a fresh face, and apparently they longed to hear of other venues. But I didn't make the grave error of saying I had come from anywhere fascinating. I made myself as dull as possible. Nor would I take sides in their instantaneously conjured arguments. Soon they were offended with me and left me alone, only murmuring the odd sulky slight behind their hands.

Black Eyed Susan, however, did not appear in the kitchen, nor any other place. All that first day, evening and night, until I was cast out of the bar at two in the morning, part of me was alert as a pair of raised antennae. But there was no trace of her at all. Finally I asked Jean, the bar waiter, if anyone else worked in the hotel, aside from the people I had seen. He answered me that of course no one else was there, what did I expect, in winter?

When at last I crawled upstairs that first night-morning, washed in the cold water, and went to my icy little room, no one was there either.

I hadn't put anything out in the room myself, partly for fear the few things I had might be stolen. The space looked miserly empty, and quite frozen in the snow-light from beyond the window. All that day the snow had descended, and been tramped for proof into the hotel. Now the town lay like a white desert. A scatter of lights burned on in distant white humps that might be houses, or only hills. Far above a scornful moon loitered in the clearing sky. Dogs barked to each other and fell silent. Cars had been banished from the roads.

The hotel however snuffled in its half-sleep. And all around a muffled roaring blew about, which might be the hot water pipes of the heating system, which worked, doubtless, everywhere but in my room.

I knew I'd better go to bed. Tomorrow I must find more blankets and perhaps an old-fashioned stone hot water-bottle.

Under the cold sheet I lay rigid, tempted to snivel at my plight, which was all my own fault anyway. But sleep overtook me before tears could. I woke at a quarter to six to the alarm call of someone thumping on my door.

"Are we on fire?" I shouted. "Go away."

"Such impertinence!" shouted back Madame Ghoule.

It turned out it was her duty to arouse from slumber all the girls who worked at *The Queen*. Having herself retired to bed at ten-thirty, I'm sure she sadistically enjoyed her morning task.

Days and nights passed then in this way. It was true I learnt the names of the three maids—Sylvie, Claude and Jasmine. I was also propositioned by one or two male customers in the bar, evaded them, and was told off by Mademoiselle Octopus—whether because she thought I'd said yes, or because I refused, I wasn't quite certain.

The snow remained on the town, sealing us in a white envelope of inertia.

❧

On my fifth evening, I saw the man from the upper corridor, the one whose door I had knocked on, and who had flown up honking for beer like a desperate goose.

He draped himself at the bar counter, and peered at Jean, who was presiding over the bottles of absinthe and cognac.

"Say, Jeanot, I want to ask you something."

"Yes, Monsieur?" Jean was always polite to guests.

"It's a bit tricky. You see, there is a woman I clapped eyes on, up in the top corridor. A real—" he lowered his voice to protect the room, though not myself, who was stood there not two feet from him—"eyeful. A stunner. Could be from Paris. Thick brown hair tied back very neat, and a brownish skin. Black eyes. Black as coal. And a figure—well. And her legs, Jeanot. What legs those are. It was the other day when I came out to see about that beer you forgot to send me up—"

"Most regrettable, Monsieur—"

"Never mind that. I'm standing in the corridor, ready to come downstairs after my drink, and there was this piece of delight, slinking along the corridor. And she had on a uniform, like your girls wear who tidy the upper floor bedrooms."

"Yes, Monsieur," said Jean, patiently.

"Well, I've never seen her before, and as you know, I've stayed at *The Queen* in the past. So I wondered who she might be? And believe me, Jeanot, old chap, I'd like to know."

"No one, Monsieur," said Jean. "There's no woman works here of that description."

"A guest then?"

"No, Monsieur. We have, at present, no women guests staying at the hotel."

Monsieur of the Beer drew back. He scowled. Then turned on me. "*You* then. If he won't say, *you* tell me. Who is she? I've only spotted her once. But that was enough."

I knew who he must mean, for the one he had detailed was none other than the woman *I* had seen on my first morning, after Madame Cora had grabbed me.

I said, "I don't know who you refer to, Monsieur."

"Oh, is it some shit of a conspiracy? Why? I've had half the other girls in this rat-hole. So why clam up over this one? Aren't I good enough now? Money not good enough?"

"Please, Monsieur," said Jean, "you are upsetting the other customers."

"Fuck the other customers. Come on, Jeanot. Is she *your* fancy piece? I *doubt* it."

The other denizens of the bar were actually quite enjoying this theatre. But at that instant, Mademoiselle Octopus, who had been absent from the room, sailed in at the doors. She loomed over the Beer Monsieur and said, in a scratchy cruel little voice, "Where are your manners? Where do you think this is? Have I to have you ejected?"

And to my amazement, the riotous Monsieur Beer subsided, blushing and begging her for leniency.

At that moment too a flock of would-be drinkers entered from the street, their shoes and boots thick to the ankle in white. As I hurried to serve them I thought, with vague wonder, *Black Eyed Susan doesn't exist—yet two of us have seen her. She must be a ghost.*

Obviously it was unreasonable that I should call her Susan. But I'd lived, even then, in England long enough a while, the phrase had sprung to my mind.

Having decided she must be a ghost, I felt I should at least reorganize her name. And so she became Suzanne des Yeux Noires.

That night the Patron of the hotel came into my room.

I had just staggered in from work and the night was young, only twelve-thirty this time, for the bar (which operated by some autonomous law regulated only by how many heavy drinkers were present) had closed up early.

"Well, now," said the Patron. "Here I am."

I looked at him, displeased yet neutral.

He said, "Is *this* the dungeon they've given you? Poor little girl. What a nasty sty—and so *cold*. Have you turned the radiator off?"

"It doesn't work," I sullenly told him.

"Dear God. You'll catch pneumonia. Well, well," he rambled on, idling round the room, as if examining my personal clutter and knick-knacks, of which, as I've said, I had few and displayed none. "What was your name again? Estelle, was it?" When I couldn't be bothered to correct him, he cogitated "No, no, that's wrong. Is it Estrellya, then?"

I said, gently, "Monsieur, please excuse me, but I'm very tired. I have to be up before six tomorrow."

"Of course, of course. Well, well," he said. He sat down on the bed, and gradually began to undo his shoes.

In bemused horror I watched this procedure, which was followed soon enough by an unknotting of his tie, a removal of his coat and waistcoat.

All the while he went on speaking.

"No, it's not Estrellya, is it? Estina. That was it? No? No, no. You see, my grandmother still believes I must want young women. She has always thought this, but in fact," he rolled his eyes at the ceiling, from which icicles might well be hanging, "in fact I married young only from duty. My wife died long ago. My mother lived longer, but then she too died. My grandmother still lives, voraciously. Well. So it goes. So it goes."

By now he had divested himself, not only of his previous character, but also of all his clothing aside from his shirt. Bulbous hairy legs, veined like the best marble, protruded beneath, also there sometimes showed the soft beak of his penis, which lay innocently already sleeping. He got up again, pulled wide the bed, and quickly coiled himself into it.

He was entirely asleep in seconds. The room rattled at his baritone snores.

I, like the fool I was, stood there in my dark uniform dress, very like, I thought, that which Suzanne des Yeux Noires had worn, save hers (despite Monsieur Beer's mention of legs) had seemed rather longer, almost to her slender ankles.

What now?

After ten minutes of standing—my room did not provide a chair— I let myself back out of the door. I poised in the corridor, which was really warmer than my room, though lit only by the snow moon at the window, considering that the dark hairs I'd found on my pillow were really not so very long, and might have belonged to the Patron (the musk of violets being probably only my imagination), and that maybe the man often slept in that bed.

It was odd. But I have met—had met even then—so much oddity.

While I was stuck there in the corridor, wondering if I should now creep down to the kitchen and sleep Cinderellerishly in the grease by the ovens, another door opened far up the passage.

Someone stole out, voluptuously stealthy in her nightgown, her hair undone and lying loose all around her, like a soft silver mist.

"Oh, has that pig gone in your room? What a pig. Come with me. It's freezing out here."

She took me by the hand and led me, in a daze, along the passage and into her own chamber. It was Sylvie.

Ah, what a transformation she'd achieved. Admittedly, her radiator worked, but all else was due to her, or so I guessed. Her bed was heaped with a glorious patchwork quilt, made of rather map-shaped pieces, colored blue and scarlet, amber and ivory. Rugs massed on the floor. Thick curtains of a dense indigo masked the icy unfriendliness of the outer streets, and her overhead lamp, though unlighted, had a shade like a lace birdcage. Meanwhile a stand of candles blazed on a table near the bed, and here too were spread cosmetics, mirrors, sweets, a bottle of wine even, and two polished glasses.

"Do you like my room?" asked Sylvie, like a clever child.

"Very much."

"I've been here three whole months. You have to do something, don't you?" I looked at her in a bedraggled way. Laziness, or some other worse element, tended to make me always feel I had better do nothing. But I nodded. She said, "Let's have a glass of wine. You can share my bed if you like. Look, it's huge. And we're just two little girls, aren't we?"

We had the wine. I'd thought she hadn't liked me. And besides she might turn like milk in the morning. But milk keeps better in winter.

I undressed behind a bird-painted screen she had, and put on one of her nightgowns. I undid my hair. Next we were in the bed, which was warm from her occupancy.

"Shall I blow out the candles?" she said. She looked playful.

"Yes," I said.

In the dark there was a brief pause, during which my blood hummed like a hive of bees. She was less than my hand's length from me.

Then she moved up close to my side.

"We'd better stay together, or we'll be cold."

"Yes."

"What fine hair you have, Esther. Oh dear, so sorry, I never meant to touch you *there*."

"That's all right, Sylvie."

"Oh! There. I've done it again. What will you think?"

"Well, perhaps..."

"Really? Oh!" Now more genuinely, "Oh—that's—wonderful—"

I felt over every inch of her through the nightgown, which presently anyway we took off, and next mine.

She had that smooth deep skin from the south, heavy and satisfying as treacle. Her hands and elbows were rough, but all the rest glided. Her breasts had centers like the smooth pink sweets on the table. I sucked them until I thought they might explode like sherbet bonbons in my mouth, and Sylvie yelped softly, pulling my hair. The core of her tasted of the sea, and had the texture of firm plums. The urge to bite her was nearly unbearable, so I bit her stomach all along its curve, leaving little marks to remind her in the morning. Before returning into the depths of the sea-plum.

She wouldn't let me make her come though, not like that. I had to lie over her, pressing her down, staring at her eyes in the dark which it seemed to me was total, thanks to the thick curtains. Our hands twisted and spasmed. At the last glorious seconds she became all I'd ever wanted. But thank God, once we had fallen together like a collapsing fan, silently screaming into each other's flesh, she became again only a charming companion in a bed warm as toast.

"That was lovely," she whispered as we turned over to sleep, spine to spine, her buttocks couched in the small of my back. "And I knew you would."

"How?"

"Just something. You know Madame was like that once? Or so they say."

"Madame—which Madame? Madame Ghoule?"

But Sylvie slept, her appetite appeased for now.

I lay awake about twenty minutes, curious, almost happy.

And long before the sadist battered on the door at a quarter to six, Sylvie and I had woken once more, and once more coupled, twining as if we had slept away our bones.

"Yes, Madame!" called out Sylvie however, at the appalling knock. I of course kept quiet.

And through the door Madame Ghoule declared, "You must wake that new one, that Estette. I have been unable. My God, how she snores—"

A delicious time then, after all, at *The Queen*. Sylvie and I. We would meet almost every night when our work was done. I bought her a few flowers and cakes, cheap beads, a comb for her hair, proper tribute, and all I could afford, smuggled in wrappers or under my outdoor coat. The town, still floured with the now-decaying snow, opened up its shops for me. By day she and I would pretend we didn't care for each other much, and sometimes she would say something faintly disparaging about me to one of the others, loud enough I couldn't fail to hear, and then she'd wink at me. At night, between the sessions of sex, she would mock the other girls. I told her to be careful, to be wary.

I didn't love her. It was more enchanting than that.

Love can be a shackle so loaded with its own imprisoning power; it hauls you to the ocean's floor and throttles you there. But this was that other sort of love, honorably ancient as dust, and light as the opening spray of champagne that, once left, soon invisibly dries.

Did I then think of the other one, the ghost, Suzanne? Yes. Now and then. Involved in this unexpected romp, that gave me besides a warm bed, and even demonstrated for me the way to make the hot water come in the bathroom (Sylvie beating with a broom-handle on the tap) that also managed to see me given slices of meat in the kitchen, and other delicacies (by telling the contra-suggestive cook I should on no account get anything of the sort), even so, unforgivably (or inevitably perhaps, if I'm honest), some part of me was still glancing round to find the pain, the elation, of an unrequited obsession, therefore the black-eyed arrogance of Suzanne, the ghost.

To that end, I began to seek out Madame Cora, the grandmother of the peculiar Patron.

After all, that first morning, it was she who had yanked me up into the corridor where I'd seen Suzanne. And surely, if Monsieur Beer had beheld the apparition too, Madame Cora must likewise have done so. (To approach Monsieur himself had been out of the question. Following his outburst in the bar and the Octopus intervention, he'd fled the hotel the next day.)

Madame Cora, though, was a handier proposition. She dined almost every evening at eight o'clock in the dining room, where I was by now nearly always expected to assist in the service of guests.

Normally the Chief Waiter tended to Madame Cora, but once I had made up my mind, which took, I admit, two or three weeks, I slipped between them like a narrow knife.

"Good evening, Madame. We have an excellent fish tonight."

"What do you say?"

"An excellent fish. The cook has prepared it carefully and several people are praising it. I hope you'll like it, Madame. May I bring you a fresh carafe of water? This one has a fly in it."

She stared into the carafe, which had nothing in it but the water. She said, "Very well. What's your name?"

"Esther, Madame. We met on my first day at the hotel."

"Est," she said, looking at her first course, a sort of mushroom creation, which she'd broken but not eaten. "The East."

The Chief Waiter was there. He leaned over us. To me he said, "What are you doing here? Table seven wishes the roast chicken with sauce."

"Excuse me. Madame's water has a fly in it."

"A fly? In winter? Never. There's no fly."

"Please look there. It's a fly."

He raised the carafe, squinting in, his large, hopeless, unfair eyes expanding through the glass into a pair of ghastly swimming eye-fish.

"Nothing," he said.

But Madame Cora flew into a temper. "Let her take it away. There's a fly! Of course! Do as you're told."

He cowered and I sped out with the decanter.

Coming back in after a moment with, of course, the same water, I saw Madame Cora was now sitting alone again, the Chief Waiter spun off like a displaced molecule to the other side of the restaurant.

When I set the carafe back down before her, she put out her hard and bony hand and gripped my wrist, as at our meeting. This time I bent willingly towards her.

"Did he have you?" she asked in a low rasping voice.

She meant the Patron.

I said, truthfully, "He spent a night in my bed, Madame."

"Ah, good, good." She nodded and let me go. "He must be appeased," she said, obscurely. Her old eyes—what was she—seventy, seventy-five?—were dark yet filmed over. Her sad and disappointed lips turned down. And yet there was to them, those lips, something that once had been gallant—the lines running upward before the depression of gravity and age pushed them earthward. "He may wish to do it again," she said. She shot me a look.

"Very well, Madame," I said, meekly.

"Good. You're a good girl."

I filled her water glass. She seemed thoughtful. I said, "Madame, that young woman who passed us that day in the corridor, she had brown hair and very black eyes. Who is she?"

Madame Cora glanced at me again, and she smiled, pressing her sad mouth upwards.

"So you *saw* her?"

I straightened. A chill ran over my back.

"Yes. I did. What—who—is she?"

Her smile closed like a secret lock. She said, still locked smiling, "I don't want the fish. Bring me some cake now, and cheese."

She saw my defeat. She seemed to take definite pleasure in it. I understood it would be currently useless to try to question her further. Even so I said, "I call her Suzanne."

"Do you?" she asked. She laughed. It was a spiteful little bark, like her grandson's, the Patron. "Suzanne? That was never her name."

She must have made some gesture to him, for the Chief Waiter was suddenly there again, hustling me aside. "Go back to the kitchen at once! What are you at, bothering Madame?"

And back to the kitchen I went.

That night, in bed with Sylvie, I let her feed me chocolate, and told her I was unhappy as I'd been thinking of my dead mother, and my father, who was a crook. This launched her into some long epic tale of her own family and its vices, and in the end I was able to avoid making love with her. That night I felt I couldn't. But in the early hours of morning, before the yammer of Madame Ghoule on the door, I seized Sylvie in my arms, waking her to sensation so violently and harshly she began to cry, though her weeping was soon lost in other passions. "You're so unkind, Esther," she told me, snuggling into my body afterwards. "Don't you like me, really?" "I think you're quite wonderful," I said. "No," she said. "But never mind. Do you know," she went on, as I was drifting off again to sleep, "who gives me these chocolates, and the wine?" "The Patron," I suggested dreamily, She giggled. She said, "Oh no, it's..." I was asleep before I heard what she said.

I dreamed I was standing by a vast expanse of water, brown and glowing, a river. Palm trees rose above me, with pleated tines like sculpted bronze. A crocodile waddled like a green sausage on legs across a mud bank, and I heard my mother's long-ago, exasperated sigh.

When I woke up, in the moments before her knocking, I thought, *It's Madame Ghoule who is this way too, and who accordingly gives Sylvie confectionary and wine.* And when the knocking came and Sylvie only stirred in my arms, I called out loudly, "Thank you, Madame. We are awake."

To her credit I heard her answer steadily, "Excellent. Please see you're both downstairs and at work in twenty minutes. "

The snow which had loosened and regrouped, now sagged, and turned to a thick dirty sorbet, that ran off the town, leaving the roofs with loud bangs like the concussion of bombs. Released, the trees lifted black arms to a wet sun, against a scudding sky. Soon feathers of new life appeared on them, a tawny northern fuzz that, in a handful more weeks, might break to pale green.

Standing in the bathroom in my slip, hammering as usual on the hot tap, I watched in astonishment as the entire faucet gave way, spewing out fairly hot water across most of the room.

By the time I'd summoned assistance, the bathroom was flooded, the water, now growing cool, spooling away down the corridor in a glowing river.

Madame Ghoule summoned me.

"This is a disgrace, Mademoiselle."

"I'm sorry, Madame."

"Sorry is no use. Do you know how much it will cost to repair the damage?"

"No, Madame."

I thought she would dock my already meager wages. Instead she proclaimed, "We haven't been at all satisfied with your work, besides. You're slapdash, tardy, off-hand with the customers and, I hear, leave bits of food stuck on the plates when you wash them." I could say nothing to that. It was all true. "The cook has said you eat too much. In addition, you were told you're allowed only one bath a week, yet I gather you've been bathing almost every day." Also undeniable. I thought to myself, Yes, and you're jealous that I get into bed with Sylvie. But Madame Ghoule didn't list that among her sequence of complaints, of which there were several more. When she concluded, I waited for the axe to fall. It fell. "I think we shall wish to dispense with your services. Indeed, I think we shall be overjoyed to dispense with them."

Spring was coming. Despite my small gifts to Sylvie, and various essentials I'd had to buy for myself, I had by now accumulated enough to tide me over. I had been at the hotel called *The Queen* for almost two slow months—I would have been off anyway before much longer.

"Very well, Madame. Can I expect any wages owing to me?"

"Certainly not. Think yourself lucky you'll be asked to contribute nothing to the repair of the bathroom and corridor. "

❦

There are few things so liberating, I've found, as being summarily sacked. Not even any guilt attaches.

I went straight upstairs to my cold room (noting in passing, the Patron had been in my neglected bed again, this time smothering the pillow with hair oil), and changed into my own clothes and high-heeled shoes. I brushed my hair and left it loose on my shoulders, and applied my reddest lipstick to my mouth.

Then I went straight down to the bar.

"What are you doing here like that?" demanded Jean, caught, I could see, between abruptly noticing me as female, and prudish slavish disapproval. "You can't wear all that rouge, or those shoes—and some drunk's sure to spill something on that dress."

"I've been fired," I announced. "I'll have a cognac. Here," and I slid the coins to him across the counter.

Bewildered by this painted fiend, who only an hour ago had been meekly pouring out alcohol or coffee beside him, Jean measured my drink and handed it to me. Behind me, I heard a dim stirring and rustle, as Mademoiselle Octopus laid down her sewing in the kiosk.

"I want to know something, Jean," I said, boldly. "That dark woman the beery Monsieur liked upstairs—who is she?" He blinked, and I went on, "I know there *was* someone, though you were at such pains to deny it. I did too, remember, to help you out. But now I'd like to be told."

Jean opened his mouth. Stubbornly closed it. Then took a breath and said, "It's none of your concern."

"Did I say it was? I just want to know."

"Oh," said Jean, also abandoning any reserves of the commonplace, "I know why *you'd* want to know. Oh yes. I've heard about your sort of girl. Oh yes. Sylvie's said to all of us, she's not safe when you're around. Had to lock her bedroom door, she said, you were so persistent."

I shouldn't have been startled by betrayal. Being betrayed, one way or another, had become symptomatic of my existence. But for an instant my guts gave a sick lurch, and I downed the cognac, and thrust the empty glass back at him. "Another. And watch your tongue, sonny. It's Sylvie you should be careful of. And that Ghoule. Also your Patron. This hotel is a madhouse."

Jean wouldn't refill my glass, so I grabbed the bottle from him, and sloshed two glasses full. Clattering down more coins I said, "Drink up, before the sewing witch comes over."

Sheepishly, used I suppose, as many of them seemed to be, here, to being overridden by women, Jean swallowed his glass-full.

He said, to the counter, "You'd better not go after that woman upstairs, though. Just better not. Not if you've been entertaining the Patron."

Unnatural woman and *also* floozy, it seemed.

"Why is that?"

"She's his regular. Class. Brown hair and black eyes and that swarthy skin from the south. That's her. He makes her dress like a chambermaid in one of the old uniforms. We all *know*. We keep quiet."

A dank disappointment listed through me. One more betrayal. For my mystic Suzanne of the Black Eyes was not a ghost, only some upstairs classy whorey convenience of the hotel owner's, of whom we must all pretend unawareness.

"I don't believe you," I said, casually. "How could you know anything about what the Patron does?"

"Well, that's where you're wrong, see. I do know. She's the widow of a living man. He's crippled, and they've fallen on bad times. Not a servant in the house. Also she can't get anything from him, in *that* way. So she comes up to visit the Patron now and then. Her name's Henriette de Vallier."

"What an invented-sounding name."

"It's not. It's her name. She lives in one of the rich houses on the rue Rassolin."

A presence was at my shoulder, breathing on me a camphor-flavored pastille. Mademoiselle Coudeban, seamstress of bags for octopuses.

"What is happening? Why is this girl here dressed in this sluttish manner? Go up at once, girl, and wash your face. "

I turned and beamed at her. "Can I buy you a drink, Mademoiselle?"

"What effrontery! It's forbidden to drink on duty in the hotel. As for you, Jeanot, I quite plainly saw you swallow a glass of brandy."

"I gave it him for the shock," I said. "I'm no longer the employee of this strange building. I can do as I please."

"And I, miss," snapped Mademoiselle Octopus, "can have you put straight out of the door."

Although she had set down her sewing, I could see it over her shoulder, lying across the chair arm in the open kiosk. It was a shape like a map of India, perhaps, and of a deep amber color. I had seen such shapes and shades in the patchwork coverlet of my lover Sylvie. Suddenly I knew quite well who else had given Sylvie presents for her favors, and who else, too, had been betrayed. In that instance, to me.

I didn't have to say a word. By some bizarre osmosis of our brains, Mademoiselle Coudeban and I immediately and completely understood each other, and that, for now, I was potentially the more dangerous.

Her thin crunched-together face turned bitter and pale like a sour fruit sucking on a sour fruit.

I said, "Won't you take a drink with me, Mademoiselle?"

"It isn't allowed. But for yourself, since you say we no longer employ you—well. You must do as you like."

❧

After my earlier onslaught on Madame Cora in the dining room, I'd done nothing else, not knowing what else I could do.

Sometimes I had, during my breaks or on some excuse, gone up to the top corridor and walked about, passing several doors unmarked, or marked *Private*, but no longer knocking. In fact at that juncture no one at all seemed to be on the top floor. The hotel guests were, all told, very scarce; one came across them only in the bar or restaurant, or very occasionally on the stairs between the second and third stories. I'd already arrived at a surreal conclusion, which was that the hotel was primarily run only in order that its own weird, deviant and deranged life might go on. The enlisting of guests—even staff—being simply camouflage.

Now I'd been manumitted from slavery to the organism, however, I stalked out into the town, warmed by the brandy, and set off towards the street Jean had stipulated. I had seen it before, gone down it once on one of my solitary, aimless walks, which only gained meaning after I began to buy gifts for the faithless Sylvie.

The houses were tall and joined, with sloping ridged pestles of roofs. Iron railings enclosed clipped cold gardens the snow had spoiled, and here and there was a courtyard, one now with a little horse standing alone in it, browsing at a tub of wintry grass. Few cars moved along the avenue.

As in the hotel's upper corridor, I went to doors and knocked. Generally a maid appeared. "Oh, excuse my troubling you. But I've lost my kitten. Have you seen it? A little ginger cat, tiny—" Some were sentimentally concerned and took up my time suggesting various means to recapture the errant feline. Some gave me a gimlet glance and saw me off with a "No, Mademoiselle. You must try elsewhere." But all managed to inform me, in roundabout ways they never noted, that theirs was not the house of Madame de Vallier.

At the fifth house along the right-hand side, where a bare peach espalier clawed at the wall, a woman answered the door who wasn't a maid.

I looked at her, her fair hair held back by clips, her white face, green eyes and narrow mouth. No Black Eyed Susan she.

"Your kitten? Well, Mademoiselle, how can you have been so careless as to lose it?"

"Oh come, Lise. Don't be harsh." This from the shadowy stair along the hall. The voice was low and eloquent, and then there came the faintest slenderest gust of violets—

I stepped back, my heart hammering like the broom-handle on the tap of my ribs, to disrupt them and let hot hope explode outwards, splashing the espalier, the blonde woman, and anything else within reach.

Why do I put myself into such positions? Quivering down some alien street, knocking at doors and lying, in case I might find the barbed blade of a perfect, dreadsome love—

Then she was in view, the second woman who had spoken.

I said, before I could prevent it, "Madame de Vallier!"

"Oh, yes," she said. "Do you know me?"

"Forgive me, Madame. Not at all. I saw you—in a shop in the town, and someone spoke your name."

"How odd," she remarked.

She stood looking at me, not five feet away, the other woman, who she had called Lise, eclipsed and slunk aside.

Madame de Vallier paused in thought. Then: "Now the best thing," Madame de Vallier said, deciding on being firm and kind, "if the little cat has a favorite food—"

As she proceeded to give me her good-natured advice, I gazed at her, dumbfounded. Here was the woman with whom the Patron slept, presumably sometimes even in the beds of hotel staff such as myself. And she was exactly as Monsieur Beer had described her. Her chestnut brown hair was strictly tied back into a snood of black velvet. Her honey skin and faultless figure encased in neat black clothes that did indeed additionally reveal slim and well-formed legs. She was apparently in sartorial mourning for the living man of whom she was a "widow." The man who couldn't give her any more sex, or servants. She was pretty, certainly, in a pre-cast, unsurprising way. And her eyes were the dark brown of damp cedar wood. But not black, not black at all. Nor was she Suzanne. That is, she wasn't, nor could I ever have mistaken her for, the black-eyed creature I'd glimpsed in the corridor during my first hour at the hotel. Monsieur Beer and I, evidently, had seen two different women.

Henriette de Vallier finished her treatise on cat-retrieval. I thanked her effusively, and paced back down the path, looking as dispirited as any girl might who had just mislaid her beloved kitten. (I heard Lise malignly whisper, "She'd been drinking, too. You could smell it on her.")

I went and sat under a plane tree in the Place de la Fontaine, which was fountainless and winter-grim.

The life of the town mechanically passed me, up and down. Everyone was so involved, slotted each into their niche, whether comfortable or not, with a kind of self-satisfied assurance. *I am angry, so angry,* would say one face going by, or another, *I am in such a hurry,* or *I am lost in my thoughts—ask me nothing.* Even the smaller children who appeared seemed already enlisted in this army of the predestined, and already in the correct uniform and with the correct rank ascribed.

Only I sat there, outlawed flotsam—or jetsam more likely, hurled from the floating insane asylum called the Hôtel Reine.

I don't believe in ghosts, or think I don't. Or didn't or thought I didn't, then.

But I *had* seen her. She *had* gone by. And if the delicate whiff of violets was only some leftover of the other presence of Madame de Vallier, Black Eyed Susan had still been as real as I, or as the dotty old Cora, hanging on my arm.

Which brought me again, of course, to the Patron's grandmother. For she alone had been with me, when that being crossed our path. And she alone had later said to me, "So you *saw* her," and "Suzanne? That was never her name."

❧

That night I dined in the restaurant of the *Queen Hotel.*

I wore my one reasonable dress, which really was quite reasonable. I had an omelet, a salad, and something that may have been pork. Also a bottle of wine.

I was scrutinized by everyone, both the waiters and the customers, who all knew me by now as "That one, that Esette."

At ten minutes to eight, Madame Cora came in, leaning slightly sideways, as if on an unseen companion, and so moving rather like a crab. She sat down at her usual table, and the Chief Waiter hastened to her side. As always happened she took a long while, questioning every dish, clicking her tongue over the cook's efforts, asking for water, saying her napkin was soiled.

They brought her a plate of eggs, and she played with it, testing it as someone does who is perhaps searching for poison. When she laid down her fork, she looked around at last. And her watery grey-black eyes alighted on me.

Rather than seem amazed, Madame Cora nodded, as if I were a somewhat inferior acquaintance of long-standing. I picked up my glass of wine, and went across to her table, hearing about me the dismayed murmurs of our fellow diners.

"Oh, sit down, sit down," she said impatiently. And down I sat. "What do you think is in this food?"

"Eggs, I believe, Madame."

"Possibly. Useless, this cook. There was one here once, a fine cook. But that was before the war. He died in the trenches," she added, with a frown of selfish annoyance. "Since then, none of them are any good." She was such a little, wizened thing. On her hands there were no rings, not even one for wedlock. She dabbed her lips and pushed the dish away. "Do you want it?"

"No thank you, Madame. I've already eaten."

"Who are you?" she said.

"My name's Esther, Madame."

"Est," she said, as before. "From the East... How old are you?"

"Twenty-eight."

"*Pouf!* You look only sixteen. A girl. If you're so old, you should be married."

"If you say so."

"Don't you like men?" I said nothing, only modestly lowered my eyes. Madame Cora went on, "I never did. Foul brutes. But there, I had no choice. I used to bribe him, my husband, bring him girls—it kept him away from me. Then, despite everything, I had a child. My God, my God, the agony. They gave it to me and crowed, 'Look. A son.' I hated it at once. It grew up to be the present Patron's father, you see. Then there was *this* one, the Patron himself. I've brought them all women. It's all they can think of, pushing themselves into some woman. Horrible, stupid. What can it all mean? The church says it's our duty. But no, no, that was then. Surely that's all changed by now."

Did she want an answer? She'd fixed her eyes on me, drawing mine up to meet them. "I'm afraid it hasn't changed," I said.

"No. Of course not. Have you borne children?"

"No," I said

"You've been lucky."

"Yes."

The Chief Waiter had reached her table again, and he said to her sternly, "Is this person pestering you, Madame?"

"Pester? *You* are the one pesters me." She flapped the clean "soiled" napkin at him. "Be off! Where's my fruit? I wished for fruit. The Patron shall hear how casually I'm treated here." The Chief Waiter bowed and left us. Obviously he was accustomed to her ways. "I sent you to my grandson, didn't I?" she asked me. When I nodded, she said, "I hope you'll forgive that. I suppose he never gave you any sort of remuneration. No? That's like him. They say he keeps a mistress in the rue Rassolin, but how can one credit that? Even so, he lavishes a lot of money somehow, and none here. This wretched place," she waved her little wooden hand at the whole room, "it's falling apart. Nothing spent on it for years. Do you know, today one of the bathrooms exploded? What a thing. The taps blew off under the pressure of the water. Then the water soaked into the passage and through into the rooms below. Thousands of francs will be needed. I tell you, little girl," she said, conspiratorial, "one more good winter snow, and the whole crumbling edifice will collapse in rubble on the street."

I had the instant image of the hotel performing this very act. Clouds of dust and snow-spray rose into a black sky speckled with watching stars; bricks and pieces of iron bowled along the road.

And suddenly, as if she saw this image too, she gave some of her sharp little barks of laughter.

"Don't think," she said, "I'd be sorry. Not even if a ceiling dropped on my head. Oh, I hate it here," she said. And as suddenly as the laughter, her eyes were luminous and nearly youthful with tears. I had the urge to take her wooden hand. I didn't risk it. "I was young once," she confided. "Do you believe me?"

I said, "We were all young once, Madame."

"*Pouf!* You're a baby still. Twenty-eight—what's that? I was in my thirties, and still young. Oh yes. *That* was my time. Oh, the naughty things I did. He never knew, my son, and my husband was dead by then, thank God. Well, it wasn't any of their business. I worked here for them both, their skivvy. But it had many benefits, that. I would get to meet all the guests, enter their rooms even, quite intimately. There was always some excuse. Yes, little one. You and I might have had some fun then."

I looked at her narrowly. Now her eyes were sly.

I said, "I'm sure we'd have got on famously."

"*Famously!* Oh you English. Yes, I can hear that you are, all right, even through your French which is so exactly fluent."

Unwisely no doubt I assured her, "In fact, Madame, I'm a Jewess."

"A Jewess. Well then. The Jews are not so popular now, are they."

"If they ever were," I said.

"An arrogant race," she said. "And yes, *you're* an arrogant little thing. Of course you're a Jewess. But I had a lover once, a Jewess."

There. It was out. She had consorted, not so much with a pariah ethnic race, but with her own, that of women.

Her tears, which had dematerialized, shone out in her eyes again, and I thought she would reminisce now over past love. But she said again, pathetically, stoically and hopelessly, "How I hate it here." And she didn't mean, I saw, only the hotel. It was the world she hated, and what she had become in it. *Here* meant also her flesh.

Just then a waiter, attended by his Chief, came to the table with a long dish of offal-stuffed sausages.

"No!" snapped Madame Cora. "Take it away. I will have fruit."

"Madame—it's winter. There are only the apple tarts and the pears in syrup."

"Bring me the pears. They will be disgusting, but it's all I can expect, now."

The two waiters went away, bearing the sausages before them.

It wasn't that she bored me. But the pressure of her sorrows (like water on the riven tap), was very great, even overwhelming. Any plan I'd had, gradually to lead her to the elusive subject of the woman I called Suzanne, had drained from me as she spoke of her life. What was this momentary spark to that bleak digression? And anyway, did I really care? "Suzanne" perhaps had only been another of my means to kill time at the hotel. In addition, I had begun to be alarmed some-one might soon summon me again to Madame Ghoule, who would then demand, since I could afford to buy myself brandy, and had dined in the restaurant, that after all I pay over all my accrued mon-ey towards the repair of the water-damage. It seemed, did it not, so much more ruinous than I'd thought.

Because of all this, I was shifting mentally, thinking up a polite rea-son to leave Madame Cora, and so make my escape from the hotel. And in that way, I almost missed the next abrupt change in her eyes.

When I defined what was happening, I was caught a moment lon-ger, staring. It was as if a sort of glittering shutter fell through her eyes, first opening them wide as windows, and then closing them fast behind itself, so only that steely, glittering façade was left behind.

She sat bolt upright, her chin on her hand, these metallic and non-human eyes fixed on something behind me.

I turned round.

And all across the dining area, I saw a slim woman dressed in elon-gated black that was not a uniform, a large black hat with a silvery feather in it perched on her dark hair. She was in the process of walk-ing out of the room. And yet—I hadn't seen her in the restaurant un-til that second. (Had she perhaps entered behind my back, while the old woman and I were talking?) Whatever else, I knew her at once. It was She from the corridor. Not Henriette de Vallier, but Black Eyed Susan.

"Pardon me, Madame—" I stuttered, rising, throwing back my chair. Madame Cora's face seemed to dress itself in a kind of leer. She found my urgency funny, of course. She knew *precisely* what I was at.

In the doorway I brushed hastily past Jean, who was coming in with a tray of drinks. He cursed me, but I scarcely noticed.

Black Eyed Susan—Suzanne des Yeux Noires—was crossing the lobby, going under the yellow electric lamp, exiting into the blowy crystal vistas of the night.

As I too dashed out on the pavement, I was glad the snow was long gone. For already *she* was far ahead of me, walking swiftly in her little high-heels, that gave at each step a flash of ankle in a clock-patterned stocking. The wind blew her hat-plume to a ripple like a sea-wave in storm.

I could smell the unborn spring, acid as new wine, tossed by the wind. I could smell a hint of musk and violet—as unlike the scent of Madame de Vallier, or the Patron's hair oil, as any perfume could be that came from the same flower.

Now I was running. Dare I call out? What would I call? Suzanne! Suzanne! Wait just one instant—

But Cora had told me anyway, Suzanne wasn't her name.

At the street's corner, under a lamp, she turned, my quarry. She looked back at me, or I thought she did. All across the distance, in the web of light, her two space-black eyes, gleaming like frost on a steely surface. Then she was around the corner.

I ran to it, and reached it in seconds. But she had disappeared.

I patrolled up and down the street a while, looking in at doorways, up at windows, lighted or un, once into a lively café.

She must live, or visit, in this street. Perhaps I should knock on doors? I didn't knock. I wandered only up and down, until a man came out of the café and offered me a drink, and I had to tell him I was waiting for my friend. "He hasn't turned up, has he?" said the man, triumphant. "Why not give me a try?" But I told him I feared my friend was ill and I must go to him, and hurried away back to the hotel.

Even from outside I saw some fresh kind of uproar was going on, the lobby full of muddled figures and someone shouting for something, I couldn't make out what.

I entered, and stood at the edge of the crowd, and Jean thrust out of it, pasty-faced, and slouched past me, though the street door and away up the street. Also I heard the telephone being used, clacking like a pair of knitting needles, and Madame Ghoule's guttural, "No, he must come. At once, if you please. This is Madame Ghoule at *La Reine*. Please make haste."

And then the entire unintelligibly chattery crowd was falling silent, and down the stairs, and into the crowd, parting it like the Red Sea, came the Patron, greasy grey, his spectacles in his hand, and looking ashamed, as if caught out in some particularly socially-unacceptable crime.

"Make way, it's the Patron." "Let him by, poor fellow."

He went on into the restaurant. And the crowd stole after him, Madame Ghoule lunging among them, crying out now in a clarion tone, "The doctor's on his way, but his car has broken down. He'll have to walk."

In the big room though, the crowd, composed only of a scurry of waiters, a selection of guests and customers from the bar, spread itself, and showed its essential thinness. A couple of people were still seated at their tables, they too looking more embarrassed and depressed than anything. Altogether it was a badly attended show, the audience not large enough, nor moved enough, to honor the tragedy.

Which tragedy then? Oh, that of Madame Cora, who, sitting at her table with her chin propped on her hard little hand, and her eyes wide open, had died in their midst without a sound.

No one had noticed, it seemed, until the Chief Waiter brought her the pears in syrup.

She must have finished that very moment I got up to run after the phantasmal Suzanne. What I'd seen occur in Cora's eyes was then after all truly an opening, and a closing. But the almost sneering amusement on her face had only been death.

It seemed she hadn't suffered. A massive apoplexy, the doctor assured everyone. Congratulating, very nearly, the indifferent Cora on such a textbook exodus. It would have been too quick for pain, he said. This I believed. Nor had she wanted to stay. If the ceiling had fallen on her, she said...Well. It had.

I packed my bags that night, unmolested, and left. I was only astounded to meet Jasmine the chambermaid in a corridor, who said to me fiercely, "Fancy going with a slut like that Sylvie. I'd have liked to be your friend. And I can keep my trap shut about things."

Surprises everywhere.

I took the train to the city, and found a room. As I was always doing. At least in this lodging I was allowed to make a fire, and the landlady offered hot coffee and bread in the mornings.

Of course, I had completely given up my search for, my pursuit of, Black Eyed Susan.

Perhaps I should invent an epilogue, in which I disclose that, before leaving the hotel, I'd found an old photograph of Madame Cora, and seen at once, with a shock so terrific I staggered, that she was the exact double of my "Suzanne."

And demonstrably therefore had *been* "Suzanne" in her youth. Hadn't she said, Madame Cora, that she longed for her youth, and her female lovers? Hadn't she said that "Suzanne" was never known by that name?

Maybe it was her ghost I saw, that is, the premonition of the ghost of Cora's past, or even her spatial spirit, finally eluding the hotel and the world and the old wizened body, clad in what Cora thought her own perfect form and age, about thirty, dark and sensuous, *carnal* in her black of mourning for a husband, in that expedient, safely deceased; ready for more adventures in some other place.

Or maybe the woman I saw, for see her—*scented* her—I definitely did, if only twice, was another secret mistress of the unusual Patron. Or even some figment of my own winter madness, which Cora recognized as such, knowing that any woman like Esther must be strange in other ways.

I think of her sometimes—of them both. Black Eyed Susan, vanishing into thin air at two turning points, a corridor, a street corner. Madame Cora vanishing also into thin air, leaving only her husk behind her leering in victory at her last laugh.

Thimble-riggery and Fledglings

STEVE BERMAN

THE SORCERER

Bernhard von Rothbart scratched at a sore on his chin with a snow-white feather, then hurled it as a dart at the chart hanging above the bookshelves. The quill's sharp end stabbed through the buried feet of the dunghill cock, *Gallus gallus faecis*, drawn with a scarab clutched in its beak.

"A noble bird," von Rothbart muttered as he bit clean his fingernails, "begins base and eats noble things."

He expected his daughter to look up from a book and answer "Yes, Papa," but there was only silence. Above him, in the massive wrought-iron cage, the wappentier shifted its dark wings. One beak yawned while the other preened. A musky odor drifted down.

Why wasn't Odile studying the remarkable lineage of doves?

Von Rothbart climbed down the stairs. Peered into room after room of the tower. A sullen chanticleer pecked near the coat rack. Von Rothbart paused a moment to recall whether the red-combed bird had been the gardener who had abandoned his sprouts or the glazier who'd installed murky glass.

He hoped to find her in the kitchen and guilty of only brushing crumbs from the pages of his priceless books. But he saw only the new cook, who shied away. Von Rothbart reached above a simmering cauldron to run his fingers along the hot stones until they came back charred black.

Out the main doors, the sorcerer looked out at the wide and tranquil moat encircling his home, and at the swans drifting over its surface. He knew them to be the most indolent birds. So much so they barely left the water.

He brushed his fingers together. Ash fell to the earth and the feathers of one gliding swan turned soot-dark and its beak shone like blood.

"Odile," he called. "Come here!"

The black swan swam to shore and slowly waddled over to stand before von Rothbart. Her neck, as sinuous as any serpent's, bent low until she touched her head to his boots.

༄

THE BLACK SWAN

Odile felt more defeated than annoyed at being discovered. Despite the principle that, while also a swan, she should be able to tell one of the bevy from the other, Odile had been floating much of the afternoon without finding Elster. Or, if she had, the maiden—Odile refused to think of them as pens, despite Papa insisting that was the proper terminology—had remained mute.

"What toad would want this swan's flesh?" her papa muttered. "I want to look upon the face of my daughter."

In her head, she spoke a phrase of *rara lingua* that shed the albumen granting her form. The transformation left her weak and famished; while she had seen her papa as a pother owl devour a hare in one swallow, Odile as a swan could not stomach moat grass and cloying water roots. No longer the tips of great wings, her fingers dug at the moss between flagstones.

"There's my plain girl." Smiling, he gently lifted her by the arms. "So plain, so sweet." He stroked her cheek with a thumb.

She could hear the love in his voice, but his familiar cooing over her rough-as-vinegar face and gangly limbs still hurt. A tear escaped along the edge of her nose.

"Why you persist in playing amongst the bevy...." He stroked her cheek with a thumb. "Come inside." He guided her towards the door. "There won't only be lessons today. I'll bring a Vorspiel of songbirds to the window to make you smile."

Odile nodded and walked with him back into the tower. But she would rather Papa teach her more of *rara lingua*. Ever since her sixteenth birthday, he had grown reluctant to share invocations. At first, Odile thought she had done something wrong and was being punished, but she now she suspected that Papa felt magic, like color, belonged to males. The books he let her read dealt with nesting rather than sorcery.

From his stories, Odile knew he had been only a few years older when he left his village, adopted a more impressive name, and traveled the world. He had stepped where the ancient augers had read entrails. He had spoken with a cartouche of ibises along the Nile and fended off the copper claws of the gagana on a lost island in the Caspian Sea.

But he never would reveal the true mark of a great sorcerer: how he captured the wappantier. His secrets both annoyed Odile and made her proud.

❧

THE WAPPENTIER

As the sole- surviving offspring of the fabled ziz of the Hebrews, the wappentier is the rarest of raptors. Having never known another of its ilk, the wappentier cannot speak out of loneliness and rarely preens its dark feathers. Some say the beast's wings can stretch from one horizon to the other, but then it could not find room in the sky to fly. Instead, this *lusus naturae* perches atop desolate crags and ruins.

The Rashi claimed that the wappentier possesses the attributes of both the male and female. It has the desire to nest and yet the urge to kill. As soon as gore is taken to its gullet, the wappentier lays an egg that will never hatch. Instead, these rudiments are prized by theurgists for their arcane properties. Once cracked, the egg, its gilded shell inscribed with the Tetragrammaton, reveals not a yolk but a quintessence of mutable form, reflected in the disparate nature of the beast. A man may change his physique. A woman may change her fate. But buried, the eggs become foul and blackened like abandoned iron.

൚

THIS SWAN MAY

When Elster was nine, her grandmother brought her to the fairgrounds. The little girl clutched a ten-pfenning tight in her palm. A gift from her papa, a sour-smelling man who brewed gose beer all day long. "To buy candy. Or a flower," said her grandmother.

The mayhem called to Elster, who tugged at her grandmother's grip wanting to fly free. She broke loose and ran into the midst of the first crowd she came upon. Pushing her way to the center, she found there a gaunt man dressed in shades of red. He moved tarnished thimbles about a table covered in a faded swatch of silk.

The man's hands, with thick yellowed warts at every bend and crease, moved with a nimble grace. He lifted up one thimble to reveal a florin. A flip and a swirl and the thimble at his right offered a corroded haller. The coins were presented long enough to draw sighs and gasps from the crowd before disappearing under tin shells.

"I can taste that ten-bit you're palming," said the gaunt man. Thick lips hid his teeth. How Elster heard him over the shouts of the crowd— "*Die linke Hand*"—she could not guess. "Wager for a new life? Iron to gold?" His right hand tipped over a thimble to show a shining mark, bit of minted sunlight stamped with a young woman's face. Little Elster stood on her toes, nearly tipping over the table, to see the coin's features. Not her mother or her grandmother. Not anyone she knew yet. But the coin itself was the most beautiful of sights; the gold glittered and promised her anything. Everything. Her mouth watered and she wanted the odd man in red's coin so badly that spittle leaked past her lips.

When she let go of the table, the iron pfenning rolled from her sweaty fingers. The gaunt man captured it with a dropped thimble.

"Now which one, magpie? You want the shiny one, true? Left or right or middle or none at all?"

Elster watched his hands. She could not be sure and so closed her eyes and reached out. She clamped her hand over the gaunt man's grip. His skin felt slick and hard like polished horn. "This one," she said. When she looked, his palm held an empty thimble.

"Maybe later you'll find the prize." When he smiled she saw that his front teeth were metal: the left a dull iron, the right gleamed gold.

A strong arm pulled her away from the table. "Stupid child." Her grandmother cuffed her face. "From now on, a thimble will be your keep."

༜

THE MESSAGE

Down in the cellar, the stones seeped with moisture. Odile sneezed from the stink of mould. She could see how her papa trembled at the chill.

The floor was fresh-turned earth. Crates filled niches in the walls. In the tower's other cage, a weeping man sat on a stool. The king's livery, stained, bunched about his shoulders.

"The prince's latest messenger." Papa gestured at a bejeweled necklace glittering at the man's feet. "Bearing a bribe to end the engagement."

Papa followed this with a grunt as he stooped down and began digging in the dirt with his fingers. Odile helped him brush away what covered a dull, gray egg. "Papa, he's innocent."

He gently pulled the egg loose of the earth. "Dear, there's a tradition of blame. Sophocles wrote that 'No man loves the messenger of ill.'"

He took a pin from his cloak and punched a hole into the ends of the egg while intoning *rara lingua*. Then he approached the captive man, who collapsed, shaking, to his knees. Papa blew into one hole and a vapor reeking of sulfur drifted out to surround the messenger. Screams turned into the frantic call of a songbird.

"We'll send him back to the prince in a gilded cage with a message. 'We delightfully accept your offer of an engagement ball.' Perhaps I should have turned him into a parrot and he could have spoken that."

"Papa," Odile chided.

"I'll return his form after the wedding. I promise." He carried the egg to one shelf and pulled out the crate of curse eggs nestled in soil. "What king more wisely cares for his subjects?"

THE PRINCE

The prince would have rather mucked out every filthy stall in every stable of the kingdom than announce his engagement to the sorcerer's daughter at the ball. His father must have schemed his downfall; why else condemn him to marry a harpy?

"Father, be reasonable. Why not the Duke of Bremen's daughter?" The prince glanced up at the fake sky the guildsmen were painting on the ballroom's ceiling. A cloud appeared with a brushstroke.

"The one so lovely that her parents keep her at a cloister?" asked the king. "Boy, your wife should be faithful only to you. Should she look higher to God, she'll never pay you any respect."

"Then that Countess from Schaumberg—"

The king sighed. "Son, there are many fine lands with many fine daughters but none of them have magic."

"Parlor tricks!"

"Being turned into a turkey is not a trick. Besides, von Rothbart is the most learned man I have ever met. If his daughter has half the mind, half the talent…."

"Speaking dead languages and reciting dusty verse won't keep a kingdom."

The king laughed. "Don't tell that to Cardinal Passerine."

Thimbleriggery and Fledglings

The Fledgling

In the silence, Odile looked up from yellowed pages that told how a pelican's brood are stillborn until the mother pecks its chest and resurrects them with her own blood. Odile had no memory of her own mother. Papa would never answer any question she asked about her.

She pinched the flame out in the sconce's candle and opened the shutters. The outside night had so many intriguing sounds. Even if she only listened to the breeze it would be enough to entice her from her room.

She went to her dresser, opened the last drawer, and found underneath old mohair sweaters the last of the golden wappentier eggs she had taken. She could break it now, turn herself into a night bird and fly free. The thought tempted her as she stared at her own weak reflection on the shell. She polished it for a moment against her dressing gown.

But the need to see Elster's face overpowered her.

So, as she had done so many nights, Odile gathered and tied bed sheets and old clothes together as a makeshift rope to climb down the outer walls of her papa's tower.

As she descended, guided only by moonlight, something large flew near her head. Odile became still, with the egg safe in a makeshift sling around her chest, her toes squeezing past crumbling mortar. A fledermaus? Her papa called them vermin; he hunted them as the pother owl. If he should spot her…. But no, she did not hear his voice demand she return to her room. Perhaps it was the wappentier. Still clinging to the wall, she waited for the world to end, as her papa had said would happen if the great bird ever escaped from its cage. But her heartbeat slowly calmed and she became embarrassed by all her fears. The elder von Rothbart would have fallen asleep at his desk, cheek smearing ink on the page. The sad wappentier would be huddled behind strong bars. Perhaps it also dreamed of freedom.

Once on the ground, Odile walked towards the moat. Sleeping swans rested on the bank. Their long necks twisted back and their bills tucked into pristine feathers.

She held up the wappentier egg. Words of *rara lingua* altered her fingernail, making it sharp as a knife. She punctured the two holes, and as she blew into the first, her thoughts were full of incantations and her love's name. She had trouble holding the words in her head; as if alive and caged, they wanted release on the tongue. Maybe Papa could not stop from turning men into birds, though Odile suspected he truly enjoyed doing so.

She never tired of watching the albumen sputter out of the shell and drift over the quiet swans like marsh fire before falling like gold rain onto one in their midst.

Elster stretched pale limbs. Odile thought the maid looked like some unearthly flower slipping through the damp bank, unfurling slender arms and long blonde hair. Then she stumbled until Odile took her by the hand and offered calm words while the shock of the transformation diminished.

They fled into the woods. Elster laughed to run again. She stopped to reach for fallen leaves, touch bark, then pull at a loose thread of Odile's dressing gown and smile.

Elster had been brought to the tower to fashion Odile a dress for court. Odile could remember that first afternoon, when she had been standing on a chair while the most beautiful girl she'd ever seen stretched and knelt below her measuring. Odile had never felt so awkward, sure that she'd topple at any moment, yet so ethereal, confidant that had she slipped, she would glide to the floor.

Papa instructed Elster that Odile's gown was to be fashioned from sticks and string, like a proper bird's nest. But, alone together, Elster showed Odile bolts of silk and linen, guiding her hand along the cloth to feel its softness. She would reveal strands of chocolate-colored ribbon and thread them through Odile's hair while whispering how pretty she could be. Her lips had lightly brushed Odile's ears.

When Papa barged into Odile's room and found the rushes and leaves abandoned at their feet and a luxurious gown in Elster's lap, he dragged Elster down to the cellar. A tearful Odile followed, but she could not find the voice to beg him not to use a rotten wappentier egg.

In the woods, they stopped, breathless, against a tree trunk. "I brought you a present," Odile said.

"A coach that will carry us far away from your father?"

Odile shook her head. She unlaced the high top of her dressing gown and allowed the neckline to slip down inches. She wore the prince's bribe but now lifted it off her neck. The thick gold links, the amethysts like frozen drops of wine, seemed to catch the moon's fancy as much as their own.

"This must be worth a fortune." Elster stroked the necklace Odile draped over her long, smooth neck.

"Perhaps. Come morning, I would like to know which swan is you by this."

Elster took a step away from Odile. Then another until the tree was between them. "Another day trapped. And another. And when you marry the prince, what of me? No one will come for me then."

"Papa says he will release all of you. Besides, I don't want to marry the prince."

"No. I see every morning as a swan. You can't—won't—refuse your father."

Odile sighed. Lately, she found herself daydreaming that Papa had found her as a chick, fallen from the nest, and turned her into a child. "I've never seen the prince," Odile said as she began climbing the tree.

"He'll be handsome. An expensive uniform with shining medals and epaulets. That will make him handsome."

"I heard his father and mother are siblings. He probably has six fingers on a hand." Odile reached down from the fat branch she sat upon to pull Elster up beside her.

"Better to hold you with."

"The ball is tomorrow night."

"What did he do with the gown I made you?"

"He told me to burn it. I showed him the ashes of an apron. It's hidden beneath my bed."

"Let me wear it. Let me come along to the ball with you."

"You would want to see me dance with him?"

Elster threaded her fingers through Odile's hair, sweeping a twig from the ends. "Wouldn't you rather I be there than your father?"

Odile leaned close to Elster and marveled at how soft her skin felt. Her pale cheeks. Her arms, her thighs. Odile wanted music then, for them to dance together dangerously on the branches. Balls and courts and gowns seemed destined for other girls.

∾

The Coach

On the night of the ball, von Rothbart surprised Odile with a coach and driver. "I returned some lost sons and daughters we had around the tower for the reward." He patted the rosewood sides of the coach. "I imagine you'll be traveling to and from the palace in the days to come. A princess shouldn't be flying."

Odile opened the door and looked inside. The seats were plush and satin.

"You wear the same expression as the last man I put in the cellar cage." He kissed her cheek. "Would a life of means and comfort be so horrible?"

The words in her head failed Odile. They wouldn't arrange themselves in an explanation, in the right order to convey to Papa her worries about leaving the tower, her disgust at having to marry a man she didn't know and could never care for. Instead she pressed herself against him. The bound twigs at her bosom stabbed her chest. The only thing that kept her from crying was the golden egg she secreted in the nest gown she wore.

When the coach reached the woods, Odile shouted for the driver to top. He looked nervous when she opened the door and stepped out on to the road.

"Fraulein, your father insisted you arrive tonight. He said I'd be eatin' worms for the rest of my days."

"A moment." She had difficulty running, because of the rigid gown. She knew her knees would be scratched raw by the time she reached the swans. Odile guided a transformed Elster to the road. The sight of the magnificent coach roused her from the change's fugue.

"Finally I ride with style." Elster waited for the driver to help her climb the small steps into the coach. "But I have no dress to wear tonight."

Odile sat down beside her and stroked the curtains and the cushions. "There is fabric wasted here to make ten gowns."

When Odile transformed her fingernails to sharp points to rip free satin and gauze, she noticed Elster inch away. The magic frightened her. Odile offered a smile and her hand to use as needles. Elster took hold of her wrist with an almost cautious touch.

The bodice took shape in Elster's lap. "We could stay on the road. Not even go to the ball. You could turn the driver into a red-breasted robin and we could go wherever we want."

"I've never been this far away from home." Odile wondered why she hadn't considered such an escape. But all her thoughts had been filled with the dreaded ball, as if she had no choice but to accept the prince's hand. She glanced out the tiny window at the world rushing past. But Papa would be waiting for her tonight. There would be studies tomorrow and feeding the wappentier, and she couldn't abandon Papa.

It was a relief that she had no black egg with her, that she had no means to turn a man into fowl. She had never done so, could not imagine the need. So she shook her head.

Elster frowned. "Always your father's girl." She reached down and bit free the thread linking Odile's fingers and her gown. "Remember that I offered you a choice."

THE BALL

The palace ballroom had been transformed into an enchanting wood. The rugs from distant Persia rolled up to allow space for hundreds of fallen leaves fashioned from silk. The noble attendees slipped on the leaves often. A white-bearded ambassador from Lombardy fell and broke his hip; when carried off he claimed it was no accident but an *atto di guerra*.

Trees, fashioned by carpenters and blacksmiths, spread along the walls. The head cook had sculpted dough songbirds encrusted with dyed sugars and marzipan beaks.

The orchestra was instructed not to play any tune not found in nature. This left them perplexed and often silent.

"Fraulein Odile von Rothbart and her guest Fraulein Elster Schwanensee." The herald standing on the landing had an oiled, thick mustache.

Odile cringed beneath the layers of twigs and parchment that covered her torso and trailed off to sweep the floor. How they all stared at her. She wanted to squeeze Elster's hand for strength but found nothing in her grasp; she paused halfway down the staircase, perplexed by her empty hand. She turned back to the crowd of courtiers but saw no sign of her swan maid.

The courtiers flocked around her. They chattered, so many voices that she had trouble understanding anything they said.

"That frock is so…unusual." The elderly man who spoke wore a cardinal's red robes. "How very bold to be so…indigenous."

A sharp-nosed matron held a silken pomander beneath her nostrils. "I hope that is imported mud binding those sticks," she muttered.

❧

THE LOVEBIRDS

Elster picked up a crystal glass of chilled Silvaner from a servant's platter. She held the dry wine long in her mouth, wanting to remember its taste when she had to plunge a beak into moatwater.

"Fraulein von Rothbart. Our fathers would have us dance."

Elster turned around. She had been right about the uniform. Her heart ached to touch the dark blue-like-evening wool, the gilded buttons, the medals at the chest, and the thick gold braid on the shoulders. A uniform like that would only be at home in a wardrobe filled with fur-lined coats, jodhpurs for riding with leather boots, silken smoking jackets that smelled of Turkish tobacco. The man who owned such clothes would only be satisfied if his darling matched him in taste.

She lowered her gaze with much flutter and curtsied low.

"I am pleased you wore my gift." The prince had trimmed fingernails that looked so pink as to possibly be polished. He lifted up one section of the necklace she wore. The tip of his pinky slid into the crease between her breasts. "How else would I know you?"

She offered a promissory smile.

He led her near where the musicians sought to emulate the chirp of crickets at dusk.

"So, I must remember to commend your father on his most successful enchantment."

"Your Imperial and Royal Highness is too kind."

Three other couples, lavish in expensive fabric and pearls and silver, joined them in a quadrille. As the pairs moved, their feet kicked up plumes of silk leaves. Despite the gold she wore around her neck, Elster felt as if she were a tarnished coin thimblerigged along the dance floor.

"I have an admission to make," she whispered in the prince's ear when next she passed him. "I'm not the sorcerer's daughter."

The prince took hold of her arm, not in a rough grasp, but as if afraid she would vanish. "If this is a trick—"

"Once I shared your life of comfort. Sheets as soft as a sigh. Banquet halls filled with drink and laughter. Never the need for a seamstress as I never wore a dress twice.

"My parents were vassals in Saxony. Long dead now." She slipped free of his hold and went to the nearest window. She waited for his footsteps, waited to feel him press against her. "Am I looking East? To a lost home?"

She turned around. Her eyes lingered a moment on the plum-colored ribbon sewn to one medal on his chest. "So many years ago—I have lost count—a demonic bird flew into my bedchamber."

"Von Rothbart."

Elster nodded at his disgust. "He stole me away, back to his lonely tower. Every morning I woke to find myself trapped as a swan. Every night he demands I become his bride. I have always refused."

"I have never stood before such virtue." The prince began to tear as he stepped back and then fell to one knee. "Though I can see why even the Devil would promise himself to you."

His eyes looked too shiny, as if he might start crying or raving like a madman. Elster had seen the same sheen in Odile's eyes. Elster squeezed the prince's hand but looked over her shoulder at where she had parted with the sorcerer's daughter. The art of turning someone into a bird would never dress her in cashmere or damask. Feathers were only so soft and comforting.

∾

THE LOST

When Odile was a young girl, her father told her terrible tales every *Abend vor Allerheiligen*. One had been about an insane cook who had trapped over twenty blackbirds and half-cooked them as part of a pie. All for the delight of a royal court. Odile had nightmares about being trapped with screeching chicks, all cramped in the dark, the stink of dough, the rising heat. She would not eat any pastry for years.

Watching Elster dance with the prince filled Odile with pain. She didn't know whether such hurt needed tears or screams to be freed. She approached them. The pair stopped turning.

"Your warning in the coach? Is this your choice?" asked Odile.

Elster nodded though her hands released the prince's neck.

The *rara lingua* to tear the swan maid's humanity from her slipped between Odile's lips with one long gasp. Her face felt feverish and damp. Perhaps tears. She called for Papa to take the swan by the legs into the kitchen and return carrying a bulging strudel for the prince.

∾

THE STRYGIAN

As a long-eared pother owl, von Rothbart had hoped to intimidate the nobles with a blood-curdling shriek as he flew in through a window. An impressive father earned respect, he knew. But with the cacophony in the ballroom—courtiers screaming, guards shouting, the orchestra attempting something cheerful—only three fainted.

Von Rothbart roosted on the high-backed chair at the lead table. He shrugged off a mantle of feathers and seated himself with his legs on the tablecloth and his boots in a dish of poached boar.

"I suppose the venery for your lot would be an inbred of royals."

No one listened.

He considered standing atop the table but his knees ached after every transformation. As did his back. Instead, he pushed his way through the crowd at the far end, where most of the commotion seemed centered.

He did not expect to find a tearful Odile surrounded by a ring of lowered muskets. One guard trembled so. The prince shouted at her. The king pulled at his son's arm.

Von Rothbart raised his arms. The faux trees shook with a sudden wind that topped glasses, felled wigs, and swept the tiles free of silk leaves. "Stop," he shouted. "Stop and hear me!"

All eyes turned to him. He tasted fear as all the muskets pointed at him.

"You there, I command you to return Elster to me." The prince's face had become ruddy with ire. His mouth flecked with spittle.

"Who?"

"No lies, Sorcerer. Choose your words carefully"

The king stepped between them. He looked old. As old as von Rothbart felt. "Let us have civil words."

"Papa—" cried Odile.

"If you have hurt my daughter in any way—"

A cardinal standing nearby smoothed out his sanguine robes. "Your daughter bewitched an innocent tonight."

"She flew away from me," said the prince. "My sweet Elster is out there. At night. All alone."

Von Rothbart looked around him. He could not remember ever being so surrounded by men and women and their expressions of disgust, fear, and hatred left him weak. Weak as an old fool, one who thought he could ingratiate his dear child into their ranks as a cuckoo did with its egg.

Only magpies would care for such shiny trappings and they were sorrowful birds who envied human speech.

He took a deep breath and held it a moment as the magic began. His lungs hurt as the storm swirled within his body. He winced as a rib cracked. He lost two teeth as the gusts escaped his mouth. The clouds painted on the ceiling became dark and thick and spat lightning and rain down upon the people.

Odile stretched and caught the wind von Rothbart sent her as the crowd fled. He took her out of the palace and into the sky. It pained him to speak so all he asked her was if she was hurt. The tears that froze on her cheeks answered yes, Papa.

❧

The Black Swain

"Von Rothbart!"

Odile looked out the window. She had expected the prince. Maybe he'd be waving a sword or a blunderbuss and be standing before a thousand men. But not the king standing by the doors and a regal carriage drawn by snorting stallions. He looked dapper in a wool suit, and she preferred his round fur hat to a crown.

"Von Rothbart, please, I seek an audience with you."

Odile ran down the staircase and then opened the doors.

The king plucked the hat from his head and stepped inside. "Fraulein von Rothbart."

"Your majesty." She remembered to curtsy.

"Your father—"

"Papa is ill. Ever since…well, that night, he's been taken to bed."

"I'm sorry to hear that. Your departure was marvelous. The court has been talking of nothing else for days." The king chuckled. "I'd rather be left alone."

She led him to the rarely used sitting room. The dusty upholstery embarrassed her.

"It's quiet here. Except the birds of course." The king winced. "My apologies."

"Your son—"

"Half-mad they say. Those who have seen him. He's roaming the countryside hoping to find her. A swan by day and the fairest maiden by night." He tugged at his hat, pulling it out of shape. "Only, she's not turning back to a maiden again, is she?"

Odile sat down in her father's chair. She shook her head.

"Unless, child, your father...or you would consent to removing the curse."

"Why should I do that, your majesty?"

The king leaned forward. "When I was courting the queen, her father, a powerful duke, sent me two packages. In one, was an ancient sword. The iron blade dark and scarred. An heirloom of the duke's family that went back generations, used in countless campaigns— every one a victory." The king made a fist. "When I grasped the hilt, leather salted by sweat, I felt I could lead an army."

"And the second package?" Odile asked.

"That one contained a pillow."

"A pillow?"

The king nodded. "Covered with gold brocade and stuffed with goose down." The king laughed. "The messenger delivered as well a note that said I was to bring one, only one, of the packages with me to dinner at the ducal estate."

"A test."

"That is what my father said. My tutors had been soldiers not statesmen. The sword meant strength, courage, to my father. What a king should, no, must possess to keep his lands and people safe. To him the choice was clear."

Odile smiled. Did all fathers enjoy telling stories of their youth?

"I thought to myself, if the answer was so clear then why the test? What had the duke meant by the pillow? Something soft and light, something womanly...."

The notion of a woman being pigeonholed so irritated Odile. Was she any less a woman because she lacked the apparent grace of girls like Elster? She looked down at the breeches she liked to wear, comfortable not only because of the fit but because they had once been worn by her father. Her hands were not smooth but spotted with ink and rubbed with dirt from where she had begun to dig Papa's grave. Their escape had been too taxing. She worried over each breath he struggled to take.

"...meant to rest upon, to lay your head when sleeping. Perhaps choosing the pillow would show my devotion to his daughter, that I would be a loving husband before a valiant king—"

"Does he love her?" Odile asked.

The king stammered, as if unwilling to tear himself from the story.

"Your son. Does he love her?"

"What else would drive a man of privilege to the woods? He's forsaken crown for thorn. Besides, a lost princess? Every peasant within miles has been bringing fowl to the palace hoping for a reward."

"A princess." Odile felt a bitter smile curl the edges of her mouth. Would his Royal Highness be roaming the land if he knew his true love was a seamstress? But then Odile remembered Elster's touch, the softness of her lips, her skin.

Perhaps Elster had been meant to be born a princess. She had read in Papa's books of birds that raid neighboring nests, roll out the eggs and lay their own. Perhaps that happened to girls as well. The poor parent never recognized the greedy chick for what it truly was. The prince might never as well.

If her own, unwanted destiny of doting bride had been usurped, then couldn't she choose her future? Why not take the one denied to her?

"The rings on your fingers."

"Worth a small fortune." He removed thick bands set with rubies and pearls. "A bride price then? I could also introduce you to one of the many eligible members of my court."

Odile took the rings, heavy and warm. "These will do," she said and told the king to follow her.

By candlelight, she took him down to the dank cellar. He seemed a bit unnerved by the empty cage. She pulled out a tray of blackened eggs. Then another. "She's here. They're all here. Take them."

The king lifted one egg. He looked it over then shook it by his ear.

"Look through the holes." She held the candle flame high.

The king peered through one end. "My Lord," he sputtered. The egg tumbled from his grasp and struck the floor, where it shattered like ancient pottery.

"There—There's a tiny man sleeping inside."

"I know." She brushed aside the shards with her bare foot. A sharp edge cut her sole and left a bloody streak on the stones. "Don't worry, you freed him."

She left him the light. "Find the princess's egg. Break all of them, if you want. There might be other princesses among them." She started up the staircase.

"She stepped on his toes a great deal."

"What was that?"

The king ran his hands over the curse eggs. "When I watched them dance, I noticed how often she stepped on my son's toes. One would think her parents were quite remiss in not teaching her the proper steps." He looked up at her with a sad smile. "One would think."

Odile climbed to the top of the tower to her papa's laboratory. Inside its cage, the wappentier screeched from both heads when she entered. Since their return, she had neglected it; Papa had been the only one who dared feed the beast.

Its last golden egg rested on a taxonomy book. She held it in her hands a moment before moving to the shutters and pushing them open. She felt the strong breeze. Wearing another shape, she could ride the air far. Perhaps all the way to the mountains. Or the sea.

The wanderlust, so new and strong, left her trembling. Abandoning a life could be cruel.

Still clutching the egg to her chest, she went down to her papa's bedroom. He had trouble opening his eyes when she touched his forehead. He tried to speak but lacked the strength.

Her thoughts held *rara lingua* with a certainty that surprised her. As she envisioned her lessons, her jaw began to ache. Her mouth tasted like the salt spray of the ocean. She looked down at her arms. Where the albumen dripped white feathers grew.

She called out, the sound hoarse and new and strange, but so fitting coming from the heavy body she wore. As a pelican, she squatted besides Papa's pillow. Her long beak, so heavy and ungainly as she moved her head, rose high. She plunged it down into her own breast, once, twice, until blood began to spill. Drops fell on to Papa's pale lips. As she hopped about the bed, it spattered onto his bared chest.

She forced her eyes to remain open despite the pain, so she could be assured that the color did return to his face, to see the rise and fall of each breath grow higher, stronger.

He raised his hand to her chest but she nudged his fingers away. Her wound had already begun to close on its own.

When she returned to human form, she touched above her breasts and felt the thick line of a scar. No, she decided it must be a badge, a medal like the prince had worn. She wanted it seen.

"Lear would be envious," Papa said in a voice weak but audible, "to have such a pelican daughter."

She laughed and cried a bit as well. She could not voice how his praise made her feel. So after she helped him sit up in bed, she went to his cluttered wardrobe. "I have to leave." She pushed aside garments until she found a curious outfit, a jacket and breeches, all in shades of red.

"Tell me where you're going."

"Tomorrow's lessons are on the road. I'll learn to talk with ibises and challenge monsters."

"Yes, daughter." Papa smiled. "But help me upstairs before you go."

In the tower library, Papa instructed Odile on how to work the heavy mechanism that lowered the wappentier's cage for feeding or recovering the eggs. The wappentier shuddered and its musty smell filled the room.

"When the time comes, search the highest peaks." Papa unlocked the latch with a white quill and swung the door open. The hinges screeched. Or maybe the wappentier cried out.

Her heart trembled inside her ribs and she pulled at her father even as he stepped back.

The wappentier stretched its wings a moment before taking flight. It flew past them—its plumage, which she had always imagined would feel harsh and rough—was gentle like a whisper. The tower shook. Stones fell from the window's sides and ledge as it broke through the wall.

Odile thought she heard screams below. Horses and men.

Her father hugged her then. He felt frail, as if his bones might be hollow, but he held tight a moment. She could not find the words to assure him that she'd return.

Outside the tower, she found the king's carriage wallowed in the moat. The horses still lived, though they struggled to pull the carriage free. After years of a diet of game meat, the wappentier may have more hungered for rarer fare. There was no sign of a driver.

She waded into the water, empty of any swans, she noticed. The carriage door hung ajar. Inside was empty. As she led the horses to land, Odile looked up in the sky and did not see the wappentier. It must no longer be starved. She hoped the king was still down in the cellar smashing eggs.

She looked back at the tower and thought she saw for a moment her father staring down from the ruined window. She told herself there might be another day for books and fathers. Perhaps even swans. Then she stepped up to the driver's seat and took hold of the reins and chose to take the road.

The Lady Who Plucked Red Flowers beneath the Queen's Window

RACHEL SWIRSKY

My story should have ended on the day I died. Instead, it began there.

Sun pounded on my back as I rode through the Mountains where the Sun Rests. My horse's hooves beat in syncopation with those of the donkey that trotted in our shadow. The queen's midget Kyan turned his head toward me, sweat dripping down the red-and-blue protections painted across his malformed brow.

"Shouldn't…we…stop?" he panted.

Sunlight shone red across the craggy limestone cliffs. A bold eastern wind carried the scent of mountain blossoms. I pointed to a place where two large stones leaned across a narrow outcropping.

"There," I said, prodding my horse to go faster before Kyan could answer. He grunted and cursed at his donkey for falling behind.

I hated Kyan, and he hated me. But Queen Rayneh had ordered us to ride reconnaissance together, and we obeyed, out of love for her and for the Land of Flowered Hills.

We dismounted at the place I had indicated. There, between the mountain peaks, we could watch the enemy's forces in the valley below without being observed. The raiders spread out across the meadow below like ants on a rich meal. Their women's camp lay behind the main troops, a small dark blur. Even the smoke rising from their women's fires seemed timid. I scowled.

"Go out between the rocks," I directed Kyan. "Move as close to the edge as you can."

Kyan made a mocking gesture of deference. "As you wish, Great Lady," he sneered, swinging his twisted legs off the donkey. Shamans' bundles of stones and seeds, tied with twine, rattled at his ankles.

I refused to let his pretensions ignite my temper. "Watch the valley," I instructed. "I will take the vision of their camp from your mind and send it to the Queen's scrying pool. Be sure to keep still."

The midget edged toward the rocks, his eyes shifting back and forth as if he expected to encounter raiders up here in the mountains, in the Queen's dominion. I found myself amused and disgusted by how little provocation it took to reveal the midget's true, craven nature. At home in the Queen's castle, he strutted about, pompous and patronizing. He was like many birth-twisted men, arrogant in the limited magic to which his deformities gave him access. Rumors suggested that he imagined himself worthy enough to be in love with the Queen. I wondered what he thought of the men below. Did he daydream about them conquering the Land? Did he think they'd make him powerful, that they'd put weapons in his twisted hands and let him strut among their ranks?

"Is your view clear?" I asked.

"It is."

I closed my eyes and saw, as he saw, the panorama of the valley below. I held his sight in my mind, and turned toward the eastern wind which carries the perfect expression of magic—flight—on its invisible eddies. I envisioned the battlefield unfurling before me like a scroll rolling out across a marble floor. With low, dissonant notes, I showed the image how to transform itself for my purposes. I taught it how to be length and width without depth, and how to be strokes of color and light reflected in water. When it knew these things, I sang the image into the water of the Queen's scrying pool.

Suddenly—too soon—the vision vanished from my inner eye. Something whistled through the air. I turned. Pain struck my chest like thunder.

I cried out. Kyan's bundles of seeds and stones rattled above me. My vision blurred red. Why was the midget near me? He should have been on the outcropping.

"You traitor!" I shouted. "How did the raiders find us?"

I writhed blindly on the ground, struggling to grab Kyan's legs. The midget caught my wrists. Weak with pain, I could not break free.

"Hold still," he said. "You're driving the arrow deeper."

"Let me go, you craven dwarf."

"I'm no traitor. This is woman's magic. Feel the arrow shaft."

Kyan guided my hand upward to touch the arrow buried in my chest. Through the pain, I felt the softness of one of the Queen's roc feathers. It was particularly rare and valuable, the length of my arm.

I let myself fall slack against the rock. "Woman's magic," I echoed, softly. "The Queen is betrayed. The Land is betrayed."

"Someone is betrayed, sure enough," said Kyan, his tone gloating.

"You must return to court and warn the Queen."

Kyan leaned closer to me. His breath blew on my neck, heavy with smoke and spices.

"No, Naeva. You can still help the Queen. She's given me the key-stone to a spell—a piece of pure leucite, powerful enough to tug a spirit from its rest. If I blow its power into you, your spirit won't sink into sleep. It will only rest, waiting for her summons."

Blood welled in my mouth. "I won't let you bind me...."

His voice came even closer, his lips on my ear. "The Queen needs you, Naeva. Don't you love her?"

Love: the word caught me like a thread on a bramble. Oh, yes. I loved the queen. My will weakened, and I tumbled out of my body. Cold crystal drew me in like a great mouth, inhaling.

~

I was furious. I wanted to wrap my hands around the first neck I saw and squeeze. But my hands were tiny, half the size of the hands I remembered. My short, fragile fingers shook. Heavy musk seared my nostrils. I felt the heat of scented candles at my feet, heard the snap of flame devouring wick. I rushed forward and was abruptly halted. Red and black knots of string marked boundaries beyond which I could not pass.

"O, Great Lady Naeva," a voice intoned. "We seek your wisdom on behalf of Queen Rayneh and the Land of Flowered hills."

Murmurs rippled through the room. Through my blurred vision, I caught an impression of vaulted ceilings and frescoed walls. I heard people, but I could only make out woman-sized blurs—they could have been beggars, aristocrats, warriors, even males or broods.

I tried to roar. My voice fractured into a strangled sound like trapped wind. An old woman's sound.

"Great Lady Naeva, will you acknowledge me?"

I turned toward the high, mannered voice. A face came into focus, eyes flashing blue beneath a cowl. Dark stripes stretched from lower lip to chin: the tattoos of a death whisperer.

Terror cut into my rage for a single, clear instant. "I'm dead?"

"Let me handle this." Another voice, familiar this time. Calm, authoritative, quiet: the voice of someone who had never needed to shout in order to be heard. I swung my head back and forth trying to glimpse Queen Rayneh.

"Hear me, Lady Who Plucked Red Flowers beneath My Window. It is I, your Queen."

The formality of that voice! She spoke to me with titles instead of names? I blazed with fury.

Her voice dropped a register, tender and cajoling. "Listen to me, Naeva. I asked the death whisperers to chant your spirit up from the dead. You're inhabiting the body of an elder member of their order. Look down. See for yourself."

I looked down and saw embroidered rabbits leaping across the hem of a turquoise robe. Long, bony feet jutted out from beneath the silk. They were swaddled in the coarse wrappings that doctors prescribed for the elderly when it hurt them to stand.

They were not my feet. I had not lived long enough to have feet like that.

"I was shot by an enchanted arrow…." I recalled. "The midget said you might need me again…."

"And he was right, wasn't he? You've only been dead three years. Already, we need you."

The smugness of that voice. Rayneh's impervious assurance that no matter what happened, be it death or disgrace, her people's hearts would always sing with fealty.

"He enslaved me," I said bitterly. "He preyed upon my love for you."

"Ah, Lady Who Plucked Red Flowers beneath My Window, I always knew you loved me."

Oh yes, I had loved her. When she wanted heirs, it was I who placed my hand on her belly and used my magic to draw out her seedlings; I who nurtured the seedlings' spirits with the fertilizer of her chosen man; I who planted the seedlings in the womb of a fecund brood. Three times, the broods I catalyzed brought forth Rayneh's daughters. I'd not yet chosen to beget my own daughters, but there had always been an understanding between us that Rayneh would be the one to stand with my magic-worker as the seedling was drawn from me, mingled with man, and set into brood.

I was amazed to find that I loved her no longer. I remembered the emotion, but passion had died with my body.

"I want to see you," I said.

Alarmed, the death whisperer turned toward Rayneh's voice. Her nose jutted beak-like past the edge of her cowl. "It's possible for her to see you if you stand where I am," she said. "But if the spell goes wrong, I won't be able to—"

"It's all right, Lakitri. Let her see me."

Rustling, footsteps. Rayneh came into view. My blurred vision showed me frustratingly little except for the moon of her face. Her eyes sparkled black against her smooth, sienna skin. Amber and obsidian gems shone from her forehead, magically embedded in the triangular formation that symbolized the Land of Flowered Hills. I wanted to see her graceful belly, the muscular calves I'd loved to stroke—but below her chin, the world faded to grey.

"What do you want?" I asked. "Are the raiders nipping at your heels again?"

"We pushed the raiders back in the battle that you died to make happen. It was a rout. Thanks to you."

A smile lit on Rayneh's face. It was a smile I remembered. *You have served your Land and your Queen,* it seemed to say. *You may be proud.* I'd slept on Rayneh's leaf-patterned silk and eaten at her morning table too often to be deceived by such shallow manipulations.

Rayneh continued, "A usurper—a woman raised on our own grain and honey—has built an army of automatons to attack us. She's given each one a hummingbird's heart for speed, and a crane's feather for beauty, and a crow's brain for wit. They've marched from the Lake Where Women Wept all the way across the fields to the Valley of Tonha's Memory. They move faster than our most agile warriors. They seduce our farmers out of the fields. We must destroy them."

"A usurper?" I said.

"One who betrays us with our own spells."

The Queen directed me a lingering, narrow-lidded look, challenging me with her unspoken implications.

"The kind of woman who would shoot the Queen's sorceress with a roc feather?" I pressed.

Her glance darted sideways. "Perhaps."

Even with the tantalizing aroma of revenge wafting before me, I considered refusing Rayneh's plea. Why should I forgive her for chaining me to her service? She and her benighted death whisperers might have been able to chant my spirit into wakefulness, but let them try to stir my voice against my will.

But no—even without love drawing me into dark corners, I couldn't renounce Rayneh. I would help her as I always had from the time when we were girls riding together through my grandmother's fields. When she fell from her mount, it was always I who halted my mare, soothed her wounds, and eased her back into the saddle. Even as a child, I knew that she would never do the same for me.

"Give me something to kill," I said.

"What?"

"I want to kill. Give me something. Or should I kill your death whisperers?"

Rayneh turned toward the women. "Bring a sow!" she commanded.

Murmurs echoed through the high-ceilinged chamber, followed by rushing footsteps. Anxious hands entered my range of vision, dragging a fat, black-spotted shape. I looked toward the place where my ears told me the crowd of death whisperers stood, huddled and gossiping. I wasn't sure how vicious I could appear as a dowager with bound feet, but I snarled at them anyway. I was rewarded with the susurration of hems sliding backward over tile.

I approached the sow. My feet collided with the invisible boundaries of the summoning circle. "Move it closer," I ordered.

Hands pushed the sow forward. The creature grunted with surprise and fear. I knelt down and felt its bristly fur and smelled dry mud, but I couldn't see its torpid bulk.

I wrapped my bony hands around the creature's neck and twisted. My spirit's strength overcame the body's weakness. The animal's head snapped free in my hands. Blood engulfed the leaping rabbits on my hem.

I thrust the sow's head at Rayneh. It tumbled out of the summoning circle and thudded across the marble. Rayneh doubled over, retching.

The crowd trembled and exclaimed. Over the din, I dictated the means to defeat the constructs. "Blend mustard seed and honey to slow their deceitful tongues. Add brine to ruin their beauty. Mix in crushed poppies to slow their fast-beating hearts. Release the concoction onto a strong wind and let it blow their destruction. Only a grain need touch them. Less than a grain—only a grain need touch a mosquito that lights on a flower they pass on the march. They will fall."

"Regard that! Remember it!" Rayneh shouted to the whisperers. Silk rustled. Rayneh regarded me levelly. "That's all we have to do?"

"Get Lakitri," I replied. "I wish to ask her a question."

A nervous voice spoke outside my field of vision. "I'm here, Great Lady."

"What will happen to this body after my spirit leaves?"

"Jada will die, Great Lady. Your spirit has chased hers away."

I felt the crookedness of Jada's hunched back and the pinch of the strips binding her feet. Such a back, such feet, I would never have. At least someone would die for disturbing my death.

⁓

Next I woke, rage simmered where before it had boiled. I stifled a snarl, and relaxed my clenched fists. My vision was clearer: I discerned the outlines of a tent filled with dark shapes that resembled pillows and furs. I discovered my boundaries close by, marked by wooden stakes painted with bands of cinnamon and white.

"Respected Aunt Naeva?"

My vision wavered. A shape: muscular biceps, hard thighs, robes of heir's green. It took me a moment to identify Queen Rayneh's eldest daughter, who I had inspired in her brood. At the time of my death, she'd been a flat-chested flitling, still learning how to ride.

"Tryce?" I asked. A bad thought: "Why are you here? Has the usurper taken the palace? Is the Queen dead?"

Tryce laughed. "You misunderstand, Respected Aunt. I am the usurper."

"You?" I scoffed. "What does a girl want with a woman's throne?"

"I want what is mine." Tryce drew herself up. She had her mother's mouth, stern and imperious. "If you don't believe me, look at the body you're wearing."

I looked down. My hands were the right size, but they were painted in Rayneh's blue and decked with rings of gold and silver. Strips of tanned human flesh adorned my breasts. I raised my fingertips to my collarbone and felt the raised edges of the brand I knew would be there. Scars formed the triangles that represented the Land of Flowered Hills.

"One of your mother's private guard," I murmured. "Which?"

"Okilanu."

I grinned. "I never liked the bitch."

"You know I'm telling the truth. A private guard is too valuable for anyone but a usurper to sacrifice. I'm holding this conference with honor, Respected Aunt. I'm meeting you alone, with only one automaton to guard me. My informants tell me that my mother surrounded herself with sorceresses so that she could coerce you. I hold you in more esteem."

"What do you want?"

"Help winning the throne that should be mine."

"Why should I betray my lover and my Land for a child with pretensions?"

"Because you have no reason to be loyal to my mother. Because I want what's best for this Land, and I know how to achieve it. Because those were my automatons you dismantled, and they were good, beautiful souls despite being creatures of spit and mud. Gudrin is the last of them."

Tryce held out her hand. The hand that accepted drew into my vision: slender with shapely fingers crafted of mud and tangled with sticks and pieces of nest. It was beautiful enough to send feathers of astonishment through my chest.

"Great Lady, you must listen to The Creator of Me and Mine," intoned the creature.

Its voice was a songbird trill. I grimaced in disgust. "You made male automatons?"

"Just one," said Tryce. "It's why he survived your spell."

"Yes," I said, pondering. "It never occurred to me that one would make male creatures.

"Will you listen, Respected Aunt?" asked Tryce.

"You must listen, Great Lady," echoed the automaton. His voice was as melodious as poetry to a depressed heart. The power of crane's feathers and crow's brains is great.

"Very well," I said.

Tryce raised her palms to show she was telling truth. I saw the shadow of her mother's face lurking in her wide-set eyes and broad, round forehead.

"Last autumn, when the wind blew red with fallen leaves, my mother expelled me from the castle. She threw my possessions into the river and had my servants beaten and turned out. She told me that I would have to learn to live like the birds migrating from place to place because she had decreed that no one was to give me a home. She said I was no longer her heir, and she would dress Darnisha or Peni in heir's green. Oh, Respected Aunt! How could either of them take a throne?"

I ignored Tryce's emotional outpouring. It was true that Tryce had always been more responsible than her sisters, but she had been born with an heir's heaviness upon her. I had lived long enough to see fluttering sparrows like Darnisha and Peni become eagles, over time.

"You omit something important," I said. "Why did your mother throw you out, Imprudent Child?"

"Because of this."

The automaton's hand held Tryce steady as she mounted a pile of pillows that raised her torso to my eye level. Her belly loomed large, ripe as a frog's inflated throat.

"You've gotten fat, Tryce."

"No," she said.

I realized: she had not.

"You're pregnant? Hosting a child like some brood? What's wrong with you, girl? I never knew you were a pervert. Worse than a pervert! Even the lowest worm-eater knows to chew mushrooms when she pushes with men."

"I am no pervert! I am a lover of woman. I am natural as breeze! But I say we must not halve our population by splitting our females into women and broods. The raiders nip at our heels. Yes, it's true, they are barbaric and weak—now. But they grow stronger. Their population increases so quickly that already they can match our numbers. When there are three times as many of them as us, or five times, or eight times, they'll flood us like a wave crashing on a naked beach. It's time for women to make children in ourselves as broods do. We need more daughters."

I scoffed. "The raiders keep their women like cows for the same reason we keep cows like cows, to encourage the production of calves. What do you think will happen if our men see great women swelling with young and feeding them from their bodies? They will see us as weak, and they will rebel, and the broods will support them for trinkets and candy."

"Broods will not threaten us," said Tryce. "They do as they are trained. We train them to obey."

Tryce stepped down from the pillows and dismissed the automaton into the shadows. I felt a murmur of sadness as the creature left my sight.

"It is not your place to make policy, Imprudent Child," I said. "You should have kept your belly flat."

"There is no time! Do the raiders wait? Will they chew rinds by the fire while I wait for my mother to die?"

"This is better? To split our land into factions and war against ourselves?"

"I have vowed to save the Land of Flowered Hills," said Tryce, "with my mother or despite her."

Tryce came yet closer to me so that I could see the triple scars where the gems that had once sealed her heirship had been carved out of her cheeks. They left angry, red triangles. Tryce's breath was hot; her eyes like oil, shining.

"Even without my automatons, I have enough resources to overwhelm the palace," Tryce continued, "except for one thing."

I waited.

"I need you to tell me how to unlock the protections you laid on the palace grounds and my mother's chambers."

"We return to the beginning. Why should I help you?"

Tryce closed her eyes and inhaled deeply. There was shyness in her posture now. She would not direct her gaze at mine.

She said, "I was young when you died, still young enough to think that our strength was unassailable. The battles after your death shattered my illusions. We barely won, and we lost many lives. I realized that we needed more power, and I thought that I could give us that power by becoming a sorceress to replace you." She paused. "During my studies, I researched your acts of magic, great and small. Inevitably, I came to the spell you cast before you died, when you sent the raiders' positions into the summoning pool."

It was then that I knew what she would say next. I wish I could say that my heart felt as immobile as a mountain, that I had always known to suspect the love of a Queen. But my heart drummed, and my mouth went dry, and I felt as if I were falling.

"Some of mother's advisers convinced her that you were plotting against her. They had little evidence to support their accusations, but once the idea rooted into mother's mind, she became obsessed. She violated the sanctity of woman's magic by teaching Kyan how to summon a roc feather enchanted to pierce your heart. She ordered him to wait until you had sent her the vision of the battleground, and then to kill you and punish your treachery by binding your soul so that you would always wander and wake."

I wanted to deny it, but what point would there be? Now that Tryce forced me to examine my death with a watcher's eye, I saw the coincidences that proved her truth. How else could I have been shot by an arrow not just shaped by woman's magic, but made from one of the Queen's roc feathers? Why else would a worm like Kyan have happened to have in his possession a piece of leucite more powerful than any I'd seen?

I clenched Okilanu's fists. "I never plotted against Rayneh."

"Of course not. She realized it herself, in time, and executed the women who had whispered against you. But she had your magic, and your restless spirit bound to her, and she believed that was all she needed."

For long moments, my grief battled my anger. When it was done, my resolve was hardened like a spear tempered by fire.

I lifted my palms in the gesture of truth telling. "To remove the protections on the palace grounds, you must lay yourself flat against the soil with your cheek against the dirt, so that it knows you. To it, you must say, 'The Lady Who Plucked Red Flowers beneath the Queen's Window loves the Queen from instant to eternity, from desire to regret.' And then you must kiss the soil as if it is the hem of your lover's robe. Wait until you feel the earth move beneath you and then the protections will be gone."

Tryce inclined her head. "I will do this."

I continued, "When you are done, you must flay off a strip of your skin and grind it into a fine powder. Bury it in an envelope of wind-silk beneath the Queen's window. Bury it quickly. If a single grain escapes, the protections on her chamber will hold."

"I will do this, too," said Tryce. She began to speak more, but I raised one of my ringed, blue fingers to silence her.

"There's another set of protections you don't know about. One cast on your mother. It can only be broken by the fresh life-blood of something you love. Throw the blood onto the Queen while saying, 'The Lady Who Plucked Red Flowers beneath Your Window has betrayed you.'"

"Life-blood? You mean, I need to kill—"

"Perhaps the automaton."

Tryce's expression clouded with distress. "Gudrin is the last one! Maybe the baby. I could conceive again—"

"If you can suggest the baby, you don't love it enough. It must be Gudrin."

Tryce closed her mouth. "Then it will be Gudrin," she agreed, but her eyes would not meet mine.

I folded my arms across Okilanu's flat bosom. "I've given you what you wanted. Now grant me a favor, Imprudent Child Who Would Be Queen. When you kill Rayneh, I want to be there."

Tryce lifted her head like the Queen she wanted to be. "I will summon you when it's time, Respected Aunt." She turned toward Gudrin in the shadows. "Disassemble the binding shapes," she ordered.

For the first time, I beheld Gudrin in his entirety. The creature was tree-tall and stick-slender, and yet he moved with astonishing grace. "Thank you on behalf of the Creator of Me and My Kind," he trilled in his beautiful voice, and I considered how unfortunate it was that the next time I saw him, he would be dead.

I smelled the iron-and-wet tang of blood. My view of the world skewed low, as if I'd been cut off at the knees. Women's bodies slumped across lush carpets. Red ran deep into the silk, bloodying woven leaves and flowers. I'd been in this chamber far too often to mistake it, even dead. It was Rayneh's.

It came to me then: my perspective was not like that of a woman forced to kneel. It was like a child's. Or a dwarf's.

I reached down and felt hairy knees and fringed ankle bracelets. "Ah, Kyan…."

"I thought you might like that." Tryce's voice. These were probably her legs before me, wrapped in loose green silk trousers that were tied above the calf with chains of copper beads. "A touch of irony for your pleasure. He bound your soul to restlessness. Now you'll chase his away."

I reached into his back-slung sheath and drew out the most functional of his ceremonial blades. It would feel good to flay his treacherous flesh.

"I wouldn't do that," said Tryce. "You'll be the one who feels the pain."

I sheathed the blade. "You took the castle?"

"Effortlessly." She paused. "I lie. Not effortlessly." She unknotted her right trouser leg and rolled up the silk. Blood stained the bandages on a carefully wrapped wound. "Your protections were strong."

"Yes. They were."

She re-tied her trouser leg and continued. "The Lady with Lichen Hair tried to block our way into the chamber." She kicked one of the corpses by my feet. "We killed her."

"Did you."

"Don't you care? She was your friend."

"Did she care when I died?"

Tryce shifted her weight, a kind of lower-body shrug. "I brought you another present." She dropped a severed head onto the floor. It rolled toward me, tongue lolling in its bloody face. It took me a moment to identify the high cheekbones and narrow eyes.

"The death whisperer? Why did you kill Lakitri?"

"You liked the blood of Jada and Okilanu, didn't you?"

"The only blood I care about now is your mother's. Where is she?"

"Bring my mother!" ordered Tryce.

One of Tryce's servants—her hands marked with the green dye of loyalty to the heir—dragged Rayneh into the chamber. The Queen's torn, bloody robe concealed the worst of her wounds, but couldn't hide the black and purple bruises blossoming on her arms and legs. Her eyes found mine, and despite her condition, a trace of her regal smile glossed her lips.

Her voice sounded thin. "That's you? Lady Who Plucked Red Flowers beneath My Window?"

"It's me."

She raised one bloody, shaking hand to the locket around her throat and pried it open. Dried petals scattered onto the carpets, the remnants of the red flowers I'd once gathered for her protection. While the spell lasted, they'd remained whole and fresh. Now they were dry and crumbling like what had passed for love between us.

"If you ever find rest, the world-lizard will crack your soul in its jaws for murdering your Queen," she said.

"I didn't kill you."

"You instigated my death."

"I was only repaying your favor."

The hint of her smile again. She smelled of wood smoke, rich and dark. I wanted to see her more clearly, but my poor vision blurred the red of her wounds into the sienna of her skin until the whole of her looked like raw, churned earth.

"I suppose our souls will freeze together." She paused. "That might be pleasant."

Somewhere in front of us, lost in the shadows, I heard Tryce and her women ransacking the Queen's chamber. Footsteps, sharp voices, cracking wood.

"I used to enjoy cold mornings," Rayneh said. "When we were girls. I liked lying in bed with you and opening the curtains to watch the snow fall."

"And sending servants out into the cold to fetch and carry."

"And then! When my brood let slip it was warmer to lie together naked under the sheets? Do you remember that?" She laughed aloud, and then paused. When she spoke again, her voice was quieter. "It's strange to remember lying together in the cold, and then to look up, and see you in that body. Oh, my beautiful Naeva, twisted into a worm. I deserve what you've done to me. How could I have sent a worm to kill my life's best love?"

She turned her face away, as if she could speak no more. Such a show of intimate, unroyal emotion. I could remember times when she'd been able to manipulate me by trusting me with a wince of pain or a supposedly accidental tear. As I grew more cynical, I realized that her royal pretense wasn't vanishing when she gave me a melancholy, regretful glance. Such things were calculated vulnerabilities, intended to bind me closer to her by suggesting intimacy and trust. She used them with many ladies at court, the ones who loved her.

This was far from the first time she'd tried to bind me to her by displaying weakness, but it was the first time she'd ever done so when I had no love to enthrall me.

Rayneh continued, her voice a whisper. "I regret it, Naeva. When Kyan came back, and I saw your body, cold and lifeless—I understood immediately that I'd been mistaken. I wept for days. I'm weeping still, inside my heart. But listen—" her voice hardened "—we can't let this be about you and me. Our Land is at stake. Do you know what Tryce is going to do? She'll destroy us all. You have to help me stop her—"

"Tryce!" I shouted. "I'm ready to see her bleed."

Footsteps thudded across silk carpets. Tryce drew a bone-handled knife and knelt over her mother like a farmer preparing to slaughter a pig. "Gudrin!" she called. "Throw open the doors. Let everyone see us."

Narrow, muddy legs strode past us. The twigs woven through the automaton's skin had lain fallow when I saw him in the winter. Now they blazed in a glory of emerald leaves and scarlet blossoms.

"You dunce!" I shouted at Tryce. "What have you done? You left him alive."

Tryce's gaze held fast on her mother's throat. "I sacrificed the baby."

Voices and footsteps gathered in the room as Tryce's soldiers escorted Rayneh's courtiers inside.

"You sacrificed the baby," I repeated. "What do you think ruling is? Do you think Queens always get what they want? You can't dictate to magic, Imprudent Child."

"Be silent." Tryce's voice thinned with anger. "I'm grateful for your help, Great Lady, but you must not speak this way to your Queen."

I shook my head. Let the foolish child do what she might. I braced myself for the inevitable backlash of the spell.

Tryce raised her knife in the air. "Let everyone gathered here behold that this is Queen Rayneh, the Queen Who Would Dictate to a Daughter. I am her heir, Tryce of the Bold Stride. Hear me. I do this for the Land of Flowered Hills, for our honor and our strength. Yet I also do it with regret. Mother, I hope you will be free in your death. May your spirit wing across sweet breezes with the great bird of the sun."

The knife slashed downward. Crimson poured across Rayneh's body, across the rugs, across Tryce's feet. For a moment, I thought I'd been wrong about Tryce's baby—perhaps she had loved it enough for the counter-spell to work—but as the blood poured over the dried petals Rayneh had scattered on the floor, a bright light flared through the room. Tryce flailed backward as if struck.

Rayneh's wound vanished. She stared up at me with startled, joyful eyes. "You didn't betray me!"

"Oh, I did," I said. "Your daughter is just inept."

I could see only one solution to the problem Tryce had created— the life's blood of something I loved was here, still saturating the carpets and pooling on the stone.

Magic is a little bit alive. Sometimes it prefers poetic truths to literal ones. I dipped my fingers into the Queen's spilled blood and pronounced, "The Lady Who Plucked Red Flowers beneath Your Window has betrayed you."

I cast the blood across the Queen. The dried petals disintegrated. The Queen cried out as my magical protections disappeared.

Tryce was at her mother's side again in an instant. Rayneh looked at me in the moment before Tryce's knife descended. I thought she might show me, just this once, a fraction of uncalculated vulnerability. But this time there was no vulnerability at all, no pain or betrayal or even weariness, only perfect regal equanimity.

Tryce struck for her mother's heart. She let her mother's body fall to the carpet.

"Behold my victory!" Tryce proclaimed. She turned toward her subjects. Her stance was strong: her feet planted firmly, ready for attack or defense. If her lower half was any indication, she'd be an excellent Queen.

I felt a rush of forgiveness and pleasure and regret and satisfaction all mixed together. I moved toward the boundaries of my imprisonment, my face near Rayneh's where she lay, inhaling her last ragged breaths.

"Be brave," I told her. "Soon we'll both be free."

Rayneh's lips moved slowly, her tongue thick around the words. "What makes you think...?"

"You're going to die," I said, "and when I leave this body, Kyan will die, too. Without caster or intent, there won't be anything to sustain the spell."

Rayneh made a sound that I supposed was laughter. "Oh no, my dear Naeva...much more complicated than that...."

Panic constricted my throat. "Tryce! You have to find the piece of leucite—"

"...even stronger than the rock. Nothing but death can lull your spirit to sleep...and you're already dead...."

She laughed again.

"Tryce!" I shouted. "Tryce!"

The girl turned. For a moment, my vision became as clear as it had been when I lived. I saw the Imprudent Child Queen standing with her automaton's arms around her waist, the both of them flushed with joy and triumph. Tryce turned to kiss the knot of wood that served as the automaton's mouth and my vision clouded again.

Rayneh died a moment afterward.

A moment after that, Tryce released me.

If my story could not end when I died, it should have ended there, in Rayneh's chamber, when I took my revenge.

It did not end there.

Tryce consulted me often during the early years of her reign. I familiarized myself with the blur of the paintings in her chamber, squinting to pick out placid scenes of songbirds settling on snowy branches, bathing in mountain springs, soaring through sun-struck skies.

"Don't you have counselors for this?" I snapped one day.

Tryce halted her pacing in front of me, blocking my view of a wren painted by The Artist without Pity.

"Do you understand what it's like for me? The court still calls me the Imprudent Child Who Would Be Queen. Because of you!"

Gudrin went to comfort her. She kept the creature close, pampered and petted, like a cat on a leash. She rested her head on his shoulder as he stroked her arms. It all looked too easy, too familiar. I wondered how often Tryce spun herself into these emotional whirlpools.

"It can be difficult for women to accept orders from their juniors," I said.

"I've borne two healthy girls," Tryce said petulantly. "When I talk to the other women about bearing, they still say they can't, that 'women's bodies aren't suited for childbirth.' Well, if women can't have children, then what does that make me?"

I forebore responding.

"They keep me busy with petty disputes over grazing rights and grain allotment. How can I plan for a war when they distract me with pedantry? The raiders are still at our heels, and the daft old biddies won't accept what we must do to beat them back!"

The automaton thrummed with sympathy. Tryce shook him away and resumed pacing. "At least I have you, Respected Aunt."

"For now. You must be running out of hosts." I raised my hand and inspected young, unfamiliar fingers. Dirt crusted the ragged nails. "Who is this? Anyone I know?"

"The death whisperers refuse to let me use their bodies. What time is this when dying old women won't blow out a few days early for the good of the Land?"

"Who is this?" I repeated.

"I had to summon you into the body of a common thief. You see how bad things are."

"What did you expect? That the wind would send a hundred songbirds to trill praises at your coronation? That sugared oranges would rain from the sky and flowers bloom on winter stalks?"

Tryce glared at me angrily. "Do not speak to me like that. I may be an Imprudent Child, but I am the Queen." She took a moment to regain her composure. "Enough chatter. Give me the spell I asked for."

Tryce called me in at official occasions, to bear witness from the body of a disfavored servant or a used-up brood. I attended each of the four ceremonies where Tryce, clad in regal blue, presented her infant daughters to the sun: four small, green-swathed bundles, each borne from the Queen's own body. It made me sick, but I held my silence.

She also summoned me to the court ceremony where she presented Gudrin with an official title she'd concocted to give him standing in the royal circle. Honored Zephyr or some such nonsense. They held the occasion in autumn when red and yellow leaves adorned Gudrin's shoulders like a cape. Tryce pretended to ignore the women's discontented mutterings, but they were growing louder.

The last time I saw Tryce, she summoned me in a panic. She stood in an unfamiliar room with bare stone walls and sharp wind creaking through slitted windows. Someone else's blood stained Tryce's robes. "My sisters betrayed me!" she said. "They told the women of the grasslands I was trying to make them into broods, and then led them in a revolt against the castle. A thousand women, marching! I had to slay them all. I suspected Darnisha all along. But Peni seemed content to waft. Last fall, she bore a child of her own body. It was a worm, true, but she might have gotten a daughter next. She said she wanted to try!"

"Is that their blood?"

She held out her reddened hands and stared at them ruefully as if they weren't really part of her. "Gudrin was helping them. I had to smash him into sticks. They must have cast a spell on him. I can't imagine...."

Her voice faltered. I gave her a moment to tame her undignified excess.

"You seem to have mastered the situation," I said. "A Queen must deal with such things from time to time. The important thing will be to show no weakness in front of your courtiers."

"You don't understand! It's much worse than that. While we women fought, the raiders attacked the Fields That Bask under Open Skies. They've taken half the Land. We're making a stand in the Castle Where Hope Flutters, but we can't keep them out forever. A few weeks, at most. I told them this would happen! We need more daughters to defend us! But they wouldn't listen to me!"

Rayneh would have known how to present her anger with queenly courage, but Tryce was rash and thoughtless. She wore her emotions like perfume. "Be calm," I admonished. "You must focus."

"The raiders sent a message describing what they'll do to me and my daughters when they take the castle. I captured the messenger and burned out his tongue and gave him to the broods, and when they were done with him, I took what was left of his body and cata-pulted it into the raiders' camp. I could do the same to every one of them, and it still wouldn't be enough to compensate for having to listen to their vile, cowardly threats."

I interrupted her tirade. "The Castle Where Hope Flutters is on high ground, but if you've already lost the eastern fields, it will be dif-ficult to defend. Take your women to the Spires of Treachery where the herders feed their cattle. You won't be able to mount traditional defenses, but they won't be able to attack easily. You'll be reduced to meeting each other in small parties where woman's magic should give you the advantage."

"My commander suggested that," said Tryce. "There are too many of them. We might as well try to dam a river with silk."

"It's better than remaining here."

"Even if we fight to a stalemate in the Spires of Treachery, the raid-ers will have our fields to grow food in, and our broods to make children on. If they can't conquer us this year, they'll obliterate us in ten. I need something else."

"There is nothing else."

"Think of something!"

I thought.

I cast my mind back through my years of training. I remembered the locked room in my matriline's household where servants were never allowed to enter, which my cousins and I scrubbed every dawn and dusk to teach us to be constant and rigorous.

I remembered the cedar desk where my aunt Finis taught me to paint birds, first by using the most realistic detail that oils could achieve, and then by reducing my paintings to fewer and fewer brushstrokes until I could evoke the essence of bird without any brush at all.

I remembered the many-drawered red cabinets where we stored Leafspine and Winterbrew, powdered Errow and essence of Howl. I remembered my bossy cousin Alne skidding through the halls in a panic after she broke into a locked drawer and mixed together two herbs that we weren't supposed to touch. Her fearful grimace transformed into a beak that permanently silenced her sharp tongue.

I remembered the year I spent traveling to learn the magic of foreign lands. I was appalled by the rituals I encountered in places where women urinated on their thresholds to ward off spirits, and plucked their scalps bald when their eldest daughters reached majority. I walked with senders and weavers and whisperers and learned magic secrets that my people had misunderstood for centuries. I remembered the terror of the three nights I spent in the ancient ruins of The Desert which Should Not Have Been, begging the souls that haunted that place to surrender the secrets of their accursed city. One by one my companions died, and I spent the desert days digging graves for those the spirits found unworthy. On the third dawn, they blessed me with communion, and sent me away a wiser woman.

I remembered returning to the Land of Flowered Hills and making my own contribution to the lore contained in our matriline's locked rooms. I remembered all of this, and still I could think of nothing to tell Tryce.

Until a robin of memory hopped from an unexpected place—a piece of magic I learned traveling with herders, not spell-casters. It was an old magic, one that farmers cast when they needed to cull an inbred strain.

"You must concoct a plague," I began.

Tryce's eyes locked on me. I saw hope in her face, and I realized that she'd expected me to fail her, too.

"Find a sick baby and stop whatever treatment it is receiving. Feed it mosquito bellies and offal and dirty water to make it sicker. Give it sores and let them fill with pus. When its forehead has grown too hot for a woman to touch without flinching, kill the baby and dedicate its breath to the sun. The next morning, when the sun rises, a plague will spread with the sunlight."

"That will kill the raiders?"

"Many of them. If you create a truly virulent strain, it may kill most of them. And it will cut down their children like a scythe across wheat."

Tryce clapped her blood-stained hands. "Good."

"I should warn you. It will kill your babies as well."

"What?"

"A plague cooked in an infant will kill anyone's children. It is the way of things."

"Unacceptable! I come to you for help, and you send me to murder my daughters?"

"You killed one before, didn't you? To save your automaton?"

"You're as crazy as the crones at court! We need more babies, not fewer."

"You'll have to hope you can persuade your women to bear children so that you can rebuild your population faster than the raiders can rebuild theirs."

Tryce looked as though she wanted to level a thousand curses at me, but she stilled her tongue. Her eyes were dark and narrow. In a quiet, angry voice, she said, "Then it will be done."

They were the same words she'd used when she promised to kill Gudrin. That time I'd been able to save her despite her foolishness. This time, I might not be able to.

～

Next I was summoned, I could not see at all. I was ushered into the world by lowing, distant shouts, and the stench of animals packed too closely together.

A worried voice cut through the din. "Did it work? Are you there? Laverna, is that still you?"

Disoriented, I reached out to find a hint about my surroundings. My hands impacted a summoning barrier.

"Laverna, that's not you anymore, is it?"

The smell of manure stung my throat. I coughed. "My name is Naeva."

"Holy day, it worked. Please, Sleepless One, we need your help. There are men outside. I don't know how long we can hold them off."

"What happened? Is Queen Tryce dead?"

"Queen Tryce?"

"She didn't cast the plague, did she? Selfish brat. Where are the raiders now? Are you in the Spires of Treachery?"

"Sleepless One, slow down. I don't follow you."

"Where are you? How much land have the raiders taken?"

"There are no raiders here, just King Addric's army. His soldiers used to be happy as long as we paid our taxes and bowed our heads at processions. Now they want us to follow their ways, worship their god, let our men give us orders. Some of us rebelled by marching in front of the governor's theater, and now he's sent sorcerers after us. They burned our city with magical fire. We're making a last stand at the inn outside town. We set aside the stable for the summoning."

"Woman, you're mad. Men can't practice that kind of magic."

"These men can."

A nearby donkey brayed, and a fresh stench plopped into the air. Outside, I heard the noise of burning, and the shouts of men and children.

"It seems we've reached an impasse. You've never heard of the Land of Flowered Hills?"

"Never."

I had spent enough time pacing the ruins in the Desert which Should Not Have Been to understand the ways in which civilizations cracked and decayed. Women and time marched forward, relentless and uncaring as sand.

"I see."

"I'm sorry. I'm not doing this very well. It's my first summoning. My aunt Hetta used to do it but they slit her throat like you'd slaughter a pig and left her body to burn. Bardus says they're roasting the corpses and eating them, but I don't think anyone could do that. Could they? Hetta showed me how to do this a dozen times, but I never got to practice. She would have done this better."

"That would explain why I can't see."

"No, that's the child, Laverna. She's blind. She does all the talking. Her twin Nammi can see, but she's dumb."

"Her twin?"

"Nammi's right here. Reach into the circle and touch your sister's hand, Nammi. That's a good girl."

A small hand clasped mine. It felt clammy with sweat. I squeezed back.

"It doesn't seem fair to take her sister away," I said.

"Why would anyone take Laverna away?"

"She'll die when I leave this body."

"No, she won't. Nammi's soul will call her back. Didn't your people use twins?"

"No. Our hosts died."

"Yours were a harsh people."

Another silence. She spoke the truth, though I'd never thought of it in such terms. We were a lawful people. We were an unflinching people.

"You want my help to defeat the shamans?" I asked.

"Aunt Hetta said that sometimes the Sleepless Ones can blink and douse all the magic within seven leagues. Or wave their hands and sweep a rank of men into a hurricane."

"Well, I can't."

She fell silent. I considered her situation.

"Do you have your people's livestock with you?" I asked.

"Everything that wouldn't fit into the stable is packed inside the inn. It's even less pleasant in there if you can imagine."

"Can you catch one of their soldiers?"

"We took some prisoners when we fled. We had to kill one but the others are tied up in the courtyard."

"Good. Kill them and mix their blood into the grain from your larder, and bake it into loaves of bread. Feed some of the bread to each of your animals. They will fill with a warrior's anger and hunt down your enemies."

The woman hesitated. I could hear her feet shifting on the hay-covered floor.

"If we do that, we won't have any grain or animals. How will we survive?"

"You would have had to desert your larder when the Worm-Pretending-to-Be-Queen sent reinforcements anyway. When you can safely flee, ask the blind child to lead you to the Place where the Sun Is Joyous. Whichever direction she chooses will be your safest choice."

"Thank you," said the woman. Her voice was taut and tired. It seemed clear that she'd hoped for an easier way, but she was wise enough to take what she received. "We'll have a wild path to tame."

"Yes."

The woman stepped forward. Her footsteps released the scent of dried hay. "You didn't know about your Land, did you?"

"I did not."

"I'm sorry for your loss. It must be—"

The dumb child whimpered. Outside, the shouts increased.

"I need to go," said the woman.

"Good luck," I said, and meant it.

I felt the child Laverna rush past me as I sank back into my restless sleep. Her spirit flashed as brightly as a coin left in the sun.

I never saw that woman or any of her people again. I like to think they did not die.

I did not like the way the world changed after the Land of Flowered Hills disappeared. For a long time, I was summoned only by men. Most were a sallow, unhealthy color with sharp narrow features and unnaturally light hair. Goateed sorcerers too proud of their paltry talents strove to dazzle me with pyrotechnics. They commanded me to reveal magical secrets that their peoples had forgotten. Sometimes I stayed silent. Sometimes I led them astray. Once, a hunched barbarian with a braided beard ordered me to give him the secret of flight. I told him to turn toward the prevailing wind and beg the Lover of the Sky for a favor. When the roc swooped down to eat him, I felt a wild kind of joy. At least the birds remembered how to punish worms who would steal women's magic.

I suffered for my minor victory. Without the barbarian to dismiss me, I was stuck on a tiny patch of grass, hemmed in by the rabbit heads he'd placed to mark the summoning circle. I shivered through the windy night until I finally thought to kick away one of the heads. It tumbled across the grass and my spirit sank into the ground.

Men treated me differently than women had. I had been accustomed to being summoned by Queens and commanders awaiting my advice on incipient battles. Men eschewed my consult; they sought to steal my powers. One summoned me into a box, hoping to trap me as if I were a minor demon that could be forced to grant his wishes. I chanted a rhyme to burn his fingers. When he pulled his hand away, the lid snapped shut and I was free.

Our magic had centered on birds and wind. These new sorcerers made pets of creatures of blood and snapping jaws, wolves and bears and jaguars. We had depicted the sun's grace along with its splendor, showing the red feathers of flaming light that arc into wings to sweep her across the sky. Their sun was a crude, jagged thing—a golden disk surrounded by spikes that twisted like the gaudy knives I'd seen in foreign cities where I traveled when I was young.

The men called me The Bitch Queen. They claimed I had hated my womb so much that I tried to curse all men to infertility, but the curse rebounded and struck me dead. Apparently, I had hanged myself. Or I'd tried to disembowel every male creature within a day's walk of my borders. Or I'd spelled my entire kingdom into a waking death in order to prevent myself from ever becoming pregnant. Apparently, I did all the same things out of revenge because I became pregnant. I eschewed men and impregnated women with sorcery. I married a thousand husbands and murdered them all. I murdered my husband, the King, and staked his head outside my castle, and then forced all the tearful women of my kingdom to do the same to their menfolk. I went crazy when my husband and son died and ordered all the men in my kingdom to be executed, declaring that no one would have the pleasure I'd been denied. I had been born a boy, but a rival of my father's castrated me, and so I hated all real men. I ordered that any woman caught breastfeeding should have her breasts cut off. I ordered my lover's genitals cut off and sewn on me. I ordered my vagina sewn shut so I could never give birth. I ordered everyone in my kingdom to call me a man.

They assumed my magic must originate with my genitals: they displayed surprise that I didn't strip naked to mix ingredients in my vagina or cast spells using menstrual blood. They also displayed surprise that I became angry when they asked me about such things.

The worst of them believed he could steal my magic by raping me. He summoned me into a worthless, skinny girl, the kind that we in the Land of Flowered Hills would have deemed too weak to be a woman and too frail to be a brood. In order to carry out his plans, he had to make the summoning circle large enough to accommodate the bed. When he forced himself on top of me, I twisted off his head.

The best of them summoned me soon after that. He was a young man with nervous, trembling fingers who innovated a way to summon my spirit into himself. Books and scrolls tumbled over the surfaces of his tiny, dim room, many of them stained with wax from unheeded candles. Talking to him was strange, the two of us communicating with the same mouth, looking out of the same eyes.

Before long, we realized that we didn't need words. Our knowledge seeped from one spirit to the other like dye poured into water. He watched me as a girl, riding with Rayneh, and felt the sun burning my back as I dug graves in the Desert which Should Not Have Been, and flinched as he witnessed the worm who attempted to rape me. I watched him and his five brothers, all orphaned and living on the street, as they struggled to find scraps. I saw how he had learned to read under the tutelage of a traveling scribe who carried his books with him from town to town. I felt his uncomfortable mixture of love, respect, and fear for the patron who had set him up as a scribe and petty magician in return for sex and servitude. *I didn't know it felt that way,* I said to him. *Neither did I,* he replied. We stared at each other cross-eyed through his big green eyes.

Pasha needed to find a way to stop the nearby volcano before it destroyed the tiny kingdom where he dwelled. Already, tremors rattled the buildings, foreshadowing the coming destruction.

Perhaps I should not have given Pasha the spell, but it was not deep woman's magic. Besides, things seemed different when I inhabited his mind, closer to him than I had been to anyone.

We went about enacting the spell together. As we collected ash from the fireplaces of one family from each of the kingdom's twelve towns, I asked him, *Why haven't you sent me back? Wouldn't it be easier to do this on your own?*

I'll die when your spirit goes, he answered, and I saw the knowledge of it which he had managed to keep from me.

I didn't want him to die. *Then I'll stay,* I said. *I won't interfere with your life. I'll retreat as much as I can.*

I can't keep up the spell much longer, he said. I felt his sadness and his resolve. Beneath, I glimpsed even deeper sadness at the plans he would no longer be able to fulfill. He'd wanted to teach his youngest brother to read and write so that the two of them could move out of this hamlet and set up shop in a city as scribes, perhaps even earn enough money to house and feed all their brothers.

I remembered Laverna and Nammi and tried to convince Pasha that we could convert the twins' magic to work for him and his brother. He said that we only had enough time to stop the volcano. *The kingdom is more important than I am,* he said.

We dug a hole near the volcano's base and poured in the ashes that we'd collected. We stirred them with a phoenix feather until they caught fire, in order to give the volcano the symbolic satisfaction of burning the kingdom's hearths. A dense cloud of smoke rushed up from the looming mountain and then the earth was still.

That's it, said Pasha, exhaustion and relief equally apparent in his mind. *We did it.*

We sat together until nightfall when Pasha's strength began to fail. *I have to let go now,* he said.

No, I begged him, *Wait. Let us return to the city. We can find your brother. We'll find a way to save you.*

But the magic in his brain was unwinding. I was reminded of the ancient tapestries hanging in the Castle Where Hope Flutters, left too long to moths and weather. Pasha lost control of his feet, his fingers. His thoughts began to drift. They came slowly and far apart. His breath halted in his lungs. Before his life could end completely, my spirit sank away, leaving him to die alone.

After that, I did not have the courage to answer summons. When men called me, I kicked away the objects they'd used to bind me in place and disappeared again. Eventually, the summons stopped.

I had never before been aware of the time that I spent under the earth, but as the years between summons stretched, I began to feel vague sensations: swatches of grey and white along with muted, indefinable pain.

When a summons finally came, I almost felt relief. When I realized the summoner was a woman, I did feel surprise.

"I didn't expect that to work," said the woman. She was peach-skinned and round, a double chin gentling her jaw. She wore large spectacles with faceted green lenses like insect eyes. Spines like porcupine quills grew in a thin line from the bridge of her nose to the top of her skull before fanning into a mane. The aroma of smoke—whether the woman's personal scent or some spell remnant—hung acrid in the air.

I found myself simultaneously drawn to the vibrancy of the living world and disinclined to participate in it. I remained still, delighting in the smells and sights and sounds.

"No use pretending you're not there," said the woman. "The straw man doesn't usually blink on its own. Or breathe."

I looked down and saw a rudimentary body made of straw, joints knotted together with what appeared to be twine. I lifted my straw hand and stretched out each finger, amazed as the joints crinkled but did not break. "What is this?" My voice sounded dry and crackling, though I did not know whether that was a function of straw or disuse.

"I'm not surprised this is new to you. The straw men are a pretty new development. It saves a lot of stress and unpleasantness for the twins and the spirit rebounders and everyone else who gets the thankless job of putting up with Insomniacs taking over their bodies. Olin Nimble—that's the man who innovated the straw men—he and I completed our scholastic training the same year. Twenty years later? He's transfigured the whole field. And here's me, puttering around the library. But I suppose someone has to teach the students how to distinguish Pinder's Breath from Summer Twoflower."

The woman reached into my summoning circle and tugged my earlobe. Straw crackled.

"It's a gesture of greeting," she said. "Go on, tug mine."

I reached out hesitantly, expecting my gesture to be thwarted by the invisible summoning barrier. Instead, my fingers slid through unresisting air and grasped the woman's earlobe.

She grinned with an air of satisfaction that reminded me of the way my aunts had looked when showing me new spells. "I am Scholar Misa Meticulous." She lifted the crystal globe she carried and squinted at it. Magical etchings appeared, spelling words in an unfamiliar alphabet. "And you are the Great Lady Naeva who Picked Posies near the Queen's Chamber, of the Kingdom Where Women Rule?"

I frowned, or tried to, unsure whether it showed on my straw face. "The Land of Flowered Hills."

"Oh." She corrected the etching with a long, sharp implement. "Our earliest records have it the other way. This sort of thing is commoner than you'd think. Facts get mixed with rumor. Rumor becomes legend. Soon no one can remember what was history and what they made up to frighten the children. For instance, I'll bet your people didn't really have an underclass of women you kept in herds for bearing children."

"We called them broods."

"You called them—" Misa's eyes went round and horrified. As quickly as her shock had registered, it disappeared again. She snorted with forthright amusement. "We'll have to get one of the historians to talk to you. This is what they *live* for."

"Do they."

It was becoming increasingly clear that this woman viewed me as a relic. Indignation simmered; I was not an urn, half-buried in the desert. Yet, in a way, I was.

"I'm just a teacher who specializes in sniffing," Misa continued. "I find Insomniacs we haven't spoken to before. It can take years, tracking through records, piecing together bits of old spells. I've been following you for three years. You slept dark."

"Not dark enough."

She reached into the summoning circle to give me a sympathetic pat on the shoulder. "Eternity's a lonely place," she said. "Even the academy's lonely, and we only study eternity. Come on. Why don't we take a walk? I'll show you the library."

My straw eyes rustled as they blinked in surprise. "A walk?"

Misa laughed. "Try it out."

She laughed again as I took one precarious step forward and then another. The straw body's joints creaked with each stiff movement. I felt awkward and graceless, but I couldn't deny the pleasure of movement.

"Come on," Misa repeated, beckoning.

She led me down a corridor of gleaming white marble. Arcane symbols figured the walls. Spell-remnants scented the air with cinnamon and burnt herbs, mingling with the cool currents that swept down from the vaulted ceiling. Beneath our feet, the floor was worn from many footsteps and yet Misa and I walked alone. I wondered how it could be that a place built to accommodate hundreds was empty except for a low-ranking scholar and a dead woman summoned into an effigy.

My questions were soon answered when a group of students approached noisily from an intersecting passageway. They halted when they saw us, falling abruptly silent. Misa frowned. "Get on!" she said, waving them away. They looked relieved as they fled back the way they'd come.

The students' shaved heads and shapeless robes made it difficult to discern their forms, but it was clear I had seen something I hadn't been meant to.

"You train men here," I ascertained.

"Men, women, neuters," said Misa. "Anyone who comes. And qualifies, of course."

I felt the hiss of disappointment: another profane, degraded culture. I should have known better than to hope. "I see," I said, unable to conceal my resentment.

Misa did not seem to notice. "Many cultures have created separate systems of magic for the male and female. Your culture was extreme, but not unusual. Men work healing magic, and women sing weather magic, or vice versa. All very rigid, all very unscientific. Did they ever try to teach a man to wail for a midnight rain? Oh, maybe they did, but if he succeeded, then it was just that one man, and wasn't his spirit more womanly than masculine? They get noted as an exception to the rule, not a problem with the rule itself. Think Locas Follow with the crickets, or Petrin of Atscheko, or for an example on the female side, Queen Urté. And of course if the man you set up to sing love songs to hurricanes can't even stir up a breeze, well, there's your proof. Men can't sing the weather. Even if another man could. Rigor, that's the important thing. Until you have proof, anything can be wrong. We know now there's no difference between the magical capabilities of the sexes, but we'd have known it earlier if people had asked the right questions. Did you know there's a place in the northern wastes where they believe only people with both male and female genitals can work spells?"

"They're fools."

Misa shrugged.

"Everyone's a fool, sooner or later. I make a game of it with my students. What do we believe that will be proven wrong in the future? I envy your ability to live forever so you can see."

"You should not," I said, surprised by my own bitterness. "People of the future are as likely to destroy your truths as to uncover your falsehoods."

She turned toward me, her face drawn with empathy. "You may be right."

We entered a vast, mahogany-paneled room, large enough to quarter a roc. Curving shelf towers formed an elaborate labyrinth. Misa led me through the narrow aisles with swift precision.

The shelves displayed prisms of various shapes and sizes. Crystal pyramids sat beside metal cylinders and spheres cut from obsidian. There were stranger things, too, shapes for which I possessed no words, woven out of steel threads or hardened lava.

Overhead, a transparent dome revealed a night sky strewn with stars. I recognized no patterns among the sparkling pinpricks; it was as if all the stars I'd known had been gathered in a giant's palm and then scattered carelessly into new designs.

Misa chattered as she walked. "This is the academy library. There are over three hundred thousand spells in this wing alone and we've almost filled the second. My students are taking bets on when they'll start construction on the third. They're also taking bets on whose statue will be by the door. Olin Nimble's the favorite, wouldn't you know."

We passed a number of carrel desks upon which lay maps of strange rivers and red-tinted deserts. Tubes containing more maps resided in cubby holes between the desks, their ends labeled in an unfamiliar alphabet.

"We make the first year students memorize world maps," said Misa. "A scholar has to understand how much there is to know."

I stopped by a carrel near the end of the row. The map's surface was ridged to show changes in elevation. I tried to imagine what the land it depicted would look like from above, on a roc's back. Could the Mountains where the Sun Rests be hidden among those jagged points?

Misa stopped behind me. "We're almost to the place I wanted to show you," she said. When we began walking again, she stayed quiet.

Presently, we approached a place where marble steps led down to a sunken area. We descended, and seemed to enter another room entirely, the arcs of the library shelves on the main level looming upward like a ring of ancient trees.

All around us, invisible from above, there stood statues of men and women. They held out spell spheres in their carved, upturned palms.

"This is the Circle of Insomniacs," said Misa. "Every Insomniac is depicted here. All the ones we've found, that is."

Amid hunched old women and bearded men with wild eyes, I caught sight of stranger things. Long, armored spikes jutted from a woman's spine. A man seemed to be wearing a helmet shaped like a sheep's head until I noticed that his ears twisted behind his head and became the ram's horns. A child opened his mouth to display a ring of needle-sharp teeth like a leech's.

"They aren't human," I said.

"They are," said Misa. "Or they were." She pointed me to the space between a toothless man and a soldier whose face fell in shadow behind a carved helmet. "Your statue will be there. The sculptor will want to speak with you. Or if you don't want to talk to him, you can talk to his assistant, and she'll make notes."

I looked aghast at the crowd of stone faces. "This—this is why you woke me? This sentimental memorial?"

Misa's eyes glittered with excitement. "The statue's only part of it. We want to know more about you and the Kingdom Where Women Rule. Sorry, the Land of Flowered Hills. We want to learn from you and teach you. We want you to stay!"

I could not help but laugh, harsh and mirthless. Would this woman ask a piece of ancient stone wall whether or not it wanted to be displayed in a museum? Not even the worms who tried to steal my spells had presumed so much.

"I'm sorry," said Misa. "I shouldn't have blurted it out like that. I'm good at sniffing. I'm terrible with people. Usually I find the Great Ones and then other people do the summoning and bring them to the library. The council asked me to do it myself this time because I lived in a women's colony before I came to the academy. I'm what they call woman-centered. They thought we'd have something in common."

"Loving women is fundamental. It's natural as breeze. It's not some kind of shared diversion."

"Still. It's more than you'd have in common with Olin Nimble."

She paused, biting her lip. She was still transparently excited even though the conversation had begun to go badly.

"Will you stay a while at least?" she asked. "You've slept dark for millennia. What's a little time in the light?"

I scoffed and began to demand that she banish me back to the dark—but the scholar's excitement cast ripples in a pond that I'd believed had become permanently still.

What I'd learned from the unrecognizable maps and scattered constellations was that the wage of eternity was forgetfulness. I was lonely, achingly lonely. Besides, I had begun to like Misa's fumbling chatter. She had reawakened me to light and touch—and even, it seemed, to wonder.

If I was to stay, I told Misa, then she must understand that I'd had enough of worms and their attempts at magic. I did not want them crowding my time in the light.

The corners of Misa's mouth drew downward in disapproval, but she answered, "The academy puts us at the crossroads of myriad beliefs. Sometimes we must set aside our own." She reached out to touch me. "You're giving us a great gift by staying. We'll always respect that."

Misa and I worked closely during my first days at the academy. We argued over everything. Our roles switched rapidly and contentiously from master to apprentice and back again. She would begin by asking me questions, and then as I told her about what I'd learned in my matriline's locked rooms, she would interrupt to tell me I was wrong, her people had experimented with such things, and they never performed consistently. Within moments, we'd be shouting about what magic meant, and what it signified, and what it wanted—because one thing we agreed on was that magic was a little bit alive.

Misa suspended her teaching while she worked with me, so we had the days to ourselves in the vast salon where she taught. Her people's magic was more than superficially dissimilar from mine. They constructed their spells into physical geometries by mapping out elaborate equations that determined whether they would be cylinders or dodecahedrons, formed of garnet or lapis lazuli or cages of copper strands. Even their academy's construction reflected magical intentions, although Misa told me its effects were vague and diffuse.

"Magic is like architecture," she said. "You have to build the right container for magic to grow in. The right house for its heart."

"You fail to consider the poetry of magic," I contended. "It likes to be teased with images, cajoled with irony. It wants to match wits."

"Your spells are random!" Misa answered. "Even you don't understand how they work. You've admitted it yourself. The effects are variable, unpredictable. It lacks rigor!"

"And accomplishes grandeur," I said. "How many of your scholars can match me?"

I soon learned that Misa was not, as she claimed, an unimportant scholar. By agreement, we allowed her female pupils to enter the salon from time to time for consultations. The young women, who looked startlingly young in their loose white garments, approached Misa with an awe that verged on fear. Once, a very young girl who looked barely out of puberty, ended their session by giving a low bow and kissing Misa's hand. She turned vivid red and fled the salon.

Misa shook her head as the echoes of the girl's footsteps faded. "She just wishes she was taking from Olin Nimble."

"Why do you persist in this deception?" I asked. "You have as many spells in the library as he does. It is you, not he, who was asked to join the academy as a scholar."

She slid me a dubious look. "You've been talking to people?"

"I have been listening."

"I've been here a long time," said Misa. "They need people like me to do the little things so greater minds like Olin Nimble's can be kept clear."

But her words were clearly untrue. All of the academy's scholars, from the most renowned to the most inexperienced, sent to Misa for consultations. She greeted their pages with good humor and false humility, and then went to meet her fellow scholars elsewhere, leaving her salon to me so that I could study or contemplate as I wished.

In the Land of Flowered Hills, there had once been a famous scholar named The Woman Who Would Ask the Breeze for Whys and Wherefores. Misa was such a woman, relentlessly impractical, always half-occupied by her studies. We ate together, talked together, slept together in her chamber, and yet I never saw her focus fully on anything except when she was engrossed in transforming her abstract magical theories into complex, beautiful tangibles.

Sometimes, I paused to consider how different Misa was from my first love. Misa's scattered, self-effaced pursuit of knowledge was nothing like Rayneh's dignified exercise of power. Rayneh was like a statue, formed in a beautiful but permanent stasis, never learning or changing. Misa tumbled everywhere like a curious wind, seeking to understand and alter and collaborate, but never to master.

In our first days together, Misa and I shared an abundance of excruciating, contentious, awe-inspiring novelty. We were separated by cultures and centuries, and yet we were attracted to each other even more strongly because of the strangeness we brought into each other's lives.

The academy was controlled by a rotating council of scholars that was chosen annually by lots. They made their decisions by consensus and exercised control over issues great and small, including the selection of new mages who were invited to join the academy as scholars and thus enter the pool of people who might someday control it.

"I'm grateful every year when they don't draw my name," Misa said.

We were sitting in her salon during the late afternoon, relaxing on reclining couches and sipping a hot, sweet drink from celadon cups. One of Misa's students sat with us, a startle-eyed girl who kept her bald head powdered and smooth, whom Misa had confided she found promising. The drink smelled of oranges and cinnamon; I savored it, ever amazed by the abilities of my strange, straw body.

I looked to Misa. "Why?"

Misa shuddered. "Being on the council would be...terrible."

"Why?" I asked again, but she only repeated herself in a louder voice, growing increasingly frustrated with my questions.

Later, when Misa left to discuss a spell with one of the academy's male scholars, her student told me, "Misa doesn't want to be elevated over others. It's a very great taboo for her people."

"It is self-indulgent to avoid power," I said. "Someone must wield it. Better the strong than the weak."

Misa's student fidgeted uncomfortably. "Her people don't see it that way."

I sipped from my cup. "Then they are fools."

Misa's student said nothing in response, but she excused herself from the salon as soon as she finished her drink.

The council requested my presence when I had been at the academy for a year. They wished to formalize the terms of my stay. Sleepless Ones who remained were expected to hold their own classes and contribute to the institution's body of knowledge.

"I will teach," I told Misa, "but only women."

"Why!" demanded Misa. "What is your irrational attachment to this prejudice?"

"I will not desecrate women's magic by teaching it to men."

"How is it desecration?"

"Women's magic is meant for women. Putting it into men's hands is degrading."

"But why!"

Our argument intensified. I began to rage. Men are not worthy of woman's magic. They're small-skulled, and cringing, and animalistic. It would be wrong! *Why, why, why?* Misa demanded, quoting from philosophical dialogues, and describing experiments that supposedly proved there was no difference between men's and women's magic. We circled and struck at one another's arguments as if we were animals competing over territory. We tangled our horns and drew blood from insignificant wounds, but neither of us seemed able to strike a final blow.

"Enough!" I shouted. "You've always told me that the academy respects the sacred beliefs of other cultures. These are mine."

The Lady Who Plucked Red Flowers...

"They're absurd!"

"If you will not agree then I will not teach. Banish me back to the dark! It does not matter to me."

Of course, it did matter to me. I had grown too attached to chaos and clamor. And to Misa. But I refused to admit it.

In the end, Misa agreed to argue my intentions before the council. She looked at turns furious and miserable. "They won't agree," she said. "How can they? But I'll do what I can."

The next day, Misa rubbed dense, floral unguents into her scalp and decorated her fingers with arcane rings. Her quills trembled and fanned upward, displaying her anxiety.

The circular council room glowed with faint, magical light. Cold air mixed with the musky scents favored by high-ranking scholars, along with hints of smoke and herbs. Archways loomed at each of the cardinal directions. Misa led us through the eastern archway, which she explained was for negotiation, and into the center of the mosaic floor.

The council's scholars sat on raised couches arrayed around the circumference of the room. Each sat below a torch that guttered, red and gold, rendering the councilors' bodies vivid against the dim. I caught sight of a man in layered red and yellow robes, his head surmounted by a brass circlet that twinkled with lights that flared and then flitted out of existence, like winking stars. To his side sat a tall woman with mossy hair and bark-like skin, and beside her, a man with two heads and torsos mounted upon a single pair of legs. A woman raised her hand in greeting to Misa, and water cascaded from her arms like a waterfall, churning into a mist that evaporated before it touched the floor.

Misa had told me that older scholars were often changed by her people's magic, that it shaped their bodies in the way they shaped their spells. I had not understood her before.

A long, narrow man seemed to be the focal point of the other councilors' attention. Fine, sensory hairs covered his skin. They quivered in our direction like a small animal's sniffing. "What do you suggest?" he asked. "Shall we establish a woman-only library? Shall we inspect our students' genitalia to ensure there are no men-women or women-men or twin-sexed among them?"

"Never mind that," countered a voice behind us. I turned to see a pudgy woman garbed in heavy metal sheets. "It's irrelevant to object on the basis of pragmatism. This request is exclusionary."

"Worse," added the waterfall woman. "It's immoral."

The councilors around her nodded their heads in affirmation. Two identical-looking men in leather hoods fluttered their hands to show support.

Misa looked to each assenting scholar in turn. "You are correct. It is exclusionist and immoral. But I ask you to think about deeper issues. If we reject Naeva's conditions, then everything she knows will be lost. Isn't it better that some know than that everyone forgets?"

"Is it worth preserving knowledge if the price is bigotry?" asked the narrow man with the sensory hairs, but the other scholars' eyes fixed on Misa.

They continued to argue for some time, but the conclusion had been foregone as soon as Misa spoke. There is nothing scholars love more than knowledge.

❧

"Is it strange for you?" I asked Misa. "To spend so much time with someone trapped in the body of a doll?"

We were alone in the tiny, cluttered room where she slept. It was a roughly hewn underground cavity, its only entrance and exit by ladder. Misa admitted that the academy offered better accommodations, but claimed she preferred rooms like this one.

Misa exclaimed with mock surprise. "You're trapped in the body of a doll? I'd never noticed!"

She grinned in my direction. I rewarded her with laughter.

"I've gotten used to the straw men," she said more seriously. "When we talk, I'm thinking about spells and magic and the things you've seen. Not straw."

Nevertheless, straw remained inescapably cumbersome. Misa suggested games and spells and implements, but I refused objects that would estrange our intimacy. We lay together at night and traded words, her hands busy at giving her pleasure while I watched and whispered. Afterward, we lay close, but I could not give her the warmth of a body I did not possess.

One night, I woke long after our love-making to discover that she was no longer beside me. I found her in the salon, her equations spiraling across a row of crystal globes. A doll hung from the wall beside her, awkwardly suspended by its nape. Its skin was warm and soft and tinted the same sienna that mine had been so many eons ago. I raised its face and saw features matching the sketches that the sculptor's assistant had made during our sessions.

Misa looked up from her calculations. She smiled with mild embarrassment.

"I should have known a simple adaptation wouldn't work," she said. "Otherwise, Olin Nimble would have discarded straw years ago. But I thought, if I worked it out…."

I moved behind her, and beheld the array of crystal globes, all showing spidery white equations. Below them lay a half-formed spell of polished wood and peridot chips.

Misa's quill mane quivered. "It's late," she said, taking my hand. "We should return to bed."

❧

Misa often left her projects half-done and scattered. I like to think the doll would have been different. I like to think she would have finished it.

Instead, she was drawn into the whirl of events happening outside the academy. She began leaving me behind in her chambers while she spent all hours in her salon, almost sleepwalking through the brief periods when she returned to me, and then rising restless in the dark and returning to her work.

By choice, I remained unclear about the shape of the external cataclysm. I did not want to be drawn further into the academy's politics.

My lectures provided little distraction. The students were as preoccupied as Misa. "This is not a time for theory!" one woman complained when I tried to draw my students into a discussion of magic's predilections. She did not return the following morning. Eventually, no one else returned either.

Loneliness drove me where curiosity could not and I began following Misa to her salon. Since I refused to help with her spells, she acknowledged my presence with little more than a glance before returning to her labors. Absent her attention, I studied and paced.

Once, after leaving the salon for several hours, Misa returned with a bustle of scholars—both men and women—all brightly clad and shouting. They halted abruptly when they saw me.

"I forgot you were here," Misa said without much contrition.

I tensed, angry and alienated, but unwilling to show my rage before the worms. "I will return to your chamber," I said through tightened lips.

Before I even left the room, they began shouting again. Their voices weren't like scholars debating. They lashed at each other with their words. They were angry. They were afraid.

That night, I went to Misa and finally asked for explanations. It's a plague, she said. A plague that made its victims bleed from the skin and eyes and then swelled their tongues until they suffocated.

They couldn't cure it. They treated one symptom, only to find the others worsening. The patients died, and then the mages who treated them died, too.

I declared that the disease must be magic. Misa glared at me with unexpected anger and answered that, no! It was not magic! If it was magic, they would have cured it. This was something foul and deadly and *natural*.

She'd grown gaunt by then, the gentle cushions of fat at her chin and stomach disappearing as her ribs grew prominent. After she slept, her headrest was covered with quills that had fallen out during the night, their pointed tips lackluster and dulled.

I no longer had dialogues or magic or sex to occupy my time. I had only remote, distracted Misa. My world began to shape itself around her—my love for her, my concern for her, my dread that she wouldn't find a cure, and my fear of what I'd do if she didn't. She was weak, and she was leading me into weakness. My mind sketched patterns

I didn't want to imagine. I heard the spirits in The Desert Which Should Not Have Been whispering about the deaths of civilizations, and about choices between honor and love.

Misa stopped sleeping. Instead, she sat on the bed in the dark, staring into the shadows and worrying her hands.

"There is no cure," she muttered.

I lay behind her, watching her silhouette.

"Of course there's a cure."

"Oh, *of course*," snapped Misa. "We're just too ignorant to find it!"

Such irrational anger. I never learned how to respond to a lover so easily swayed by her emotions.

"I did not say that you were ignorant."

"As long as you didn't say it."

Misa pulled to her feet and began pacing, footsteps thumping against the piled rugs.

I realized that in all my worrying, I'd never paused to consider where the plague had been, whether it had ravaged the communities where Misa had lived and loved. My people would have thought it a weakness to let such things affect them.

"Perhaps you are ignorant," I said. "Maybe you can't cure this plague by building little boxes. Have you thought of that?"

I expected Misa to look angry, but instead she turned back with an expression of awe. "Maybe that's it," she said slowly. "Maybe we need your kind of magic. Maybe we need poetry."

For the first time since the plague began, the lines of tension began to smooth from Misa's face. I loved her. I wanted to see her calm and curious, restored to the woman who marveled at new things and spent her nights beside me.

So I did what I knew I should not. I sat with her for the next hours and listened as she described the affliction. It had begun in a swamp far to the east, she said, in a humid tangle of roots and branches where a thousand sharp and biting things lurked beneath the water. It traveled west with summer's heat, sickening children and old people first, and then striking the young and healthy. The children and elderly sometimes recovered. The young and healthy never survived.

I thought back to diseases I'd known in my youth. A very different illness came to mind, a disease cast by a would-be usurper during my girlhood. It came to the Land of Flowered Hills with the winter wind and froze its victims into statues that would not shatter with blows or melt with heat. For years after Rayneh's mother killed the usurper and halted the disease, the Land of Flowered Hills was haunted by the glacial, ghostly remains of those once-loved. The Queen's sorceresses sought them out one by one and melted them with memories of passion. It was said that the survivors wept and cursed as their loved ones melted away, for they had grown to love the ever-present, icy memorials.

That illness was unlike what afflicted Misa's people in all ways but one—that disease, too, had spared the feeble and taken the strong.

I told Misa, "This is a plague that steals its victims' strength and uses it to kill them."

Misa's breaths came slowly and heavily. "Yes, that's it," she said. "That's what's happening."

"The victims must steal their strength back from the disease. They must cast their own cures."

"They must cast your kind of spells. Poetry spells."

"Yes," I said. "Poetry spells."

Misa's eyes closed as if she wanted to weep with relief. She looked so tired and frail. I wanted to lay her down on the bed and stroke her cheeks until she fell asleep.

Misa's shoulders shook but she didn't cry. Instead, she straightened her spectacles and plucked at her robes.

"With a bit of heat and...how would obsidian translate into poetry?..." she mused aloud. She started toward the ladder and then paused to look back. "Will you come help me, Naeva?"

She must have known what I would say.

"I'll come," I said quietly, "but this is woman's magic. It is not for men."

What followed was inevitable: the shudder that passed through Misa as her optimism turned ashen. "No. Naeva. You wouldn't let people die."

But I would. And she should have known that. If she knew me at all.

☙

She brought it before the council. She said that was how things were to be decided. By discussion. By consensus.

We entered through the western arch, the arch of conflict. The scholars arrayed on their raised couches looked as haggard as Misa. Some seats were empty, others filled by men and women I'd not seen before.

"Why is this a problem?" asked one of the new scholars, an old woman whose face and breasts were stippled with tiny, fanged mouths. "Teach the spell to women. Have them cast it on the men."

"The victims must cast it themselves," Misa said.

The old woman scoffed. "Since when does a spell care who casts it?"

"It's old magic," Misa said. "Poetry magic."

"Then what is it like?" asked a voice from behind us.

We turned to see the narrow man with the fine, sensory hairs, who had demanded at my prior interrogation whether knowledge gained through bigotry was worth preserving. He lowered his gaze onto my face and his hairs extended toward me, rippling and seeking.

"Some of us have not had the opportunity to learn for ourselves," he added.

I hoped that Misa would intercede with an explanation, but she held her gaze away from mine. Her mouth was tight and narrow.

The man spoke again. "Unless you feel that it would violate your ethics to even describe the issue in my presence."

"No. It would not." I paused to prepare my words. "As I understand it, your people's magic imprisons spells in clever constructions. You alter the shape and texture of the spell as you alter the shape and texture of its casing."

Dissenting murmurs rose from the councilors.

"I realize that's an elementary description," I said. "However, it will suffice for contrast. My people attempted to court spells with poetry, using image and symbol and allusion as our tools. Your people give magic a place to dwell. Mine woo it to tryst awhile."

"What does that," interjected the many-mouthed old woman, "have to do with victims casting their own spells?"

Before I could answer, the narrow man spoke. "It must be poetry—the symmetry, if you will. Body and disease are battling for the body's strength. The body itself must win the battle."

"Is that so?" the old woman demanded of me.

I inclined my head in assent.

A woman dressed in robes of scarlet hair looked to Misa. "You're confident this will work?"

Misa's voice was strained and quiet. "I am."

The woman turned to regard me, scarlet tresses parting over her chest to reveal frog-like skin that glistened with damp. "You will not be moved? You won't relinquish the spell?"

I said, "No."

"Even if we promise to give it only to the women, and let the men die?"

I looked toward Misa. I knew what her people believed. The council might bend in matters of knowledge, but it would not bend in matters of life.

"I do not believe you would keep such promises."

The frog-skinned woman laughed. The inside of her mouth glittered like a cavern filled with crystals. "You're right, of course. We wouldn't." She looked to her fellow councilors. "I see no other option. I propose an Obligation."

"No," said Misa.

"I agree with Jian," said a fat scholar in red and yellow. "An Obligation."

"You can't violate her like that," said Misa. "The academy is founded on respect."

The frog-skinned woman raised her brows at Misa. "What is respect worth if we let thousands die?"

Misa took my hands. "Naeva, don't let this happen. Please, Naeva." She moved yet closer to me, her breath hot, her eyes desperate. "You know what men can be. You know they don't have to be ignorant worms or greedy brutes. You know they can be clever and noble! Remember Pasha. You gave him the spell he needed. Why won't you help us?"

Pasha—kin of my thoughts, closer than my own skin. It had seemed different then, inside his mind. But I was on my own feet now, looking out from my own eyes, and I knew what I knew.

When she'd been confronted by the inevitable destruction of our people, Tryce had made herself into a brood. She had chosen to degrade herself and her daughters in the name of survival. What would the Land of Flowered Hills have become if she'd succeeded? What would have happened to us hard and haughty people who commanded the sacred powers of wind and sun?

I would not desecrate our knowledge by putting it in the hands of animals. This was not just one man who would die from what he learned. This would be unlocking the door to my matriline's secret rooms and tearing open the many-drawered cupboards. It would be laying everything sacrosanct bare to corruption.

I broke away from Misa's touch. "I will tell you nothing!"

The council acted immediately and unanimously, accord reached without deliberation. The narrow man wrought a spell-shape using only his hands, which Misa had told me could be done, but rarely and only by great mages. When his fingers held the right configuration, he blew into their cage.

An Obligation.

It was like falling through blackness. I struggled for purchase, desperate to climb back into myself.

My mouth opened. It was not I who spoke.

"Bring them water from the swamp and damp their brows until they feel the humidity of the place where the disease was born. The spirit of the disease will seek its origins, as any born creature will. Let the victims seek with their souls' sight until they find the spirit of the disease standing before them. It will appear differently to each, vaporous and foul, or sly and sharp, but they will know it. Let the victims open the mouths of their souls and devour the disease until its spirit is inside their spirit as its body is inside their body. This time, they will be the conquerors. When they wake, they will be stronger than they had been before."

My words resonated through the chamber. Misa shuddered and began to retch. The frog-skinned woman detached a lock of her scarlet hair and gave it, along with a sphere etched with my declamation, to their fleetest page. My volition rushed back into me as if through a crashing dam. I swelled with my returning power.

Magic is a little bit alive. It loves irony and it loves passion. With all the fierceness of my dead Land, I began to tear apart my straw body with its own straw hands. The effigy's viscera fell, crushed and crackling, to the mosaic floor.

The narrow man, alone among the councilors, read my intentions. He sprang to his feet, forming a rapid protection spell between his fingers. It glimmered into being before I could complete my own magic, but I was ablaze with passion and poetry, and I knew that I would prevail.

The fire of my anger leapt from my eyes and tongue and caught upon the straw in which I'd been imprisoned. Fire. Magic. Fury. The academy became an inferno.

❧

They summoned me into a carved rock that could see and hear and speak but could not move. They carried it through the Southern arch, the arch of retribution.

The narrow man addressed me. His fine, sensory hairs had burned away in the fire, leaving his form bald and pathetic.

"You are dangerous," he said. "The council has agreed you cannot remain."

The council room was in ruins. The reek of smoke hung like a dense fog over the rubble. Misa sat on one of the few remaining couches, her eyes averted, her body etched with thick ugly scars. She held her right hand in her lap, its fingers melted into a single claw.

I wanted to cradle Misa's ruined hand, to kiss and soothe it. It was an unworthy desire. I had no intention of indulging regret.

"You destroyed the academy, you bitch," snarled a woman to my left. I remembered that she had once gestured waterfalls, but now her arms were burned to stumps. "Libraries, students, spells…." Her voice cracked.

"The council understands the grave injustice of an Obligation," the narrow man continued, as if she had not interjected. "We don't take the enslavement of a soul lightly, especially when it violates a promised trust. Though we believe we acted rightfully, we also acknowledge we have done you an injustice. For that we owe you our contrition.

"Nevertheless," he continued, "It is the council's agreement that you cannot be permitted to remain in the light. It is our duty to send you back into the dark and to bind you there so that you may never answer summons again."

I laughed. It was a grating sound. "You'll be granting my dearest wish."

He inclined his head. "It is always best when aims align."

He reached out to the women next to him and took their hands. The remaining council members joined them, bending their bodies until they, themselves, formed the shape of a spell. Misa turned to join them, the tough, shiny substance of her scar tissue catching the light. I knew from Misa's lessons that the texture of her skin would alter and shape the spell. I could recognize their brilliance in that, to understand magic so well that they could form it out of their own bodies.

As the last of the scholars moved into place, for a moment I understood the strange, distorted, perfect shape they made. I realized with a slash that I had finally begun to comprehend their magic. And then I sank into final, lasting dark.

∽

I remembered.

I remembered Misa. I remembered Pasha. I remembered the time when men had summoned me into unknown lands.

Always and inevitably, my thoughts returned to the Land of Flowered Hills, the place I had been away from longest, but known best.

Misa and Rayneh. I betrayed one. One betrayed me. Two loves ending in tragedy. Perhaps all loves do.

I remembered the locked room in my matriline's household, all those tiny lacquered drawers filled with marvels. My aunt's hand fluttered above them like a pale butterfly as I wondered which drawer she would open. What wonder would she reveal from a world so vast I could never hope to understand it?

"To paint a bird, you must show the brush what it means to fly," my aunt told me, holding my fingers around the brush handle as I strove to echo the perfection of a feather. The brush trembled. Dip into the well, slant, and press. Bristles splay. Ink bleeds across the scroll and—there! One single graceful stroke aspiring toward flight.

What can a woman do when love and time and truth are all at odds with one another, clashing and screeching, wailing and weeping, begging you to enter worlds unlike any you've ever known and save this people, this people, this people from king's soldiers and guttering volcanoes and plagues? What can a woman do when beliefs that seemed as solid as stone have become dry leaves blowing in autumn wind? What can a woman cling to when she must betray her lovers' lives or her own?

A woman is not a bird. A woman needs ground.

All my aunts gathering in a circle around the winter fire to share news and gossip, their voices clat-clat-clatting at each other in comforting, indistinguishable sounds. The wind finds its way in through the cracks and we welcome our friend. It blows through me, carrying scents of pine and snow. I run across the creaking floor to my aunts' knees which are as tall as I am, my arms slipping around one dark soft leg and then another as I work my way around the circle like a wind, finding the promise of comfort in each new embrace.

Light returned and shaded me with grey.

I stood on a pedestal under a dark dome, the room around me eaten by shadow. My hands touched my robe which felt like silk. They encountered each other and felt flesh. I raised them before my face and saw my own hands, brown and short and nimble, the fingernails jagged where I'd caught them on the rocks while surveying with Kyan in the Mountains where the Sun Rests.

Around me, I saw more pedestals arranged in a circle, and atop them strange forms that I could barely distinguish from shade. As my eyes adjusted, I made out a soldier with his face shadowed beneath a horned helmet, and a woman armored with spines. Next to me stood a child who smelled of stale water and dead fish. His eyes slid in my direction and I saw they were strangely old and weary. He opened his mouth to yawn, and inside, I saw a ring of needle-sharp teeth.

Recognition rushed through me. These were the Insomniacs I'd seen in Misa's library, all of them living and embodied, except there were more of us, countless more, all perched and waiting.

Magic is a little bit alive. That was my first thought as the creature unfolded before us, its body a strange darkness like the unrelieved black between stars. It was adorned with windows and doors that gleamed with silver like starlight. They opened and closed like slow blinking, offering us portals into another darkness that hinted at something beyond.

The creature was nothing like the entities that I'd believed waited at the core of eternity. It was no frozen world lizard, waiting to crack traitors in his icy jaws, nor a burning sun welcoming joyous souls as feathers in her wings. And yet, somehow I knew then that this creature was the deepest essence of the universe—the strange, persistent thing that throbbed like a heart between stars.

Its voice was strange, choral, like many voices talking at once. At the same time, it did not sound like a voice at all. It said, "You are the ones who have reached the end of time. You are witnesses to the end of this universe."

As it spoke, it expanded outward. The fanged child staggered back as the darkness approached. He looked toward me with fear in his eyes, and then darkness swelled around me, too, and I was surrounded by shadow and pouring starlight.

The creature said, "From the death of this universe will come the birth of another. This has happened so many times before that it cannot be numbered, unfathomable universes blinking one into the next, outside of time. The only continuity lies in the essences that persist from one to the next."

Its voice faded. I stretched out my hands into the gentle dark. "You want us to be reborn?" I asked.

I wasn't sure if it could even hear me in its vastness. But it spoke.

"The new universe will be unlike anything in this one. It will be a strangeness. There will be no 'born,' no 'you.' One cannot speak of a new universe. It is anathema to language. One cannot even ponder it."

Above me, a window opened, and it was not a window, but part of this strange being. Soothing, silver brilliance poured from it like water. It rushed over me, tingling like fresh spring mornings and newly drawn breath.

I could feel the creature's expectancy around me. More windows opened and closed as other Sleepless Ones made their choices.

I thought of everything then—everything I had thought of during the millennia when I was bound, and everything I should have thought of then but did not have the courage to think. I saw my life from a dozen fractured perspectives. Rayneh condemning me for helping her daughter steal her throne, and dismissing my every subsequent act as a traitor's cowardice. Tryce sneering at my lack of will as she watched me spurn a hundred opportunities for seizing power during centuries of summons. Misa, her brows drawn down in inestimable disappointment, pleading with me to abandon everything I was and become like her instead.

They were all right. They were all wrong. My heart shattered into a million sins.

I thought of Pasha who I should never have saved. I thought of how he tried to shield me from the pain of his death, spending his last strength to soothe me before he died alone. For millennia, I had sought oblivion and been denied. Now, as I approached the opportunity to dissipate at last…now I began to understand the desire for something unspeakably, unfathomably new.

I reached toward the window. The creature gathered me in its massive blackness and lifted me up, up, up. I became a woman painted in brushstrokes of starlight, fewer and fewer, until I was only a glimmer of silver that had once been a woman, now poised to take flight. I glittered like the stars over The Desert which Should Not Have Been, eternal witnesses to things long forgotten. The darkness beyond the window pulled me. I leapt toward it, and stretched, and changed.

The Children of Cadmus

ELLEN KUSHNER

THE DAUGHTER SPEAKS:
The daughters of Cadmus have a duty to their father's house, and so do all of the sons, as well. And thus it is that we can never be truly happy, my brother and I. For he loves the night, the strange time when all men are asleep. He loves the swoop and glitter of the stars that the gods have set in the heavens, loves to watch the heroes and the monsters cartwheel their way across until rosy-fingered Aurora strokes them away before Apollo's chariot. Only then will he fall into bed, my big brother, sprawled out on his couch half the day until the sun has passed the zenith of the heavens, when he comes lumbering out of his chamber, blinking and rubbing his eyes, looking for something to eat. I can usually

find him something. It's a wonder my brother and I ever meet at all. For I love the cold gray dawn, when the grass is still wet with dew. I love to be up before everyone except the household slaves and the keepers of the hounds, readying for the hunt, which I love best of all. The chase through the woods through the waking dawn, the dappled trees and morning shadows, the chase of the sweet, swift animals that we love even as we seek to break them and bring them to their knees to furnish our tables and our bellies and our feasts. I love to run with my spear and my hounds in my short chiton, legs free and arms free. ...But those days are finished for me. I am Creusa, the daughter of Autonoë, the daughter of Cadmus, king of Thebes. I am of an age to be married, now.

You will have heard of our grandfather, Cadmus: he who sowed the serpent's teeth, and brought forth a race of warriors to build our fair city of Thebes. He did not do all this alone. The god Phoebus Apollo told Cadmus where to find his fate, and Pallas Athena herself stood by him as he scattered the dragon's teeth across the fields of Boetia. The gods love our grandfather Cadmus.

And we, in return, must love and honor them.

And so I do. I make my sacrifices to Zeus the Thunderer, to Hera of the Hearth, and to red Mars, fierce in War, who is father to my grandmother Harmonia, whose mother is seaborn Aphrodite.

But it is Artemis, virgin goddess of the hunt, I love. And that is my despair.

❧

THE SON SPEAKS:

My sister Creusa is quite mad. I said as much to my tutor, Chiron the Centaur, and he chided me, as he so often does. He is always whisking his tail at me—it stings but does not really hurt. And I would take ten times that sting to remain his pupil. For while Cadmus and my parents think the great centaur is teaching me hunting, we left that behind long ago. Chiron is a noble archer, true, and I'm not a bad shot thanks to him. But Chiron is a master of the art of healing and knows the movements of the stars.

The stars tell stories. Some of the stars are our own people, taken from the pains of this life up into the heavens. The stars make patterns, too, and surely it all means something. Here on earth, there is pain and blood and strife. But the stars move in an orderly way, pacing out a huge dance across time that no man has seen the end of.

If I watch long enough, I think I might learn.

As it is, I am often forced out of my bed into a cold and drippy day and expected to run about, shouting, following smelly dogs howling to wake the dead. They are perfectly nice dogs, ordinarily, but they become monsters when we hunt. And so I run after poor wild beasts that never did me any harm, to open great wounds in their sides with my spear or my arrows—if the dogs' teeth don't get to them first—to rip open their sleek and beautiful hides and ruin them forever, letting out their life's blood in the process while the poor animals writhe and froth trying to escape.

When I leave this earth, I would not mind becoming a star, or even a full constellation. People will look up at me, and tell my story. And I will become part of the great pattern, the great dance.

Chiron says that I should not mock my sister's dreams. He says that our dreams are our truth, even if we cannot achieve them. He says that I should help my sister, if I can, to bear the fate the gods choose for her. I'll try.

◦∾

THE DAUGHTER SPEAKS:

I cannot bear it. I cannot bear to think, because I am a girl, almost a woman now, that my fate will be to become the wife of any man. I wish to follow the goddess. I wish to run with her in the hunt by day, and lie with her and her nymphs by night. Instead, a man's hands on me? A man's mouth on my lips, a man's body on mine?

The only rough hair and rough skin I want anywhere near me is that of my kill. Rather than yield to a man's touch, I would *become* a lion, a boar, a hare, or a deer, myself.

Such transformations are not unheard of. The stories abound of men and women turned to animals, to trees or flowers or even stars, in order to escape a more terrible fate. The gods can be cruel, but they have always helped our house.

Whom shall I pray to, then?

To Phoebus Apollo, who desired and chased the fair nymph Daphne, she who ran from him—as I would run, even from a god—screaming for help? Just as his hands reached her, Daphne turned into a laurel tree. Her toes became roots, her skin bark, her hair leaves, leaving the god unsatisfied…. I don't want to be a tree. I want to run, and run free.

To the great Zeus, lover of the beautiful mortal Io? He was powerless when his angry wife, Hera, turned pretty Io into a cow, afflicted by flies and unable to speak her torment. No help from the gods, then, and what goddess would hear my prayers? Hera, goddess of wives and hearths, wants me for her own. Wise Athena would mock me. And Aphrodite…her kind of rapturous love is not for me. Only Artemis the Hunter can save me.

All my life I have prayed to her. But if she has heard me, she does not care.

Is it because of my impiety? Do I love the goddess too much? There is a marble statue in her temple, with high round breasts and long white thighs. Once, when I was alone there, I reached out and touched them, running my fingers along all that whiteness, cool as stone but smooth as perfect flesh. Nobody saw me, I'm sure. I dream of touching them again. But I'm afraid of how even the thought makes me feel, all hungry with a hunger there is no food for, and aching like pain, only strangely sweet. All I have to do is think about touching her, to feel that way again. I don't think there's even a name for how I feel. It fills me utterly, and I am almost powerless before it. So I dare to call it love. Maybe this is why Zeus could not leave pretty Io alone, though it meant her doom. Or why Apollo ran after the screaming Daphne.

Maybe the goddess does not want such love from me. But it is hers, all the same.

THE SON SPEAKS:

My sister grows pale. It is terrible to see. She weeps and spins, and burns herbs at the altar of Artemis. Now Creusa wants to build her own special altar to the goddess. Yesterday she begged me to bring her horns from a mighty stag, the finest in the forest.

I'll do a lot for poor Creusa. So I suppose I'll take a good sharp saw, and hack away at the next deer we kill. It's not really the season for the great-horned stags. The older ones are cunning in the hunt, and the young ones not yet grown. But for my sister, I will make a stag appear, if I can. If it will make her happy.

THE DAUGHTER SPEAKS:

The suitors are coming. Four from the north, three from the south, and two from the east. They will expect hospitality befitting the House of Cadmus. I must be here to welcome them when they come.

Or I must flee.

What will I do, oh, what will I do? Choose the least horrible of them, and submit?

Or could I leave the safety of our city and of my mother's house, to live outcast and alone in some wasteland without people? Live all by myself in a cave by a spring, devoting my life and my virginity to her who hunts by day and shines by night? My hair would grow tangled, my clothing or the skins of the beasts I caught. I would drink only water, eat the flesh of my prey. The only fire I'd ever see would be my own, the only voice the voices of my dogs, and of my kills. Can I do it?

THE SON SPEAKS:

I found Creusa with a knife in her hand, lifting her blade to her own neck.

"Stop!" My hand is so much bigger than hers, now. It was not hard to circle hand and knife in my grasp. "Sister, I beg you! No matter how hard this life is, it is better than wandering with the starless shades."

"You big star-gazing ox," she said, but she wasn't angry. "I was just cutting my hair."

She wore a short chiton, and her cloak was on the chest next to her, even though the weather was very hot.

I saw it then. "You're going?"

"Yes," she whispered. "It is my fate."

"A nameless, homeless wanderer? Oh, Creusa, no!"

"What else can I do? Grandfather will not let me dedicate myself to Artemis and live chaste. While I am under his roof, I must obey his will." She patted my hand, releasing her knife into it. "And so I'm leaving. I will seek the goddess all my life, and maybe she will take pity on me and let me find her."

"And if she doesn't? Creusa, what then?"

Her eyes filled with tears. "I don't know. I don't know what else to do."

I took both her hands. They were so cold. I looked hard into her eyes, which shone with unshed stars. "Don't go. Not yet. Once you have gone, you can never come back. There's still time."

"Time for what?"

"I'll think of something," I promised her. "I'll watch the skies. There is a pattern, there is a dance...."

She shook her head. She doesn't believe the night skies hold any answers. But she put her knife down, pinned up her hair again, and folded up her cloak.

～

THE DAUGHTER SPEAKS:

What a fool I've been! The answer to my escape has been before me all along.

As I sat spinning under the great tree in the courtyard, in he walked, grandfather's old friend, gray and gnarled as the staff he stretches before him to find his way.

The seer Tiresias. I flung myself at his feet, kneeling in supplication, clutching the hem of his robe. I would not rise, but made the old seer bend down to hear my whispered plea: "Prophet, blinded by the gods for what you saw—I beg you, tell me the secret of your transformation!"

"Rise," he said, "and sit with me. Does the daughter of the House of Cadmus wish to become a prophet? Or blind, or old? Those last two may be easily achieved, given enough years and patience."

"I don't have years!"

"Nor patience, either, it would seem."

I picked up my spindle and put it down. But then I placed it in his hands. "Remember this?" I said. "Remember when you wore a woman's body as your own?"

I had always doubted the tale. Tiresias is so dry, so unlovely, so gnarled and hairy and *male*. But when he took the spindle from me, he naturally maintained the tension and the twist with a sureness no man's hands could ever know.

"It's true," I marveled. "You were a woman seven years, before you came again to your manhood."

"But it is not my manhood you seek, little princess."

"Yes, it is!" The prophet eased away from me in his seat uncomfortably, and I laughed. "Not that. Never that."

Tiresias shrugged, and laughed himself. "What, then?"

"I wish to leave my father's house."

"And so you shall, when you are wed."

"I do not wish to marry. I wish to follow the goddess."

"Have you asked your family's permission?"

"They only laugh at me. They say a girl never knows her own mind." The old man nodded. "But when I say I *do* know, they tell me a princess must wed, to carry on a noble line."

"You think they are wrong?"

I hung my head, ashamed of what I must ask. "Is it possible, Seer, for someone to be born into the wrong body?" I waited, tense, to see if he would pull away. But he turned the spindle in his hands. He did not spin.

"Go on."

I leaned closer, whispered in the grizzled hair that fell over his ears. "I don't want what women want. I don't want a husband, or children, or a house. I want—what I want is what men want!" There. I had said it. My heart hammered, and my cheeks were hot. But I felt strangely glad, and lighter, now. The words came tumbling out of me: "I want to run free, to hunt, to kill, to glory in my fleetness and my strength! If I can't have them as a woman, then let me have them as a man!"

Hardly knowing what I was doing, I grasped his old shoulders between my hands. "Tell me your secret! Tell me what you did, how you changed your shape, and how I may do it too!"

Tiresias did not move. But his blind eyes turned up to mine. "And if I do? What is it you hunt, Child of Cadmus? What is your true desire?"

"Artemis," I whispered, her very name a prayer I breathed into his face. "I would seek Artemis of the Hunt."

I don't know where he found the strength to push me away. It was as if another touched me, threw me backward to the ground. Tiresias towered above me, his staff raised, a howl like an animal's coming from his throat: "*Woe!* Woe to the House of Cadmus! Blood and terror, terror and blood and the great deer running!"

"Stop!" I crawled to the edge of his robe, pulling on it to draw his attention, but it was as if I were not even there.

"O terrible transformation!" He flung up his arm again, as though to hide the vision from his sightless eyes.

"The hunter hunted and the terror loosed! Alas for a house made barren! Alas for a seed made cold!"

The prophecy was terrible enough. But what if people heard the shouting, and came running to listen?

"I didn't mean it," I babbled. "I beg you, stop, I didn't mean it—"

Slowly, the prophet lowered his staff until he was leaning his full weight on it. His knees were shaking. "Oh, little princess, what I saw!" Slowly, he lowered himself to his knees before me. "I beg you, for your grandfather's sake and mine, do not pursue the goddess. Such a terrible transformation. Death and madness. Terrible, terrible…."

The old man was weeping at my feet. I had to kneel before him myself, and clasp his ankles and promise I would never seek to become other than that I am.

But what is that?

❧

THE SON SPEAKS:

My sister rose in the middle of the night to tell me of the bloody prophecy. She found me up on the roof, where I'd gone to watch the progress of Saturn as it met for the first time in my life with Alpha Serpentis.

Her face was the color of the moon, silver, all the blood washed away by starlight. She did not weep, but I held her by her stiff shoulders to comfort her anyway, in the cold night air.

"I dare not go," she said. "I dare not run." She looked out over the sleeping fields to the woods beyond. "And yet, I almost wish I could. To seek the goddess, to look on her once before I die…."

"Creusa!"

"It's the way I feel. I can't explain."

"No need," I said. "I just don't want you to die, that's all."

She smiled, and touched my cheek. "You big star-gazing ox."

That's when I realized how I could help her. I was a fool not to have thought of it before. Chiron was right: the gods decide our fate, but it is ours to look squarely on it, to take up what we have been given, and to use it the best way that we can.

If fate decreed me for a hunter, why then, I would hunt.

But my quarry would be for my sister's sake. The goddess loves one who hunts with spirit and true purpose.

Creusa yawned. She really isn't much good at night. "I'd better get to bed," she said sadly. "The suitors are coming, and I have household matters to attend to."

"I'd better get to bed, myself." I forced a yawn, too. "The hunt starts bright and early, and I've got a lot of meat to catch for all your suitors."

She said, "I hope they like rabbit; it's all you're likely to get this time of year."

"Whatever it is, I'll dedicate my catch to you, and to your future happiness."

That's what I told her. But my true quarry, *that* I'll keep a secret, until I can return to my sad sister with news to turn her pale cheeks bright with joy.

❧

THE DAUGHTER SPEAKS:

Actaeon is gone. He's been gone for five days and four nights. The skies have been clear. Maybe he has finally wandered off, star-struck, star-gazing, at last.

His companions say they lost him on the second day of the hunt. They'd been running hard, and their nets and spears were full of the blood of the wild animals they'd caught. It was midday, sunny and hot, and even in the tangle of bushes and scrub, the shadows were short. Hunting was over for the day.

They cast themselves down in whatever shade they could find, and drank from streams and cleaned their nets. They'd begin again early the next morning.

They say my brother wandered away, following the music of a rocky stream that led deep into the shady wood. They saw him disappear into a grove of pines and cypress, and that was all.

Hours passed, and he did not return. They thought he'd fallen asleep in the shade somewhere, and let him be. Then a wonderful thing happened so late in the day: a huge stag came running out of the pines, scattering bright drops of water from its brows. The dogs were excited; it was as if they'd been waiting all day for this particular stag, as if they'd already had its scent. Weariness forgotten, all gave it chase.

The stag ran blindly, crashing through the brush in terror.

But the brave dogs were always on its trail, never resting or letting go. When the great stag finally turned to face the dogs, as brave ones will, instead of attacking them with its horns, it stretched out its neck and bellowed, as if its voice were calling them to stop! The dogs fell back, confused, but the men surrounded it, urging them on.

"Where's Actaeon?" they cried. "He really should see this. Actaeon! Actaeon!" The forest rang with my brother's name.

The deer turned its head then, and cried again, a noise almost like a human voice. Its eyes rolled wildly from one to the other of them, looking for escape, but the circle was too tight.

As the hounds closed round it, the deer fell to its knees, for all the world as though begging them to save it. But the dogs brought it down at last, tearing at its flanks until it could cry no more. There really was nothing to save, by the time the dogs were done; the men were distracted, calling for my brother, who never came, not even to see the kill. But then, I know he never really liked hunting. He was just pretending, so as not to shame our house.

They have set the dogs to follow his scent. But the dogs will only go so far into the grove of pine and cypress before they become confused and frightened and lose the scent. They keep returning to the place they slew the deer. Silly creatures.

Chiron has searched the stars. He is not there.

༄

THE DAUGHTER SPEAKS AGAIN:

Artemis has come to me at last.

She came in all her beauty, bathed in moonlight so clear it looked like water—or was it water so bright it was like the moon? I saw her body clearly through it, curved and strong like a bow.

"Follow me now," she said, "if you will."

I rose from my couch and followed her on the moon's path, which led from my chamber window to the meadow beyond my grandfather's house. Where her feet trod, night flowers bloomed, and small animals, the mice and voles and even rabbits—for she carried no bow but the moon's curve on her brow—looked up to adore her.

At the edge of the wood, the goddess paused.

"Here, I am the only light. Will you follow?"

I nodded.

The woods were dark, but she was the moon, and I moved fearless by the light of her body between the trees. I heard the sound of rushing water, then. A fountain, gushing naturally from the rock, formed a sweet pool where ferns grew amongst the stones.

Artemis stood at the edge of the pool. The water reflected her brightness now so strongly that I could hardly see. One foot was in the water, the other on a rock. She turned her back to me, and smiled over her shoulder as she undid one sandal, and then the other. The curve of her back, drawn like a bow, the hair pulled up from the nape of her neck….

"Look your fill, virgin daughter of the House of Cadmus. To such as you, nothing is forbidden."

I felt the hungry ache I had known for so long grow in me a hundred hundredfold. The more I gazed on her, the more it grew, until my legs shook so I could hardly stand. The silver water stood between us.

The goddess held out her hand. "Will you cross the water and come to me?"

I would have crossed fire for her. I set one foot on the edge of the pool.

"But remember," she said, "there is a price to be paid by mortals who look upon the goddess in her nakedness. Will you remember that?"

I nodded. She dipped one white hand in the water. Moonstruck drops flew through the air into my face.

My whole body shivered. I felt my skin shudder on my bones, as if trying to shake them off. I felt strange, and light, and my balance left me. I pitched forward but caught myself on the edge of a stone.

And then I saw my own face in the pool.

I screamed, and heard a deer's cry tear the night air. Saw the black mouth and black tongue of a doe parting to give that cry again.

The goddess leapt on my back. Her thighs straddled my flanks like fire, and her weight on my spine was a terrible glory.

I fled through the night woods, more terrified than I have ever been, and more completely consumed by a happiness I hope I never feel again.

It might have been hours, or it might have been years. I remember nothing of where I've been. Until she guided me back to the pool, urging me on until I submerged my panting, sweating, hairy body in its icy silver waters, and came to, gasping and trembling and choking to the surface of the water, in my own form again.

"You shiver, daughter of Cadmus."

I tried to hide my nakedness with my hands, my hair. I was so ashamed. Ashamed of what I'd been; ashamed of what I was.

The goddess took my face in her hands and kissed me. I felt the deer's power coursing through my veins, the deer's joy in its own wildness running in my own body. But my hands were my hands, my voice my voice as I moaned my pleasure. It might have been heartbeats, it might have been years. My aching turned to sweet pain, and then only to sweetness. And so, finally, I knew what it was to have my strange hunger satisfied.

The goddess cradled my head in her hands. "In the full heat of the day, when I rested with my maidens, and bathed in the cool water, your brother came to me here." Her lips spoke against my lips. "And so he saw what is forbidden men to see. And paid the price. Do you remember the price, Child of Cadmus? Do you understand what I say?"

I understood. Woe to the House of Cadmus, the terrible transformation. I tasted my own tears on both our lips.

"Do you understand, then, that his own dogs savaged him while his friends looked on and cheered?"

Woe to the House of Cadmus, the terror and the blood. I felt my own groan twist against her body.

"But before the power of human speech left him, he cried out your name. And before his hands became hooves, he held them out, begging me to pity him. And so I came to find you, and to tell you of your brother's fate."

Her arms were around me then, holding what was left of me together while I shivered into little pieces.

"You should have come to me," the goddess said. "You should never have sent a man to do your work for you."

I heard a high mewing keen like the lost birds that fly in from the sea.

"Do you still wish to be my votary? To serve me all your days?"

She had given me everything I thought I ever wanted, and taken from me what I held most dear. The gods love our house, and we must love them.

"Speak," she said. "You still have the power of human speech."

My voice was hoarse. "I do."

"And?"

"I will be your servant always."

"Will you come with me into the woods? I will make you forget all human sorrow, and your name will be a whisper on the wind."

I yearned for her. "And my brother's name?"

"The same."

"I must go home. They are waiting for him. I must speak of my brother's fate, that all may mourn him, and know what price is paid for your terrible glory."

"Go, then, Child of Cadmus. I accept your service. And serve me still."

Her kiss on my brow burned like silver horns, the twin crests of the moon.

I felt no different when I returned to Cadmus's house. But the suitors were all sent quietly away, with gifts. I serve the goddess now, as she has promised. I sing songs in her honor, and keep the fires lit at my brother's shrine. I hunt what I can: the flies that buzz around sleeping babies' eyes on hot days; the sun that robs the color of our wool; the mice that steal the grain. I speak for the goddess, and no one contradicts me.

The Guest

ZEN CHO

Yiling was riding home on her motorcycle when she saw the cat. It was late evening and the air was thick with smells, but the scent of the cat rang out like the clang of a temple bell, cutting through the stench of exhaust and the oil-in-the-nose smell of fried food wafting from the roadside stalls.

Yiling turned off the road and parked her motorcycle on the grassy verge next to the stalls. She bought two pyramidal packets of nasi lemak, each neatly wrapped in banana leaf, and some kuih: the sticky green kind layered with white santan, and triangles of pink-and-white kuih lapis. She thought of buying a durian—she liked to entertain well and did not get the chance to do it often—but she already had too much to carry.

As she walked back to her motorcycle she scooped up the cat. It had been looking elsewhere and by the time Yiling grasped it by the back of the neck it was too late for it to escape.

The cat's claws came out; it hissed in indignation. Yiling ignored it. She put it on her lap and steered her motorcycle one-handed for the rest of the ride home.

It was not really home. Her parents lived in another house with her two siblings. Yiling rented a room in a terrace house with an acquaintance of her grandmother's. The presence of the auntie went some way towards comforting her parents.

The auntie was not generous and the rent was high considering Yiling only had a bedroom to herself—the auntie did not even like Yiling to cook in the kitchen, or to watch TV in the living room. But the auntie was not interested in Yiling's life and that suited Yiling.

She had never raised the issue of pets but would have been surprised if the auntie had welcomed the idea. Fortunately the auntie was not at home when Yiling got back and she got the cat up the stairs without incident.

Her room was not big, but there wasn't much in it. It was made to look barer by the depressing quality of the light from the fluorescent lamp. The pale white light was unsteady as a drunken man and it gave everything a greyish, dirty look. This was even though everything in the room was very clean, from the scuffed parquet flooring to the pimpled whitewashed walls. Yiling had a bed, a cupboard for her clothes, and two chairs, one for herself and one for clients. She also had a small television which showed only three channels with any reliability.

When she set the cat down it began to explore, sniffing around the room. Yiling unwrapped one of the packets of nasi lemak and set it on the floor. She did not feel like going down the unlit stairs and through the dark abandoned house to the kitchen, so she sat on one of her chairs and ate her packet of nasi lemak with her hands. Her mother was nyonya, so she knew how to eat like this, using only her right hand to scoop up the food. From a corner of the room the cat watched her suspiciously, but after a while it came out and started on its rice.

Yiling had never liked cats. Even as a small child having dinner at a restaurant with her family, she jumped and screamed whenever a stray cat brushed past her legs under the table. Her brother and sister had liked to feed the cats surreptitious scraps from the table, but Yiling used to draw her feet up to her chair and refuse to let them down until she felt safe from that soft tickle of cat fur.

This cat could not have appealed even to a cat lover. It had a gaunt, scheming look and could have done with at least three baths. One of its hind legs was injured and it limped as it walked. Fortunately there was nothing wrong with its eyes. The diseased strays of her youth had often had eye problems and the dried liquid matting the fur around their filmy eyes had disgusted her more than anything else.

She was between jobs so that night she had nothing to do. She ate her kuih while watching TV. It was almost like being at home again: the buzz from the TV, the silence lying between her and the other living being in the room. The cat's silence was less heavy than her parents' silence, its breathing less of a repeating threat. That was an improvement on home.

She laid a sheet of plastic on the floor and for every piece of kuih she ate, she put one piece down on the sheet. While she stared at the TV she could sense the cat coming close to her leg and nibbling daintily at the kuih.

Before she went to bed she took a duvet out of her closet, which she did not use because she never turned on the air conditioning. She folded the duvet in half and then in half again and placed it on the floor. It made a high soft bed for any cats that might want one. She turned off the light and went to sleep without waiting to see if it was going to be used.

The next morning Yiling did not dare leave the door open for the cat in case it escaped. On the way out she told the auntie offhandedly that she had got a pet. She was out of the door before the auntie could begin to remonstrate.

Yiling held a diploma in Business Management from a local college. She worked at a small family-owned company which sold medicinal foot creams. Her precise role was not clear, but she did all sorts of things: kept the accounts, dealt with suppliers, and wrote marketing copy in Chinese, Malay and English.

Shortly after she had got the job the owners had retired and their daughter had taken over the management of the company. She was not much older than Yiling. She had got an MBA from an overseas university and sometimes still sounded mildly Australian, especially when speaking to customers. She rebranded Yiling as a marketing executive, which would sound well if Yiling ever moved to another job.

The daughter had a serious, pale face with fine skin and straight eyebrows like bridges over the dark water of her eyes. Yiling was strangely disappointed when she brought her well-off young friends to the office and they had loud conversations about the size of a friend's engagement ring: "Must cost at least his three months' salary or he doesn't love you," the daughter had said. A bubble of high meaningless laughter had drifted from her room.

Yiling had been living with the cat for two weeks when the memory of this incident came to her. Suddenly she felt sorry. It was unfair of her to think that because someone was beautiful, she must be interesting. Or that something must be interesting to her to be worthwhile. Really she had this feeling because she had so little in her life. She clung onto this sense of superiority to give herself significance. But there was nothing to be proud of in being different. There was nothing special about being lonely.

Returning to her empty room had always reminded her of this fact but somehow it did not bother her so much with the cat around. After three or four days she started leaving the bedroom door open. It was a gamble, but it paid off. The cat did not leave.

After a while when she came home she would see it curled up on top of the pillar next to the gate. When she got off her motorcycle to unlock the gate it would open one disdainful eye and peer at her, as if to say, "Oh, are you back?" Then it would jump off the wall and stalk into the house to make the point that it had not been waiting for her to return.

In this way affection returned to her life, so that the next time she met a client she was in a softened frame of mind. The client told a common story. She came, she said, because she had heard through a family friend that Yiling could do wonderful things. Her mother's friend had had trouble with her son and Yiling had been able to fix it. Now she, Priya, also had trouble with a man, but this was a boyfriend rather than a son.

The boyfriend had first been her coworker, but they had become close because they had so much in common. He was clever and ambitious; he had a sense of humour; he was the kindest, most giving person. In the beginning they were only friends but it was no surprise that they should have fallen in love. Unfortunately the boyfriend already had a girlfriend. This was proving a minor obstacle to their romance.

"How come he don't want break up with her?" said Yiling.

He wanted to, but things were complicated. It was a complicated relationship. Assuredly he and the girlfriend did not love each other, Priya said. He was always telling Priya about how the two of them fought, even before Priya had confessed her love to him. And the girlfriend—what a bitch, so heartless, so capricious it was difficult to see what had drawn him to her in the first place. She had no respect for his opinions, no interest in his ideas. She could not even fulfill him…you know…in that way. She could not make him happy.

And yet they were still together. Sometimes Priya's beloved would say he could not spend time with Priya because he had an appointment with the girlfriend. But he did not even like her! He longed to break up with her, but his parents were fond of her and would be heartbroken if he dumped her. Besides, there was the girlfriend to think of. For all her faults, she was still someone he cared for. He did not want to hurt her feelings. She was very stressed at work. If he broke it off now, it might tip her over the edge.

Yiling felt doubtful of her power to help in such a situation, but when Priya wiped her eyes and said, "I don't know what to do, I just want to be happy with him," she felt a startling surge of sympathy. What a fragile necessary thing love was. She told Priya she would try to help her, but Priya must bring her something that smelled of her boyfriend.

"I work primarily with smells," said Yiling. In fact she worked only with smells, but she felt pleased with the "primarily"—it had a crisp, businesslike, American feel to it.

When the consultation was over, Yiling let Priya out and went to find the cat. The cat was in the garden and withdrew when Yiling tried to pick it up. It refused to be conciliated even when Yiling tempted it with fried fish bought specially for the purpose. It eventually came back into the house but sat itself down next to the auntie in the living room to watch TV—the auntie had cable and had come to be on cordial terms with the cat.

Yiling left the door of her room open and went to bed feeling melancholy. She woke up in the middle of the night to a shadow hovering over her face. The only light in the room was from the streetlamp outside, filtered through the curtains. The windows were two dark glowing rectangles in the wall. In that non-light Yiling saw that the black blob was the cat, perched at the head of the bed and looking down at her. Yiling sat up and scratched behind the cat's ears and rubbed its face while the cat purred. After a while they both lay down and went to sleep.

The next time Priya came, Yiling decided to let the cat stay in the room for the meeting. After all there was no way she would be able to keep the resulting work from the cat. If it was complex the job might take weeks.

The cat had fine manners. It pretended to sleep on its duvet throughout the interview.

Priya brought a football jersey which belonged to her boyfriend.

"It's not so easy to do anything when the smell is not so strong," said Yiling. Priya smiled in an embarrassed way.

"Hopefully it's strong enough," she said. "I never wash it since he wore it."

She handed Yiling the jersey. There was no "hopefully" about the odour that came off it. Yiling did not look at the cat because she was a professional and used to such things, but the temptation was strong.

Yiling was not about to ask how Priya had come to be in the possession of the boyfriend's worn football jersey, but Priya seemed to feel that it begged an explanation. There was one night, she said shyly, when the girlfriend was outstation and Priya and the boyfriend had gone for a date. They had stayed at a mamak stall till late, and he had insisted on seeing her home because he was a gentleman. And one thing had led to another.... Priya's parents lived in Ipoh and she had come to KL for work. She lived alone.

"Nowadays these things don't matter," said Yiling, thinking, they did matter if the man had another girlfriend.

"Yes, yes," said Priya. "We are both very modern about this kind of thing." But her smiling eyes looked uncertain.

"So," said Yiling. She shook out the jersey and the scent gusted out. It smelled of sweat. Under that lay the smell of good intentions, indecision. "What do you want me to do for you?"

"I want him to," said Priya. She hesitated.

"You want him to choose you, is it?" said Yiling. Priya looked pained. Of course she told herself that he had already chosen her, and it was only external factors—his parents, his tender heart, his girlfriend's late nights at the office—that kept him from declaring it to the world.

"I want him to be free to be with me," said Priya.

"Har," said Yiling. "Difficult."

But the girl was lonely. At least Yiling had the cat.

"I see what I can do," she said. "But no promises, OK?"

People had odd ideas about what she was able to do, but then to be fair her skill was not a conventional one. No one had ever heard of a smell magician, which was why her parents had not supported her in trying to make a career of it.

And even she was still in the process of figuring out what she could and could not do. She could craft things out of smells, but she could only make certain things. You could not make tomyam out of a block of pecorino cheese; similarly, you could not turn the smell of a philandering asshole into a loving boyfriend. She could reproduce a philandering asshole from the smell, but she did not think this was what Priya wanted.

Over the next few weeks she worked on the job in the evenings, after she had come home from work. The cat did not like the smell of the jersey and stayed away when Yiling was working, even though it was madly curious. Crouching on the floor like a tiny Sphinx, it gazed at her as she moved her hands over the fabric, her eyes half-closed and her mouth murmuring snatches of spells.

When she had done all she thought she could do, she arranged another meeting with Priya.

Priya did not say anything at first when she came. She sat down on the other chair, opened her mouth, then put her hand over it. Her eyes went red.

"He's getting married to the girlfriend," she said. "It's over."

"That bastard," said Yiling.

"He's not a bastard," sobbed Priya. "It's his parents, they are forcing him to do this."

Yiling gave Priya the jersey. She had folded it and wrapped it in paper like something precious. She also gave Priya a piece of tissue paper.

Priya thanked her and blew her nose. She clutched the parcel as if her salvation lay in it. "What have you done with it?"

"I washed it," said Yiling. She tapped the parcel. "That's free, don't worry. I had to do laundry anyway.

"Ma'am," said Yiling. "I work very hard on this but I cannot do anything. When somebody is grown up already, they must make their own decision. I cannot change their mind for them."

Priya stared at her through eyelashes beaded with tears.

"But you helped my mother's friend," she cried. "You changed Vijay's mind—he went to America and he didn't want to come back."

"I brought back her son, but her son never went to America. Her son died," Yiling said. "I know this will sound very funny. But it is easy for me to make a person from a smell. When I give her back her son, he was the same person he use to be when he was alive. But your ex is still alive and he is already one kind of person. I cannot make a different kind of person from his smell. I cannot change this alive person's heart.

"I'm sorry," she said. "But I really spend so many hours on this. And I won't charge you. OK? You will move on. There is plenty of fish in the sea."

Priya flashed her a look of hatred.

"Everybody says that," she said. "But I only want one fish."

Apart from this outburst she was polite enough. After all it would really have been fair for Yiling to charge her. She never made promises in terms of results. It was understood that the client took the risk.

When Priya had left, the cat said from behind Yiling's back,

"That was generous of you."

Yiling had known that this must happen sooner or later. Even so, it was difficult to make herself turn around. In fact it was the hardest thing she had ever done. It was not that she was afraid, but that she was shy.

When she finally managed to turn around, she saw that the cat was blushing. This made things a bit more comfortable.

The cat had long hair, curling in a wonderfully pretty way at the ends. She had round dark eyes and skin the colour of sandalwood. She was sitting in the bed and had covered herself with the blanket because she had no clothes. Yiling noted that she was Malay, but that would not be a problem. It was not like they could get married anyway.

Yiling sat back down on her chair. She felt oddly formal.

"Actually, Puan Thanga already paid me double to tell Priya her boyfriend is useless," she said. "She knew Priya from small. Her son Vijay used to date Priya in school. She said Priya only start liking this new guy after Vijay so-called went to America. Now he is back Puan Thanga is hoping they will start to like each other again. She told me she always wanted a daughter and when Priya and Vijay were going out she felt like Priya is her own daughter. She thinks they are perfect for each other."

"Sibuk," said the cat disapprovingly. "So busybody."

Yiling shrugged. It was in the nature of aunties to be busybodies.

"This Vijay is a good guy," said Yiling. "I can tell from his smell. I never remake a dead person unless I think they are a good person. Enough useless people in the world already."

"So you lied?" said the cat. "You could change the boyfriend's mind if you want?"

"I don't lie to my clients," said Yiling sternly. "Everything I said was true. But it's not my business if my clients want to pay me extra for doing something sensible."

She looked at the cat for a while, just for the pleasure of it, and the cat looked at her. The cat was still thin, but not as thin as she had been when Yiling had first taken her home.

"I'm sorry I kidnap you," said Yiling. The cat waved one elegant hand.

"Not to worry," she said. "I would have run away if I wanted to. But we must stop living like this. You don't eat properly. Hawker food is okay, but not every day. I can cook for you, I am a very good cook. It's good you like Malay food. We will move to our own apartment so that auntie cannot know all our business. She always come into this room in the afternoon to snoop around."

"Oh," said Yiling.

"Never mind, she never find out anything. You don't own anything interesting also," said the cat. "That's one more thing, you must have a nicer room. Living in one room like this, how to be comfortable? We will make sure you have an office for your work in our new place. I will set up the business for you. With your talent you don't have to only work for scheming aunties. If you advertise your talent better you can get more customers, earn more money."

"But an apartment will be expensive," said Yiling, because she could not think of anything better to say.

"No! One bedroom, one room for the office, kitchen and bathroom," said the cat. "We don't need so much to start with. Simple-simple enough already."

"One bedroom?" said Yiling.

The cat was surprised. She looked at her intently. Then she sat up, reached over and took Yiling's hand.

"Of course," said the cat. "That's why I ran away from my parents' house. Somebody told my boss at work and I got fired and I panic and ran away. Ended up no money, no house, must sleep on the street. So I thought it was safer to be a cat. That's the only thing I can do. I'm not so clever as you, I cannot do all this spell or what. What happen to you?"

Yiling stared at their joined hands. She did magic and she liked girls. She lived alone because she was not the kind of daughter any-one would have asked for.

"Nothing happen," said Yiling.

She had just packed a bag one day, stepped out of her parents' house, and never gone back. There had been no precipitating event behind it, no big fight with her parents. She had not even had a girl-friend to leave for.

"Nothing happen," she said again. "I just don't like lying."

"Good," said the cat. "My name is Ada. You knew, right?" She did not mean her name.

"I always know who people are," said Yiling. "By their smell. That's the one thing nobody can lie about."

But Ada was not listening to this philosophising. She was of a prac-tical bent. She said,

"But first, before we do all this thing, you must get me some clothes, OK, sayang?—Can I call you sayang?"

"Please," said Yiling. "Feel free."

Rabbits

CSILLA KLEINHEINCZ

The air was boiling above the highway, whipping up the smell of dust from the car seats, as if the road led into the past instead of to Lake Balaton.

"You don't look so well," said Vera, glancing to her right. She leaned on the wheel almost as if she was afraid that without holding on, the car would leave her behind. "Why don't you roll down the window a bit?"

Amanda was wondering whether what she felt was nausea. It was difficult to tell. The smell of the dust made her woozy. She wanted to ask the little girl on the backseat if she was sick, too, but then rejected the idea. The girl couldn't speak. Or maybe she could, but no one had yet the guts to ask her anything.

"I spread the tarot for our vacation," said Vera. "It was all swords. What do you think it means?"

"If you can't read it why do you lay it out?" Amanda decided not to risk being sick; the air whistled in the window and tore the words from her mouth bite by bite.

"Because when I spread it and clean it and light a candle, it calms me. Plus it is super-mysterious. If someone were to see me, he would think I'm a witch."

Amanda frowned. Vera knew as little about tarot as about everything else; she dipped in it because it interested her, but only tried it on briefly like a new dress.

The wind felt good, it invigorated Amanda, the nausea was blown out of her. She felt empty. Now she saw Vera and the curly locks stuck to her forehead more clearly.

"And if no one sees you?"

"Then I imagine that someone does." Vera laughed but Amanda was in no mood to join her. Hi, my witch. This is me you are talking to. I look right through you like an X-ray.

She would not have minded if it had been so. Vera would become transparent like glass, Amanda would see the car door behind her and could reach into her like into an aquarium, and then she would pull out what was wrong with her. Presto. A routine operation, madam, you may go back to your girlfriend.

"Swords is an air element," she said. "Which cards were they?"

"Does it matter? I did the spread, seemed like a good idea. I am sure it had some meaning. It is enough to know that, isn't it...?"

Amanda looked at her to elicit some explanation but her friend didn't notice it.

"It is enough to know it means something," said Vera loudly over the wind, and she leaned even more on the wheel.

They set off an hour earlier, and yet they hadn't left the highway yet. Vera must have been the slowest driver on the whole stretch of road and if she could, she would have driven in the service lane. She feared for the car, which was new as her driver's license.

Well, Vera certainly isn't her old self, either, thought Amanda sadly and cranked up the window. Her ears hurt from the whistling wind.

They passed harvested wheat fields, the stubble shining golden on the face of the sleeping earth. Amanda's nausea returned; she felt as if their journey to Lake Balaton had been a succession of swigs from stale water.

"You shouldn't have eaten both of those fried eggs."

She shouldn't have, but fried eggs were a symbol just like Vera's tarot spread. Each morning they fried something for breakfast and Amanda did the same this morning to pretend they were still together. She doggedly ate the eggs and bacon while Vera waited for her, then took her bag and they were off.

As an experiment she put her hand on Vera's knee, but her girlfriend apologetically took her wrist and pushed it away. For a while the silence was cold.

They stopped at a gas station at the beginning of the Balaton road. Vera stepped out to fill up the car and make a call. Amanda turned back to the child.

The little girl didn't say a word during the journey. She sat with a chocolate doughnut in her hand and smears on her face.

Clean your face, Amanda thought hard, wondering if she could make the girl speak. Maybe the child was silent for the same reason. Maybe she just thought hard about the things she wanted to say.

The girl did not wipe the chocolate off her face. She just stared with eyes as blue as cornflowers, as those of Amanda. Her curly hair— so very like Vera's— was matted with chocolate. She dropped the doughnut into her lap, onto the white skirt.

"We are on the road, yes, almost there…. Of course…." Shrill laughter. Amanda looked out the open door at Vera. "Yes, I would love it…. Hmm? You say you can magic yourself here?" Laughter again. "Yes, Tintin. Kisses."

Tintin. What kind of nickname was that for a grown man? And who was called Jusztin nowadays? Amanda was sure it was a stagename, required by the circus, but Vera was adamant that it was real.

"Did you ever see his ID? Did it say Jusztin?"

"Yours says Amanda, so why not?"

Vera got back in the car, smiling nonchalantly, and started the engine.

"Hey," said Amanda later, when they were at Siófok. "Do you remember Panna?"

"Hmm?"

"Our daughter?"

Vera looked up in the rearview mirror, then turned on the turn signal. Their street was still far away, but she was cautious.

"Oh, that. It was a nice game. I mean, pretending she existed."

Amanda looked back. The girl shrugged as if to say she didn't care, then faded away. The chocolate doughnut remained a little while longer above the seat, then it also disappeared.

Only the headache remained, and the feeling of dejection.

༈

Tintin was a traveling circus magician. Vera said he was too young to get offers from bigger companies.

And not handsome enough, added Amanda, first in thought and later in words. She thought that Jusztin—no Tintin for her, thank you—had carrot hair and small, unpleasantly gleaming eyes. Vera liked him though. This only showed that Amanda didn't know her girlfriend as well as she believed: if these Jusztin-types were acceptable—and what's more: delightful, enchanting, sexy—then perhaps in Vera's eyes she was not who she really was.

Two weeks ago, in the town of Fót, Jusztin literally enchanted Vera: he turned her into a rabbit, then caught her with a lasso. He winked, smiled at her, and in the next minute it was Vera who shuffled her feet at the end of the rope. Jusztin wanted her to bow, then released her.

Vera thought this romantic. Amanda said it was love magic, a low one at that, but the only one she could ask about it was her enchanted girlfriend.

As they strolled on the beach and inspected ice cream vendors, Amanda watched Vera walk, watched for the signs that her steps faltered when Amanda peeled the panties of her bikini off with her gaze. Once, her girlfriend had said Amanda could ignite an ant with her gaze. Now Vera hardly even noticed. You see? Amanda looked at the little girl who followed them mute and grimy. The child glanced back, shook her Vera-hair and raised her hand. Her fingers were closed as if she had been following a string.

Her face remained calm, though as they walked the Balaton promenade, she faded and started to lose herself. When her feet melted away and her pink legs walked on blunt ends, Amanda turned away.

"Do you like ghosts?" she asked Vera. The little girl was sitting on the grass in front of them. She was playing with sticks, fencing with them, as if they were swords. Amanda didn't like that; the rattle gave her a headache.

"Sure."

Vera held her cell phone in her hand and smiled dreamily at it as she was punching its buttons.

"Not ghosts of dead people. But ghosts of people we create by the force of our mind."

"Hmm."

"Vera."

"Tintin says ghosts live in his sleeves, in his opera-hat, in his tail-coat. He stuffed them into his wand, like the scarves, gave them as fodder to his rabbits. When I was a bunny I think I saw them." She paused. "Then it turned out they were only feathers, he makes bouquets from them and conjures them out of his buttonhole. Tintin says because the ghosts live with him, they do not exist. He told me to imagine them existing and not existing at the same time."

"Balderdash."

"He is good at it, yes," said Vera.

Sometimes it would have been better if she had quarreled. Or struck back. Or at least gave a sign that she knew that Amanda didn't like Jusztin. Acknowledged, and then filed it. Then they could have gone on, closed the file. Instead, this was an endless interrogation with Amanda as the inquisitor.

"He doesn't really love you," said Amanda crossly.

"What's your problem? I came with you, didn't I?"

"But when you go back…he won't love you."

"We'll see."

Vera's face was smooth and calm, not bothered by anything. It was possible that her heart remained a rabbit's even after the trick, and was interested only in grass and fucking, maybe that was why she loved the carrot-haired Jusztin and his carrot so much.

Amanda watched the little girl knock the sticks together, with her pink tongue stuck out in concentration. The child annoyed her. She would have shouted at her, but you don't shout at imaginary children, especially when there are others around.

The little girl appeared after one of their lovemakings when they stretched lazily and naked on the rug. Their hands drew slow circles on each other's belly and breasts, and they were whispering so softly that only they and the rug could hear them. Then abruptly the girl was there on the sofa, picking her nose. She wasn't bothered by their nudity, her face was devoid of emotion, of either smile or frown.

Amanda's aunt, who was almost admitted to a ghost-researching course of a professedly Tibetan sect that was in truth run by Hungarian pensioners, once said that spontaneous spiritbirths were common, and added that they were nothing to fuss about. They existed only in the mind and if one wanted to get rid of them, one only had to purge them from within. Garlic was good, said the aunt seriously. Our ancestors knew that, although they were mistaken when they believed that garlic had to be hung in the room. You had to eat it to shoo ghosts away. They didn't care for stinky breath. Amanda laughed at that.

The little girl unnerved her. The child's shin was short as if it had melted away. Her eyes sparkled red.

"I'm going inside."

"Hmm," mumbled Vera and put the cell phone to her ear.

"I'm staying outside," said Amanda in the same voice.

"Aham," said Vera, then her face lit up. "Oh, *Tintin!*"

Amanda wished to strangle her, but didn't because of Jusztin. She felt him watching them from the distance through his magic wand like through a telescope, his breath ruffled the grass at their feet. She would behave nicely in front of him.

In fact, very nicely.

She leaned forward and kissed Vera's nape. He girlfriend shot a glance at her.

"And what was the performance like?"

When she bit Vera's nape, she got a light slap in the face. Amanda growled back.

"What…? Yes, a doggie."

Amanda turned up her nose. *You won't mislead Jusztin, he saw what I did. He is here with us. More and more real every minute.*

She hesitated a little in front of the bungalow, then went inside to open the bottle of whisky she had brought herself.

❧

She smelled their perfumes in every room. Vera was Kenzo Air, Amanda was Summer. The two glasshouse scents made the world feel stuffy. Two hothouse flowers without stamens, Amanda thought.

In the bedroom, under the bedcover, the perfume mixed with the smell of soap. Amanda wanted to snuggle closer but didn't dare. She felt someone lying between them: a long, heavy body, pressing down the quilt, but still invisible. Vera was dreaming of Jusztin.

Amanda watched Vera, and in turn Jusztin's ghost watched her. He was only a heavy void in the air: invisible, but she could feel his gaze upon her. He conjured himself here, thought Amanda, to keep an eye on me. He is a cheater. *I* don't ogle them when *they* are sleeping together.

Defiant, she slid closer, pushed away the ghost and slipped her hand under Vera's cover. Her girlfriend's skin was warm and soft. She moved her hand up to Vera's breasts and massaged them gently. Vera sighed.

Hearing a soft hiss, Amanda smiled. Take that, Jusztin.

She slid her hand lower, inside Vera's pajamas. The faint stubble prickled her but the opening was invitingly wet.

"I thought we have discussed this," muttered Vera sleepily.

Amanda's fingers groped further down.

"We can stay friends without this." Vera took Amanda's wrist and squeezed it.

"I don't remember anything like that."

"I told you I have Tintin now."

"And did you tell him you have Amanda?"

Vera pulled her hand out of her pajamas.

"Be a good girl."

Amanda looked around. She didn't see either the child or the void in the place of Jusztin's ghost.

"He is not here to see!"

"Just don't do it, okay?"

Amanda pulled her hand back and pushed it into her own pajamas. She closed her eyes and pretended it was Vera. If her girlfriend heard her gasping, she didn't show it.

She couldn't reach release. Sometime during her caressing herself, Jusztin lay back between them, his presence cold and sobering. Amanda felt she would never have an orgasm. With a sigh, she pulled her hand out of her pajamas.

She turned her back on them and tried to sleep. She had a headache, maybe from the whisky, maybe from something else. She was nauseated, but when the white-dressed, red-eyed child appeared under the window and squatted down, the nausea had passed.

The little girl didn't walk after them anymore. Her legs and arms had melted to drumsticks and she hopped forward. Whenever she saw something interesting, she stopped and sniffled it. Her hair was falling badly, and under the curly locks she was downy like a newborn baby or a chick. Amanda felt sorry for her but didn't know what to do. When she tried to caress the child, her hand passed through her, and she couldn't bear the reproachful gaze the girl cast at her.

"What's the matter? You look upset," said Vera.

"Do you know that Panna dies this way? If you leave?"

"Aren't you too old for an imaginary daughter?" asked Vera.

They walked on the Balaton beach among the other people enjoying their holidays. Amanda would have stopped at the corncob-seller, but her girlfriend hurried on. She walked with quick, jerking steps as if something drew her.

"*Our* imaginary daughter," emphasized Amanda.

"Whatever."

They walked a step away from each other. They never held hands, not even before, because of the strange stares they got, but now Amanda longed for it more than ever. Just to show the world. She had enough of love confined between walls.

Pink-skinned people buzzed around them, wearing ice cream-colored clothes, holding fashion-colored ice creams. Not far away on the lawn, vividly painted wagons stood. The crowd pressed close around them. Poles speared the sky.

"Hey!" Amanda stopped. "Aren't they...?"

"What?"

Vera stopped and turned around. Her face was red. She smiled but her smile never reached her eyes.

"The circus came this way, is it okay if I say hello?"

Amanda opened her mouth, closed it, then shouted at Vera.

"Do you believe that if you pretend we don't have a problem you won't be a stupid bitch?"

People stopped for a moment around them, then started walking again. None of their business. Vera paled, turned around and ran towards the half-erected circus tent.

Amanda bit her lip and looked around. The child disappeared.

In the end she followed Vera. She knew her; she would calm down, forgive and smile—almost like letting her close—even though she was the most distant in those moments.

The frame of the circus tent was already erect, the dirty, blue-yellow tarp was half-pulled over it like a coat. Fat women in heavy make-up shepherded the children away, worried they would be hit if something fell, like a tilting pole. The tarp was rolled back from the cages; scraggy bears, ostriches and monkeys watched the humans with bored eyes.

Amanda saw neither Vera's curly blonde hair nor Jusztin's red head. She was lost among the spectators, but in the end, she was swept towards the cages together with the children. Rancid bear stink wrung her nose, ostriches clacked their beaks. Jusztin's ghost watched her from the eyes of the gum-chewing monkeys and swam in and out of the animals' ears.

You don't deceive me, Amanda thought. I see you. I know you are watching.

The attention upset her. Jusztin's ghost had no business here, he was with Vera, so why was he watching *her*?

In front of the rabbit cage, a big, white and fluffy dog stood on his hind legs with his paws on the wire mesh. When Amanda turned, she saw it was the little girl. The child waved her stubby arm, then plopped down on the ground. She was melting disturbingly fast.

Soon there will be nothing left, thought Amanda, watching the girl reproachfully. You should try to stay. At least fight a little!

The ghost of the girl sat down in front of the rabbit cage and licked her white hand. She either didn't hear Amanda or was not interested.

❧

"Tintin says once he tried to magick himself from one end of the ring to the other."

"The ring is circular, it has no ends."

"Stop nit-picking." Vera gazed down at the half-peeled potato in her hand. She didn't look angry. "So he attempted it and part of him teleported but the rest stayed where it was. He said he doesn't mind it, because it was his faults that went forward." She giggled.

Amanda stared at her.

"Is this a joke?"

"Yes. Just imagine, he can make jokes!" Vera raised her voice and looked at Amanda for the first time. "Would you bring the carrots from the car?"

Amanda shrugged and left the house. As she was walking through the garden towards the car, she was followed by the hopping girl on one side and by Jusztin's ghost on the other. She looked at neither of them, just opened the trunk, grabbed the bag and hurried back.

They followed in silence. When she stopped, they stopped, too. They touched her a little as if they needed to feel her.

She took the bag inside, grabbed a knife and started to clean the garlic.

"Do you remember last year, when we were here and your bra snapped on the beach?" asked Vera. She seemed to carry a conversation that didn't include Amanda; perhaps she started it when her friend went out for the grocery.

"Of course. You covered my tits until I refastened it," said Amanda gruffly. Her throat was dry. When was the last time Vera touched her breasts?

"Sorry," said Vera. "It's just…."

"I cannot do magic."

"I'm not saying…."

"And I won't. I don't think it's fair."

A small pause.

"If you ask me, he cannot do magic either. Magicians are just quick, you know? Very quick," said Vera.

"I wouldn't know about that."

They were silent. Strange, Amanda thought, we seem to do the most talk when we are not speaking.

"Why so much garlic?"

"To eat it."

Vera stared as Amanda popped the first three cloves into her mouth and forced herself to chew them. Vera grimaced.

"You want to sleep in the same bed as me smelling like that?"

"Why would we sleep in the same bed?" asked Amanda. "You won't eat me out anyway." She flung the knife on the table and ran out. The garlic stung her tongue but she forced it down.

The ghosts were standing beside a shrub. Jusztin looked almost like himself, although transparent. The girl sat at his feet, white and shapeless. Only her eyes sparkled red and familiar. Amanda walked to them and breathed at them.

Their shapes blurred and hollowed, their pose faltered.

Amanda opened her mouth, breathing in and out. In and out. The smell of garlic enveloped her and the ghosts retreated a step.

Good.

She was not sure it was the garlic that made them fade or her will, and she didn't know whether they would be back or not, but she didn't really care.

She stood and breathed garlic until the girl and Jusztin disappeared, then went back into the kitchen and flushed Vera with thick garlic stench.

"Silly," said Vera.

"I am blowing Jusztin out of you."

"You wish."

"I love you," said Amanda.

Vera made no answer. After a while she said: "Brush your teeth." She turned away indifferently, but Amanda heard from her voice that she wouldn't kiss her even if she did brush her teeth.

They were not the only adults in the circus tent without children— this was Lake Balaton, nothing was considered embarrassing here— but they were the only lesbian couple.

The only ex-lesbian couple, thought Amanda.

"We are ex-bians," she told Vera.

Her girlfriend laughed politely.

"Tintin says there are no real lesbians. Only women who haven't met him yet."

Amanda didn't laugh.

"Tintin has to have an opinion of everything."

Vera shrugged.

The auditorium darkened and the purple-coated ringmaster walked forward in a circle of light to announce the program. The children shouted, their parents whispered in their ears to shut up and listen, soon the bears would come.

What am I doing here, Amanda asked herself, but couldn't find an answer. Even Vera upset her. She looked around to see the little girl among the babbling, beaming children, but couldn't tell them apart in the semidarkness. She is not here. Amanda hadn't seen her since afternoon when she breathed garlic on her. Did she banish her together with Jusztin? Did that really work?

She felt slightly sorry.

In the ring, bears circled on unicycles. Their acrid stench mixed with the smell of popcorn and floss candy. The tent was stuffy and noisy; the racket and the lack of air made Amanda's head throb.

Vera almost slipped from the seat as she leaned forward. Thanks to Jusztin's tickets they were sitting at the edge of the ring, and every time the bears passed in front of them, driven by the whip of their handler, the stink overwhelmed them. The wheels stirred up dust and one of the bears sneezed. It sounded almost human.

After the bears came the strongman. The children chattered during his performance and demanded more animals. Amanda stared at the slowly flexing, oiled muscles and watched herself intently to see if the sight of the man made her skin tingle. She was not surprised by the lack of reaction and glanced enviously at Vera. If they both had their men, she a strongman, her girlfriend a magician, perhaps they wouldn't need to part. At night, when the men were sleeping, they could sneak into a shared bed.

The strongman was followed by a pair of nicely trimmed poodles that rolled around on red balls and jumped through hoops. Their handler—a fat, blonde woman—shrieked her commands and bowed after each trick, her breasts straining against her dress. The men whistled.

Then came Jusztin. He wore a black tailcoat and a tophat. Wrinkles lined his long horse-face as he raised his wand and waved it. White doves flew out of his sleeves, then circled and disappeared under the tent, as if the canvas had been as high as the sky. Amanda had a feeling the tentpole was higher than the moon. She didn't see the far wall.

She watched Jusztin and he watched her. First Amanda thought he was looking at Vera, but the small, deep eyes locked at her. It was a familiar gaze, the ghost had watched her like this before she blew him into oblivion.

The doves were followed by paper flowers and scarves; objects were raining from Jusztin's ears and mouth. Vera clapped her hands enthusiastically, her palms were already red. Amanda hugged herself and watched Jusztin sternly.

You won't enchant me. Using magic is not fair.

The magician played just for them. The children cried in awe when suddenly fish appeared in an aquarium and then jumped into the air and disappeared again.

Jusztin bowed and took off his hat. His red hair was ruffled and his ears were sticking out on either side. He glanced up, nodded, then hit his hat with the wand and stepped to the edge of the ring.

The children behind Amanda and Vera stretched toward Jusztin and cried: "Me! Me! I want to!"

Jusztin paid them no heed and presented the hat to Vera. Amanda glanced at her girlfriend: her face was red and her smile was cruel to see. Vera gingerly reached into the hat and pulled out a white rabbit.

The audience roared with delight. Jusztin stepped back with a satisfied smile.

Amanda was staring at the rabbit. She knew it. The red eyes of the bunny locked at her and her ears twitched when Vera lifted it up for others to see. Its downy fur was almost like a real rabbit's, but Amanda saw that here and there curly, blonde hairs were sticking to it, and that it was smeared with chocolate.

She looked back at Jusztin who received the applause with arms opened wide, then gestured and two assistants pulled a long, wheeled crate to the center. Red stars sparkled on its blue velvet cover and the swords, laid down on top in a star, shone brightly.

Jusztin raised his hand.

"And now, for the next trick, I would like to have a volunteer!'

Vera jumped up, with the rabbit in her hands.

"Me!"

"Me! Me!" cried the children.

Jusztin turned around, looking for someone who fit the decorated crate most perfectly. Amanda knew he had already chosen, he just turned around to key up the expectation.

I see through you like an X-ray.

She thought Jusztin would choose Vera, but the long finger pointed at her. From the magician's eyes, the ghost was looking back at her.

She felt strangely relieved. She calmly rose and stepped onto the ring with ease. Amid the applause she walked to Jusztin.

"I know you are cheating," she told him, then hopped on the wheeled platform of the crate and handed the swords to Jusztin. The assistants opened the crate. The walls of the circus tent flew away. Amanda didn't recognize Vera's face among the white dots. Maybe she wouldn't have found her even if she had gone back now.

With a calculated movement, she lay down into the crate. She couldn't do anything else anyway. Jusztin showed the audience the swords.

When the lid closed, Amanda thought that with a little bit of luck she could turn into a rabbit as well. A humanoid bunny, like Vera. Then perhaps she could also forget everything except grass and carrots.

The drums boomed louder, then stopped altogether. This is already the trick, she thought and laced her fingers. She held back her breath and waited in the dark of the crate for something to happen.

Anything at all.

The Egyptian Cat

CATHERINE LUNDOFF

Erica turned over the last page of the manuscript with a sigh. Somehow, a collection like *Hairballs Over Innsmouth* should have been more fun to edit. She wondered why writers were having such a hard time writing humorous cat-related horror stories that included an homage to H. P. Lovecraft. It should have been a snap. But perhaps the rewrites would look much better.

The thought cheered her enough to go and get the mail, even though it might contain yet more manuscripts. And it did. But along with the envelopes with addresses written in crayon and the one that seemed to contain nothing but melted chocolate, there was a box. She looked at it carefully, noting that although her name and address were printed on a mailing label, the return address was completely illegible.

She wondered if she should contact the bomb squad or something before she opened it. You couldn't be too careful these days. Some of the writers who she'd turned down for her last anthology, *Catnip and Hashish*, had been pretty irate.

Finally, she decided she was overreacting. Her writers were cat people, after all; their limited attention span would have moved on to some new source of fascination or irritation by now. She swept up all the mail and dumped it on the dining room table.

She opened the bills first, of course, then the manuscripts, but her gaze was drawn repeatedly back to the mysterious box. Something about it spoke of unfathomable mysteries beyond human ken.

So after she had opened everything else, separated the mail into piles and fed the cats when their cries became too inconvenient to ignore, she reached for it. First she held it up to her ear to listen for telltale ticking sounds. The brown paper crackled reassuringly but apart from that, the package made no other sound. She cut open a flap in the paper on one side. Nothing leaped out or blew up.

She slowly removed the paper to reveal a completely nondescript cardboard box. Maybe it was shoes. Would a fan have sent her something as useful as a new pair of shoes? She doubted it. One of the cats uttered a piercing whine and she jumped. The cat, a large tabby named Sarnath, rubbed himself ingratiatingly against her leg while she pondered the box. *Open it*, the cat seemed to be saying. *It might be treats.*

"It might be a bad thing too, Sarny. You just never know." She reflected that living alone had left her with the unfortunate habit of talking to her cats. And listening to them. Sarnath's inscrutable slitted gaze met hers and she reached for the box as if under a spell. She opened it, though not without a remaining qualm or two.

But if she had hoped to see its contents immediately, she was doomed to disappointment. Whatever it was, it was buried under styrofoam peanuts that crinkled and rolled beneath her questing fingers.

But at last, they encountered something hard. She shivered, then forced herself to grasp whatever it was and pull it from its nest. For a brief instant, she looked away only to find herself looking deep into Sarnath's eyes. The cat had begun to purr, a deep, rumbling noise that should have been reassuring but somehow only served to fill her with a vague apprehension.

With an effort, she turned her head to look at the contents of the package, now cradled gingerly in her right hand. Slitted emerald eyes stared back at her and she very nearly dropped whatever it was. Regaining control, she found her jaw falling open in astonishment. Her unknown admirer had sent her a statue of a cat. And what a statue it was!

Clearly of Egyptian origin, it was made of some sort of black stone and covered with carvings that appeared to be hieroglyphs. A single gold earring hung from one ear and the eyes were greenest glass. Or were they tiny emeralds? She couldn't be sure. She set it down so that it met her gaze with an impassive expression, filling her with both a nameless dread and an unexpected excitement, as if her life could be completely transformed at any moment.

It was at that same moment, the doorbell rang, causing Erica to start from her reverie. Surely it couldn't be Mr. McGillicuddy from next door again. He'd already dropped by three times this week and one could only borrow so many cups of sugar. Perhaps Phyllis and Felicia from her bridge club were right and he was interested in more than the contents of her kitchen. She groaned. If only…but there was no point in dwelling on what might have been.

The doorbell rang again, impatience clear in the length of the chime that echoed through the hall. Erica resigned herself to answering it. "Coming! Give me a minute." She remembered to look through the gauzy curtain that hung over the door before she opened it. Even in Foggy Harbor, Massachusetts, there were criminals inclined to prey on a woman living alone.

But all she could see was that the person on her doorstep was broad of shoulder and wearing an elegant suit and a hat that covered her/his hair. He or she also had their back to the door and was looking out over the garden. She did catch a glimpse of dark golden brown skin as the person, whoever they were, raised one hand to brush away some speck on the beautiful dark gray suit. Erica's pulse raced and she tried in vain to catch her breath. *It couldn't be....*

She admonished herself to stop acting like a schoolgirl. Rashida Simmons was gone for good, along with any hopes she'd had in that quarter. Still she trembled as she reached for the knob and opened the door.

Her visitor turned, almost reluctantly, as if they too feared what they might see. An involuntary cry escaped Erica's lips. The woman on her doorstep pulled off her hat and ran her fingers through her short curls. She didn't look up from the threshold as she spoke, "Hello, Erica. I'm sorry for dropping by like this. I'd have called if…I had the number."

At that moment, Erica forgot the ten years that stretched between them, forgot the professional editor that she'd become and spoke her mind without hesitation or forethought. "Rashida Simmons, you get your ass in here right now! You've got some explaining to do!" She reached out with the strength born of desperation and yanked the other woman's arm, pulling her inside. With shaking hands she locked the door behind her, sealing off any chance of easy escape.

Only then did she turn, chest heaving with pent-up indignation. Her quarry met her eyes this time as she took a deep breath and murmured, "It wasn't like that, Erica. I had to leave Foggy Harbor. Let me try and explain but before I go any further, I have to ask: did you receive a package in the mail today?"

"You just drop by after no word for ten years to inquire about the local postal service? Things a little slow wherever you've been keeping yourself?" Erica shook in every limb, part of her longing to hurl herself into Rashida's arms, part of her wanting to throw her out, never to be seen again.

Rashida winced but persisted. "Did it?"

"Yes. Why? Was it from you? Not that a token of affection wouldn't have been too much to ask." Erica uttered a most unladylike snort.

"Where is it?" Rashida ignored the snort, spinning around on her heels as if the statue would be lying around the foyer. She strode around purposefully, looking into each room as if she were welcome to do so. Erica sputtered indignantly after her as she discovered the study. "At last!" she cried out as she dropped into the chair in front of the statue.

The words were a spear through Erica's heart. She forced that organ to harden around a rapidly widening hole. "Well, now that you've found what you came for, I suggest you take it and get out."

Rashida studied her with large golden eyes, almost amber in the afternoon light. Erica strangled stillborn the memory of what they looked like at dawn when her former lover first awakened. She tapped her foot impatiently, waiting for Rashida to take her statue and go.

Instead, the other woman leaned her arms on the table and gave her a serious look. "I know you better than that, Erica. You could never have changed this much. Besides, you're editing cat horror anthologies. You have to know why I'm here; you'll never be able to sleep until you find out."

So Rashida had been following her career? The idea was somehow soothing, warming the coldness of the hard-edged hole in the center of Erica's being. Perhaps…but no. She forced the hope away. Still, it would be nice to know what all this was about. Rashida was right about that much.

She forced her response out between frozen lips: "Oh, very well. But you'll leave after you're done explaining. I suppose you want tea?" Not gracious certainly, but far more than she intended. She cursed the good manners she'd been brought up with.

"Tea would be wonderful. Thank you." Rashida smiled, and it was like watching dawn over the harbor. Erica very nearly melted, only just forcing herself to flee the room in search of cups and hot water. Rashida trailed after her into the kitchen, giving her no time to recover.

"You've done a lot with the place since your aunt died. I like it." She held the words out like a peace offering and Erica grimaced, knowing that the ceiling was covered with cracked and peeling paint and the random stains of old leaks. Her small inheritance and the income from her books was scarcely enough to pay the property taxes and her own needs, certainly not enough for upkeep in a place this big.

A great rage filled her. "I'm engaged. To be married. To Mr. McGillicuddy next door." She blurted the words out, unable to stop herself.

Rashida's dark face paled and she looked away, as if from something she could not bear to see. At last, she murmured, "Congratulations," so softly that Erica barely caught the word.

She cursed the impulse that made her invent such a patent falsehood and longed to throw herself at Rashida's feet to beg for forgiveness. But pride held her upright, made her pour the tea and seal her lips.

Rashida rose, pacing, as she blew on her tea to cool it, her agitation clear. "I had hoped…well, never mind about that now. Can we go back to the other room? I hate to let the statue out of my sight for long." She walked out the door and down the hall without a backward glance or even the saucer that Erica held out to her.

Erica followed her down the hallway, already making up her mind to admit that she'd told a little fib about Mr. McGillicuddy. But when she got to the study, Rashida was sitting at the table, eyes fixed on the cat, and she found she couldn't say it. Instead, she picked up Rashida's cup and smacked it onto the saucer with unnecessary force. "All right, so it's clear that you didn't come back to see me. What's the story with the statue?"

Rashida brought both hands up to her face and rubbed her cheeks as if suddenly exhausted. "All right. You remember when my mother disappeared?"

As if Erica could forget the most traumatic moment of their high school years. Mrs. Simmons had vanished into the night, leaving only the briefest of notes for her husband and teenage daughter. She had assured them that she'd be back and told them not to worry. They never heard from her again.

Erica had spent months consoling Rashida; it had been what had drawn them together. How ironic that Mrs. Simmons' disappearance was somehow instrumental in today's events, too. "Of course I re-member. The FBI never found a thing. Your father became a private detective but was never able to find any trace of her. Why? Have you heard something?"

Rashida reached into the front pocket of her immaculately tailored suit and pulled out a crumpled envelope. Wordlessly, she handed it to Erica. For an instant, Erica contemplated refusing to read what-ever it was. After all, what did it matter now? But her curiosity was aroused. She took it, opening the envelope slowly and carefully as if something inside might bite her. A distant part of her brain noted the two-year-old postmark.

The letter inside was typed on an actual typewriter; there were even smudges where the correction tape failed.

My dearest daughter,

I hope you can forgive me. There's no time to try to explain it all now—it wouldn't be good enough for what you've lost any-way. Just know I always meant to come back and that I love you and your father very much. If I hadn't left, I'd have lost both of you.

Now I have to ask you to do something for me. My family, gen-eration upon generation back to our ancestors' time in Nubia of old, were appointed as the guardians of a sacred relic. It is an object of great power and it must be protected from those who would misuse it. The time has come when I must pass it on to you, my child. I know you have started your training and are almost ready to take on this great burden. I will come to you soon to tell you more.

If you do not hear from me again, know that I am prevented from coming by forces beyond my control. I will send the object into safekeeping with friends who will guard it until you are ready. Return to the beginning to seek what you need.

Your loving mother,

Keira

"I never heard from her again. I believe that she may have run afoul of forces trying to find the statue. I think my aunt and uncle knew what befell her, but feared to tell me in case her fate frightened me from performing my duties," Rashida offered up in spectral tones.

"Not to be overly skeptical, Rashida, but are you sure that your mother was quite…right when she wrote this? Or that this letter is even from her? What 'training'? What sacred relic?" Erica's questions all rushed together until they emerged almost as a single sentence. She bit back a few others. *Nubia? The Simmons family has been here in Foggy Harbor for generations.*

"Still the same old cautious Erica." Rashida smiled wistfully as she took the letter from Erica's hand and carefully folded it before putting it in the envelope and tucking it back in her suit. "My aunt and uncle came to visit about a week before I left town. They told me some of this back then but I didn't believe it either. Not at first. But then they showed me some things and I…had to leave with them. It was my duty. Can I trust you with one of my family's greatest secrets, Erica?" Her face was grave and her eyes didn't waver from her former lover's.

Erica bit back a few more responses and thought about it through the numb cloud currently filling her mind. Even if she suspected Rashida was now as crazy as the letter writer, who would she tell? Her bridge club? Her publisher? Not likely. Besides, how different could this story be from anything she'd read recently? There was even a cat in it. She shrugged and sat down at the table. "Disclose away." She sipped at her tea and waited.

Rashida stood and closed all the blinds and curtains, shrouding the room in twilight gloom. Then she walked over to the table and the cat. She raised her hands to shoulder height and a distant look crossed her features, as if she traveled across time. Her lips parted to emit a chant in a language that Erica did not recognize, one that was at once guttural and musical. The hairs stood up on Erica's nape and she shivered despite herself, filled with a heretofore unknown sense of eldritch dread.

Rashida's eyes were pools of molten gold, her face that of a warrior goddess of old. Erica could not tear her gaze away, though her heart cried out in fear that this new Rashida could never be hers again. The statue's eyes began to glow as the hieroglyphics on its sides were outlined in light. A strange humming sound filled the room, vibrating its way through Erica's china cabinet. The hieroglyphs blazed brilliantly, far too bright to look at, and Erica threw her arm over her face.

The humming lasted a moment more before dying away into silence, and the room went dark once again. "It's safe to look now." Rashida's voice was reassuring but Erica still hesitated a moment before lowering her arm. The cat's inscrutable emerald eyes glowed back at her.

She found her voice with an effort. "So does it do anything besides glow and hum?"

Rashida gave her a look of disbelief. "Of course it does. It's an object of destiny, a source of ancient and terrible power."

"Okay. So what does it actually do?" Erica was beginning to remember one of Rashida's less desirable traits, namely a tendency toward the unnecessarily dramatic.

"It can be used as a weapon of awesome destructive power. And it can bring back what was lost and change fate, perhaps even raise the dead if the user is powerful enough."

Or it could just be battery-powered and you might be a few scarabs shy of a full complement. Erica stopped the words before they escaped her lips, focusing instead on Rashida's first statement. "What do you mean, 'it can be used as a weapon'? What kind of weapon? Used by whom?"

"Only the followers of Set himself, clearly nothing you'd be worried about." Rashida glared at her and Erica realized that she had been using the same voice she used on Mrs. Grayson, her neighbor who had early onset Alzheimer's. "Very well," Rashida said finally. "I can see that you don't believe me. I'll take the statue and go. I have one last task to perform in Foggy Harbor, then we need never see each other again."

"No, wait. What are you going to do next? At least let me cook dinner for you before you go. For old time's sake." Perhaps she could find a way to bring Rashida back to a little of her old, saner self, she thought. Or get her to spend the night. She squelched the second thought.

The doorbell rang again and Erica rolled her eyes. "Let me just get rid of whoever it is and we can have a cozy chat. I'd really like to hear about what you've been up to." *At least I hope I'll like it.* She skirted around the statue as she headed for the front door. No point in taking too many chances. At least it wasn't changing fate right now, and Rashida wasn't bolting for the door.

The doorbell rang again and Erica found herself looking into Alex McGillicuddy's faded blue eyes through the glass pane. She could have screamed with frustration. Instead she made herself open the door. "Hello, Mr. McGillicuddy. I'm afraid I can't stop to chat. I have a guest. Did you need something?" *Such as a shove off my porch?* She held the words back. Clearly Rashida's return was doing nothing for her good nature.

"Well, hello there, neighbor. I didn't mean to intrude—I was just hoping to get that recipe from you again, the one for that wonderful chicken dish you dropped off when I moved in. I seem to have misplaced the copy you gave me. But it can wait. I've got a frozen pot pie I can just heat up." Alex gave her a look of pure longing that nearly made Erica roll her eyes before he turned away, shoulders slumped with rejection.

Damn the man. "Wait a minute, Alex. We can't have you resorting to the microwave every night. Just follow me back to the kitchen and I'll give you another copy of the recipe." She ushered him, trying not to cringe at his beaming smile.

That was the moment when Rashida emerged from the study. Erica couldn't help the tremor that went through her. After all, Rashida still thought.... "Hello. I'm Rashida Simmons," she announced before Erica could say anything. "I understand that congratulations are in order." She gave Alex a stiff, wooden smile and clutched his hand in a death grip, white knuckles clearly visible.

Alex looked surprisingly alert, if a bit baffled. "How do you do? I was just stopping by for a recipe. Congratulations, you say?"

Rashida chose that moment to twist their hands so that Alex's wrist was exposed. Erica caught a brief glimpse of a snakelike tattoo before he yanked his arm away and pulled his sleeve down. Rashida and Alex glared at each other as if they were about to engage in mortal combat.

Desperate to end the standoff, Erica began to babble. "Let's talk about that later, Alex. Rashida and I were just going to sit down to dinner and chat about old times. Why don't we head back to the kitchen so you can get on with your own dinner?" She seized Alex's arm and steered him down the hallway with unnecessary force.

She couldn't help but notice the glance he sent after Rashida as she receded down the hallway in the distance. Had he always possessed that gleam of pure malice in his faded blue eyes? It made her think of ancient temples, their walls oozing with ichor and unspeakable evil. And snakes. She couldn't abide snakes. The thought made her scowl fiercely at him. He blinked innocently back, which made her scowl more.

She snatched her recipe box from the stove and yanked the card from the front. "Here you go. Just copy it over and give it back to me when you get around to it. Have a lovely evening!" She flung her back door open and gave him a smile that contained no ambiguities whatsoever.

"Your friend seems very nice and of course I don't mean to intrude, but perhaps we could all dine together. She seems as though she'd be very interesting to talk to." Alex smiled ingratiatingly at her and made no move toward the door.

"Perhaps another time. We have a lot to catch up on. Now, if you'll excuse me...." Erica glanced pointedly from the door to her neighbor.

At a glacial pace, he stepped toward the door, mumbling words like "sorry" and "intrude." Erica smiled and nodded, making it clear that her mind was somewhere else entirely. Finally, after what seemed an eternity, he oozed out of her kitchen. She watched him make his way down the garden path and out the gate with a fierce enthusiasm.

Then she raced back to the study. An empty room met her eyes: both the statue and Rashida were gone. Erica delivered herself of several unladylike comments before she noticed the note at the edge of the desk. As she reached for it, a part of her could not help but notice that the room felt better somehow. There was no sense of dread, eldritch or otherwise, only her familiar comfortable furniture and her sleeping cats. She glanced at them as if hoping for answers, but only got gentle snores in response.

She opened the note, knowing what it would say. Rashida was gone for good, driven away by some nonsensical quest and the stupid lie that Erica had told her. In a moment of stunning clarity, she recognized that perhaps even a somewhat deranged Rashida was worth having, at least to her, and she knew despair even before she began reading. The actual text only confirmed her fears.

> *Dear Erica,*
> *I'm sorry to have intruded on you like this. I had forgotten how people's lives change. Please know that I wish only the best for you in your future life and rest assured that I will not burden you again.*
> *Yours,*
>
> *Rashida*

Erica was just slumping into the chair Rashida had recently occupied when she remembered something that the other woman had said. Something about "one last task." Where could the long lost scion of Nubian priests guarding a sacred relic perform a task here in Foggy Harbor? She wouldn't have gone back to the old Simmons place, surely. Mr. Simmons had passed on a few years back and the family who bought the place had done a drastic remodeling job. That left his old office and…Mrs. Simmon's mausoleum! Of course, why hadn't it occurred to her before?

Erica leapt to her feet and threw caution to the winds. She grabbed her purse and her shoes. Following some instinct she hadn't known she possessed, she bolted down the hall to the kitchen and obtained a small flashlight and, after a moment of hesitation, a box of matches, several packages of salt, and a longish kitchen knife.

Had there been anyone to ask her why she chose those items, she would not have been able to answer them. Perhaps it was one of her own ancestors advising her, maybe a long forgotten Goodie Somebody or Other who narrowly avoiding meeting her death in Salem. Or perhaps it just was editing too many cat horror anthologies. But whatever the reason, the knife felt good and comforting in her hand and the rest felt like essential tools.

She seized her coat from the hook and made sure the cats had enough to eat in case she was gone for a while. The bridge club would take them in if need be, she reminded herself sternly. Then she was off like a shot on her bicycle, pedaling as if her life depended on it toward the Shady Oaks Resting Place out on the edge of town. Rashida would be there already, if that's where she was headed. Erica hoped for the best and rode as she had never ridden before.

Fortunately, the cemetery was not far away and traffic was light. Erica skidded to a halt in front of the locked gates moments later and wondered how she was going to get inside. Then she remembered that Rashida had another way in, a gap in the fence some ways down that she used when she wanted to visit the family tomb after hours. She rode her bike on a bit further, then chained it to a post near where she thought the hole was.

With a deep breath, she straightened out her coat and marched up to the fence. Her memory had served her well. An impossibly skinny opening met her searching gaze and she despaired. Then she heard the noise of an engine, one that sounded vaguely threatening, if an engine could be described that way. She shrank into the shadows and glanced around.

Alex was parking his car on the street near the cemetery entrance. And he wasn't alone. There were two men with him, neither of them familiar, but both of an aspect that would have caused a braver heart than Erica's to quail. They got out of the car and made for the locked gates of the cemetery.

For an instant, she thought of going home and calling the police. But what would she tell them? Then she thought of the way Alex had looked at Rashida when they met. There had been something in his expression that filled her with urgency. She found that if she held her breath and twisted just right, she was able to squeeze through the fence to fall, gasping, onto the soft green grass on the other side.

She could hear an ominous clicking noise from the entrance; they must be cutting or picking the lock. Brushing herself off, she rose and sprinted for the deeper shadows under the trees. Then she pulled out her little flashlight, and shielding it as much as she could with her fingers, she dashed forward through the tombstones and trees toward the Simmons mausoleum.

It took longer than she expected and she got lost once, but she finally found it. To the amazement of Foggy Harbor, Rashida's grandfather had built the family tomb as a small stone pyramid in the midst of the more standard marble structures. It was trimmed with black stone and guarded by statues of Anubis and Bastet. There were even hieroglyphs, which everyone else in Foggy Harbor thought was an unbearable pretension. Erica had thought so herself upon occasion. Now her nerves were so agitated, it was all she could do to approach the structure.

As she got closer, she noticed that the hieroglyphs were glowing faintly. Could Rashida be inside, unaware of her danger? Still, she mustn't overreact. She couldn't be absolutely sure that Alex presented any kind of threat. Perhaps he just enjoyed late night visits to cemeteries with large male friends. Large terrifying male friends.

Erica squared her shoulders and tried to remember where the catch for the door was hidden. Then she reached into the recess next to the door and opened it. The mechanism still worked flawlessly after all these years. Without stopping to marvel at that minor miracle, she slipped inside and let it click shut behind her.

She had expected to walk into Stygian gloom but to her surprise, the interior was lit with a pale golden glow. It was bright enough to illuminate the names on the memorials, including those of Rashida's parents. Erica wondered who, if anyone, was buried in her mother's tomb before she turned away, shivering a bit.

In the middle of the floor, one of the great marble slabs was pulled aside and a flight of steps led downward. From below, she thought she could hear the sound of muted chanting, and it sent chills up her already frozen spine. She considered demanding that Rashida stop all this nonsense and come upstairs to talk to her, but the words would not cross her immobile lips.

Instead, Erica closed her eyes and remembered Rashida as she had been, back when they were first together at Foggy Harbor State, before that first fateful Egyptology class. She caressed the memory of Rashida's golden eyes in the sunset and the way she felt when—she made herself stop and shuffle toward the steps. There would be time for trips down Memory Lane later, once all this was over. Alex and his thugs could only be minutes behind her.

Even so she crept down the stairs at a snail's pace. The sight that met her eyes when she reached the bottom was not one that even her books could have prepared her for. Rashida stood before an altar presided over by the cat statue. The air was thick with incense and the smoke of many candles. Her former lover was naked to the waist, though she still wore her gray wool pants. Above those, she was clad only in massive gold jewelry: a collar, several arm rings, huge earrings. She raised a blood-covered knife as she chanted. Erica could see shallow gashes in her arms, and the sight made her shudder all over.

Rashida was completely unaware of her, her golden eyes rimmed with kohl and focused on another world. Erica shrank back for a moment, too terrified to approach her friend. She could see that there was a dish of blood in front of the statue and for a ghastly moment, she feared that her friend had come to sacrifice herself to the mysterious statue. That thought was enough to break through her fears. "No!" she cried, her voice cutting through the smoke and the chanting like a blade.

Rashida faltered, and Erica could feel the air of the chamber tense and coil, becoming suddenly dangerous to the point of madness. Something unfathomably evil lurked there, somehow, just outside the realm of human senses. Using all of her strength, Erica leaped forward and pulled Rashida to the floor, knocking the knife from her hands and covering her with her trembling body in a vain effort to protect her.

It was at that moment Alex and his minions burst into the tomb. They thundered downstairs just as Erica thought the air itself was about to strike them all down. Alex laughed, a cold mirthless sound in the murk of the chamber. "It seems you received a package intended for me, Guardian." He stepped forward, towering over them, his eyes cold and clearer than Erica had ever seen them.

Well, she thought, somewhat hysterically, *if it's just a post office mix-up, we can all go home. No harm done.* Her glance fell on one of the men with Alex and she was quiet. Harm would be done tonight and it was only a matter of time before it was clear who would be the recipient of it.

Rashida stirred from underneath her, easing Erica off to one side. "It is not for you, oh Servant of Set! It is my sacred mission to guard it and guard it I shall," Rashida's lips were set, a deep fury burning in her eyes. She had not yet looked at Erica, but the latter was not looking forward to the moment when her attention shifted.

She had to cut the tension somehow. "Really, Alex, if I'd known you had such an interest in antiquities, I'd have gone to the museum with you when you asked. Perhaps we can continue this discussion over dinner?" Erica asked hopefully.

"Let her go, she knows nothing about this." Rashida's eyes never left Alex's.

"On the contrary, she has some suspicions about me. And she is curious enough that it is only a matter of time before she wants to know more. Isn't that right, my dear?" Alex gave Erica a mock flirtatious leer that made her grimace in disgust.

Alex McGillicuddy is a minion of Set? It wasn't all that hard to believe, really, what with all the annoying attentions he'd been paying to her. Clearly she was better off staying single, not that that appeared to be her biggest concern at the moment.

But whoever or whatever he was, Alex was annoying her more than usual. She said the most outrageous thing she could think of. "That's it. The wedding's off." She glared at Alex and scrambled to her feet as Rashida did the same. The air around them seemed to have thinned a bit, as if the chanting had stopped calling whatever it was bringing into this world from one beyond.

Alex looked baffled. "The wedd—oh, never mind." His gaze fell on the statue and his eyes brightened with dark emotions. "Take the cat, boys, and we'll just seal up our little friends in their tomb. I'm sure they can comfort each other for a while, at least until the air runs out."

"Wait," Rashida held up her hand. "This is not your Lord's. Its powers will not obey you." Erica could feel a force coiling around them again, could feel something coming to a summons she could not hear. She reached into her handbag and found the packets of salt. As slowly and carefully as she could, she pulled them out. She glanced sidelong at Rashida and noticed that the latter seemed to be preparing to attack Alex.

The cat glowed even brighter as one of the thugs approached it. Alex hadn't answered Rashida's challenge, which was not surprising, since his attention seemed wholly fixed on the statue. But he had a gun out now and was pointing it at them.

Erica reached into her bag with excruciating slowness and pulled out the knife. She handed it to Rashida who gave her a bemused but still angry glance. "Athame," Erica muttered as softly as she could, using the only word she could remember from *Kitties in the Witch House*, her very nearly best-selling anthology.

Rashida smiled and it was an expression that made her face beautiful and terrible all at once. Following the strange instinct that had driven her since she left the house, Erica tore open the packets of salt and threw their contents out around them in a rough circle. "Hold it!" Alex barked at them just as his minion touched the cat.

The air above the altar grew dark as Rashida began to chant again. It swirled around the man, something glowing in its depths that Erica could not bear to look at. She closed her eyes and ducked as a bullet from Alex's gun whizzed past. The words flowing from Rashida's lips were like the ones she'd been chanting when Erica first entered, but they were different in timbre somehow. She was still terrified but she felt protected, as if whatever powers Rashida was calling were no longer harmful. At least to them.

A high-pitched, piercing cry of utter pain and terror filled the room. Erica covered her ears and flinched away and even Rashida stumbled in her chant. The air thickened and tightened above the altar, reminding Erica of nothing so much as a giant serpent. Or a very sinuous cat. Alex's henchman waved his arms and flailed as if trying to fend off some invisible foe. Then with a scream horrific in its finality, he fell to the floor, motionless.

Alex trained his gun on Rashida. "Call it off, witch. Your creature can't kill me before I fire this again." His eyes were icy in the murk of the chamber, even though his remaining thug shook with fear at his side.

Erica gave Rashida a panicked look. She couldn't lose her now, not like this. Rashida laughed, the rich mellow sound filling the chamber around them. The thing above the altar hovered, its face taking shape and growing pointed ears. The face hovered above the bowl of Rashida's blood, a ghastly phantom tongue lapping at its contents. Rashida glanced at it before meeting Alex's eyes. "Bets?" she inquired in a somewhat bored voice.

Erica's eyes widened in horror as she saw Alex's finger tighten on the trigger, then change his mind and point the gun at her. Rashida whispered something that might have been a prayer or a curse. She brought the kitchen knife down in a slashing moment as Alex pulled the trigger. A white cloud rose from the circle of salt around them and Erica watched as the bullet slowed to a crawl, stopping inches from her shoulder. Rashida reached out and flicked it with her finger, sending it to roll on the floor.

Alex's eyes narrowed and his thin lips parted in a chant of his own. Rashida gestured, and the cloud edged closer to his remaining minion. The man stood his ground a moment, then glanced at his fallen comrade, and fled up the stairs. The cloud appeared to have grown paws now, and it circled Alex, a glow that might have been eyes fixed on his upraised hands.

The sounds that fell from Alex's lips were cold and cruel, an ancient evil walking among them. Erica nearly covered her eyes before deciding that she couldn't bear not to watch. A second shadow arose from the cat statue, this one clearly a serpent with a fiery eyes. The cat shadow turned toward it, its spectral mouth opened in a silent hiss.

Then the two were joined in battle as their acolytes chanted at each other across the tomb. Erica glanced from one to the other, wondering what, if anything, she should do. The circle of salt still glowed faintly around them, which was reassuring. She watched the shadows battle for a moment and considered whether or not to simply sit down and wait it out. But that seemed cowardly somehow.

Rashida's face looked strained when she glanced back, and a new sense of urgency filled Erica at the sight. She wondered if she could learn an ancient chant in the next minute or two and help that way, but languages had never been her forte. Next she speculated that there might be something she could do to help the shadow kitty win its battle, but that too seemed unlikely.

Then she looked up at Alex. He seemed stronger, his face twisted in an expression of pure evil. He was also closer than she'd realized, only a few feet away from the edge of their protective circle. There wasn't much time and a deus ex machina did not seem forthcoming.

It was then that Erica had an idea. It was a weird sort of idea, but she thought it just might work. She reached into her purse and took out her book of matches. Then she took off her sweater and wrapped it around her fake leather purse. She lit several matches and with only the slightest of qualms, she held the sputtering flame to her favorite sweater. As the wool caught on fire, she studied the distance between them and Alex with narrowed eyes.

When at last she made her throw, she threw it underhand, just "like a girl" as Rashida would have said in disgust back when they played college softball. She lobbed it with care and skill, though, and no one could argue with the results. The ball of flaming wool and plastic landed at Alex's feet, sparks catching on his pants. He hesitated, his chant faltering for a breath, then two, as he stamped and shook his foot to put out the flames which engulfed his cuffs.

With a hiss that knocked Erica to her knees, the cat shadow found some hidden source of strength. When she looked up, she could see the serpent dangling from its spectral kitty jaws. She looked at Rashida, hoping to see that her friend had found the same strength. But to her horror, Rashida seemed nearly spent.

A loud noise distracted her, and she looked at Alex in time to see him drop his gun. She gathered herself and hopped out of the salt circle. Immediately, mighty forces assailed her and she walked forward as if in a gale. But walk forward she did until she was able to reach the gun. She managed to pick it up and hold it out in front of her with hands that shook convulsively. "All right," she said in a voice that shook nearly as badly. "Enough of this nonsense."

She pointed the gun in Alex's general direction and pulled the trigger, the recoil knocking her to the floor. Her shot missed, but it was enough to make him flinch. Rashida's words fell like hail, faster and more powerful, than before and Alex dropped to his knees, hands pressed over his ears, silent at last. A great rushing sound tore through the chamber and both cat and serpent vanished. The glow of the hieroglyphs faded until only the candles and the fiery sweater still provided light.

Rashida stepped forward and raised the kitchen knife above Alex, her face transformed into the countenance of a goddess of death. "No!" Erica shouted.

Her friend seemed to shift, as if another person was working their way to the surface. "I know you were engaged to him and all, but really Erica, I'm sure you can see he's not the greatest catch."

Erica's jaw dropped open. "I was never engaged to him! I just said that because I was angry with you. That's no reason to kill him." She staggered to her feet. "You won't call on powerful dark forces from beyond this world again, will you, Mr. McGillicuddy?"

Alex hissed something that might have been agreement. His eyes were dead now, as if the spirit which drove him was gone. Looking into them, Erica had another idea. "Besides, maybe he knows what happened to your mother."

Rashida's face shifted, becoming more Rashida again. "Do you, Set-spawn? Do you know something?" She waved the knife threateningly in front of his dazed looking face.

It seemed to be enough to bring him back to life, and his lips twisted in a snarl. "My Lord consumed her, body and spirit, just as he will consume you!" Then he twisted around and kicked out with desperate strength. Rashida jumped back as he pulled himself to his feet. Then he charged forward, straight at the cat on the altar. Rashida lunged after him, but not quickly enough, as he darted past her and placed his hands on the statue.

For a moment, nothing happened. His face twisted and it seemed to Erica as if he was drawing on some unseen source of power. The statue began to glow a little, then a bit more. A tendril of shadow reached out from it and wrapped itself around his body in a hideously companionable fashion. He threw back his head and laughed, and the shadow slipped into his mouth. His laughter changed to a choking cough and he fell to the floor, his body convulsing, until just as suddenly, he was still.

The statue fell with him, meeting the stone floor with a crash. The head broke loose and shadows poured out. They surged out in a mighty gray wave, then just as quickly dissipated. In their wake, they left two corpses and two exhausted women. "Well, looks like that might be it for your task," Erica said in awed but relieved tones.

Rashida stared at her in disbelief, then picked her way across the floor to the statue. She picked up the head and held it as if seeking answers to questions only she could hear. The green eyes twinkled in the cat's face but volunteered nothing. A single tear worked its way down Rashida's cheek.

Erica ran over to comfort her. She wrapped her arms around her friend and held her tightly, and in that brief instant, both of them touched the cat. The statue quivered and shook, light pouring from it instead of shadows this time. It engulfed them, then swept through the chamber and up the stairs into the mausoleum. Then it too vanished as the shadows had done.

"We've released all that it held," Rashida whispered. "There is nothing more to guard."

Erica kissed her bare shoulder and turned her around so she could kiss the tears from her cheeks. "Where are the rest of your clothes, by the way?"

Rashida pointed up wordlessly. Erica took the pieces of the statue and tucked them into her capacious pockets. Then she took Rashida's hand in hers and towed her along as she walked over to pick her house keys out of the smoldering wreckage of her purse. "Let's go home for dinner." She smiled reassuringly at Rashida, but the latter seemed lost in her thoughts.

Erica pulled her up the stairs behind her. There was a faint knocking coming from Keira Simmons' tomb. They looked at each other, and Erica shrugged and nodded, the experiences of the evening having completely exhausted her capacity for terror. Rashida pulled on her shirt and jacket before they approached the tomb. They looked deep into each other's eyes for a long moment, then they pushed the lid away. Keira Simmons sat up, clearly alive, her face that of someone waking from a long sleep.

"Hello, Mother," Rashida choked out at last. "I asked Bastet to help me find you, and she has." Rashida burst into tears.

Erica nodded politely to Mrs. Simmons as she and her daughter tearfully embraced. She gave Rashida a wan smile before turning and walking out of the tomb. She had no place in this part of Rashida's story. Still, she ached at the thought that she might never see Rashida again. In an acute state of emotional turmoil, she retrieved her bike, and went home, where she tumbled into bed and slept for many hours.

She was sitting at her kitchen table the next morning reading stories with titles like "Kittens in the Walls" when the doorbell rang. She shuffled slowly down the hall and flung the door open without bothering to check to see who it was.

Rashida looked back at her, golden eyes calm and peaceful. "I was thinking," she said without preamble, "that I missed you." Then she stepped up and took the astonished Erica in her arms for a long kiss. And Erica kissed her back, right there on the doorstep in front of all of Foggy Harbor. Then she took Rashida's hand and pulled her inside, shutting the door behind her.

World War III Doesn't Last Long

NORA OLSEN

(for Eamon Hart 1977-2009)

"Felicia darlink, it's me. Open up!"

No one called her Felicia except her neighbors, who read the name off her mailbox. "Just a second," Fell said. She flipped the lock and opened the door. Mrs. Sziemencewicz was waiting in the hallway. Mrs. Abreu from 3L stood beside her. The two women had become awfully chummy since the disaster started. Fell couldn't remember them ever talking before. It seemed that catastrophe really did bring people together in mutual aid.

At least until the eating-each-other stage started, Fell thought.

"We've been watching the television, and we just wanted to let you know the good news," Mrs.

Sziemencewicz said. "Everything is fine. Just keep staying inside, they said. Help is on the way."

Mrs. Abreu beamed and bobbed her head. "The Red Cross," she said.

"The paratroopers, dear," corrected Mrs. Sziemencewicz. "The 101st Airborne."

"No, that was this morning," Mrs. Abreu insisted.

"Thank you," Fell said. "That's great, I'm glad to hear it. Thanks for keeping me updated."

"It's nothing," said Mrs. Sciemencewicz. "Don't mention it, darlink. You know, we're keeping an eye on you. Making sure everything is OK. Don't be so worried."

Mrs. Abreu stepped forward and actually patted Fell's cheek. How are you supposed to respond to having your cheek patted, Fell wondered. She tried to smile.

"There is one thing," Mrs. S. said. "You know, I didn't get a chance to go to the store before all this business started. I was wondering if I could borrow a little something for supper."

Fell opened her mouth and then closed it. "Why not," she said. She was standing in her kitchen and it was only three steps to the cupboard, where she got a blue can of Annie's brand organic ravioli. She handed it to Mrs. S., then noticed Mrs. A's glittering eyes. She quickly got the second can and gave it to Mrs. A.

"Oh thanks so much," Mrs. S. said, grabbing the door and swinging it closed as if she were afraid Fell would change her mind. "We'll let you know what we hear. It's a pity you have no TV."

The door slammed. Fell clicked the lock behind her.

Why had she given them the food?

Every time they gave her an update, it was always the same. The details changed, but the essentials remained. The radiation will only harm you if you go outside. Don't worry. At the appropriate time, the police or the army will come and get you and bring you food. She wondered if her neighbors really believed it. Everyone had stopped doing their jobs and gone home to stay with their families or friends.

So who was going to come save us? Fell figured that all the police and soldiers were huddling at home with their kids like everyone else.

Fell had always boasted about how prepared she was for any disaster. When water stopped coming out of the tap, that was okay because Fell had lots of bottles stockpiled. If all else failed there was clean water in the toilet tank. There was still electricity, but no more phone or cable or internet. Fell could accept that, maybe some lines had gone down. Maybe everyone else had service except for Clay Street. It wasn't like Verizon was going to come fix things. But why was everyone's cell service out? Wasn't cell phone service kind of automatic, even if no one was doing a job? Just satellites in the sky or something?

Fell's girlfriend would know. Soo Jin would scold Fell. She would say, "You're a college graduate? Oh right, Political Science. Yeah. You should crack open a science book sometime. A children's book. *How Things Work.*"

Here's what Fell's political science knowledge told her: the people in charge had cut off all the phone and internet. They didn't want the people communicating.

Here's what else Fell knew.

She had given food away to the neighbors because she was leaving. It had taken a while for Fell's heart to catch up with her brain. Did she really believe that her Tyvek walls were going to keep out the Evil Radiation? With these leaky window frames that the wind whistled through all winter? Please. Did Fell want to die alone in her three-room railroad apartment? Or did she want to spend her last days in Astoria, Queens, with the woman she loved, in *her* three-room apartment? Mrs. Abreu had told her there were $500 fines for going outside, but who exactly was going to be giving out tickets?

Once Fell made up her mind, she packed quickly. Only the things that she thought were really necessary. Water, some tinned food and a can opener, a lighter, first aid kit, a shiny reflective blanket. A jar of Nutella. Fell just loved the stuff and she'd be damned if she was going to die without eating as much of it as she could. A charger and lot of batteries. Soo Jin never had any batteries.

Fell copied out the same note twice:

SOOJ, I WENT TO YOUR PLACE (THURSDAY AT 2PM.) -F.

The idea that Soo Jin might come looking for her and they could miss each other was a depressing one. Fell taped one note to her apartment door and the other to the front door. She saw the curtains in Mrs. S's apartment twitch and knew she was being watched.

At the last minute, Fell felt in her pocket for a Sharpie and scrawled the date on the note. "Thursday" might not be helpful. Then she wondered how Soo Jin would feel if she came all the way here and saw this terse note. She added lots of little hearts and XXs and OOs. Great, now it was a note from a twelve year old.

Fell turned away from the note before she could fiddle with it any more.

It was so strange to be outdoors. She wondered if everyone was observing her, not just Mrs. S. Fell had watched the streets a lot the last few days and hadn't seen a single person.

It smelled a lot worse out here. It was really foul. Fell knew this was from the Newtown Creek sewage treatment plant, now neglected. She pulled the bandanna she'd tied around her neck up over her mouth and nose. Didn't really help much.

Despite the bad smells, she felt her spirits lift. It was so good to be outside. It was a gorgeous summer day. The bricks of the factory across the street were bright in the sunlight. Fell unlocked her bike from the sign post in front of the factory and thought about how she would likely never see Clay Street again. Not everyone would say that the combination of industrial buildings and three-story residences of various colors was beautiful, but Fell was very fond of it.

At the corner of the street was the Pulaski Bridge, which passed over Newtown Creek and brought you into Queens. Fell was dismayed when she looked up and saw the roadway of the Pulaski Bridge sticking straight up into the sky. The Pulaski was a drawbridge, and it was raised. Why? To allow tall rescue boats to chug down the creek? Just to mess up Fell's plans?

There was another small drawbridge a few blocks away. Fell decided to cruise past and see if that one was raised as well. No, she saw from Greenpoint Avenue that this bridge was up too.

It would have to be the Gore Memorial Bridge, then. On the way to Meeker Avenue, Fell saw a dog tied up to a lamp post. It barked feebly at her. She thought of letting it loose but she was a little afraid of dogs. She found a ramp leading onto the BQE. After several days of sitting in her apartment doing nothing, Fell was winded and out of shape. She had to get off her bike and walk it up the ramp.

Once on the BQE, it was kind of fun to be riding where usually only cars could go. The BQE led onto the Gore Memorial Bridge. Fell had ridden her bike over the Gore many times since it was built in 2014, but of course only on the bike path. Now was her chance to really own the nine-lane bridge! To get a better view of the skyline of Manhattan, she lifted her bike over the concrete divider. Now she was on the side that should have had oncoming traffic. Below was Newtown Creek. It seemed to have more oily swirls in it than usual, and that was saying a lot for the little creek that had been designated a Superfund site.

Just as Calvary Cemetery began to loom into view on the Queens side, Fell saw a car idling on the road, parked perpendicularly smack in the middle of the roadway. As she drew closer, Fell saw that the car was running but there was no one in it. Fell couldn't see anyone around, and she peddled as fast as she could. The driver must have jumped. Only as she was whizzing down the ramp past Calvary Cemetery did it occur to her that she could have taken the car and driven to Soo Jin's. But she didn't want anything to do with that spooky car. What if there was someone hiding in it?

The giant vista of graves that was Calvary Cemetery seemed to go on forever. She'd heard that in the nineteenth century, twenty-five immigrant children were buried there every day. No one was going to be buried anymore in this city, unless you counted apartment buildings as big tombs. Fell started wondering if Soo Jin even really loved her. Why did Fell have to be the one to go and find her? It suddenly seemed clear that she cared much more about Soo Jin than Soo

Jin cared about her. Fell remembered that Soo Jin's ex also lived in Astoria. What if her ex strolled over to make amends so she could die with a clean conscience? Fell recalled that the ex was a lingerie model and wondered if Soo Jin ever really got over her.

Fell was pretty sure she was in Sunnyside now, but her knowledge of Queens geography was a bit underdeveloped. She wished the Citigroup building was still standing. It had been such a good landmark, the only really tall building in Queens. It had been like a polestar that told you where you were. Fell remembered shopping in Chinatown with Soo Jin and giggling at gaudy commemorative wall plaques of the Citigroup building that were for sale on Canal Street. They had joked that soon there wouldn't be a skyscraper left in the city, just lots of commemorative plaques. Soo Jin had worked as a math tutor to a little girl whose parents both worked in the Citigroup building. Soo Jin never heard from them again after the attack, and refused to look at the names of the dead.

The thing was, it was a pretty big declaration of love to travel across the city when the government was telling you to stay indoors because of the radiation. Fell didn't know if she was ready for that yet. The declaring her love part. She might be marginally more ready for radiation. Lesbians were supposed to move really fast. The cliche was that the second date was renting a U-Haul truck so they could move in together. But it hadn't been that way with Fell and Soo Jin. If only she could have had a chance to talk to Soo Jin when the bombs fell on Pennsylvania. They could have made some kind of plan. But Fell had only been able to speak to her father in California, and then the phones had stopped working. She should have called Soo Jin first. She didn't even really care about her father all that much. Just thinking about this was making Fell feel nauseated.

Every way Fell turned she was confronted by a fence with some train tracks behind it. It seemed to go on and on, and Fell was getting frustrated. Then she started hearing music. She knew it might be a mistake to go to it, but she was curious. It was hard to tell where the sound was coming from. Then she turned on to Skillman Avenue and saw the playground.

The two men in the park looked so natural that Fell wasn't even surprised to see them. They were two middle-aged black men. One was doing chin-ups on the jungle gym. The other, less fit-looking, was sitting reading the *Daily News*. It must have been an old copy, but the man seemed engrossed. A boom pod was next to him, blasting out the music on its tiny, high-quality speakers.

Fell approached cautiously. The chin-up man saw her and acknowledged her with a slight nod. He continued his workout, dropping from the bars to knock off a few pushups.

"This guy wrote to Dear Abby," newspaper guy said. "He's in prison and suspects his girlfriend is seeing another man. He's got two more years and he's asking her what should he do."

"There's nothing he can do," chin-up man said, not even out of breath. "He'll sit there in prison one way or the other."

"My point exactly. Two years is a long time. He went and bought a stamp from the commissary, and sent off this letter to Dear Abby. Now he's waiting in his jumpsuit for her reply so he can find out what he's supposed to do!" The man slapped his newspaper and laughed.

"That's off the hook," said the other man. He was finally panting. He lay down on his back and begins to do some sort of sit-up.

"Excuse me, do either of you have cell phones that work?" Fell ventured.

Chin-up man barked out a laugh. "No one does," he said. "And I'll tell you something. That's a satellite station we're listening to. No DJ, all music. So the radiation isn't interfering with no waves."

It was what Fell expected, but she was disappointed. "Can you tell me the way to Steinway Street in Astoria?"

"Just keep going the way you're going and take a right on 39th Street," chin-up man said. "That'll take you over Sunnyside Yard. You cross Northern Boulevard and boom, you're there."

"You have a blessed day," newspaper guy said sternly, as if he knew she would disobey him and not have a blessed day.

"Thanks, you too," she said. Was that the right thing to say? It didn't sound right. The man's directions were excellent. Soon Fell was coasting along Steinway Street, lined with its familiar shops. A black car with TLC plates was speeding along the other way, and honked at her as he passed. The car was going so fast that a blowback breeze made Fell's hair stand up. The only moving car she had seen all day.

Fell turned off onto 25th Avenue and there was Soo Jin's building. More classy than her own, brick not aluminum siding. Now she was sick to her stomach with nervousness. If Soo Jin wasn't there, she had no Plan B.

She dismounted and leaned her bike against the fence of the building next door. There was a sign reading **NO BIKES!** but what were they going to do to her? She locked the bike, feeling extremely silly as she did so.

Fell walked up to Soo Jin's front door with its fancy glass paneling. The panel was an oval with three beveled triangles inside. Fell had never noticed that before. If she'd been on a witness stand, she'd have testified that it was rectangular. Was she losing her mind? Above the door was a stained glass transom depicting flowers. That looked more familiar. She and Soo Jin had argued about it. Fell thought it was elegant but Soo Jin said it was cheap, American-style crap.

Fell realized that she was standing in front of the door, staring at it. What was the matter with her?

She rang Soo Jin's bell and waited.

"Hello?" crackled Soo Jin's voice.

"It's me. Fell."

Soo Jin buzzed her in. As Fell pushed the door open, she heard a door slam upstairs and then feet pounding down the steps.

They both reached the bottom of the steps at the same time.

"I was just in the neighborhood," Fell joked. She lifted Soo Jin up off the bottom step and hugged her.

Another door opened. It must be Awilda, Soo Jin's landlady. She was stingy with the heat in the winter and often had complaints about noise, particularly the door slamming.

Fell didn't turn around, just kept hugging Soo Jin.

"Oh, it's you!" Awilda said. "If only I could be so lucky, and my Ernesto came back to me."

Fell didn't care about the widow Awilda's problems. She kissed Soo Jin and presently Awilda's door clicked shut again.

"Put me down," Soo Jin demanded, kicking her feet.

Fell did. Soo Jin led her upstairs and into her apartment, letting the door slam again. Just like in Fell's apartment, the first room you walked into was the kitchen.

Clothes, food and various items of electrical equipment were scattered all over the room. There were used matches and burnt paper all over the kitchen table. "What is all this?"

"I got worried," Soo Jin said. "I was packing up to go look for you."

"What's all this Radio Shack junk? You building a robot or something?"

"No, bozo, I had a few ideas about making the phone lines work." Soo Jin kissed Fell again. This time Fell got a hint of menthol from Soo Jin's Blistex.

"Oh, you're overheated, you poor thing," Soo Jin said, running her hands over Fell's forehead and the back of her neck.

Suddenly Soo Jin was crying. This unnerved Fell every time. She sat down on the rickety chair and pulled Soo Jin onto her lap.

"It's going to break," Soo Jin complained. "Where am I going to get a new chair under these circumstances?"

Fell brushed tears off Soo Jin's cheek with her thumb.

"I've been so upset thinking about my family," Soo Jin said.

"Really?" Soo Jin's parents lived in Korea. She hadn't been in touch with them in years. They had quarreled over Soo Jin's sexuality, lack of Christian beliefs, career aspirations, and anything else they ever discussed. Soo Jin hardly ever mentioned about them.

"Yes. I wish I could make things right with my parents. I've been writing messages and burning them all day. Do you think that my mother can somehow sense that I'm thinking of her? Do you think she understands how I feel?"

"I'm sure she does, Sooj," Fell lied. "She's probably thinking of you right now too. I expect she's thinking the same thing."

It was sort of alarming to hear Soo Jin talking woo woo spiritual garbage like this. Fell had nothing against that sort of thing, everyone should live the way they wanted to live. But it was really out of character for Soo Jin, her little cynic. She hoped Soo Jin wasn't cracking up.

Soo Jin let out a long, shuddering breath.

"Of course," she said. "That makes sense. I feel so much better talking to you. The version of you that's in my head is not as nice as the real thing. I'm not bonkers, you know. Burning the papers isn't literal, like smoke signals or something. It's supposed to be symbolic. I just thought there should be a ceremony for this unprecedented situation. I burnt messages to Hyun-ki too. I feel okay about him. I'm glad he doesn't have to go through this Book of Revelation-style crap."

Fell kissed her cheek. Hyun-ki was Sooj's little brother, who had died many years ago.

"Did you burn messages to me?" Fell asked.

"No, don't be silly!" Soo Jin said, and laughed. "I didn't have to do that. I knew you were coming."

Fell laughed too. This was more like it. How could she have thought Sooj would run off with the lingerie model?

"Then why were you packing up?"

"I panicked!" Soo Jin said. "I was sure today was the day you would decide to come and that you wouldn't leave any later than 3pm. So I had set a little deadline in my head, and you were half an hour late!"

"That was the Sunnyside Yards' fault!" Fell complained. "I would have been right on schedule, but I didn't know about them. It was in my way! How did you know when I would leave?"

"Oh, there's no mystery there. I know how your mind works. Don't get me wrong, it wasn't your job to come get me or anything. It's just I knew you would. It's the kind of thing you'd do. So it would have been stupid of me to go too. Oh, I don't suppose you got any word from your father?"

"I did talk to him right after the bombs fell," Fell said. "He sounded fine, he was going to stay with his poker buddy who lives in the same building. Kind of out of it, you know what he's like."

The chair made an ominous creaking sound. Soo Jin leaped up. Fell was glad, her legs had fallen asleep. Soo Jin was such light, but she could still squish you.

"Take off that sweatshirt," Sooj ordered. "You're all red, and you're burning up."

"No, it's freezing in here," Fell said. She stood up and immediately regretted it. First the room was swimming around. Then the room was still and only her head was swimming.

"Actually, I'm awfully tired from the ride," Fell said. "I think I'll take a little nap."

Soo Jin looked upset. "I don't know if I should let you sleep. You just got here. I want to spend some more time together."

"You can wake me up in half an hour," Fell suggested.

Soo Jin frowned. Then her face cleared. "Maybe I'll take a nap too. I don't feel that great either. Do you want some Nutella? I've been saving it for you."

Fell shook her head.

"Here, have some juice anyway."

Fell drained a glass of orange juice, which tasted terrible. Then she and Soo Jin lay down spoon-style in the dark bedroom. Soo Jin had some strings of Christmas lights up around the room and they looked pretty.

"We'll make love like bunnies when we wake up," she promised Soo Jin, putting an arm around her and petting her stomach.

"Good," said Soo Jin.

Fell was so terribly tired, but there was something important she was forgetting. What was it?

"Oh yeah!" she said. "Sooj, are you still awake? I have to tell you something important."

She felt Sooj tense up. "What?"

"I love you."

Soo Jin laughed. "That's all? I know. I mean, I love you too."

"It's just I never told you that before," Fell explained.

"I know! But it's fine. You're the strong, silent type." Soo Jin giggled again. "Not cheap with your words and all that."

"Fine. I won't tell you again."

Soo Jin kicked her. "Again! Tell me now!"

So Fell told her again. Then they did fall asleep.

The Effluent Engine

N. K. Jemisin

New Orleans stank to the heavens. This was either the water, which did not have the decency to confine itself to the river but instead puddled along every street; or the streets themselves, which seemed to have been cobbled with bricks of fired excrement. Or it may have come from the people who jostled and trotted along the narrow avenues, working and lounging and cursing and shouting and sweating, emitting a massed reek of unwashed resentment and perhaps a bit of hangover. As Jessaline strolled beneath the colonnaded balconies of Royal Street, she fought the urge to give up, put the whole fumid pile to her back, and catch the next dirigible out of town.

Then someone jostled her. "Pardon me, miss," said a voice at her elbow, and Jessaline was forced to stop, because the earnest-looking young man who stood there was white. He smiled, which did not surprise her, and doffed his hat, which did.

"Monsieur," Jessaline replied, in what she hoped was the correct mix of reserve and deference.

"A fine day, is it not?" The man's grin widened, so sincere that Jessaline could not help a small smile in response. "I must admit, though; I have yet to adjust to this abysmal heat. How are you handling it?"

"Quite well, monsieur," she replied, thinking, *What is it that you want from me?* "I am acclimated to it."

"Ah, yes, certainly. A fine negress like yourself would naturally deal better with such things. I am afraid my own ancestors derive from chillier climes, and we adapt poorly." He paused abruptly, a stricken look crossing his face. He was the florid kind, red haired and freckled with skin so pale that it revealed his every thought—in point of which he paled further. "Oh, dear! My sister warned me about this. You aren't Creole, are you? I understand they take it an insult to be called, er…by certain terms."

With some effort Jessaline managed not to snap, *Do I look like one of them?* But people on the street were beginning to stare, so instead she said, "No, monsieur. And it's clear to me you aren't from these parts, or you would never ask such a thing."

"Ah—yes." The man looked sheepish. "You have caught me out, miss; I'm from New York. Is it so obvious?"

Jessaline smiled carefully. "Only in your politeness, monsieur." She reached up to adjust her hat, lifting it for a moment as a badly-needed cooling breeze wafted past.

"Are you perhaps—" The man paused, staring at her head. "My word! You've naught but a scrim of hair!"

"I have sufficient to keep myself from drafts on cold days," she replied, and as she'd hoped, he laughed.

"You're a most charming ne—woman, my dear, and I feel honored to make your acquaintance." He stepped back and bowed, full and proper. "My name is Raymond Forstall."

"Jessaline Dumonde," she said, offering her lace-gloved hand, though she had no expectation that he would take it. To her surprise he did, bowing again over it.

"My apologies for gawking. I simply don't meet many of the coloured on a typical day, and I must say—" he hesitated, darted a look about, and at least had the grace to drop his voice. "You're remarkably lovely, even with no hair."

In spite of herself, Jessaline laughed. "Thank you, monsieur." After an appropriate and slightly awkward pause, she inclined her head. "Well, then; good day to you."

"Good day indeed," he said, in a tone of such pleasure that Jessaline hoped no one had heard it, for his sake. The folk of this town were particular about matters of propriety, as any society which relied so firmly upon class differences. While there were many ways in which a white gentleman could appropriately express his admiration for a woman of colour—the existence of the *gens de couleur libre* was testimony to that—all of those ways were simply Not Done in public.

But Forstall donned his hat, and Jessaline inclined her head in return before heading away. Another convenient breeze gusted by, and she took advantage of it to adjust her hat once more, in the process sliding her stiletto back into its hiding place amid the silk flowers.

This was the dance of things, the *cric-crac* as the storytellers said in Jessaline's land. Everyone needed something from someone. Glorious France needed money, to recover from the unlamented Napoleon's endless wars. Upstart Haiti had money from the sweet gold of its sugarcane fields, but needed guns—for all the world, it seemed, wanted the newborn country strangled in its crib. The United States had guns but craved sugar, as its fortunes were dependent upon the acquisition thereof. It alone was willing to treat with Haiti, though Haiti was the stuff of American nightmare: a nation of black slaves who had killed off their white masters. Yet Haitian sugar was no less sweet for its coating of blood, and so everyone got what they wanted, trading 'round and 'round, a graceful waltz—only occasionally devolving into a knife-fight.

It had been simplicity itself for Jessaline to slip into New Orleans. Dirigible travel in the Caribbean was inexpensive, and so many travelers regularly moved between the island nations and the great American port city that hardly any deception had been necessary. She was indentured, she told the captain, and he had waved her aboard without so much as a glance at her papers (which were false anyhow). She was a wealthy white man's mistress, she told the other passengers, and between her fine clothes, regal carriage, and beauty—despite her skin being purest sable in color—they believed her and were alternately awed and offended. She was a slave, she told the dockmaster on the levee; a trusted one, lettered and loyal, promised freedom should she continue to serve to her fullest. He had smirked at this, as if the notion of anyone freeing such an obviously valuable slave was ludicrous. Yet he, too, had let her pass unchallenged, without even charging her the disembarkation fee.

It had then taken two full months for Jessaline to make inquiries and sufficient contacts to arrange a meeting with the esteemed Monsieur Norbert Rillieux. The Creoles of New Orleans were a closed and prickly bunch, most likely because they had to be; only by the rigid maintenance of caste and privilege could they hope to retain freedom in a land which loved to throw anyone darker than tan into chains. Thus more than a few of them had refused to speak to Jessaline on sight. Yet there were many who had not forgotten that there but for the grace of God went their own fortune, so from these she had been able to glean crucial information and finally an introduction by letter. As she had mentioned the right names and observed the right etiquette, Norbert Rillieux had at last invited her to afternoon tea.

That day had come, and....

And. Rillieux, Jessaline was finally forced to concede, was an idiot.

"Monsieur," she said again, after drawing a breath to calm herself, "as I explained in my letter, I have no interest in sugarcane processing. It is true that your contributions to this field have been much appreciated by the interests I represent; your improved refining methods have saved both money and lives, which could both be reinvested in other places. What we require assistance with is a wholly different matter, albeit related."

"Oh," said Rillieux, blinking. He was a savagely thin-lipped man, with a hard stare that might have been compelling on a man who knew how to use it. Rillieux did not. "Your pardon, mademoiselle. But, er, who did you say you represented, again?"

"I did not say, monsieur. And if you will forgive me, I would prefer not to say for the time being." She fixed him with her own hard stare. "You will understand, I hope, that not all parties can be trusted when matters scientific turn to matters commercial."

At that, Rillieux's expression turned shrewd at last; he understood just fine. The year before, Jessaline's superiors had informed her, the plan Rillieux had proposed to the city—an ingenious means of draining its endless, pestilent swamps, for the health and betterment of all—had been turned down. Six months later, a coalition of city engineers had submitted virtually the same plan and been heaped with praise and funds to bring it about. The men of the coalition were white, of course. Jessaline marveled that Rillieux even bothered being upset about it.

"I see," Rillieux said. "Then, please forgive me, but I do not know what it is you want."

Jessaline stood and went to her brocaded bag, which sat on a side-table across the Rillieux house's elegantly-apportioned salon. In it was a small, rubber-stopped, peculiarly-shaped jar of the sort utilized by chemists, complete with engraved markings on its surface to indicate measurements of the liquid within. At the bottom of this jar swirled a scrim of dark brown, foul-looking paste and liquid. Jessaline brought it over to Rillieux and offered the jar to his nose, waiting until he nodded before she unstoppered it.

At the scent which wafted out, he stumbled back, gasping, his eyes all a-water. "By all that's holy! Woman, what is that putrescence?"

"That, Monsieur Rillieux, is effluent," Jessaline said, neatly stoppering the flask. "Waste, in other words, of a very particular kind. Do you drink rum?" She knew the answer already. On one side of the parlor was a beautifully made side table holding an impressive array of bottles.

"Of course." Rillieux was still rubbing his eyes and looking affronted. "I'm fond of a glass or two on hot afternoons; it opens the pores, or so I'm told. But what does that—"

"Producing rum is a simple process with a messy result: this effluent, namely, and the gas it emits, which until lately was regarded as simply the unavoidable price to be paid for your pleasant afternoons. Whole swaths of countryside are afflicted with this smell now as a result. Not only is the stench offensive to men and beasts, we have also found it to be as powerful as any tincture or laudanum; over time it causes anything exposed to suffocate and die. Yet there are scientific papers coming from Europe which laud this gas' potential as a fuel source. Captured properly, purified, and burned, it can power turbines, cook food, and more." Jessaline turned and set the flask on Rillieux's beverage stand, deliberately close to the square bottle of dark rum she had seen there. "We wish you to develop a process by which the usable gas— methane—may be extracted from the miasma you just smelled."

Rillieux stared at her for a moment, then at the flask. She could tell that he was intrigued, which meant that half her mission had been achieved already. Her superiors had spent a profligate amount of money requisitioning a set of those flasks from the German chemist who'd recently invented them, precisely with an eye towards impressing men like Rillieux, who looked down upon any science that did not show European roots.

Yet as Rillieux gazed at the flask, Jessaline was dismayed to see a look of consternation, then irritation, cross his face.

"I am an engineer, mademoiselle," he said at last, "not a chemist."

"We have already worked out the chemical means by which it might be done," Jessaline said quickly, her belly clenching in tension. "We would be happy to share that with you—"

"And then what?" He scowled at her. "Who will put the patent on this process, hmm? And who will profit?" He turned away, beginning to pace, and Jessaline could see that he was working up a good head of steam, to her horror. "You have a comely face, Mademoiselle Dumonde, and it does not escape me that dusky women such as yourself once seduced my forefathers into the most base acts, for which those men atoned by at least raising their half-breed children honorably. If I were a white man hoping to once more profit from the labor of an honest Creole like myself—one already proven gullible—I would send a woman like you to do the tempting. To them, all of us are alike, even though I have the purest of French blood in my veins, and you might as well have come straight from the jungles of Africa!"

He rounded on her at this, very nearly shouting, and if Jessaline had been one of the pampered, cowed women of this land, she might have stepped back in fear of unpleasantness. As it was, she did take a step—but to the side, closer to her brocade bag, within which was tucked a neat little derringer whose handle she could see from where she stood. Her mission had been to use Rillieux, not kill him, but she had no qualms about giving a man a flesh wound to remind him of the value of chivalry.

Before matters could come to a head, however, the parlor door opened, making both Jessaline and Norbert Rillieux jump. The young woman who came in was clearly some kin of Rillieux's; she had the same ocherine skin and loose-curled hair, the latter tucked into a graceful split chignon atop her head. Her eyes were softer, however, though that might have been an effect of the wire-rimmed spectacles perched atop her nose. She wore a simple gray dress, which had the unfortunate effect of emphasizing her natural pallor, and making her look rather plain.

"Your pardon, Brother," she said, confirming Jessaline's guess. "I thought perhaps you and your guest might like refreshment?" In her hands was a silver tray of crisp square beignets dusted in sugar, sliced merliton with what looked like some sort of remoulade sauce, and tiny wedges of pecan penuche.

At the sight of this girl, Norbert blanched and looked properly abashed. "Ah—er, yes, you're right, thank you. Ah—" He glanced at Jessaline, his earlier irritation clearly warring with the ingrained desire to be a good host; manners won, and he quickly composed himself. "Forgive me. Will you take refreshment, before you leave?" The last part of that sentence came out harder than the rest. Jessaline got the message.

"Thank you, yes," she said, immediately moving to assist the young woman. As she moved her brocade bag, she noticed the young woman's eyes, which were locked on the bag with a hint of alarm. Jessaline was struck at once with unease—had she noticed the derringer handle? Impossible to tell, since the young woman made no outcry of alarm, but that could have been just caution on her part. That one meeting of eyes had triggered an instant, instinctual assessment on Jessaline's part; *this* Rillieux, at least, was nowhere near as myopic or bombastic as her brother.

Indeed, as the young woman lifted her gaze after setting down the tray, Jessaline thought she saw a hint of challenge lurking behind those little round glasses, and above that perfectly pleasant smile.

"Brother," said the young woman, "won't you introduce me? It's so rare for you to have lady guests."

Norbert Rillieux went from blanching to blushing, and for an instant Jessaline feared he would progress all the way to bluster. Fortunately he mastered the urge and said, a bit stiffly, "Mademoiselle Jessaline Dumonde, may I present to you my younger sister, Eugenie?"

Jessaline bobbed a curtsy, which Mademoiselle Rillieux returned. "I'm pleased to meet you," Jessaline said, meaning it, *because I might have enjoyed shooting your brother to an unseemly degree, otherwise.*

It seemed Mademoiselle Rillieux's thoughts ran in the same direction, because she smiled at Jessaline and said, "I hope my brother hasn't been treating you to a display of his famous temper, Mademoiselle Dumonde. He deals better with his gadgets and vacuum tubes than people, I'm afraid."

Rillieux did bluster at this. "Eugenie, that's hardly—"

"Not at all," Jessaline interjected smoothly. "We were discussing the finer points of chemistry, and your brother, being such a learned man, just made his point rather emphatically."

"Chemistry? Why, I adore chemistry!" At this, Mademoiselle Rillieux immediately brightened, speaking faster and breathlessly. "What matter, if I may ask? Please, may I sit in?"

In that instant, Jessaline was struck by how lovely her eyes were, despite their uncertain coloring of browny-green. She had never preferred the looks of half-white folk, having grown up in a land where, thanks to the Revolution, darkness of skin was a point of pride. But as Mademoiselle Rillieux spoke of chemistry, something in her manner made her peculiar eyes sparkle, and Jessaline was forced to reassess her initial estimate of the girl's looks. She was handsome, perhaps, rather than plain.

"Eugenie is the only other member of my family to share my interest in the sciences," Rillieux said, pride warming his voice. "She could not study in Paris as I did; the schools there do not admit women. Still, I made certain to send her all of my books as I finished with them, and she critiques all of my prototypes. It's probably for the best that they wouldn't admit her; I daresay she could give my old masters at the *École Centrale* a run for their money!"

Jessaline blinked in surprise at this. Then it came to her; she had lost Rillieux's trust already. But perhaps....

Turning to the beverage stand, she picked up the flask of effluent. "I'm afraid I won't be able to stay, Mademoiselle Rillieux—but before I go, perhaps you could give me your opinion of this?" She offered the flask.

Norbert Rillieux, guessing her intent, scowled. But Eugenie took the flask before he could muster a protest, unstoppering it deftly and wafting the fumes toward her face rather than sniffing outright. "Faugh," she said, grimacing. "Definitely hydrogen sulfide, and probably a number of other gases too, if this is the product of some form of decay." She stoppered the flask and examined the sludge in its bottom with a critical eye. "Interesting—I thought it was dirt, but this seems to be some more uniform substance. Something made this? What process could generate something so noxious?"

"Rum distillation," Jessaline said, stifling the urge to smile when Eugenie looked scandalized.

"No wonder," Eugenie said darkly, "given what the end product does to men's souls." She handed the flask back to Jessaline. "What of it?"

So Jessaline was obliged to explain again. As she did, a curious thing happened; Eugenie's eyes grew a bit glazed. She nodded, "mmm-hmming" now and again. "And as I mentioned to your brother," Jessaline concluded, "we have already worked out the formula—"

"The formula is child's play," Eugenie said, flicking her fingers absently. "And the extraction would be simple enough, if methane weren't dangerously flammable. Explosive even, under certain conditions…which most attempts at extraction would inevitably create. Obviously any mechanical method would need to concern itself primarily with stabilizing the end products, not merely separating them. Freezing, perhaps, or—" She brightened. "Brother, perhaps we could try a refinement of the vacuum-distillation process you developed for—"

"Yes, yes," said Norbert, who had spent the past ten minutes looking from Jessaline to Eugenie and back, in visibly increasing consternation. "I'll consider it. In the meantime, Mademoiselle Dumonde was actually leaving; I'm afraid we delay her." He glared at Jessaline as Eugenie made a moue of dismay.

"Quite right," said Jessaline, smiling graciously at him. She put away the flask and tucked the bag over her arm, retrieving her hat from the back of the chair. She could afford to be gracious now, even though Norbert Rillieux had proven intractable. Better indeed to leave, and pursue the matter from an entirely different angle.

And, as Norbert escorted her to the parlor door with a hand rather too firm upon her elbow, Jessaline glanced back and smiled at Eugenie, who returned the smile with charming ruefulness and a shy little wave.

Not just handsome, pretty, Jessaline decided at last. And that meant this new angle would be *most enjoyable* to pursue.

❧

There were, however, complications.

Jessaline, pleased that she had succeeded in making contact with a Rillieux, if not the one she'd come for, treated herself to an evening out about the Vieux Carre. It was not the done thing for a lady of gentle breeding—as she was emulating—to stop in at any of the rollicking music halls she could hear down side streets, though she was intrigued. She could, however, sit in on one of the new-fangled vaudevilles at the Playhouse, which she quite enjoyed though it was difficult to see the stage well from rear balcony. Then, as nightfall finally brought a breath of cool relief from the day's sweltering humidity, she returned to her room at the inn.

From time spent on the harder streets of Port-au-Prince, it was Jessaline's longtime habit to stand to one side of a door while she unlocked it, so that her shadow under the door would not alert anyone inside. This proved wise, as pushing open the door she found herself facing a startled male figure, which froze in silhouette before the room's picture window, near her traveling-chest. They stared at one another for a breath, and then Jessaline's wits returned; at once she dropped to one knee and in a single smooth sweep of her hand, brushed up her booted leg to palm a throwing-knife.

In the same instant the figure bolted, darting toward the open balcony window. Jessaline hissed out a curse in her own Kreyòl tongue, running into the room as he lunged through the window with an acrobat's nimbleness, rolling to his feet and fetching up against the elaborately ironworked railing. Fearing to lose him, Jessaline flung the knife from within the room as she ran, praying it would strike, and heard the thunk as it struck flesh. The figure on her balcony stumbled, crying out—but she could not have hit a vital area, for he grasped the railing and pulled himself over it, dropping the short distance to the ground and out of sight.

Jessaline scrambled through the window as best she could, hampered by her bustle and skirts. Just as she reached the railing, the figure finished picking himself up from the ground and turned to run. Jessaline got one good look at him in the moonlight, as he turned back to see if she pursued: a pinch-faced youth, clearly pale beneath the bootblack he'd smeared on his face and straw-colored hair to help himself hide in the dark. Then he was gone, running into the night, though he ran oddly and kept one of his hands clapped to his right buttock.

Furious, Jessaline pounded the railing, though she knew better than to make an outcry. No one in this town would care that some black woman had been robbed, and the constable would as likely arrest her for disturbing the peace.

Going back into her room, she lit the lanterns and surveyed the damage. At once a chill passed down her spine. The chest held a number of valuables that any sensible thief would've taken: fine dresses; a cameo pendant with a face of carved obsidian; the brass gyroscope that an old lover, a dirigible-navigator, had given her; a pearl-beaded purse containing twenty dollars. These, however, had all been shoved rudely aside, and to Jessaline's horror, the chest's false bottom had been lifted, revealing the compartment underneath. There was nothing here but a bundle of clothing and a larger pouch, containing a far more substantial sum—but that had not been taken, either.

But Jessaline knew what *would* have been in there, if she had not taken them with her to see Rillieux: the scrolls which held the chemical formula for the methane extraction process, and the rudimentary designs for the mechanism to do so—the best her government's scientists had been able to cobble together. These were even now at the bottom of her brocade bag.

The bootblack-boy had been no thief. Someone in this foul city knew who and what she was, and sought to thwart her mission.

Carefully Jessaline replaced everything in the trunk, including the false bottom and money. She went downstairs and paid her bill, then hired a porter to carry her trunk to an inn two blocks over, where she rented a room without windows. She slept lightly that night, waking with every creak and thump of the place, and took comfort only from the solid security of the stiletto in her hand.

The lovely thing about a town full of slaves, vagabonds, beggars, and blackguards was that it was blessedly easy to send a message in secret.

Having waited a few days so as to let Norbert Rillieux's anger cool—just in case—Jessaline then hired a child who was one of the innkeepers' slaves. She purchased fresh fruit at the market and offered the child an apple to memorize her message. When he repeated it back to her word for word, she showed him a bunch of big blue-black grapes, and his eyes went wide. "Get word to Mademoiselle Eugenie without her brother knowing, and these are yours," she said. "You'll have to make sure to spit the seeds in the fire, though, or Master will know you've had a treat."

The boy grinned, and Jessaline saw that the warning had not been necessary. "Just you hold onto those, Miss Jessaline," he said back, pointing with his chin at the grapes. "I'll have 'em in a minute or three." And indeed, within an hour's time he returned, carrying a small folded square of cloth. "Miss Eugenie agrees to meet," he said, "and sends this as a surety of her good faith." He pronounced this last carefully, perfectly emulating the Creole woman's tone.

Pleased, Jessaline took the cloth and unfolded it to find a handkerchief of fine imported French linen, embroidered in one corner with a tiny perfect "R." She held it to her nose and smelled a perfume like magnolia blossoms; the same scent had been about Eugenie the other day. She could not help smiling at the memory. The boy grinned too, and ate a handful of the grapes at once, pocketing the seeds with a wink.

"Gonna plant these near the city dump," he said. "Maybe I'll bring you wine one day!" And he ran off.

❧

So Jessaline found herself on another bright, sweltering day at the convent of the Ursulines, where two gentlewomen might walk and exchange thoughts in peace without being seen or interrupted by curious others.

"I have to admit," said Eugenie, smiling sidelong at Jessaline as they strolled amid the nuns' garden, "I was of two minds about whether to meet you."

"I suppose your brother must've given you an earful after I left."

"You might say so," Eugenie said, in a dry tone that made Jessaline laugh. (One of the old nuns glowered at them over a bed of herbs. Jessaline covered her mouth and waved apology.) "But that wasn't what gave me pause. My brother has his ways, Mademoiselle Jessaline, and I do not always agree with him. He's fond of forming opinions without full information, then proceeding as if they are proven fact." She shrugged. "I, on the other hand, prefer to seek as much information as I can. I have made inquiries about you, you see."

"Oh? And what did you find?"

"That you do not exist, as far as anyone in this town knows." She spoke lightly, Jessaline noticed, but there was an edge to her words, too. Unease, perhaps. "You aren't one of us, that much anyone can see; but you aren't a freedwoman either, though the people at your old inn and the market seemed to think so."

At this, Jessaline blinked in surprise and unease of her own. She had not thought the girl would dig that deeply. "What makes you say that?"

"For one, that pistol in your bag."

Jessaline froze for a pace before remembering to keep walking. "A lady alone in a strange, rough city would be wise to look to her own protection, don't you think?"

"True," said Eugenie, "but I checked at the courthouse too, and there are no records of a woman meeting your description having bought her way free anytime in the past thirty years, and I doubt you're far past that age. For another, you hide it well, but your French has an odd sort of lilt; not at all like that of folk hereabouts. And for thirdly—this is a small town at heart, Mademoiselle Dumonde, despite its size. Every time some fortunate soul buys free, as they say, it's the talk of the town. To put it bluntly, there's no gossip about you, and there should have been."

They had reached a massive old willow tree which partially overhung the garden path. There was no way around it; the tree's draping branches had made a proper curtain of things, nearly obscuring from sight the area about the trunk.

The sensible thing to do would have been to turn around and walk back the way they'd come. But as Jessaline turned to meet Eugenie's eyes, she suffered another of those curious epiphanies. Eugenie was smiling, sweet, but despite this there was a hard look in her eyes, which reminded Jessaline fleetingly of Norbert. It was clear that she meant to have the truth from Jessaline, or Jessaline's efforts to employ her would get short shrift.

So on impulse Jessaline grabbed Eugenie's hand and pulled her into the willow-fall. Eugenie yelped in surprise, then giggled as they came through into the space beyond, green-shrouded and encircling, like a hurricane of leaves.

"What on earth—? Mademoiselle Dumonde—"

"It isn't Dumonde," Jessaline said, dropping her voice to a near-whisper. "My name is Jessaline Cleré. That is the name of the family that raised me, at least, but I should have had a different name, after the man who was my true father. His name was L'Ouverture. Do you know it?"

At that, Eugenie drew a sharp breath. "Toussaint the Rebel?" she asked. "The man who led the revolution in Haiti? *That* was your father?"

"So my mother says, though she was only his mistress; I am natural-born. But I do not begrudge her, because her status spared me. When the French betrayed Toussaint, they took him and his wife and legitimate children and carried them across the sea to torture to death."

Eugenie put her hands to her mouth at this, which Jessaline had to admit was a bit much for a gently-raised woman to bear. Yet it was the truth, for Jessaline felt uncomfortable dissembling with Eugenie, for reasons she could not quite name.

"I see," Eugenie said at last, recovering. "Then—these interests you represent. You are with the Haitians."

"I am. If you build a methane extraction mechanism for us, Mademoiselle, you will have helped a nation of free folk *stay* free, for I swear that France is hell-bent upon re-enslaving us all. They would have done it already, if one of our number had not thought to use our torment to our advantage."

Eugenie nodded slowly. "The sugarcane," she said. "The papers say your people use the steam and gases from the distilleries to make hot-air balloons and blimps."

"Which helped us bomb the French ships most effectively during the Revolution, and also secured our position as the foremost manufacturers of dirigibles in the Americas," Jessaline said, with a bit of pride. "We were saved by a mad idea and a contraption that should have killed its first user. So we value cleverness now, Mademoiselle, which is why I came here in search of your brother."

"Then—" Eugenie frowned. "The methane. It is to power your dirigibles?"

"Partly. The French have begun using dirigibles too, you see. Our only hope is to enhance the maneuverability and speed of our craft, which can be done with gas-powered engines. We have also crafted powerful artillery which use this engine design, whose range and accuracy is unsurpassed. The prototypes work magnificently—but the price of the oil and coal we must currently use to power them is too dear. We would bankrupt ourselves buying it from the very nations that hope to destroy us. The rum effluent is our only abundant, inexpensive resource...our only hope."

But Eugenie had begun to shake her head, looking taken aback. "Artillery? *Guns*, you mean?" she said. "I am a Christian woman, Mademoiselle—"

"Jessaline."

"Very well; Jessaline." That look was in her face again, Jessaline noted; that air of determination and fierceness that made her beautiful at the oddest times. "I do not care for the idea of my skills being put to use in taking lives. That's simply unacceptable."

Jessaline stared at her, and for an instant fury blotted out thought. How dare this girl, with her privilege and wealth and coddled life.... Jessaline set her jaw.

"In the Revolution," she said, in a low tight voice, "the last French commander, Rochambeau, decided to teach my people a lesson for daring to revolt against our betters. Do you know what he did? He took slaves—including those who had not even fought—and broke them on the wheel, raising them on a post afterwards so the birds could eat them alive. He buried prisoners of war, also alive, in pits of insects. He *boiled* some of them, in vats of molasses. Such acts, he deemed, were necessary to put fear and subservience back into our hearts, since we had been tainted by a year of freedom."

Eugenie, who had gone quite pale, stared at Jessaline in purest horror, her mouth open. Jessaline smiled a hard, angry smile. "Such atrocities will happen again, Mademoiselle Rillieux, if you do not help us. Except this time we have been free for two generations. Imagine how much fear and subservience these *Christian* men will instill in us now?"

Eugenie shook her head slowly. "I…I had not heard…. I did not consider…." She fell mute.

Jessaline stepped closer and laid one lace-gloved finger on the divot between Eugenie's collarbones. "You had best consider such things, my dear. Do you forget? There are those in this land who would like to do the same to you and all your kin."

Eugenie stared at her. Then, startling Jessaline, she dropped to the ground, sitting down so hard that her bustle made an aggrieved creaking sound.

"I did not know," she said at last. "I did not know these things."

Jessaline beheld the honest shock on her face and felt some guilt for having troubled her so. It was clear the girl's brother had worked hard to protect her from the world's harshness. Sitting beside Eugenie on the soft dry grass, she let out a weary sigh.

"In my land," she said, "men and women of *all* shades are free. I will not pretend that this makes us perfect; I have gone hungry many times in my life. Yet there, a woman such as yourself may be more than the coddled sister of a prominent scientist, or the mistress of a white man."

Eugenie threw her a guilty look, but Jessaline smiled to reassure her. The women of Eugenie's class had few options in life; Jessaline saw no point in condemning them for this.

"So many men died in the Revolution that women fill the ranks now as dirigible-pilots and gunners. We run factories and farms too, and are highly-placed in government. Even the houngans are mostly women now—you have vodoun here too, yes? So we are important." She leaned close, her shoulder brushing Eugenie's in a teasing way, and grinned. "Some of us might even become spies. Who knows?"

Eugenie's cheeks flamed pink and she ducked her head to smile. Jessaline could see, however, that her words were having some effect; Eugenie had that oddly absent look again. Perhaps she was imagining all the things she could do in a land where the happenstances of sex and caste did not forbid her from using her mind to its fullest? A shame; Jessaline would have loved to take her there. But she had seen the luxury of the Rillieux household; why would any woman give that up?

This close, shoulder to shoulder and secluded within the willow tree's green canopy, Jessaline found herself staring at Eugenie, more aware than ever of the scent of her perfume, and the nearby softness of her skin, and the way the curls of her hair framed her long slender neck. At least she did not cover her hair like so many women of this land, convinced that its natural state was inherently ugly. She could not help her circumstances, but it seemed to Jessaline that she had taken what pride in her heritage that she could.

So taken was Jessaline by this notion, and by the silence and strangeness of the moment, that she found herself saying, "And in my land it is not uncommon for a woman to head a family with another woman, and even raise children if they so wish."

Eugenie started—and to Jessaline's delight, her blush deepened. She darted a half-scandalized, half-entranced look at Jessaline, then away, which Jessaline found deliciously fetching. "Live with—another woman? Do you mean—?" But of course she knew what Jessaline meant. "How can that be?"

"The necessities of security and shared labor. The priests look the other way."

Eugenie looked up then, and Jessaline was surprised to see a peculiar daring enter her expression, though her flush lingered. "And…."

She licked her lips, swallowed. "Do such women...ah...behave as a family in...*all* matters?"

A slow grin spread across Jessaline's face. *Not so sheltered in her thoughts at least, this one!* "Oh, certainly. All matters—legal, financial, domestic...." Then, as a hint of uncertainty flickered in Eugenie's expression, Jessaline got tired of teasing. It was not proper, she knew; it was not within the bounds of her mission. But—just this once—perhaps—

She shifted just a little, from brushing shoulders to pressing rather more suggestively close, and leaned near, her eyes fixed on Eugenie's lips. "And conjugal," she added.

Eugenie stared at her, eyes huge behind the spectacles. "C-conjugal?" she asked, rather breathlessly.

"Oh, indeed. Perhaps a demonstration...."

But just as Jessaline leaned in to offer just that, she was startled by the voice of one of the nuns, apparently calling to another in French. From far too near the willow tree, a third voice rose to shush the first two—the prying old biddy who'd given Jessaline the eye before.

Eugenie jumped, her face red as plums, and quickly shifted away from Jessaline. Privately cursing, Jessaline did the same, and an awkward silence fell.

"W-well," said Eugenie, "I had best be getting back. I told my brother I would be at the seamstress', and that doesn't take long."

"Yes," Jessaline said, realizing with some consternation that she'd completely forgotten why she'd asked for a meeting in the first place. "Well. Ah. I have something I'd like to offer you—but I would advise you to keep these out of sight, even at home where servants might see. For your own safety." She reached into the brocade bag and handed Eugenie the small cylindrical leather container that held the formula and plans for the methane extractor. "This is what we have come up with thus far, but the design is incomplete. If you can offer any assistance—"

"Yes, of course," Eugenie said, taking the case with an avid look that heartened Jessaline at once. She tucked the leather case into her purse. "Allow me a few days to consider the problem. How may I contact you, though, once I've devised a solution?"

"I will contact you in one week. Do not look for me." She got to her feet and offered her hand to help Eugenie up. Then, speaking loudly enough to be heard outside the willow at last, she giggled. "Before your brother learns we've been swapping tales about him!"

Eugenie looked blank for a moment, then opened her mouth in an "o" of understanding, grinning. "Oh, his ego could use a bit of flattening, I think. In any case, fare you well, Mademoiselle Dumonde. I must be on my way." And with that, she hurried off, holding her hat as she passed through the willow branches.

Jessaline waited for ten breaths, then stepped out herself, sparing a hard look for the old nun—who, sure enough, had moved quite a bit closer to the tree. "A good afternoon to you, Sister," she said.

"And to you," the woman said in a low voice, "though you had best be more careful from now on, *estipid*."

Startled to hear her own tongue on the old woman's lips, she stiffened. Then, carefully, she said in the same language, "And what would you know of it?"

"I know you have a dangerous enemy," the nun replied, getting to her feet and dusting dirt off her habit. Now that Jessaline could see her better, it was clear from her features that she had a dollop or two of African in her. "I am sent by your superiors to warn you. We have word the Order of the White Camellia is active in the city."

Jessaline caught her breath. The bootblack man! "I may have encountered them already," she said.

The old woman nodded grimly. "Word had it they broke apart after that scandal we arranged for them up in Baton Rouge," she said, "but in truth they've just gotten more subtle. We don't know what they're after, but obviously they don't just want to kill you, or you would be dead by now."

"I am not so easily removed, madame," Jessaline said, drawing herself up in affront.

The old woman rolled her eyes. "Just take care," she snapped. "And by all means, if you want that girl dead, continue playing silly lovers' games with her where any fool can suspect." And with that, the old woman picked up her spade and shears, and walked briskly away.

Jessaline did too, her cheeks burning. But back in her room, ostensibly safe, she leaned against the door and closed her eyes, wondering why her heart still fluttered so fast now that Eugenie was long gone, and why she was suddenly so afraid.

❧

The Order of the White Camellia changed everything. Jessaline had heard tales of them for years, of course—a secret society of wealthy professionals and intellectuals dedicated to the preservation of "American ideals" like the superiority of the white race. They had been responsible for the exposure—and deaths, in some cases—of many of Jessaline's fellow spies over the years. America was built on slavery; naturally, the White Camellias would oppose a nation built on slavery's overthrow.

So Jessaline decided on new tactics. She shifted her attire from that of a well-to-do freedwoman to the plainer garb of a woman of less means. This elicited no attention as there were plenty such women in the city—though she was obliged to move to yet another inn that would suit her appearance. This drew her well into the less-respectable area of the city, where not a few of the patrons took rooms by the hour or the half-day.

Here she laid low for the next few days, trying to determine whether she was being watched, though she spotted no suspicious characters—or at least, no one suspicious for the area. Which, of course, was why she'd chosen it. White men frequented the inn, but a white face that lingered or appeared repeatedly would be remarked upon, and easy to spot.

When a week had passed and Jessaline felt safe, she radically transformed herself using the bundle that had been hidden beneath her chest's false bottom. First she hid her close-cropped hair beneath a lumpy calico headwrap, and donned an ill-fitting dress of worn, stained gingham patched here and there with burlap. A few small pillows rendered her effectively shapeless—a necessity, since in this disguise it was dangerous to be attractive in any way. As she slipped out in the small hours of the morning, carrying her belongings in a satchel and shuffling to make herself look much older, no one paid her any heed—not the drowsy old men sitting guard at the stables, nor the city constables chatting up a gaudily-dressed woman under a gaslamp, nor the young toughs still dicing on the corner. She was, for all intents and purposes, invisible.

So first she milled among the morning-market crowds at the waterfront awhile, keeping an eye out for observers. When she was certain she had not been followed, she made her way to the dirigible docks, where four of the great machines hovered above a cluster of cargo vessels like huge, sausage-shaped guardian angels. A massive brick fence screened the docks themselves from view, though this had a secondary purpose: the docks were the sovereign territory of the Haitian Republic, housing its embassy as well. No American-born slave was permitted to step upon even this proxy version of Haitian soil, since by the laws of Haiti they would then be free.

Yet practicality did not stop men and women from dreaming, and near the massive ironwork gate of the facility there was as usual a small crowd of slaves gathered, gazing enviously in at the shouting dirigible crews and their smartly-dressed officers. Jessaline slipped in among these and edged her way to the front, then waited.

Presently, a young runner detached herself from the nearby rope crew and ran over to the fence. Several of the slaves pushed envelopes through the fence, commissioning travel and shipping on behalf of their owners, and the girl collected these. The whole operation was conducted in utter silence; an American soldier hovered all too near the gate, ready to report any slave who talked. (It was not illegal to talk, but any slave who did so would likely suffer for it.)

Yet Jessaline noted that the runner met the eyes of every person she could, nodding to each solemnly, touching more hands than was strictly necessary for the sake of her work. A small taste of respect for those who needed it so badly, so that they might come to crave it and eventually seek it for themselves.

Jessaline met the runner's eyes too as she pushed through a plain, wrinkled envelope, but her gaze held none of the desperate hope of the others. The runner's eyes widened a bit, but she moved on at once after taking Jessaline's envelope. When she trotted away to deliver the commissions, Jessaline saw her shuffle the pile to put the wrinkled envelope on top.

That done, Jessaline headed then to the Rillieux house. At the back gate she shifted her satchel from her shoulder to her hands, re-tying it so as to make it square-shaped. To the servant who then answered her knock—freeborn; the Rillieuxs did not go in for the practice of owning slaves themselves—she said in coarse French, "Package for Mademoiselle Rillieux. I was told to deliver it to her personal."

The servant, a cleanly-dressed fellow who could barely conceal his distaste at Jessaline's appearance, frowned further. "*English*, woman, only high-class folk talk French here." But when Jessaline deliberately spoke in butchered English, rendered barely comprehensible by an exaggerated French accent, the man finally rolled his eyes and stood aside. "She's in the garden house. Back there. There!" And he pointed the way.

Thus did Jessaline come to the overlarge shed that sat amid the house's vast garden. It had clearly been meant to serve as a hothouse at some point, having a glass ceiling, but when Jessaline stepped inside she was assailed by sounds most unnatural: clanks and squealing and the rattling hiss of a steam boiler. These came from the equipment and incomprehensible machinery that lined every wall and hung from the ceiling, pipes and clockworks big enough to crush a man, all of it churning merrily away.

At the center of this chaos stood several high worktables, each bearing equipment in various states of construction or dismantlement, save the last. At this table, which sat in a shaft of gathering sunlight, sat a sleeping Eugenie Rillieux.

At the sight of her, Jessaline stopped, momentarily overcome by a most uncharacteristic anxiety. Eugenie's head rested on her folded arms, atop a sheaf of large, irregular sheets of parchment that were practically covered with pen-scribbles and diagrams. Her hair was amuss, her glasses askew, and she had drooled a bit onto one of her pale, ink-stained hands.

Beautiful, Jessaline thought, and marveled at herself. Her tastes had never leaned towards women like Eugenie, pampered and sheltered and shy. She generally preferred women like herself, who could be counted upon to know what they wanted and take decisive steps to get it. Yet in that moment, gazing upon this awkward, brilliant creature, Jessaline wanted nothing more than to be holding flowers instead of a fake package, and to have come for courting rather than her own selfish motives.

Perhaps Eugenie felt the weight of her longing, for after a moment she wrinkled her nose and sat up. "Oh," she said blearily, seeing Jessaline. "What is it, a delivery? Put it on the table there, please; I'll fetch you a tip." She got up, and Jessaline was amused to see that her bustle was askew.

"Eugenie," she said, and Eugenie whirled back as she recognized Jessaline's voice. Her eyes flew wide.

"What in heaven's name—"

"I haven't much time," she said, hastening forward. She took Eugenie's hands in quick greeting, and resisted the urge to kiss her as well. "Have you been able to refine the plans?"

"Oh—yes, yes, I think." Eugenie pushed her glasses straight and gestured toward the papers that had served as her pillow. "This design should work, at least in theory. I was right; the vacuum-distillation mechanism was the key! Of course, I haven't finished the prototype, because the damned glassmaker is trying to charge pirates' rates—"

Jessaline squeezed her hands, exhilarated. "Marvelous! Don't worry; we shall test the design thoroughly before we put it into use. But now I must have the plans. Men are searching for me; I don't dare stay in town much longer."

Eugenie nodded absently, then blinked again as her head cleared. She narrowed her eyes at Jessaline in sudden suspicion. "Wait," she said. "You're leaving town?"

"Yes, of course," Jessaline said, surprised. "This is what I came for, after all. I can't just put something so important on the next dirigible packet—"

The look of hurt that came over Eugenie's face sent a needle straight into Jessaline's heart. She realized, belatedly and with guilty dismay, what Eugenie must have been imagining all this time.

"But...I thought...." Eugenie looked away suddenly, and bit her lower lip. "You might stay."

"Eugenie," Jessaline began, uncomfortably. "I...could never have remained here. This place...the way you live here...."

"Yes, I know." At once Eugenie's voice hardened; she glared at Jessaline. "In your perfect, wonderful land, everyone is free to live as they please. It is the rest of us, then, the poor wretched folk you scorn and pity, who have no choice but to endure it. Perhaps we should never bother to love at all, then! That way, at least, when we are used and cast aside, it will at least be for material gain!"

And with that, she slapped Jessaline smartly, and walked out. Stunned, Jessaline put a hand to her cheek and stared after her.

"Trouble in paradise?" said a voice behind her, in a syrupy drawl.

Jessaline whirled to find herself facing a six-shooter. And holding it, his face free of bootblack this time, was the young man who had invaded her quarters nearly two weeks before.

"I heard you Haitians were unnatural," he said, coming into the light, "but this? Not at all what I was expecting."

Not me, Jessaline realized, too late. *They were watching Rillieux, not me!* "Natural is in the eye of the beholder, as is beauty," she snapped.

"True. Speaking of beauty, though, you looked a damn sight finer before. What's all this?" He sidled forward, poking with the gun at the padding 'round Jessaline's middle. "So that's it! But—" He raised the gun, to Jessaline's fury, and poked at her breasts none-too-gently. "Ah, no padding *here*. Yes, I do remember you rightly." He scowled. "I still can't sit down thanks to you, woman. Maybe I ought to repay you that."

Jessaline raised her hands slowly, pulling off her lumpy headwrap so he could see her more clearly. "That's ungentlemanly of you, I would say."

"Gentlemen need gentle*women*," he said. "Your kind are hardly that, being good for only one thing. Well—that and lynching, I suppose.

But we'll save both for later, won't we? After you've met my superior and told us everything that's in your nappy little head. He's partial to your variety. I, however, feel that if I must lower myself to baseness, better to do it with one bearing the fair blood of the French."

It took Jessaline a moment to understand through all his airs. But then she did, and shivered in purest rage. "You will not lay a finger upon Eugenie. I'll snap them all off fir—"

But before she could finish her threat, there was a scream and commotion from the house. The scream, amid all the chaos of shouting and running servants, she recognized at once: Eugenie.

The noise startled the bootblack man as well. Fortunately he did not pull the trigger; he did start badly, however, half-turning to point the gun in the direction of Eugenie's scream. Which was all the opening that Jessaline needed, as she drew her derringer from the wadded cloth of the headwrap and shot the man point-blank. The bootblack man cried out, clutching his chest and falling to the ground.

The derringer was spent; it carried only a single bullet. Snatching up the bootblack man's sixgun instead, Jessaline turned to sprint toward the Rillieux house—then froze for an instant in terrible indecision. Behind her, on Eugenie's table, sat the plans for which she had spent the past three months of her life striving and stealing and sneaking. The methane extractor could be the salvation of her nation, the start of its brightest future.

And in the house—

Eugenie, she thought.

And started running.

❧

In the parlor, Norbert Rillieux was frozen, paler than usual and trembling. Before him, holding Eugenie about the throat and with a gun to her head, was a white man whose face was so floridly familiar that Jessaline gasped. "Raymond Forstall?"

He started badly as Jessaline rounded the door, and she froze as well, fearing to cause Eugenie's death. Very slowly she set the sixgun on a nearby sideboard, pushed it so that it slid out of easy reach, and raised her hands to show that she was no threat. At this, Forstall relaxed.

"So we meet again, my beauteous negress," he said, though there was anger in his smile. "I had hoped to make your acquaintance under more favorable circumstances. Alas."

"*You* are with the White Camellia?" He had seemed so gormless that day on Royal Street; not at all the sort Jessaline would associate with a murderous secret society.

"I am indeed," he said. "And you would have met the rest of us if my assistant had not clearly failed in his goal of taking you captive. Nevertheless, I too have a goal, and I ask again, sir, *where are the plans?*"

Jessaline realized belatedly that this was directed at Norbert Rillieux. And he, too frightened to bluster, just shook his head. "I told you, I have built no such device! Ask this woman—she wanted it, and I refused her!"

The methane extractor, Jessaline realized. Of course—they had known, probably via their own spies, that she was after it. Forstall had been tailing her the day he'd bumped into her, probably all the way to Rillieux's house; she cursed herself for a fool for not realizing. But the White Camellias were mostly philosophers and bankers and lawyers, not the trained, proficient spies she'd been expecting to deal with. It had never occurred to her that an enemy would be so clumsy as to jostle and *converse with* his target in the course of surveillance.

"It's true," Jessaline said, stalling desperately in hopes that some solution would present itself to her. "This man refused my request to build the device."

"Then why did you come back here?" Forstall asked, tightening his grip on Eugenie so that she gasped. "We had men watching the house servants, too. We intercepted orders for metal parts and rubber tubing, and I paid the glasssmith to delay an order for custom vacuum-pipes—"

"*You* did that?" To Jessaline's horror, Eugenie stiffened in Forstall's grasp, trying to turn and glare at him in her affront. "I argued with that old fool for an hour!"

"Eugenie, be still!" cried Norbert, which raised him high in Jessaline's estimation; she had wanted to shout the same thing.

"I will not—" Eugenie began to struggle, plainly furious. As Forstall cursed and tried to restrain her, Jessaline heard Eugenie's protests continue. "—interference with my work—very idea—"

Please, Holy Mother, Jessaline thought, taking a very careful step closer to the gun on the sideboard, *don't let him shoot her to shut her up.*

When Forstall finally thrust Eugenie aside-she fell against the bottle-strewn side table, nearly toppling it—and indeed raised the gun to shoot her, Jessaline blurted, "Wait!"

Both Forstall and Eugenie froze, now separated and facing each other, though Forstall's gun was still pointed dead at Eugenie's chest. "The plans are complete," Jessaline said to him. "They are in the workshop out back." With a hint of pride, she looked at Eugenie and added, "Eugenie has made it work."

"What?" said Rillieux, looking thunderstruck.

"What?" Forstall stared at her, then Eugenie, and then anger filled his expression. "Clever, indeed! And while I go out back to check if your story is true, you will make your escape with the plans already tucked into your clothes."

"I am not lying in this instance," she said, "but if you like, we can all proceed to the garden and see. Or, since I'm the one you seem to fear most—" She waggled her empty hands in mockery, hoping this would make him too angry to notice how much closer she was to the gun on the sideboard. His face reddened further with fury. "You could leave Eugenie and her brother here, and take me alone."

Eugenie caught her breath. "Jessaline, are you mad?"

"Yes," Jessaline said, and smiled, letting her heart live in her face for a moment. Eugenie's mouth fell open, then softened into a small smile. Her glasses were still askew, Jessaline saw with a rush of fondness.

Forstall rolled his eyes, but smiled. "A capital suggestion, I think. Then I can shoot you—"

He got no further, for in the next instant Eugenie suddenly struck him in the head with a rum-bottle.

The bottle shattered on impact. Forstall cried out, half-stunned by the blow and the sting of rum in his eyes, but he managed to keep his grip on the gun, and keep it trained more or less on Eugenie. Jessaline thought she saw the muscles in his forearm flex to pull the trigger—

—and then the sixgun was in her hand, its wooden grip warm and almost comforting as she blew a hole in Raymond Forstall's rum-drenched head. Forstall uttered a horrid gurgling sound and fell to the floor.

Before his body stopped twitching, Jessaline caught Eugenie's hand. "Hurry!" She dragged the other woman out of the parlor. Norbert, again to his credit, started out of shock and trotted after them, for once silent as they moved through the house's corridors toward the garden. The house was nearly deserted now, the servants having fled or found some place to hide that was safe from gunshots and madmen.

"You must tell me which of the papers on your desk I can take," Jessaline said as they trotted along, "and then you must make a decision."

"Wh-what decision?" Eugenie still sounded shaken.

"Whether you will stay here, or whether you will come with me to Haiti."

"*Haiti*?" Norbert cried.

"Haiti?" Eugenie asked, in wonder.

"Haiti," said Jessaline, and as they passed through the rear door and went into the garden, she stopped and turned to Eugenie. "With me."

Eugenie stared at her in such dawning amazement that Jessaline could no longer help herself. She caught Eugenie about the waist, pulled her near, and kissed her most soundly and improperly, right there in front of her brother. It was the sweetest, wildest kiss she had ever known in her life.

When she pulled back, Norbert was standing at the edge of her vision with his mouth open, and Eugenie looked a bit faint. "Well," Eugenie said, and fell silent, the whole affair having been a bit much for her.

Jessaline grinned and let her go, then hurried forward to enter the workshop—and froze, horror shattering her good mood.

The bootblack man was gone. Where his body had been lay Jessaline's derringer and copious blood, trailing away…to Eugenie's worktable, where the plans had been, and were no longer. The trail then led away, out the workshop's rear door.

"No," she whispered, her fists clenching at her sides. "No, by God!" Everything she had worked for, gone. She had failed, both her mission and her people.

"Very well," Eugenie said after a moment. "Then I shall simply have to come with you."

The words penetrated Jessaline's despair slowly. "What?"

She touched Jessaline's hand. "I will come with you. To Haiti. And I will build an even more efficient methane extractor for you there."

Jessaline turned to stare at her and found that she could not, for her eyes had filled with tears.

"Wait—" Norbert caught his breath as understanding dawned. "Go to Haiti? Are you mad? I forbid—"

"You had better come too, brother," Eugenie said, turning to him, and Jessaline was struck breathless once more by the cool determination in her eyes. "The police will take their time about it, but they'll come eventually, and a white man lies dead in our house. It doesn't really matter whether you shot him or not; you know full well what they'll decide."

And Norbert stiffened, for he did indeed know—probably better than Eugenie, Jessaline suspected—what his fate would be.

Eugenie turned to Jessaline. "He *can* come, can't he?" By which Jessaline knew it was a condition, not an option.

"Of course he can," she said at once. "I wouldn't leave a dog to these people's justice. But it will not be the life you're used to, either of you. Are you certain?"

Eugenie smiled, and before Jessaline realized what was imminent, she had been pulled rather roughly into another kiss. Eugenie had been eating penuche again, she realized dimly, and then for a long perfect moment she thought of nothing but pecans and sweetness.

When it was done, Eugenie searched Jessaline's face and then smiled in satisfaction. "Perhaps we should go, Jessaline," she said gently.

"Ah. Yes. We should, yes." Jessaline fought to compose herself; she glanced at Norbert and took a deep breath. "Fetch us a hansom cab while you still can, Monsieur Rillieux, and we'll go down to the docks and take the next dirigible southbound."

The daze cleared from Norbert's eyes as well; he nodded mutely and trotted off.

In the silence that fell, Eugenie turned to Jessaline.

"Marriage," she said, "and a house together. I believe you mentioned that?"

"Er," said Jessaline, blinking. "Well, yes, I suppose, but I rather thought that first we would—"

"Good," Eugenie replied, "because I'm not fond of you keeping up this dangerous line of work. My inventions should certainly earn enough for the both of us, don't you think?"

"Um," said Jessaline.

"Yes. So there's no reason for you to work when I can keep you in comfort for the rest of our days." Taking Jessaline's hands, she stepped closer, her eyes going soft again. "And I am so very much looking forward to those days, Jessaline."

"Yes," said Jessaline, who had been wondering just which of her many sins had earned her this mad fortune. But as Eugenie's warm breast pressed against hers, and the thick perfume of the magnolia trees wafted around them, and some clockwork contraption within the workshop ticked in time with her heart…Jessaline stopped worrying. And she wondered why she had ever bothered with plans and papers and gadgetry, because it was clear she had just stolen the greatest prize of all.

∾

The Storytellers

STEVE BERMAN has written many pieces of queer speculative fiction. His story in this volume was inspired by taking his mother to the ballet. He hopes that women reading this story realize that they can fulfill their heart without chasing after princes or crowns.

❧

GEORGINA BRUCE hates writing her author biography, and usually ends up writing something incredibly pretentious and quirky that in no way reflects her real personality. In real life, she is not the least bit quirky. If she had to sum herself up in one word, it would probably be "grumpy." Or "fat." If she were an animal, she would be a dog. If she were a piece of cutlery, she would be a knife. She thinks this should tell you all you really need to know about her.

Georgina has been writing since forever, but has only recently started to get good at it. There was a brief detour into screenwriting which messed with her head and gave her delusions of grandeur, but which also taught her a lot about how to tell a story. Her favourite kind of stories to write are about worlds within worlds and stories inside stories.

The things she has done for money include cleaning, cooking, selling double glazing, audio typing, bookselling and bellydancing. She has lived and worked in Japan, Egypt, Morocco, and Turkey. She currently lives in Birmingham, England, which she suspects is a punishment for the sins of her past lives, and she teaches English to people who need to learn it, which is not the worst job in the world. She also teaches screenwriting and creative writing, whenever and wherever she gets the chance.

Her other stories can be found in *Steam-Powered: Lesbian Steampunk Stories*, *Strange Horizons*, *Shimmer*, and various other places in

print and around the internet, including her website, georginabruce.
com.

❧

ZEN CHO was born and raised in Malaysia, read law at Cambridge,
and is now based in London. Her fiction has been featured or is forthcoming in various venues including *Strange Horizons, The Selangor
Times, Fantastique Unfettered, GigaNotoSaurus*, and *Steam-Powered
II: More Lesbian Steampunk Stories*. Her short story "First National
Forum on the Position of Minorities in Malaysia" was a finalist in the
2011 Selangor Young Talent Awards.

❧

JEWELLE GOMEZ is the author of seven books, including the double
Lambda Literary Award-winning novel *The Gilda Stories*. She also
authored the theatrical adaptation of the novel *Bones and Ash*. Her
fiction and poetry is included in over one hundred anthologies. She
has written literary and film criticism for numerous publications including *The Village Voice, The San Francisco Chronicle, Ms. Magazine*,
and *Black Scholar*. Her most recent novel, *Televised*, is looking for a
home and her newest play, "Waiting for Giovanni," which explores a
moment in the mind of James Baldwin, had its world premier at New
Conservatory Theatre Center in the fall of 2011. Visit her website
jewellegomez.com.

❧

N. K. JEMISIN is an author of speculative fiction short stories and
novels who lives and writes in Brooklyn, NY. Her work has been
nominated for the Hugo (twice), the Nebula (twice), and the World
Fantasy Award; shortlisted for the Crawford, the Gemmell Morning-
star, and the Tiptree; and she has won a Locus Award for Best First
Novel as well as the *Romantic Times* Reviewer's Choice Award.

Her short fiction has been published in professional markets such
as *Clarkesworld, Postscripts, Strange Horizons*, and *Baen's Universe*;
semipro markets such as *Ideomancer* and *Abyss & Apex*; and podcast
markets and print anthologies. Her short story "Non-Zero Probabil-
ities" received Hugo and Nebula Nominations.

Her first two novels, *The Hundred Thousand Kingdoms* and *The Broken Kingdoms*, are out now from Orbit Books. As of mid-2011, *The Hundred Thousand Kingdoms* has been nominated for ten literary awards, winning Best First Novel from *Locus Magazine*. The final book of the Inheritance Trilogy, *The Kingdom of Gods*, was released October 2011.

In addition to writing, she is a counseling psychologist (specializing in career counseling), a sometime hiker and biker, and a political/feminist/anti-racist blogger.

∽

CSILLA KLEINHEINCZ is a Hungarian-Vietnamese writer living in Kistarcsa, Hungary. Although having a Master's Degree in agricultural engineering, all her work is now centered around literature. She translates fantasy and science fiction (Peter S. Beagle, Kelly Link, and Ursula K. Le Guin, for instance) and is an editor at Delta Vision, a major Hungarian fantasy publisher. As editor she launched two series, one, "Masters of Imagination," featuring iconic works from the SF/F genre, the other, "Delta Workshop," introducing young and talented Hungarian writers from the science fiction, fantasy, and horror genres and collecting their works in annual thematic anthologies (*77* and *Erato*). She is also founding editor of the online magazine *SFmag* (http://sfmag.hu). She has written poems, two novels (an urban fantasy focusing on dreaming and a YA fantasy based on Hungarian fairy tales), and a short story collection in Hungarian. Her short stories appeared in English and in various European languages.

∽

ELLEN KUSHNER's first novel, *Swordspoint: A Melodrama of Manners*, quickly became a cult book that some say initiated the queer end of the "fantasy of manners" spectrum. She returned to the same setting in *The Privilege of the Sword* and its sequel, *The Fall of the Kings* (written with her partner, Delia Sherman), as well as a growing number of short stories. Her second novel, *Thomas the Rhymer*, won the Mythopoeic Award and the World Fantasy Award.

Her most recent work includes the anthology *Welcome to Border-town*, co-edited with Holly Black, and a "feminist-shtetl-magical-realist" musical audio drama, "The Witches of Lublin" (written with klezmer artists Yale Strom and Elizabeth Schwartz). She is currently recording the audiobook version of *Swordspoint*.

Kushner was for many years the host of public radio's *Sound & Spirit*. Her work for kids includes *The Golden Dreydl*: a Klezmer "Nutcracker" for Chanukah. Kushner has taught writing at the Clarion and Odyssey workshops, and at Hollins University. She is a co-founder of the Interstitial Arts Foundation, an organization supporting work that falls between genre categories. She and her partner, author and educator Delia Sherman, had a huge wedding in Boston in 1996, followed by a legal marriage ceremony there in 2004. They now live in New York City, with a lot of books, airplane tickets, and no cats whatsoever. EllenKushner.com.

∽

MICHELLE LABBÉ is named after a Beatles song. She was raised by a librarian and a chemist in the suburban wastelands of Springfield, Virginia. She is certain that this explains everything.

Michelle received her B.A. in English from the University of Mary Washington in 2009 and her M.A. in Publishing and Writing from Emerson College in 2011. Her illustrious post-graduate career has thus far consisted of writing freelance articles, forgetting to change out of her pajamas, and scouring the job market for entry-level editorial positions. She likes to imagine that this will make for an excellent inspirational rags-to-riches story someday, if she ever happens to become rich and famous.

In her spare time Michelle enjoys bike-riding, baking perfect soufflés, and trying to write the kind of lesbian fantasy novel she has always wanted to read. Michelle's short fiction has appeared in journals such as *Renard's Menagerie* and *Reflection's Edge*, as well as *Microchondria*, an original flash fiction anthology published by Harvard Book Store. Michelle lives in Somerville, Massachusetts, with assorted roommates, a very fluffy cat, and a TARDIS cookie jar.

She would like to take this opportunity to thank her mentor, Dr. Warren Rochelle. This one's for you.

∽

TANITH LEE is one of the more acclaimed British writers of speculative fiction alive today. She has penned over seventy novels and 250 short stories as well as numerous poems. The recent collection *Disturbed By Her Song*, which featured "Black Eyed Susan," was a finalist for the Lambda Literary Award. But don't fret for her...as Lee has won multiple World Fantasy Awards as well as the British Fantasy Award (the first woman to ever do so).

❧

CATHERINE LUNDOFF is a transplanted Brooklynite who now lives in scenic Minnesota with her wife, bookbinder and conservator Jana Pullman, and their cats, the latter of which are ostensibly Egyptian in origin. In former lives, she was an archaeologist and a bookstore owner, though not at the same time. These days, she does arcane things with computer software at large companies.

She is the two-time Goldie Award-winning author of *Night's Kiss* and *Crave: Tales of Lust, Love and Longing* as well as her latest collection, *A Day at the Inn, A Night at the Palace and Other Stories*. She is the editor of *Haunted Hearths and Sapphic Shades: Lesbian Ghost Stories*, designated as a Best Other Work at the 2010 Gaylactic Spectrum Awards, and co-editor, with JoSelle Vanderhooft, of *Hellebore and Rue: Tales of Queer Women and Magic*. She periodically teaches writing classes at The Loft Literary Center in Minneapolis and elsewhere. Her website is catherinelundoff.com.

❧

NORA OLSEN writes science fiction for teenagers. She lives in New York State with her lovely girlfriend Áine Ní Cheallaigh. Her debut novel *The End* was published by Prizm Books in December 2010.

❧

RACHEL SWIRSKY's short fiction has appeared in venues including Tor.com, *Subterranean Magazine*, *Fantasy Magazine*, *Weird Tales*, and the *Konundrum Engine Literary Review*, and been selected for inclusion in year's best collections from Jonathan Strahan, Rich Horton, and the VanderMeers. *Through the Drowsy Dark*, a mini-collection of Swirsky's feminist poems and short stories, was released in Aqueduct Press's conversation pieces series in 2010.

Swirsky blogs about feminist science fiction at Ambling Along the Aqueduct, about politics at Alas, a Blog, about writing at Big Other, and about a combination of all of the above at her personal blog, That Which Deranges the Senses.

Aɒꝺ

JoSELLE VANDERHOOFT was born in 1980 in Framingham, Massachusetts, when Leo ruled but Gemini was on the rise. By no means
a young woman yet, she nonetheless migrated West to Salt Lake
City just like her pioneering Mormon ancestors. She wrote her first
produced play at sixteen and graduated from the University of Utah
with honors bachelor degrees in English and Theatre Studies. While
studying here she received the Steffenson-Cannon fellowship, which
she held from 1999-2001. She also served as literary intern and/or
dramaturgy intern for several theatres including New Dramatists,
The Women's Project and Productions and the Actors Theatre of
Louisville.

A dramaturge and something of a lapsed playwright, Vanderhooft
now works as a freelance journalist, poet and fiction writer. To date,
she has published seven poetry books, numerous short stories, and
a novel, *The Tale of the Miller's Daughter.* She has edited the lesbian
anthologies *Sleeping Beauty, Indeed, Steam-Powered: Lesbian Steampunk Stories, Bitten by Moonlight,* and (with Catherine Lundoff)
Hellebore & Rue.

She currently lives in Florida with her partner and several boister-
ous cats.

CPSIA information can be obtained at www.ICGtesting.com
Printed in the USA
BVOW071725291211

279385BV00001B/3/P